elegy for the east

elegy for the east

A story of blood and broken dreams

DHRUBAJYOTI BORAH

Translated by the author from the Assamese original
KALANTARAR GADYA

THORNBIRD
NIYOGI BOOKS

Published by
NIYOGI BOOKS
Block D, Building No. 77,
Okhla Industrial Area, Phase-I,
New Delhi-110 020, INDIA
Tel: 91-11-26816301, 26818960
Email: niyogibooks@gmail.com
Website: www.niyogibooksindia.com

Editor: Vibha Chakravarty Kumar
Layout: Shashi Bhushan Prasad
Cover design: Misha Oberoi

ISBN: 978-93-89136-66-1
Publication: 2020

Printed at: Niyogi Offset Pvt. Ltd., New Delhi, India

To Loy and his mother, Sharodi

CONTENTS

ABOUT PRABHAT

I

Prabhat was hurrying back home.

Dusk was descending. A curtain of darkness was about to envelop the city below. The neon and halogen lights that flickered to life along the wide roads tried to push back the veil of darkness.

At the end of a routine day like any other, Prabhat was on his way home from his tuitions. As he walked along the dark road, his eyes opened wider.

What struck one about Prabhat when one looked at his face were his large eyes. With well-shaped eyebrows, his eyes were his most attractive feature. Barring them, his face was the ordinary, sweet face of a young boy in his teens. But people were easily drawn to his pensive pair of eyes.

His name was ordinary too—Prabhat. Apparently, he had been born early in the morning; hence, the name Prabhat, meaning dawn. An undergraduate student in college, he had never been able to excel academically despite studying regularly and attentively. He played cricket with his friends, but never found a place on any team apart from the class team. He occasionally read a detective novel, and stories that appeared in the special puja supplements of newspapers and magazines. The books he had read so far had not been able to leave any impression on his mind; perhaps, he was yet to come across or discover such a book. Every morning after breakfast, he would board a bus to college and regularly present himself in the classroom.

Like most other boys his age, he had just learnt to shave. When he saw pretty girls in college, he would experience a mysterious delight. But unlike his friends, he could not muster the courage to flirt harmlessly with the girls—let alone tease them. His fantasies about women were still very simple, almost innocent. He liked listening to ghazals and subsequently experiencing a sense of self-indulgent desolation.

Prabhat was an ordinary college-going young man.

From the wide road to Prabhat's house, one had to walk for almost 200 metres. That was a narrow stretch, though one could make out that it had been paved once upon a time. All that remained now were stones and potholes. Several small alleys branched out from that narrow road, with houses packed against the alleys on either side. As he crossed the first alley, the familiar odour assailed his nostrils. That odour given off by piles of rotting garbage. A part of that road was unoccupied and the residents of the neighbourhood had made it their garbage dump. A sickeningly foul smell emanated from the pile of accumulating garbage—a smell so nauseating that it churned one's insides and made them gag. People who took that road regularly had got used to the smell. They found it uncomfortable, but unlike the new passers-by, they did not gag. Once in a while, municipality trucks would cart the garbage away. A crowd of labourers, with their noses covered, would shovel the garbage onto the trucks. The odour from the dump, prodded and pushed, would spread wide on that day.

When he reached that spot, Prabhat picked up speed out of habit. When he was a young boy, he used to be scared of crossing that spot, because of the few snarling feral dogs who would be nosing the dump.

Was somebody following him in the darkness? Suddenly, Prabhat had that feeling. He looked over his shoulders. Darkness was enveloping the road.

Barring a few, most of the street lights were yet to come on. Where was he? There was no one in sight. Then the street light in front of a house next to the road blazed to life. A man stood there. Prabhat was right; his instinct about somebody following him was correct.

The man was looking at him. Prabhat hurried into his house.

'*Baba* (affectionate term often used interchangeably with given names in Bengali), there you are,' his father called out from the porch. Perfunctorily acknowledging his father's greeting, he made his way inside, calling out to his mother. In spite of being in college, he was like a little boy, his father thought to himself. 'Listen, I would like a cup of tea,' he said to his wife. It was getting cold. Gathering his shawl, he made himself comfortable on the bamboo chair with the day's newspaper. Now that his son was home, he was relieved. He could read his newspaper in peace. All he wanted was a hot cup of tea. What was this fragrance emanating from the kitchen? Fried papads? Right, it was fried papad. Smiling under his moustache, he started reading his paper.

Sitting next to his mother in the kitchen, Prabhat started having tea and fried papads.

How different were our school and college days! About 20-30 years ago?

The letters on the newspaper blurred.

The world then seemed so simple, enclosed in comprehensible patterns. Success in life was defined by the ability to study a technical subject such as medicine or engineering. 'Taking a line'... that was known as taking a line then. If you could take a line, your future was secure. A government job, marriage, an undramatic sex life approved by society, children, a house or two, a good second-hand if not a new car, and finally—a quiet demise. On the day of the funeral, the daily newspaper would carry an obituary penned by an overenthusiastic nephew or a friend of the children. It was then that the world discovered that such a man lived.

There were very few occurrences to disrupt this uneventful life. The news of somebody's child marrying outside the caste was a sufficiently significant piece of social news.

Every 10 years, there would be an agitation over language and medium. At places, there would be fisticuffs between the Assamese and the Bengalis. After a few days it would subside, and life would go on in its familiar orbit. After some time, the demands to build a bridge over the Brahmaputra or an oil refinery would heat the air.

Life was quite peaceful then.

Back then, nobody took politics so seriously. Politics was left to a class of soft-spoken, khadi-clad, lawyer-like men. The socialists talked about revolution in their meetings and the communists organized armed protests among farmers, but their activities created few ripples in the lives of men like Narayan Hazarika. The deputy commissioner seemed to be the most important man around.

Today, Prabhat and his friends lived in a completely different era. The world had transformed beyond recognition before their eyes. Now, there were no celebrations among young men without liquor, and no politics without guns.

Yes, time had changed. And people like Prabhat's father, the Narayan Hazarikas, found themselves in trouble. They straddled two worlds uncomfortably; the old world was changing fast and they were unable to find their bearings in the new.

With a heavy sigh, Narayan Hazarika flipped the pages of the daily newspaper. Sipping his hot tea and munching fried papads, he began scanning the paper for some juicy news.

It was then that he heard the knock on the door. Hazarika started at the unexpected sound.

Who was it at this hour? What might be the time? He looked at his watch; it was past eight. Who was this visitor knocking at such late hour? Hazarika was a little annoyed. He had had a hard day at work. It was already evening by the time he had got home after the day's grocery shopping. The winter days were short too. And who had turned up now?

'Paresh, *baba*, can you check who's at the door?' he called out to his younger son.

Prabhat's brother Paresh was in high school, and was studying in the next room. He rose to answer the door.

A stranger stood in the verandah. With a smile, he asked for his father. Paresh ushered the man indoors. Scanning the room, the man gave out a long yawn. Before he finished yawning, Prabhat's father had stepped in.

With a namaskar, he asked the man, 'I am sorry, but have we met?'

'I am from the police intelligence,' the man replied, rising to his feet and reciprocating Hazarika's greetings.

Prabhat's father was surprised. Police? Why was a man from the Police Intelligence calling on him? A sense of dread gripped him; the fear showed on his face.

'Please have a seat. Why are you here, if I may ask? I mean, you are from the police...'

'I am making routine enquiries,' the man answered matter-of-factly. 'You know how bad it is right now. And it will only get worse. The things we are forced to do now are beyond our imagination. I have been calling on many houses in this area.'

'But what have you been calling on about in this area? This is a very peaceful nieghbourhood.'

'You are right, there have been no disturbances in this area,' the man nodded in agreement. 'But there are a lot of people here, the houses are cheek-by-jowl. And almost every house has tenants. Many of these tenants are school and college students. We have to keep an eye on such houses.'

'This is a very old, middle-class area. A gentleman's area. Everybody knows everybody else. They are all Assamese people who have lived here for a long time.'

'What about the tenants?'

'Yes, there are quite a few tenants, but most of them are professionals. You know, this was a very good area once upon a time, but it has deteriorated now. Do you see the state of the roads? And that awful garbage dump? It is difficult to use that road because of the stench. This neighbourhood is deteriorating and nobody is paying attention. This has become a very neglected area, you know.'

'Unfortunately, these are the places we have been forced to keep an eye on. This is where the terrorists get the most support.'

'Terrorists!' Prabhat's father was stunned. His eyes widened and his mouth gaped in amazement. 'Terrorists? Here?'

'How would you know that they aren't here? And if they are here, all of us have had it. That is why I am here, asking for your help. I am looking for some information.'

'What information will you find in my house?' There was a note of panic in Hazarika's voice.

'Isn't Prabhat Hazarika your elder son? Please call him,' said the man in a commanding voice.

Prabhat's father felt very uncomfortable. Fear rose in his heart as he looked helplessly at the man. Who was he? Was he really from the police? Police Intelligence? Why, he had not even produced an identity card. Hazarika had a strong urge to throw the man out, but he could not muster the courage to do so. Would he be wise in offending the authorities? Would it be right to antagonize the police? How the man stared. A voice inside Hazarika spoke: 'Save Prabhat, keep him away from this man.'

The man kept staring at him.

Narayan Hazarika turned indoors and called out helplessly, 'Prabhat, *baba*, come here for a minute.'

Prabhat walked out, dressed in a shirt and an old pair of pyjamas. He looked inquiringly at his father and the stranger.

'Isn't your name Prabhat? Here, do sit down. Let's have a small talk.'

'Don't you know anybody associated with the terrorists?' asked the man with a hint of mockery in his voice. 'Have any of your friends from college joined them? You must have heard some of them talking about arms and ammunition… Guns? Revolvers? No? Has no one ever mentioned them? I know you won't lie. Have any of your classmates joined any extremist organization? Have any of them suddenly come into a lot of money—buying new jeans, expensive shoes, tape recorders? Money which their parents cannot provide? Haven't you noticed?'

Narayan Hazarika was furious. What sort of questions was this man asking Prabhat? Even though his voice was low and conversational, was this the proper way to talk?

Wrapping his shawl closer to him, he got on his feet pointedly. The man looked at him once. Then he spoke to Prabhat, 'Keep your distance from the extremists. They have infiltrated schools and colleges. One does not know how many there might be among your classmates.' The man then looked at his father and said, 'Times are bad, Hazarika. It is better to be careful.' Turning to Prabhat again, he ordered, 'Pay attention to your studies, but keep your eyes and ears open, always.' He then stood up and spoke to Hazarika with an air of authority, 'Today is Friday. At 11 am on Monday, Prabhat needs to come to the police station. Do you understand? Send him across sharp at 11. He has to ask for me when he gets there.'

After he left, Hazarika stood rooted to the spot for a long time, staring at the door. He seemed to have lost all strength to move. Prabhat stood where he was, apparently unable to move, too.

The seconds ticking by on the wall clock in the next room broke through the silence.

'Has the guest left?' asked his wife as she walked into the room with a cup of tea.

Hazarika started. He looked at his wife. Then he pounced on his son.

'What kind of friends do you have nowadays?' he exploded in anger, helplessness, and sorrow.

His mother quickly moved to stand between father and son, spilling the tea in her haste.

'What is wrong? Why are you behaving like this? Is this the way to treat your son?'

Paresh and his younger sister Pratima hurried out, fear and surprise writ large on their faces.

'He has joined the terrorists! Do you hear me? Your son has joined the terrorists!'

'What are you taking about? Who was that man?'

'He was from the police!'

'Police! What was he doing here?'

'That is what I have been trying to explain... He told me that your son has contact with terrorists.'

'Lies, Deuta. Ma, these are all lies.'

'Lies?' Rage welled up in Narayan Hazarika. 'What did that man say? Guns, revolvers, pistols. You will be the death of all of us. You will destroy us. Listen to me, if you have really taken these things up, you should know that there is no place for you in this house,' his voice broke.

'What inauspicious words are these? Do you have to lose your head over whatever anybody says? I wonder who that man really was. He was not even in a policeman's uniform! Go inside, baba. And you two, go to the table, as dinner is ready,' said the lady of the house.

Like any other day, after the children had finished their meals, Hazarika and his wife sat down to eat. 'You know, he has been asked to go to the police station,' Hazarika spoke up almost immediately, as if to himself.

'To the station? But why?'

'I have no clue. To answer some questions, I suppose. He was asked quite a few today. Prabhat said he did not know anything. I wonder why they have called him again…'

'Has somebody been spreading lies about him out of jealousy?' asked the wife.

'Apparently the terrorists have set up dens in areas such as ours. Those boardings for boys, it seems they are dangerous. Does he visit these boardings?'

'I do not think so. He had told me once that some boys from his college boarded nearby.'

'Those…those might be the dens. Ask him to be careful. Ask him not to go out and just stay at home.'

'How do you expect a grown-up boy to stay put indoors? In any case, he does not really go out too often. Tuitions, besides college. And then he visits his friends sometimes. How do I stop him every day?'

'These friends are the cause of all trouble. They give him all the wrong ideas.'

'Have your meal, you are only picking at your food. Baba did not eat properly either. Have another piece of fried fish, please.'

'Do you remember that nephew, or was it a brother, of our tenant? Is he still around? Don't you recall what a burly fellow he was? Had the built of a wrestler. How can you be sure that he was not a terrorist? Is the boy still around?'

'No, he left the day before yesterday. He said goodbye before he left.'

'You have to be very careful. Keep your distance from strangers, young men in particular. You women are taken in very easily. It is hard to say where these extremists lurk with their bombs and guns. The boys who lodge with the Borahs? Are they around?'

'I have no idea. I think you are worrying unnecessarily. They will probably ask *baba* a few more questions at the police station, and that would be it. Didn't you tell me that the man appeared to believe him when he said he did not know anything?'

'That's what he said. I wonder if he really meant it.'

'I wish you would not worry unnecessarily. You have not touched your food at all. All this talk about terrorists…this is the first I am hearing of it.'

'Hasn't anything come up in the *namghar* (prayer house for congregational worship associated with the Assamese community)?'

'Not at all,' shrugged the wife. But quietly, she remembered that Mrs Barua had brought it up... Apparently, young men were taking up arms to free the state. Mrs Das had told her later that Mrs Barua's youngest son had joined them. Did that mean that they had infiltrated their neighbourhood? Had Prabhat joined them as well? Her heart missed a beat. But she mentioned nothing to her husband.

'Do you have to worry so much just because he has been called to the station? Why don't you go with him?' she said, while clearing the table.

Hazarika rose to his feet with a long sigh. Washing his hands, he helped himself to some *saunf* (anise) from the jar on the kitchen shelf. Wrapping his shawl around him, he went out to lock the gate.

He locked the iron gate and then shut the glass-paned front door. From the dark room, he peeped through the glass. There was a light fog. The streetlight in the distance flickered, throwing the road near the house alternately into light and shadow. Two boys were hurrying ahead, slipping in and out of the shadows with every flicker of light.

Who are they? Where are they going at this time of the night? Are they terrorists? A shudder ran down his spine. Hurriedly pulling down the curtains, he went indoors.

'Listen,' he called out to his wife, 'why are the lights in the house switched on for so long? Turn them off, we have to sleep. All of us must to go to bed early.'

Lowering the mosquito net, he got into bed. On other days, getting into bed, he would switch on the table lamp and read a book. *Ramkrishna Kathamrit* or Swami Vivekananda's essays. As he read, he would wait in eager anticipation for his wife to join him. After finishing her chores in the kitchen and checking on her sleeping children, his wife would walk into the bedroom, carrying a glass of water. When she shut the wooden bedroom door, Hazarika would be aware of her presence. The words on the book open in front of him would mist over. When his wife put the glass of water on the table next to the bed, he would steal a glance of her face, reflected in the light from the lamp. Sometimes, if her eyes caught his, she would smile and Hazarika would feel a little embarrassed. After she'd get into bed, he would start a conversation with her, using the book he was reading as a topic or any other topic he could think of—minor domestic topics which only a husband and a wife talk about.

Today, Hazarika did not reach for his book. When his wife got into bed, he switched off the lamp and said, 'It is better to turn in early, you see. It is not good to keep the lights on very late.'

His wife did not reply. They stretched out in silence on either side of the bed. Time ticked by. The wall clock struck 11, 12, 1, 2. Suddenly a long whistle shattered the night's silence. Where did it come from? The police? Hazarika sat up startled.

'You do hear whistles at night sometimes,' his wife said.

'Aren't you asleep?' Hazarika asked his wife. Then, with a faint sigh, he said, 'Go to sleep. It's 2 am.'

II

'But why did you insist on Prabhat going to the police station?'

'There was no way out. How could he not go after being summoned with a date and time?'

Narayan Hazarika was talking to Partha, the journalist, seated on the verandah in front of his house. Partha observed that Hazarika had dark circles under his eyes and his forehead wore a permanent wrinkle. He appeared to be battered by a sense of uncertainty and anxiety.

'What did he have to say?' asked Partha.

Hazarika went on to narrate the whole dialogue that took place between him and his son.

'Prabhat said to me that he did not want to go to the police station; that the man who had come the other day had asked him all sorts of questions which he knew nothing about. He asked me, "Do I have to go just because they have summoned me?"'

'Then what did you say to him?' asked Partha.

'I told him he had no choice! That he had to go, because he had been asked to by the police! And he retorted that nobody just goes if called like that, that he just wouldn't go!'

'And then?' Partha asked.

'I tried to explain to him that this was all about law and order, and that the country's citizens have to follow its laws. He then asked me what the law was behind such arbitrary orders. I told him that there must be one, otherwise why would they call him. A faint suspicion did creep into my mind though, and I wondered if such a law actually existed. Then I tried to put some sense into his head and said that the police had called him only for some routine enquiries, not to sentence him.'

'Did he finally understand?' Partha enquired.

'No! He was still adamant and refused to go. "I mean it when I say I am not going. Nobody else would force me to go the way you are forcing me to" was his stance!'

'So, what was settled then?' Partha asked.

'I don't know. I got a little paranoid. I started asking him if he had told anybody, about being called to the station, that I had told him many times not to tell anybody because it's not something that people should know about since there might be trouble. He simply said that he hadn't told anybody. And once again, the same old—that he wasn't going.'

'And why do you want to keep this under wraps anyway?' asked Partha.

Narayan Hazarika was silent for some time. He stared sadly into the distance. Then he spoke, almost as if to himself, 'I thought it was best to keep it a secret from other people. It involves the police, after all. And they had only wanted to ask him a couple of questions.'

'How did you convince him to go, considering he was so adamant?' Partha asked with curiosity.

'Well, his mother spoke to him.'

'I see. What did she have to say?'

'She said "What if the police come looking for you and turn our house upside down? What if they take your father away?"'

There was already a lot of pressure on Prabhat. The psychological pressure to submit to and cooperate with the existing system had begun at home itself. A long sigh escaped Partha. It would never occur to a man like Narayan Hazarika to question the legality of the police's actions. It was the natural reaction of the middle class to comply and cooperate with the system. The question of reason or unreason did not always arise, it provided perhaps the assurance of security, a false expectation of justice.

Partha looked at Narayan Hazarika. The man seemed weary and exhausted. A contented, middle-class family with three children. A thrifty family that throve in spite of its few wants. The fact that they could live in a place like Guwahati without having to pay rent was a huge relief. The man must have renovated his father's old house.

'Who built this house?' Partha asked.

'I did. Long ago…about 20 years at least. Building a house was cheap in those days. I had initially built three rooms with half-walls using used sal wood. It had cost me only 7,000 rupees. I built the front part later, bit by bit.'

It was clear from Hazarika's words that building the house was a great achievement for him.

'What happened to the old house?'

'It is very much there, at the back, adjacent to this house. We have turned one of the rooms into a kitchen, and have rented the other two rooms. A man stays there. We have also built him another small kitchen and a bathroom.'

Partha returned to the old topic of conversation, 'So you went to the police station, too?'

'I did.'

'At 11 am?'

'We went earlier. I had to miss office that day.'

'What happened next?'

Hazarika narrated:

He told Partha that he couldn't help worrying on his way to the station; that when they got there, they found that the man who had paid them a visit was nowhere to be seen. There was another police officer there instead, but no trace whatsoever of the man who had visited them.

'What happened? Do you want to lodge a complaint? Has your maid run away?' asked a burly constable, when he saw them looking around nervously. 'Go ahead, you will find our officer inside. Make an entry.'

'No, that's not what we are here for. We had been asked to come here at 11 am today.'

'And who asked you?' enquired the constable.

Hazarika was taken aback. He did not know the man's name; he had not even asked him his name.

'An officer from the police station had paid us a visit on Friday night. He had asked us to come down today.'

'Is that so? Why don't you talk to sir inside? He might know something.'

Hazarika sidled inside. The officer sitting at the table looked up and said, 'Please come in. How can I be of service?'

Once again, Hazarika was caught off-guard. He repeated his words to the constable.

'Who asked you to come down to the station?'

'One of your officers. He said he was from the Police Intelligence. I am sorry I did not ask him his name.'

'I see. Do you have any information to share?'

'No, no such thing,' Hazarika almost broke into a sweat. 'I wonder why he asked us to come down.'

He did not want to reveal much. How surprising! They had been expressly asked to report at the station, but nobody seemed to know anything about it.

'You had been asked to report at 11 am... Sir isn't around. He will be here shortly. Do have a seat...on that bench,' said the officer.

While Hazarika sat down on the bench, Prabhat waited by the door. He beckoned Prabhat to sit next to him. He looked at the clock. It was not yet 11.

'Is he with you?' the officer asked, yawning.

Hazarika nodded.

With another yawn, the officer stared wearily out of the window. He pulled a file towards him and flicked through it. Then, suddenly, as if he remembered something, he picked up a stick and strode into the next room.

'Sir will be here. Hey, Lakshman, take them to meet sir when he comes.'

Narayan Hazarika gazed after him. There was the sound of a door opening. Human voices emanated from the next room; somebody was speaking in a harsh tone. Must be the officer. Was that the lock-up? Then there were thuds. Yes, he must be beating somebody up. Somebody screamed a frightening, tortured sound. Twice.

Narayan Hazarika's heart beat faster. His mouth was dry. He looked around helplessly. There was nobody in sight. When he looked at Prabhat, he saw that his eyes were wide with fear. 'Must be a thief or a dacoit,' he said, as if to console himself. Father and son sat in silence on the bench. A bit later, there was the sound of a scooter. The police station immediately seemed to spring into action. A few constables materialized on the verandah; another few climbed up to the verandah and walked into the adjacent room. It was almost 12 noon. Hazarika stepped out into the verandah.

It was then that a policeman told them that the Officer-in-Charge (OC) was looking for them.

He hurried into the OC's room with Prabhat.

'Please come in. What brings you here?'

For the third time, Hazarika explained the reason for his presence in the police station.

'Oh, let me see.' The officer fished out a paper from a diary. 'What did you say his name was? Prabhat Hazarika, son of Narayan Hazarika, isn't it? Yes, I got it.'

Hazarika felt a sense of relief.

'So, you are Prabhat.'

Prabhat nodded.

'Okay. We will ask you a few questions and you will have to give us the answers. Then you can leave. There is nothing to worry about. Hazarika, why don't you leave? You might be late for work. Just do me a favour... Could you put your name, work details, and home and office address down in this file before leaving?'

'File? But what for?'

'Where am I supposed to record what this young man says if not in a file? Don't worry, this is routine work.'

Hazarika could not find fault with the man's logic. But he found it hard to accept the fact that his son's name would henceforth be found in a police file. Grudgingly, he wrote down the required information, and turned to his son and said, 'I am leaving. Head straight for home, once you are done. You don't need to go to college today.'

Turning to the OC, he said, 'Well, goodbye.'

'Goodbye. You need not worry...your son will reach home safe and sound in an hour's time...*sahi salamat*. Ha, Ha, Ha.' The officer was a humorous man. Hazarika laughed with him and walked out.

'So, you weren't present when Prabhat was interrogated in the station for the first time?' Partha asked.

'No. They asked me to leave.'

'So, you do not know what they asked him...'

'I wonder. I did not go to work that day. I went home from the station. Prabhat reached home, too, in about an hour's time. I talked to him in detail about the happenings at the station.'

'What did he have to say?'

Hazarika narrated the conversation that took place with Prabhat:

'So? What happened at the police station? What all did they ask you after I left?' Hazarika shot the questions at Prabhat the moment entered the house that day.

'They did not ask me too many questions. They first asked me my name, and a few questions about my family. Then they asked me about my school, matric examinations, college...'

'What did they ask you about your school? Try to remember every little detail.'

'Which school I had studied in. The name of the principal. They took down the names of my classmates. I did not remember all of their names and addresses. I only remembered a few of them. They asked me if I knew where they were and what they were doing now.'

'What else? Anything about college?'

'The same stuff. They asked me the same things about college.'

'What about the terrorists?'

'Wanted to know if any of my classmates had gone underground.'

'What did you say?'

'I said I had no idea.'

'And what else?'

'That's it.'

'And then they asked you to leave?'

'Yes, they did not ask me questions, which I had answered at home. But they asked me to come back on Saturday.'

'Again? To the station? But why?'

'I have no clue.'

'I do not like these summonses to the police station at all,' Hazarika told Partha. 'They add to my sense of foreboding. The questions were simple. Fairly straightforward. What else remained to be asked?'

'Didn't you make enquiries about it at the station?'

'I did. Of course, I did. But I never met the man who had come home again, so I asked the OC.'

'What did he say?'

'He asked me not to worry, said these were routine formalities. All routine,' Hazarika said with a sigh.

III

Once the visits to the police station began, they continued endlessly. On each visit Prabhat would be given another date to report to at the station. Once in every 7 or 10 days—nothing was fixed. He would be in low spirits a day before the scheduled date, but cheered up for a couple of days after that.

Sometimes, he would not be asked anything at the station. At times, they would ask him a few simple questions. It was only on some days that he was asked about a particular classmate of his. He was interrogated more about his schoolfriends than his current college friends. The officer would record his answers in the file bearing his name, his presence would be recorded on days when there was no interrogation still. Then the officer would look at the calendar, fix a date, and ask him to report on that day.

'Evenings are fine, too. You can drop in on your way back from college.'

Prabhat would leave without a word.

After a few chats with Partha, Hazarika felt an affinity for the young journalist. Perhaps, because he had been able to unburden himself to him. Partha had told him clearly that he will never write anything in the newspaper without his approval, but he would like to know a bit more about Prabhat's case.

'What else? Don't they ask him anything specific?' asked Partha.

'I don't think so, at least nothing that I can remember. Did they ask you about anything else, baba?'

That day Partha had asked Prabhat to join the conversation.

'No, nothing else. But once they had shown me a couple of photos.'

'Photos? Whose photos?'

'Photos of a few men and some boys.'

'Did you recognize anybody in those photographs?'

'No, I didn't.'

'Did you tell the OC that clearly?' Hazarika intervened.

'I did.'

'Did anybody in those photographs seem remotely familiar?'

Prabhat thought for a little while. Then he spoke slowly, 'One of them looked like a boy from my school, but the boy in the photograph had a long beard.'

'Did you say so to anybody at the station?' Hazarika asked desperately.

'No, I didn't.'

'Don't...don't disclose that to anyone.' Hazarika looked at Partha helplessly.

'You are not sure, are you, that that young man in the photograph is your old schoolmate? You did the right thing by not talking about it. Now don't mention it to anybody. There will be unnecessary complications.'

Hazarika gave him a look of gratitude.

'You can go back to your studies, son,' Partha sent Prabhat back to his room.

'We are all very disturbed, you see. The whole family is deeply troubled. The boy has almost abandoned his studies, and his mother is in bad shape. My daughter, who is in the eighth standard, now consoles her mother. My younger son is scared too. I would rather not talk about myself. We are very disturbed, deeply disturbed.'

Partha felt sorry for the man. He felt sorry for Prabhat too. What trap had the family fallen into? It did not seem as if Prabhat had ties with any secret militant organization; surely, he had none. But these repeated visits to the station and the enquiries, showing him photographs, opening a file—what was happening? Was this a planned and deliberate plan, or had something carelessly begun received a momentum of its own? Was this a blind momentum, something whose course and end could not be predicted?

As a journalist, it would not be appropriate for him to get personally involved. It would also be unprofessional. No, he would only observe the course of things. But he felt sympathy for the family stir within him...and a tenderness too. One wondered how many families there were in similar situations.

'Have you talked about these things with anybody else, or sought advice?'

'Nobody except that lawyer,' said Narayan Hazarika. After being silent for a while, he continued, 'Who else can I talk to? I can't even think of someone who can help. Do you have anybody in mind?'

'No, I am only asking you.' Partha did not want to get involved. He added, 'It would be a good idea to confer with a few people of experience. There might be a way out.'

Hazarika heaved a sigh in reply.

After a brief desultory conversation, Partha left. The evening stretched out before him.

From his chair on the verandah, Hazarika stared into the distance. It was quite cold and he felt like holding on, as long as possible, to the decreasing warmth of the sunlight falling on the verandah. He sat without moving, soaking in the soft warmth. Today was a holiday, the second Saturday; tomorrow would be a

Sunday. Earlier, he used to go shopping every Sunday morning. He would carefully purchase a kilo of mutton or chicken, and some fresh produce from the market. The sight of fresh meat in the morning would cheer everybody up. Prabhat's mother enjoyed cooking…putting the meat to boil, she would go to the yard to pick mint leaves. Till a couple of years ago, Prabhat would demand from his mother that the liver and the bones be set aside for him.

For the last few Sundays, Hazarika had not shopped for food or bought meat. Since the visits to the station had begun, he had lost interest in shopping and his wife did not comment on it. She made do with dry vegetables from the vegetable-seller who pushed his cart from house to house, and eggs from the paan-shop nearby. 'Tomorrow is Sunday, I will get fresh meat first thing in the morning,' Hazarika suddenly came to a decision.

'It would be better to seek advice; the journalist was right. From another lawyer, another man...whom should I talk to? I need to think this over. Somebody might be able to give me some ideas. Surely a way out could be found. These station visits have to be stopped. This current lawyer has totally discouraged me,' Hazarika was talking to himself quietly.

His wife walked up to him with a cup of tea in her hand and stood by his side. Reaching out for the cup, Hazarika said, 'Thank you! I was longing for a cup of tea. Do sit down. Where is your cup? Why don't you get it here?'

Her husband seemed in a better mood today. Mrs Hazarika was a little surprised. She cheered up a little. She immediately got her cup from the kitchen, pulled up a cane stool next to him and sat down.

'I will go to the market tomorrow. It's been a while since I went to the market. Have our mint bushes withered?'

A small smile lit up Mrs Hazarika's face. 'No, they haven't.'

'You know, it would be a good idea to discuss Prabhat's visits to the police station with someone. That lawyer was of no help, somebody else might be able to give us some good advice,' said Malati, the wife.

'It would be better if we could ask somebody we knew. What about Manohar dada (suffix for big brother in Bengali)? He's an IAS officer, and his wife's very nice too. Do you remember, they had come over to invite us to their daughter's wedding?'

'Yes. We seem to have lost touch nowadays with members of our own family. We live in the same city, but we hardly meet. This is very bad. I remember she had told me, "You never come over—the wedding would be a good pretext. You should be there for all the celebrations, Malati, and you should stay with us. We have a big house, but hardly any people."'

'Well, I am glad you reminded me. He is the commissioner now. He would be able to make sense of these government snares,' Hazarika told his wife.

From inviting guests to hosting the *athmangala* (wedding feast) for the bride and bridegroom, Mrs Hazarika had been a great help at the wedding. Mr Hazarika had gone down to the bride's house quite a few times. The family had profusely acknowledged the help they had received from the Hazarikas.

'Tomorrow is Sunday. I will go tomorrow. It would be nice to meet them on a holiday,' announced Hazarika.

'No, not on a holiday; people rest on holidays. Why don't you call on him on Monday at about 8 pm? If you go on a working day, he might be able to phone a few people for information,' advised Malati.

'You are right. Monday would be ideal.'

Evening dawned. The afternoon sunlight had faded long ago, and it was growing dark and cold. The Hazarikas sat for a long while on the verandah, talking. It was time to get dinner ready, and a number of household chores remained too, but Mrs Hazarika did not feel like getting up. It was after ages that she was conversing so freely with her husband. She did not want to lose these moments, but after a certain point, she told him, 'I should be getting up now. I did not give the kids anything to eat in the afternoon. Dinner is some time away...so they will create a fuss soon. I will make Maggi. Would you like some?'

'Yes, please.'

From his seat on the verandah, Hazarika had a view of the houses across the narrow alley in front of their house, and a bit of the sky above the trees as well. The sky was turning dark purple in colour, and there were no stars yet. The family must be under the influence of some unfavourable star, Hazarika thought to himself. 'Stars, when unfavourable, cause a lot of havoc in our lives. They have to be appeased if respite needs to be gained from their effects,' Pundarikaksha Mishra from his office had said. Hazarika was aware that Mishra practised astrology; he had a reputation as an astrologer, too. He would have to consult him so he could make his calculations and find out what was wrong.

Prabhat's mother was cooking dinner...the egg and potato curry that everybody loved. The children were at their tables, studying. Hazarika was in the living room, reading a book, when he heard a knock.

Upon opening the door, he saw a police constable.

'Isn't this Prabhat Hazarika's house? Sir has asked him to come down to the station at once.'

'Now? At this time in the night?' Hazarika exploded. 'Is this some sort of a joke? How can you call him at such odd hours? Who is this, sir? Who is he, why is he calling my son?' he shot at the constable.

'OC is calling him. I do not know why. He just asked me to get him.'

'Well, that isn't good. He can't just call him on a whim. I will complain to higher authorities about this. Prabhat is not going anywhere. Go and tell your OC that his father won't allow him to go anywhere at night. You can go now!'

Narayan Hazarika slammed the door shut. He switched off the front light and made his way to the kitchen, grumbling. Gulping down a glass of water, he told his wife, 'Look at how they are harassing us! They call him to the station whenever they want to. I told the constable I will not allow my son to go. Let them do what they want. I will complain.'

His wife looked at him rather helplessly.

'Impossible. They have crossed all limits.' Sitting down at the dining table, Hazarika continued grumbling. His younger son came into the room. 'Deuta (father in Assamese), the policeman is still here.'

Hazarika stood up.

'Don't act in a temper, and think about what you are doing,' his wife called out after him.

Hazarika went out. True, the policeman was standing in the verandah. He had just lit himself a beedi. Hazarika opened the door.

'You can go. I will accompany my son. Tell him that.'

'Don't be late, sir is waiting.'

Hazarika did not reply. Closing the door, he made his way to Prabhat's room. Prabhat was sitting at the table. A book lay open in front of him, but he was not reading.

'Come on, baba, we have to go to the station,' Hazarika said gently. Prabhat obediently got up from the table. Hazarika felt a pang.

Father and son walked to the police station. He would complain to the OC, Hazarika thought, he would protest against his boy being summoned to the police station at odd hours.

'Why did you abuse the constable I had sent? He had gone there only because I had asked him to. We have your best interests at heart, but you always misunderstand us. How many times has your son been to the police station? Has anybody harmed him? Spoken a harsh word to him? The military should have found your boy, they would have beaten the life out of him by now. You would have learnt your lesson then. We have kept him safe,' the officer spoke harshly.

Hazarika was taken aback. Fumbling for words, he responded to the OC, 'We were upset because you keep calling him…and so late at night as well.'

'We called him for work! Do you think we have called him for a chat?' The officer was still angry. Then he calmed down a little.

'You can leave now. You need not worry about your son. Don't disturb us by waiting for him unnecessarily. We will drop him home. Now, please, leave.'

Hazarika did not know what to do. Putting his hand on Prabhat's shoulder, the OC led him inside. Hazarika slunk away. As he walked away from the compound of the police station, he felt very helpless. What should I do now, he wondered. A sob rose in his chest. He could not go back home. He found a paan shop a little bit away from the police station, and took up vigil there.

A long while elapsed. Probably an hour or more. The paan shop had shut down. What was Prabhat doing at the station?

Seating Prabhat inside a room, the OC had left. Prabhat sat there for a long time. The OC looked very grim today; he had not said a single word to him. Fear gripped him. Finally, a policeman came for him and led him across a couple of dark rooms to another room. When he walked in, he saw the OC and the man who had paid them a visit that first night sitting there. Both of them wore grim expressions. Prabhat's sense of foreboding grew.

The officer got up and almost hustled him to another door. He said, 'There are two men inside…take a good look.'

Opening the door, he shone a torch inside a small, dark room. Prabhat saw that the bare room held two boys. One of them lay prone on the ground, and the other sat leaning against the wall. Their hair was disheveled and they did not have a stitch on. Their faces were battered and swollen. It was obvious that they had been brutally beaten. When he caught sight of them, Prabhat began to shiver.

'Take a good look,' said the officer. He shone the torch on the boys' faces and bodies. When the light fell on him, the boy sitting with his back to the wall opened his eyes. His eyes were bloodshot. The other showed no signs of life. Prabhat was terrified. After a little while, the man led him out of the room and shut the door.

'Do you know any of them?'

Prabhat shook his head in denial.

'There was a boy called Subrata in your school. He was older than you.'

Prabhat nodded.

'Was he your classmate or was he senior?'

'He was my classmate in the 12th standard.'

'Is either of those boys in there Subrata?'

'No.' Prabhat replied clearly.

The OC and the other man exchanged glances. Then the OC took him outside and said to him, 'Don't breathe a word of what you have seen to anybody. Do you understand? You'll be in trouble and I won't be able to help. Not even to your family.' Turning to a constable, he said, 'Islam, take this young man home on your scooter.'

'You can go now. I hope you remember what I told you. When have you been asked to report next? Tuesday, isn't it? Come on Tuesday,' said the OC, and left.

When the scooter crossed him, Narayan Hazarika could make out that Prabhat was riding pillion. He chased after the scooter, almost breaking into a run. When he reached home, out of breath, the policeman had already left. Walking in through the open door, he saw that Prabhat lay in bed, his eyes closed. His mother and sister sat by his side. Paresh was handing his mother a fan.

Hazarika signalled to his wife and asked, 'What happened?'

'He has a high fever. He is shivering, and delirious, too.'

Hazarika sat down beside Prabhat and put a hand on his forehead. 'God, he is burning with fever. Get some water. We have to give him cold compresses.'

'They were beaten...badly beaten,' Prabhat suddenly mumbled.

IV

Partha was sitting in his office in his house, reading a report he had written the previous day. Barely six months ago, he had moved to Guwahati as a special correspondent for the North-East of a New Delhi-based newspaper. After a year in Delhi as a trainee journalist, the editor had spoken to him about relocating to Guwahati. That was the time when the unrest in Assam had succeeded in attracting the attention of a number of newspapers outside the state.

'We ought to observe the phenomenon of insurgency carefully. It would help to have a local there. Why don't you go to Guwahati? New posting with promotion. (A punishment posting, thought Partha, not many preferred going to the North-East to work.) Do you have any problems with that, young man?' the editor had asked Partha.

'No, sir, not at all. I am genuinely grateful to you. But I do have a regret.'

'You do? What regret?'

'I will miss the weekly editorial conferences with you.'

'Ha! Ha! Ha! It will be a challenging assignment. You will gain lots of experience.'

'Sir.'

'Get ready to go there. As soon as possible.'

'OK, sir.'

'I will recommend a better scale for you, with all the perks. Take the order papers from Miss Verma in the evening.'

'Yes, sir.'

'Best of luck.'

'Thank you very much, sir.'

'Godspeed, my boy,' shaking his hand, the editor bade him goodbye.

The conversation with the editor came back to Partha as he read his report. He was, in fact, thrilled to be back home after all those years spent away from Assam. His parents were quite proud of him for being the special correspondent of a national daily. A glamorous job with good money. The editor was impressed by his reporting too.

'Buy a car. A client has informed me about a Maruti in good condition,' his lawyer father had told him after his return.

A thrifty old man. If he wanted to, he could have bought me a new car, he thought to himself.

'Oh, these random thoughts!' he spoke out loud to himself while shaking his head, and tried to concentrate on his report.

What caused these organizations to be born? The whims of a few emotional, idealistic young men or was it deeper than that? A birth in a social vacuum, perhaps? Why did they fan out like flames?

That implied that there must have been gaps in society which these organizations promised to address. Or was it an easy solution for impotency for a group of young men—a quick way to glamour and power? But these came later. What came first?

These were the questions he wanted to raise in his report. There were no easy answers to them. He had failed to find any. The editor would probably find little to approve in this particular report; he might even refuse to publish it. Everybody preferred answers that were easily understood. But, one should, with sensitivity and sincerity, appreciate the fact that not all questions have easy answers. Let me send it across, and ask for the old man's opinion, Partha thought.

The politics of a group of youth going underground had had an unbelievable impact on society. This seemed to have escaped people's notice. Recently, Partha had had a novel experience.

It was a Sunday, and he had gone to see a lawyer he knew. Once upon a time, Hariprasanna Kalita used to be his father's junior. Now, he had graduated to his own practice. However, he still worked with his father on the bigger cases. His father was very fond of Hariprasanna. 'One of the best', he would often say. Hariprasanna treated Partha with affection too.

On that day, Partha had reached Hari-dada's house early. Along with other topics, the conversation veered to politics and resistance. He liked to hear everybody's opinions. It was then that a man walked into the lawyers' chambers.

'What a surprise, Hazarika. Any new developments in office?'

'No, this has nothing to do with the office. I am here for something else.'

The government branch Hazarika worked for had its retainership with Hariprasanna. Hazarika occasionally saw Kalita about some case or the other. This is something Partha found out later.

'Are you planning to file cases now, Hazarika? Ha, Ha!'

'No, this is not about a case. I wanted to clarify a few things. Personal.'

'Go ahead. This is Partha, sir's son.'

'I have a problem.'

'Anything wrong in office?'

No. It's the police.

Kalita and Partha immediately grew wary.

'One evening, about three months back, a man from the Police Intelligence suddenly paid us a visit. Apparently, he had come to make enquiries about the presence of extremists in our neighbourhood. He asked for our son, who is a BA final year student, asked him if any of his classmates were terrorists. My son said he knew nothing about these things. Then the man also asked him if he knew anybody in contact with the underground rebels, and if anybody discussed guns and pistols in college. Prabhat answered in the negative. My son is occupied with his home, classes, tuitions, and some sports; he has no interest in anything else. This was the first time we were hearing of these things. Then he was asked to report at the police station the following Monday. I accompanied him. The OC took down my name and address and sent me away. He then asked Prabhat a few questions too, and then ordered him to come back after a week. After that, they have been calling him repeatedly. They ask him a couple of questions, and sometimes they don't even ask him anything, but just give him a date and order him to come back. This has been going on for almost two months. He has been to the police station several times. The family is under a lot of stress because of this. That's why I have approached you. I need some advice.'

'Hmmm.' Hariprasanna Kalita made a sound.

Partha was listening to the narration with wonder.

'The boy has lost interest in his studies. He is always depressed. His mother is in bad shape too; the poor woman is dying of anxiety.'

'Hmm.'

For a few moments they were silent.

Partha remembered that day very well.

'He hasn't been arrested?' Kalita enquired.

'No.'

'Have they brought any specific charge against him?'

'No.'

'How would you know?'

'I asked the OC. He said it was routine enquiry and nothing much.'

'Have they questioned him about any particular incident or individual?'

'No, only about the boys he knows.'

'Have they found any incriminating evidence against your son?'

'I wouldn't know. I had asked the OC that too. He didn't say anything. Every day, he has the same thing to say—routine enquiry; that my son has nothing to fear. But then they keep calling him.'

Hariprasanna Kalita fell into deep thought. Then he said, 'The case is complicated, Hazarika, it has a few problems. Do you have any papers for these visits to the police station…like summons?'

'No, they never gave us any written summons. But my boy is innocent. He is not involved in these things.'

'That is the problem. You see, Hazarika, your son has not been arrested by the police. Had they arrested him, they would have had to produce him before a judge… I mean, charge sheet him. We would have found out for sure what the charge was and would have been able to tell you what to do. We could have appealed in the court for a solution. We can only move for bail petitions after an arrest. If the police had not produced the accused in court in time or had detained him, we could have appealed for habeas corpus for producing the prisoner. That would have been granted, too.'

'But he has not been arrested.'

'That's what I meant, therein lies the problem. Your son stays with you; he has not been arrested, and he has not been mistreated either. They only keep calling him to the station.'

'Almost every week...'

'I understand, it must be very painful. But I can't see a way out so soon. Please don't worry so much, Hazarika. The police have started off unofficially. He has been called to the station by a police officer, but unofficially.'

'But this is injustice, harassment.'

'Hazarika, I admit that their actions aren't legal. The police cannot arbitrarily call anybody to the station; summons have to be issued under a particular statute of the law. Or an arrest should precede interrogation. The police have to obey laws too. But times are so bad…these are unnatural times, Hazarika. I should tell you that a court appeal will have one outcome. They will not be able to call him to the station like this. They will only be able to take him to the station by arresting him or by issuing summons. If you wish you can appeal in the court.'

Arrest. Court. Hazarika's heart missed a beat.

'Hazarika, to be honest, I cannot think of an effective way out of this situation except through bribes. But please don't worry, let me make some enquiries on my own. You should give it some thought too, and let me know. Keep in touch. We must do something.'

Partha was listening to their conversation with interest.

Narayan Hazarika was very disheartened. Hariprasanna Kalita walked him to the gate. When he came back to his chambers, he looked worried. He told Partha, 'The problems start when the authorities take the indirect route, instead of the direct.'

'What do you mean?'

'I mean the police cannot unnecessarily harass any citizen; for purposes of investigation, they can conduct a reasonable enquiry. But it is becoming increasingly difficult to say where the reasonable enquiry ends and harassment begins.'

'If the police are so interested in the boy, they must have surely found some evidence,' Partha said.

'Not necessarily. It might be only suspicion. But then they need very little to get suspicious. Then they begin the process to find evidence where there is none. That's what these people from the Police Intelligence do. Most of the time their suspicions are found to be baseless; but sometimes, if they persist for long, they get results. They must have begun a similar blind process with Hazarika's son,' explained Kalita.

'That sounds dangerous,' Partha said, somewhat worried and shocked.

'Well, that's how things are.'

After the meeting he had witnessed, Partha grew interested in the whole incident. He wanted to know what course it would take. It had the makings of a good story. Collecting the address from Hariprasanna Kalita, he made his way to Hazarika's house one day. He liked the man; in fact, he liked the whole family. He felt a surge of sympathy towards them for facing an unexpected crisis. He also understood that Hazarika liked confiding in him—it helped him unburden himself.

Mulling over the report in his office, Partha was thinking about these things. He had an office in his own house; it was a big house, and there were several unused rooms. He also had two phones. His office had asked him to take an office-cum-residence if necessary, but there was no need to do so; the office was also supposed to give him a fax machine.

He would go to Hazarika's house today. A month had passed, hadn't it? Yes, almost a month. How things would have developed in this time?

In the evening, Partha drove to Hazarika's house. When he advanced on the road, with its stones and potholes, the odour from the garbage dump floated up to him. He hurriedly rolled up the windows of his Maruti. His father had actually bought him a second-hand red Maruti car, an old model. He was embarrassed to take it. He wondered which buddy of his father had supplied him with the car. Had he paid for it in full? But it was a good car, he could vouch for that.

It was of no use. The nauseating stench had seeped inside the car. It seemed to cling to his nose, his clothes, and the car, like grease. He hurriedly fished out a cigarette. But before he could light it, he had reached Hazarika's house. Parking the car in the yard, he lit the cigarette.

When he knocked, somebody switched on the light in front and peeped at him through the glass. Then the door opened. It was Mrs Hazarika.

'Isn't Mr Hazarika home?'

'No, he isn't.'

'How long will he be?'

'He has gone to Jorhat. Please come in.'

Partha hesitated. Deciding that some information was better than none, he walked into the simply furnished living room and sat down. The lady excused herself and went in. Partha walked out onto the verandah and snuffed out his cigarette. He did not feel like smoking in front of Mrs Hazarika. A few minutes later, she walked in with a tray bearing two cups of tea and a plate of crisp spinach pakoras. With a cup of tea in her hand, she sat down, too.

'This wasn't necessary.'

'Please have some tea. I had already made it.'

The tea and the hot pakoras tasted good.

'So, Mr Hazarika has gone to Jorhat.'

'Yes, he has taken Prabhat with him.'

'A social trip?'

'He has taken Prabhat along to cheer him up. A distant cousin is getting married. He need not have attended—he has gone only because he wanted Prabhat to have a change of scene.'

Anger, disgust, and helplessness washed over the lady's face.

'He is in a very bad state. You know everything; you are from the press. Please do something if possible... We are under a lot of stress. What is going to happen to my boy?'

'Has something else happened?' enquired Partha.

Malati Hazarika fell into memories...

'Why are you in bed in the afternoon? What's wrong? Aren't you feeling well?'

Prabhat did not answer. He turned his face away. His mother sat down by his side and stroked his hair. After some time, she noticed that he was sobbing. Her heart fluttered. What was wrong with the boy?

'What's wrong, baba? Why are you crying?'

Prabhat threw his arms round his mother.

'Come on, tell me what's wrong.'

'I won't stay here any longer. I won't go to college; I won't go for tuitions.'

'Eh, what are you saying? Tell me what has happened.'

A heavy load seemed to crush her heart.

'Did you go to the station today? They didn't call you today, did they?'

'No.'

'Did something happen in college?'

'No.'

'Then?'

'Pinaki and his friends…' he sobbed again.

'Pinaki and his friends…what did they do?'

Wasn't Pinaki Mrs Barua's youngest son? Yes, the one Mrs Das had said was close to the underground rebels. Her heart beat faster. Wasn't he a couple of years older than Prabhat?

'What did they do to you? Who was in the group?'

'Pinaki, Neerav, Chandra—the three of them.'

All of them were known to be the neighbourhood's troublemakers. At the time of the Assam agitation, the police had thrashed them quite a few times. What did they say to Prabhat?

'Come on, baba, tell me. What did Pinaki say to you?'

Prabhat recounted exactly what had happened to his mother:

'Here, Prabhat, come here, you seem to go the police station very often nowadays. What's the matter?' Pinaki questioned him.

Prabhat was startled. Squirming, he said, 'Just a couple of times...'

'But why do you keep going there?' Neerav shot at him.

'They call me to the station.'

'Who calls you? The police?' Chandra joined the interrogation, too.

'Yes, the police.'

'Do they call you every time?' Pinaki interrogated.

'Yes. They called me the first time. When I went there, I was called again. Now, they call me every week.'

'Why do they call you? Don't lie to us.'

'To ask me a few questions. They say it's because of an investigation.'

'Questions? What questions?' all three of them barked together.

'Whether I know someone, any of the underground rebels...' Prabhat said, in a scared voice. The boys surrounded him.

'And what do you say?'

'I tell them I don't know anyone; I don't know anything.'

'Is that the truth? What else? Have you been beaten up?'

'I swear. No, nothing else. They haven't laid a finger on me so far.'

'Did they ask about anybody in particular?'

'No.' (He did not tell them about the photographs and the two unknown young men.)

'Look here, Prabhat,' said Pinaki, playing with a button on his shirt, 'we consider you to be a nice boy. You will have to tell us what you are asked at the station. And I warn you, they shouldn't find out that you have been talking to us. Listen, Prabhat, you are one of us and we do not want you to come to harm. But if we find out that you have been spying or brokering for the police, then you have had it. Consider this a timely warning.'

V

'Then the boy has turned into a spy.'

'Not yet, but he is on the verge of becoming one.'

Neelratan Choudhury clicked his tongue, as if in disappointment.

'And for no fault of his. Isn't this an illogical turn of events?'

Closing his eyes, Choudhury nodded as if he was in complete agreement with what Partha had said. Choudhury was the North-East representative of a prominent news agency, a 'guru' to all budding journalists. They often called on him for a chat. Partha was narrating Prabhat's story to him.

'The boy is repeatedly summoned to the police station. These unnecessary calls have put him in a great deal of trouble. The other boys of the neighbourhood are now suspicious of him. They have questioned, even warned him! He has started believing that everybody suspects him now. Apparently, he has been followed a couple of times. The boy is in very bad shape. Can something be done about it?'

'I beg your pardon?' Opening his eyes, Choudhury emerged from his state of meditation. 'I have seen such incidents happen in many places. It's a tragedy, you see. I have had many similar experiences while covering insurgency in the North-East. There's a saying in Assamese: the squirrel eats nuts; the mongoose is caught and flayed. But you know, it is a different matter altogether. When society is in a state of turmoil, especially when there is a movement like insurgency and there is government repression, there is an air of suspicion everywhere. The common man becomes suspicious too. I have seen huge tragedies taking place in such situations.'

'But he has no ties with the organization.'

'That is the genesis of the tragedy. It would have been different if he actually had any ties.'

'Can anything be done about it?'

'I will have to think about it. There's isn't much hope.' Choudhury remarked unenthusiastically.

'What do you think will the outcome be? I mean, this problem in Assam…' Partha changed the subject.

'What can it be, eh?' Choudhury made no secret of his indifference to the whole topic. For some time, he stared out of the window. Then he glared at Partha, 'All that is happening in the name of armed struggle…does anybody seriously believe that it will work?'

'Do you mean to say that armed struggle is the wrong means to an end?' Partha decided to bait him a little.

'Why would I say that? But, baba, where is this "armed revolution?" (his words dripped with sarcasm.) He paused for a moment, then continued, 'A couple of bank robberies, extorting money at gunpoint, murdering people with conflicting viewpoints—can such scattered violence be called armed struggle? Come on, tell me. An armed struggle is not carried out by a group of people hiding in the jungles, or by an organization. People, the masses, are responsible for it. But where are your masses? It is difficult to involve people in a Gandhian, non-violent movement today; imagine how difficult it would be to motivate them to take part in an armed struggle. Do you see any such movements taking seed? I don't. So, I am unable to take the issue of armed struggle seriously, even if I wanted to. Can you?'

He picked up a paper cutter from the table and started fingering it. Partha observed him. He was a complex character. He had a reputation of being a very professional journalist, and he advised Partha and his friends to be professional as well.

'Do not ever get personally involved with news and incidents. It is not your job to reform a wrongdoer. Your job is to help correctly guide society by discovering the truth behind a particular incident.'

The old man sometimes gave long speeches. When Partha had begun talking about Prabhat, he had initially looked at him with some annoyance. Choudhury really was a complex character. He had been reporting on insurgency in the North-East for more than 20 years. He had submitted some excellent reports. He had such a reputation that people—in particular those in power—listened to him, though most of the political leaders secretly detested him.

'Your boys did not learn anything from the North-East insurgency experiences. Arre bhai, an armed struggle does not happen if you only pick up guns. You need a massive social movement for that. Massive, Partha, do you understand? There has to be a mass awakening. Even if you have to take up arms, you would need a mass involvement.'

After a pause, the conversation continued.

'Nagaland, Mizoram…these are very small states. Initially, the movements in those states had plenty of mass support. But the population there is small, there is no strength of numbers. On the one hand, you have few men—brave fighters, superior terrain—and on the other, lakhs of soldiers and crores of rupees. A very unequal fight. But Assam is not like that. There are lakhs of people here, the terrain is good too, but they hide in forests cut off from humanity. Guns by choice and scattered violence. Ha!' A glass appeared magically in Choudhury's hands. The old man must have been drinking.

'To be or not to be, violence or non-violence. Is that the question?' Partha paid a little homage to Shakespeare.

'Don't murder the Queen's English, Partha. Violence was never the question. Violence is the reaction of a repressed people. The question is, what kind of violence?'

What kind of violence? Partha released a dramatic expression.

'Not scattered violence. If violence it has to be, it should be the violence of the awakened public that can sweep away the obstacles confronting you (he spread his hands in a dramatic gesture). The violence of a group deteriorates to anarchic violence and eventually alienates the people; they fail to understand the expressions of such violence. Personally, if you ask me, I will tell you that I have no confidence in violence...but then again, I do. I suppose violence cannot be avoided totally.'

Partha was silent for a while.

Dusk fell slowly over a dust-covered Guwahati. Through the window, one caught glimpses of the sky drained of its colour, anticipating the night.

'Why don't you write about these things?'

'Why should I? I am a professional journalist, not the ideological leader of any organization. Ho, ho, ho (his laugh was most unusual, staccato). My job is to know and to let the readers, buying their papers from the agency I submit my reports to, know. I let them know what others are doing or trying to do, I don't tell them what to do.'

Choudhury glared at Partha for a long time. Then pouring himself another drink and taking a sip, he said, 'Let me tell you a story... I was quite junior at that time and I was covering the insurgency; I won't tell you where. You can guess the name of the place. What happens when the military launches operations to suppress insurgency had happened there too. Innocent people were harassed on a large scale. People were recklessly shot, tortured, and what have you. There were a few rapes as well—all in the name of hunting down the insurgents. I was a young journalist then. My blood boiled. I thought of doing something. Couldn't they be stopped? I reported the incidents. The news from the agency appeared in a column in important newspapers. Nothing came of it. I wrote about them, with no effect. Then, we did not even have a 10th of the interest the country's newspapers have in the North-East today.'

There was a slight interval, a sip at the drink, a cigarette lit.

'One day, I thought there was only one way to end this torture.'

'What was that?' Partha was visibly curious.

'Unless, after every incident of harassment, the insurgents did not launch retaliatory counterattacks and scare the people of the armed forces—who worked hard for a living—to prove "if you harass us once, we'll take revenge 10 times greater", the harassment would not stop.'

'Most interesting. What did you do about it?'

'I couldn't possibly write that. Then, one day, I met a distinguished gentleman. Respected by either camp—the insurgents and the government. I met him and interviewed him like the journalist I was. I narrated the incidents of harassment; he had heard about them earlier. After listening to me, he flared up and burst out, "The perpetrators must be punished for their acts of injustice! People should punish them. Instead, the government gives them protection. Men who shoot innocent people like cats and dogs should be gunned down as well!" I couldn't have asked for more. And the headline flashed, quoting the distinguished gentleman. If you have to stop harassment, its perpetrators have to be punished.'

'In less than a month, the counterattacks had started. The idea was picked up quickly. The attacks and counterattacks lasted for some time. The people suffered a good deal. But gradually, the word spread that if the civilians are harassed, the insurgents take violent revenge. Gradually, after a few days, the tortures ceased. They might not have ceased completely, but they practically came to an end.'

Partha listened to Choudhury in surprise.

'Now, tell me what the moral of the story is. No idea? Okay, I will tell you: that journalists cannot say certain things as journalists. But they can make others say them. Don't say things, make others do it for you. I had not planned to make the leader talk. He did it himself. That's when I realized that if you can create the proper atmosphere, you can elicit certain responses. Ho, ho! I have given you a gem of wisdom, a trick of the trade today. It is a very dangerous weapon, keep that in mind. The 'Pashupat', the most powerful weapon of mythology, if you cannot control it you will be in deep trouble. Exercise caution when you use it. Ho, ho, ho!'

How strange was his laughter? He sounded like a fox with a bad throat! Have you ever heard a fox with a bad throat? No, but surely if such a fox laughed, he would sound like this. The cynical old man, a store house of tricks. Partha was highly amused by his words.

Dusk had enveloped the Guwahati sky. It now wore a dirty ashen colour. Through the window, one could see a pinch of the sky. The crows were heading to their nests...hundreds of them in scattered formations.

There was a knock on the door. Choudhury's servant answered the door. A stocky, short-haired man walked in, smiling. He had an enormous nose, it seemed to Partha as if the nose preceded him in the room. Also, he had eyes like those of a predatory bird. The fragrance of Brute cologne accompanied him.

'Welcome, Jagmohan! Have you met Partha?'

'Unfortunately, not!' Partha stood up and extended his hand.

'Jagmohan is the Intelligence boss of this region, and Partha here is a journalist,' Choudhury introduced the two men to each other.

'Excellent!' Mr Stocky seemed pleased to see him.

'I have got something for you,' Mr Stocky bore a packet in his hands. It was a bottle of scotch. He raised the bottle and showed them the golden liquid; the bottle sparkled in the light.

'Great!' Choudhury sounded elated. 'Partha, please get us three glasses from the cabinet in the next room, will you?'

Golden liquor in three elegant glasses that danced in the light.

'Scotch should be had neat. At most, you can add ice cubes, but nothing else! The uncivilized add soda or water.' Choudhury pushed the glass in front of Stocky.

The dark sky was visible through the window. The crows were nowhere to be seen anymore. In the room, in the soft glow of dusk's fading light, the small talk between an Intelligence officer and a journalist continued.

'Have you seen the political announcement made by the underground—that of scientific socialism?' Choudhury asked.

'They have been saying that for a long time.'

'This time, they have explained it more clearly.'

'Where?'

Choudhury waved a small booklet like a flag.

'Their journal for publicity.'

'Let me have a look. I haven't seen it!' exclaimed Jagmohan.

'What do you mean you haven't seen it? You are someone from the Intelligence! This came out a while ago. A month, maybe two, isn't it, Partha?'

'Seriously, I haven't. I want a copy of this. Do you have a spare copy? No, let me xerox it. Please call your boy.' Jagmohan fished a wallet out of his pocket.

'Look here, we should be getting such things from you bosses of the Intelligence. And you take them from us journalists! Ho, ho, ho...strange. A failure of the Intelligence, I say!'

'Arre, you get a lot of information...lot of stuff too. You never let us know, do you?'

'And why should we? The information we receive can be found in the reports we submit.'

'Not everything, if I am right.' The last words were cast at Partha. The smile on his face reminded Partha of one on a crocodile's jaws.

Of all the documents published by the absconding rebels, this was the most significant. And the Intelligence boss did not know about its existence till now. It had been distributed quite openly. This was the state of the Police Intelligence! Perhaps that is why some blind processes like summoning Prabhat to the station had been established repeatedly. Groping in the dark—you never knew when you might find something!

'What is your comment on this?'

'Will be published in the papers tomorrow. A long article. A special article. Please read it.'

'Sure. Why don't you give me the summary?'

'You will find the summary in the papers. Facts too. Everything.'

Jagmohan was a little miffed. It occurred to Partha that had Choudhury provided him with the summary, Jagmohan might not have read the article at all. Mr Stocky might not have made that effort after all. Now he was forced to read it, so he was miffed.

They sipped the golden liquor. The ice cubes had melted slightly.

'What else is happening? I have been out of town for quite some time.'

'Why don't you tell him, Partha? That's Partha's story,' Choudhury suddenly said.

Partha narrated Prabhat's story. Jagmohan listened to him mostly in silence, interrupting only to ask a few basic questions like the name of the police station and of the officer, and Prabhat's address.

'Look, Jagmohan, this is foolishness. If such incidents have become widespread, I am convinced we are in for trouble. And you know, irrational and injudicious acts alienate people from the State like nothing else; they debilitate the very foundation of the State. They are unnecessary, and top brass such as you should be more careful.'

Mr Stocky listened attentively, and said, 'I am aware that there is an investigation in progress regarding a top leader. I don't know the details. I promise I will make enquiries.'

Partha wanted to say something, but fell silent when he saw Choudhury's face.

It was dark all around by now.

Looking at his watch, Partha rose to his feet. He had to send a late dispatch for the city edition. Mr Stocky and the fox with the bad throat sat with the scotch. As he descended the stairs, he heard them break into loud laughter—the laughter that slipped out of the cracks in the door and chased Partha.

'Creatures of the establishment,' Partha said to himself when it suddenly struck him. Mr Stocky, directly, and the old fox with a sore throat, indirectly, were both diligent guardians of the State.

He felt as if he had made a small, but significant, discovery.

VI

'So, I take it that the visits to the police station have stopped?'

'Yes, thank God.' Hazarika sounded elated.

Partha was meeting him after one and a half months. He had often thought about them, but had been unable to pay a visit because of his work. His reporting had taken him to Delhi once, to upper Assam twice, and to Manipur once as well. In a place called Oinam in Manipur, the military had been perpetrating severe atrocities. A few Human Rights activists had uncovered the ugly situation and the case was now in court.

'He does not have to go regularly to the police station anymore. I have only been asked to inform them if he happens to go out of Guwahati.'

'But how did this happen? Did the top official you know, the commissioner perhaps, helped?' Partha asked.

'Not at all. He did nothing at all. These people are of no use,' Hazarika's voice was full of bitterness. 'I did not want to meet him. I was forced to go because of Prabhat's mother.'

'What did he have to say?'

Hazarika recounted the tale:

'He must have some connection with the terrorists. Why would the police suspect him otherwise? They must have some proof,' said the commissioner.

'But he is innocent. He has not even been remotely involved in such activities!'

'You can't trust them, Hazarika, you can't trust them. Each young man is a potential extremist nowadays. That's what the police think, too. And they have their reasons. Little boys are shooting people, robbing banks, crossing borders to set up camps in other countries. The underground groups they join in foreign lands—the Burma Kachins, Karen, Shan—they are all drug smugglers. Aren't you aware of these happenings?'

Hazarika felt very helpless. 'But he is not involved,' he remained firm.

'Good for him,' said the commissioner, indifferently.

Dressed in a floral shirt and a pair of pyjamas, the commissioner sat on the spacious verandah in front of his house. Two cars were parked on the portico—a personal car and a red light-flashing official car. A uniformed policeman stood at the gate. Sitting on a cane chair, the officer was fidgeting, obviously in some discomfort. Hazarika had turned up at his house when he was seeing off a Marwari gentleman. Hazarika had heard that it was very difficult to meet the commissioner, that he would keep people waiting for at least half an hour.

'Did you explain Prabhat's case to him in detail?' Partha asked.

'I did, right from the beginning. But he showed no interest.'

Hazarika continued recounting:

'I am not very well, you see,' the commissioner said, belching loudly, and pinching himself gently all over his stomach. 'I am thinking of giving office a miss today. There was a departmental promotion meeting scheduled. I have asked that to be cancelled. My wife's ordered some *magur* fish and curry leaves; apparently, they are good when you have indigestion. You see, I am not very fond of allopathic medicine.'

A stale odour ensued from where the commissioner sat. Hazarika felt very uncomfortable. The commissioner got to his feet. Hazarika held out a piece of paper to him. 'I have written the important details here,' he said, handing it to the commissioner.

'All right, I will see what I can do. If there are no specific charges, the police won't bother him once they are done with their investigation.'

Hazarika left. From a distance, he saw the man talking to the policeman at the gate, crumpling the piece of paper into a small ball.

'That's when I decided to act. It's futile to rely on others. Nobody is going to help you. So, I...' Hazarika said, angry and empowered at the same time.

'And what did you do?' Partha asked excitedly.

'I decided to find out for myself what Prabhat's crime was. Why he was being repeatedly called to the station. The police never give any explanations; they only tell me that an investigation is in progress, and call Partha again and again. But they must have something in mind. So, I now tried to find out what his crime was.'

'How did you do that?'

'I started with Prabhat. I pestered him for details on what the police had asked him.'

'And what did he say?'

Hazarika started to recount his conversation with Prabhat to Partha:

'I don't remember everything,' Prabhat said.

'Do try to remember. Did they question you about anybody in particular? For instance, Pinaki or any of his friends from our neighbourhood?' pressed Hazarika.

'No.'

'What about your classmates?'

'They did not mention any names. They only wanted to know if I knew anybody connected to the underground.'

'And the photographs they showed you...'

'But I don't know anybody in those photographs.'

'Didn't they ask you about one of your classmates?'

Prabhat thought for a while. 'Yes, they had asked me about Subrata.'

'They wanted to know if any of the boys at the station was Subrata, didn't they?'

'Yes. But none of those boys was Subrata. They were beaten so cruelly...'

'Who is this Subrata?'

'He was my classmate in Higher Secondary.'

'Did you know him well?'

'I did. Don't you remember? He used to come to our house.'

'Did he?'

'Yes, a couple of times. That boy who looked much older than us. You had asked me once what a boy much older than me was doing in our class.'

'Now I remember. I do remember him. Is that Subrata underground now? Where is he?'

'He went home after his first year of Higher Secondary.'

'Why did he leave?'

'I have no idea. In any case, he was not very interested in studies. He would regularly bunk classes.'

'And why did you make friends with such boys?'

'No, no, he used to read a lot. He owned a lot of books.'

'Now wait, has he gone underground?'

'I have no idea. Possibly.'

'I figured it out,' Narayan Hazarika told Partha. 'This Subrata was the culprit. It was because of him that the police kept bothering Prabhat. So now, I started making enquiries about this boy called Subrata.'

Partha was amused by Hazarika's account of his amateur detective efforts.

'And how did you go about your investigation?'

'Ha ha. You are right. It was investigation of a kind. You know, I feel like telling you things. But you are a newspaper man... Please don't go and publish everything that I tell you. I thought that the best sources of information would be the boys who were close to the fugitives. So, I decided to talk to them.'

Partha drew his chair closer to Hazarika. The suspense was gradually building. Hazarika continued, 'There are a few boys in our neighbourhood who are rumoured to have close ties to the underground. I don't know how close they really are, but people say that they are involved. Pinaki, for example. He is Barua's son. He was, in fact, the one who warned Prabhat. I thought of talking to him.'

'So, did you talk to him?'

'Yes, I did.'

'What did you ask him?'

Hazarika recounted:

'Here, Pinaki, I would like to have a word with you.'

'Go ahead, uncle.'

'I am in serious trouble, Pinaki. Only you can help me.'

'I am listening, uncle.'

'I think you know it already. It's Prabhat's problem. It's causing us a lot of trouble.'

'I knew you were going to talk about Prabhat, uncle. I expected you to come much earlier though.'

'You have warned him. He is very scared, you know.'

'It's not a warning, uncle, we have only cautioned him. We know that Prabhat is a nice boy, a really nice boy. We haven't been able to make out why the police keep calling him to the station. Prabhat is a simple boy, the police might ask him something and he might end up saying something else, something that would land us in trouble.'

'No, no, not at all. Why would he say anything that will cause you trouble?' Hazarika protested, loudly. 'Why would he talk about you? He hasn't been asked about you, you know.'

'What do they want to know?'

'They have asked him about Subrata, in a roundabout way.'

'Subrata? Who is Subrata?'

Hazarika was confused. He did not know if he had acted wisely in mentioning Subrata's name. He grew a little apprehensive.

'That Subrata, he was their classmate in Higher Secondary. He had come to our house a couple of times. He looked much older than the rest of them. A healthy boy. He was a tenant here, somewhere. Apparently, he dropped out of college.'

Pinaki thought for a while. He looked at Hazarika sitting in front of him. The man looked harassed. He was also looking at him with a lot of expectation. Pinaki felt sorry for him.

'Uncle, let me tell you something. Between us, Prabhat has nothing to be afraid of. Really, he has nothing to fear. Please don't worry. We were a little suspicious that the police might ask him questions about Subrata. If he had told us himself, there would have been nothing to worry about.'

'He still doesn't know that he is being interrogated because of Subrata. That's my guess, because he has been asked about Subrata in particular twice.'

'Uncle, please listen to me. This boy called Subrata…he is a top leader now. He holds an important position.'

'Where is he?'

'How would I know? Sometimes he comes to Guwahati. I had heard that he was here a few months ago. His name is Bharat, Arindam Phukan.'

'Not Subrata?'

'That's his old name. No wonder I couldn't place him when you said Subrata. But uncle, this is strictly between us.'

'Yes, of course. Let's assume that we have never had this talk. But I would like to tell you something, too. You are like my own son, so I request you to look after Prabhat, please. The boy is very simple.'

'Please don't worry, uncle.'

'Pinaki, if you let him know yourself, the boy would be reassured.'

'So, the famous Arindam Phukan was your son's classmate, Subrata!'

'That's right.' Hazarika sounded worried. He was a little uncomfortable about having told all this to Partha. He was a reporter, after all. He hoped he would not publish their conversations. At the same time, he felt much lighter after talking to the young man.

'You are a journalist. I hope you will not spread it.'

'No, I won't. Please don't worry about it.'

'I am not worrying. You know what it has been like for us from the beginning. One can't help feeling a little frightened.'

'What did you do after you found out Subrata's identity?'

'For a few days, nothing. But they started calling Prabhat to the station frequently. It seems they took him somewhere once. Things did not look good. His mother's health was getting affected...high blood pressure'.

'Really! How is she now?'

'She is on medication.'

'What did you do after that?'

'What else could I do? I couldn't watch the boy and his mother suffer before my eyes. I went to the station and met the OC. I asked him why he was harassing my son. Told him that the boy named Subrata the police have been troubling my son about has had no contact with him for the last three years. That my son doesn't know till today that that boy is Arindam Phukan, a top leader. I let the commissioner know that that's what I had found out, and that I was telling him because I would like an end to this. But I did not tell the OC where I got my information from. He did not ask me either.'

'What did the OC do?'

'He did not say much. He took out Prabhat's file and jotted down what I had told him.'

'In the file?'

'Yes, in the file. But he did tell me that if that was the case, it was clear that my son was innocent. After a couple of days, when Prabhat went to the station, he was told not to come anymore. But I have told you that already...'

'When was that?'

'About a month ago.'

Partha did a quick mental calculation. The summons to the station had stopped about a week after he and Choudhury had given Jagmohan the details of the case. But he did not reveal this to Hazarika.

'That's great news. So, it's all behind you now!'

'I couldn't agree more. I can't explain to you what a huge relief it is. I was really very scared. But going to the station and telling them everything clearly helped, didn't it? However, I have been a little worried about something...'

'What is that?'

'After I spoke to the OC, my name was put down on Prabhat's file as an informer. Do you think that might create any problems?'

A GREEN WORLD SWEPT BY THE CAR WINDOW

I

A cloudless blue sky.

The peaks of mountains stretching across horizons, as if they were standing arm-in-arm. Each mountain slope glowed in the bright light; the erosions were yellow chasms in dark blue. From a distance, they looked like paths leading up the mountain. In the evenings, the mountains would turn grey in colour, with just a hint of blue.

As far as he could see, a sea of green paddy stretched out in front of him. The roads cutting through the fields were covered by the heads of the paddy, bowed with the weight of the grains. Occasionally, a solitary tree stood on a small mound, like a lone sentinel. Scattered all over were the bamboo bushes. The pictures on the windows of the gypsy danced as the car travelled over the winding road.

Partha tore his gaze away from the world outside, and turned to the boy driving the car. The boy, wearing a cap with a long shade, drove with deep concentration. How old was he? About 17 or 18? Close to that. A film of hardness had obscured the youthful charm of his face. He was chewing gum intently.

Partha fished out a packet of chewing gum from his bag. He popped one into his mouth and offered another to the boy sitting at the back of the car. What was he up to? He was cleaning a gun. Was it loaded? What if it went off? Partha handed the remaining pieces of chewing gum to the driver. Spitting out the gum in his mouth, he popped in the new pieces and smiled at Partha like a little boy. His eyes, a bright brown, sparkled. For a moment, the hard muscles on his jaws relaxed; he was just a child.

From the beginning of the journey, they had not said a word to Partha. All his efforts at conversation had bounced off their monosyllabic answers. After a point, he had given up and taken to staring out of the window in silence—looking at the sea of green paddy, the range of mountains turning a gradual grey, the solitary trees in the fields, and a village surrounded by clusters of bamboo.

Partha had got off at a small town, after an overnight journey by bus. An elderly man, clad in a Hawaiian shirt over a dhoti, picked him out correctly from among the crowd of passengers descending from the bus. 'I am Deba Gohain. I hold a minor post in the Panchayat department,' he introduced himself to Partha. On their way back from the bus stop in an autorickshaw, he added, 'We will go to my house now. You can take some rest. I hope your journey was not very uncomfortable.'

'No, not at all. I slept most of the time,' Partha said.

'That's good. I find it hard to sleep on night buses.'

'How is the heat? Has it been raining?'

'It's fairly hot. It has been raining, too. In fact, it rained heavily yesterday night.'

The world was soaking wet. The leaves of trees, washed by the rain, glistened in the morning sun. At one end of the small town, Gohain owned a spacious 'Assam type' house. There were a variety of trees in his sprawling yard—mangos, areca nut, jackfruit, et al.

'Please make yourself comfortable.' Gohain was an attentive host.

A boy sat on the bench in the verandah, swinging his legs. He smiled at Partha hesitantly and whispered a question into Gohain's ears. Gohain nodded vigorously. The boy hurriedly stepped down from the verandah. Mounting the Honda parked near the gate, he sped out of the yard. The roar of the motorcycle rang in Partha's ears for a long time.

'They have been informed about your arrival. A car will pick you up. Maybe you can take some rest now.'

'Plenty of oil has been discovered around here, hasn't it? I saw a number of oil rigs on the way.'

'You are right, and that has been our undoing. All the waste that comes up while drilling for oil is emptied into the ponds, in our fields. Our fields have become poisonous. All the fish were killed long ago, now it's the paddy's turn.'

Partha was genuinely surprised.

'The oil companies belong to the government. And the government is giving the public a hard time. It's the greed of the high-ups, you see.'

'Any compensation?' asked Partha.

'Compensation indeed. They even trick you out of the oil in your garden.

'What?'

'Oh yes. If the oil companies discover that there is oil in your yard, they will not drill for oil there. They would have to purchase your land then, spend money. What they do instead is install pipes in public land and slant the pipes by a degree or two so that a thousand feet into the ground, the pipes would find their way into your land. And you wouldn't even know. A bunch of cheats.'

Partha listened to Gohain in surprise. He did not want to believe him but deep down he knew that Gohain was telling the truth, and he felt a wave of misery sweep over him.

As darkness descended, the mountains became a blur. Dusk gathered on the bamboo trees lining the road; it would slowly spread to the bosom of the open fields. The boy driving the car switched on the headlights, but only one light came to life. 'I thought I had got it repaired. What a pain this is,' he said.

In the single beam, the surrounding darkness deepened. Apart from the route of light, nothing else could be seen.

Partha had been waiting for the boys for almost the whole day. Against his will, he had to take an early dinner at Gohain's insistence. The duck meat, cooked in pepper, had been delicious. He had killed time by reading insignificant bits of news from the old newspaper in the drawing room. When a motorcycle sped into the yard, Gohain had stepped out hurriedly. From the drawing room, Partha could see him talking to the rider. 'You have to be ready; the car that's going to pick you up is almost here.' Gohain had told him.

Half an hour later, Partha had climbed into the Maruti Gypsy, which bore the name of a government department. A little later, the car left the paved roads for the road winding through the village. The afternoon sun was about to set.

It all seemed unreal to Partha; like a dream. Every part of Gohain's house bore the clear imprint of a young woman's hands; the indistinct sound of a sweet voice floated in occasionally. Who was the mysterious young lady? This car with a government stamp, the boy roaring on his Honda, the gypsy speeding through the village, the marks of several wheels on the roads—the hide-and-seek between secrecy and openness—all these seemed like a part of an illusion. Was this a project undertaken in seriousness?

When he had been invited to conduct a secret interview with the underground leaders, Partha was elated. He had been requested to maintain complete secrecy. But he had felt a little uncomfortable when the two boys, who met him at the press club, had spirited him away to talk about the meeting before the questioning glances of the other reporters.

Partha had met Choudhury. 'I know you have interviewed a number of underground leaders; I might have a similar opportunity soon. I would just like to know a little more about the interview techniques.'

Choudhury, as always, made a number of facetious remarks. He seemed a little envious, too.

'They are a bunch of cheats. What use is it to interview them?'

Partha kept quiet.

'Don't show any unnecessary enthusiasm,' Choudhury finally seemed inclined to talk, 'Be professional. Remember that the underground leaders are insecure men. Don't accept any gifts, in particular costly gifts, or money. Reject them as politely as you can. Remember that only professionals are respected.'

Snapping out of his memories, Partha saw that it was raining again. The windscreen blurred. In the light from the headlight, the raindrops looked like arrows.

'It rained heavily yesterday night. We had a clear day though,' said one of the boys. Gradually, the rain increased. The wipers of the car did not work; the car slowed down. Finally, it was almost impossible to drive. The boy stopped the car under a huge tree. There was no thunder or lightning, and so, little danger in parking under a tree. The headlights were switched off. The rain beat down steadily on the hood.

'Have you ever come to any of our "places", Kakaideu (elder brother in Assamese)?' the boy in the driver's seat spoke up in the darkness.

'No, I haven't. Is your house somewhere nearby?'

'We just left it behind.'

Partha remembered a boy, driving into a village enveloped by darkness, trying his best to peer though the dark…

'Kakaideu, what do you think about our revolution?'

The boys, who had been unwilling to talk for so long, now initiated a conversation. The rain-filled darkness had perhaps relaxed their guard a little. It was dark outside, and pouring; were they looking for a sense of comfort in talk?

'I do not know much about it,' Partha replied, honestly. 'I hope to learn a lot from this journey. Why don't you tell me about it yourselves?'

'We believe in armed revolution. What do you think, Kakaideu?'

'Why do you believe in it?' Partha dodged their question.

'Where do you see real democracy, Kakaideu? Aren't the elections a means of granting legitimacy to rule by exploitation? Is it possible to reform a society such as this, Kakaideu?'

'When elections are held by the police-military at gunpoint, it is difficult to say who is going to vote,' said the boy sitting in the back of the car. 'In a country where a government forms in spite of an election boycotted by all major democratic parties—where one becomes a minister with only a hundred votes—is there any respect left for democracy in such a country? Does it inspire any confidence?'

'Weren't proper elections held just two years after that?'

The boys' loud laughter was expressive.

'Kakaideu, in that election, we were the voters as well as the volunteers. How old were we then? About 14, at the most 15.'

'So, you have abandoned thought of all means except for armed revolution,' Partha commented.

'Does the public have faith in any other means? Does the current system hold any charm anymore? And Kakaideu, do you really think that the rights of the people, and the rights over resources, can be established without armed revolution? Haven't the public experimented with democracy many, many times in the last 40 years?'

The two boys seemed more forthcoming now and a little agitated; words streamed out of their mouths. Partha listened to them with attention. But he also wondered what he was doing at their age… Leading a self-centered life, empty of thought. A life spent in studying, playing, having fun. And look at these young boys! One of them had grown up in a remote village, where there was no electricity even today. Weren't they searching for something new in their lives with all the passion and focus of youth?

'Kakaideu, haven't you noticed how the idea of armed revolution has fired the youth? Only this can end the attitude of slavery in the minds and bodies of our people,' said the boy sitting at the back. The boy in the driver's seat rolled down the windows to check the rain.

'The rain's letting up. We can move.' The gypsy's engine thundered to life and the car jolted to a start.

Partha looked out of the window; it was pitch black. In the bushes lining the road, not even a firefly could be seen. The headlights cut a solitary path through that darkness. Partha was thinking about armed revolution. With his limited experience and bookish knowledge, he found it difficult to acknowledge armed revolution to be the only way to freedom. But why not? What was the world's experience? Barring a few special situations, wasn't it a history of failure all along? Come to think of it, it had been successful in those countries where widespread political activity had preceded armed revolution. And what about the circumstances? The armed battle in China had succeeded against local belligerent leaders and foreign attackers, in the absence of a strong central authority. But armed struggle in a tiny part of a huge country ruled by a powerful central government... Could a small group of people initiate armed struggle? Mechanically, without any reference to reality? Wasn't this a crucial political decision for any individual or organization?

The road curved almost from 90 to a 100 degrees. Light filtered through the trees; an orange glow lit up the sky. A few flames, red and yellow, danced over the ground in abandon. A gust of wind occasionally threatened to blow out the flames, without success. What were those flames, like the flames of hell?

'What is that?'

'That's the gas from the oil fields burning. Have you never seen gas being burnt? No? These gases are not waste, they are priceless natural gas. The oil companies are only interested in taking the oil, they have no interest in investing money to make use of the gas. In upper Assam, you would see such fires burning on both banks of the Brahmaputra.'

Partha watched the fire, entranced. The driver said, 'When the wind blows towards this road, you would hear a dreadful wail from the burning flames, as if the earth is in mourning.'

Partha shuddered. So, this was the real face of the industry. Natural resources were coolly extracted, what was redundant was destroyed. Such industry had brought about no change in the lives of the local people, no progress. What it created, instead, was the pain of unemployment and widespread resentment even in the presence of unlimited resources. It had no contribution to make to art or commerce. Was there not any relation between this sense of resentment and armed struggle?

The people witnessing the burning of the fires, yet alienated from its warmth even in the cold of the winter...why would not they resent and detest the system? Why would not they want to take up arms?

Am I trying to justify armed struggle? Partha thought to himself. What was Choudhury's advice? As a journalist, do not jump to conclusions, do not try to justify any incident based on your ideas, that that is bound to colour your report. Collect facts. If your collection is accurate, truth would surface. Always be professional.

'What is the aim of your armed struggle?'

'A free country based on scientific communism.'

Predictable. Clichéd answer to a clichéd question.

'What are the main obstacles to beginning an armed struggle?'

Partha was under the impression that the two boys would say something about the problems with collecting arms, government or military resistance, or the lack of proper awareness among people.

'There is such a variety of people in our state, so many tribes and races. They are all so distinct. It won't do if they can't be united.'

'How do you propose to do it?'

'All identities should be united into one Assamese identity. Otherwise we would find it hard to proceed against the enemy, Kakaideu.'

Was it possible—such ahistorical, unscientific, utopian fantasies?

Entering the world of armed struggle, they had found themselves up against the wall of ethnic consciousness of different tribes and races. They might have realized that the ideas that persisted through time were after all, shallow. They were confused to see the divisions that existed among the large Assamese community, which they had considered to be an indivisible unit. But it was unfortunate that, in the absence of a deep understanding of history and social realism, they had found a solution in denationalization. Partha wanted to tell them that they were wrong; social change did not grow out of some self-created ideas, that social reality could not be changed at will. Unity would perhaps only be possible if every tribe's aspirations were respected. But he kept quiet; he remembered Choudhury, and tried to look at things professionally.

'We are almost there, Kakaideu,' the boy driving the car said.

He drove the car into another road branching off the main road. The headlight shone on both sides of the narrow road. A little ahead lay a village sunk in darkness. He honked his horn at front of a gate.

'Here we are, Kakaideu.'

Partha opened the gate and accompanied the boy into the dark yard. A bamboo door creaked open. A beam of light from a lamp fell on the yard. Two silhouettes stood at the door.

The boy who had been driving the car clicked his heels in a salute and said, 'Sir, our guest is here.'

Holding out his hand, a man walked towards Partha. 'Welcome. I hope you had a comfortable journey. Please come in, we have made arrangements for you to rest here tonight.'

II

A solitary tree, that stood like an ancient sentry on a small mound. As it rose over the ground, it bent slightly and, after a point, grew in the opposite direction. There were two huge protrusions in the bend, full and round like a woman's breasts. Like a misshapen giant, the tree towered over the other trees. Partha stared at it for a long time. For some strange reason, this unnatural tree made him uneasy.

Uneven forest land, with deep spots interspersing the mounds, full of tall grass and shrubs. There were pits and swamps too. A remote land, with an air of inaccessibility.

It was afternoon when Partha had reached this remote area.

The previous night, he had slept early. As he lay in bed, he heard the gate open, the car turn in the yard and drive away in the rain with a mild roar. Had the boys left? He had not even asked their names; they would fade into nameless memories… Sleep descended over random thoughts.

Somebody shook him awake. It was the boy who had greeted him yesterday, holding a cup of tea in his hands. He was still dressed in his camouflage uniform. Partha took a sip of hot tea. Yes, he had slept well. Lunch was served by a girl with Oriental features—steaming hot rice, vegetables, and fried pork; bright red chilies too. The girl serving him, and her companion—who sat at the hearth, cooking—wore no expressions on their faces. They worked lethargically and in complete silence. A small boy, about six or seven years old, was staring at the cold, blue metal of the gun placed on the bed. Stretching his hand cautiously, he fingered the wooden part of the gun. The girl shouted at him, and the boy instantly sprinted indoors.

The journey began after lunch. It was some distance away to the village from where Partha had arrived the day before. One was often in danger of slipping on the muddy uneven roads. Partha was tired. The boys escorting him slowed down, and said to his mild embarrassment:

'Should we rest for a while, dada?'

A relief. Partha greedily flopped down on a trunk lying on the road and lit a cigarette. He did not even know the name of the boy who had been attending to him since yesterday.

'May I know your name?'

'Alok.'

Alok turned and said something to the boy carrying a gun. Plucking a piece of bamboo out of a grove nearby, he cut a stave out of it and handed it to Partha.

'Here you are, dada. This will help you on slippery roads.'

Partha accepted the stick gratefully.

The boy smiled bashfully. A simple boy from the village... anybody could see that.

'Shall we proceed, dada?'

'Yes, of course.'

Indeed, the road was very slippery. It would have been difficult to walk without the stick. After sometime, they had to wade through a muddy stream too. They moved with their pants rolled up above their knees, shoes in their hands, their feet treading on soft sand. Gradually, the water rose to their thighs.

The forest grew denser. There were unknown trees on either side. At one point, a tree lay across the stream and they had to clamber over it. At places, at a distance, one could see ponds covered with hyacinths and weeds. Alok and his companion were attentive to Partha.

'Dada, there are leeches here. But please don't be afraid. We are here.'

At the sound of the word, a shiver ran up Partha's spine. With fear and repulsion, he looked at the water covering his feet and the wet grass on the banks.

'This must be very hard for you, dada,' said Alok.

'A little. But I quite like the experience,' Partha said truthfully.

They reached their destination in the afternoon. The stream wound between a few small mounds, and small shelters stood on them—built out of bamboos and covered with green or black plastic sheets. A few boys, dressed in camouflage and carrying single-barreled guns, perched on the mounds.

Partha was taken to a spacious dugout. Seating him on a bamboo cot, Alok disappeared for a long time. What had happened? Where was he? What were the boys doing setting up camps in such remote, godforsaken areas?

The leaders who had called Partha to interview them only made an appearance towards the evening.

'We are really sorry for making you wait. Please forgive us. I am Bharat Hazarika (Bharat Hazarika. The notorious leader who was absconding!). And this is our camp commander Rondip, Rondip Baruah. (No, he had never heard that name before. This wasn't a real name; it must be an alias.) Partha shook hands with them enthusiastically. Their fit bodies were enclosed in camouflage fatigues, and caps sat on their heads.

'You must have gone through a lot of trouble to get here. Wading through mud and water. We were actually planning to go down to the village to meet you, but I got stuck elsewhere. Have you washed your hands and feet? What about some tea?' Bharat Hazarika seemed genuinely concerned.

'No trouble at all. It was a new experience for me,' said Partha.

They all laughed aloud.

They were all sitting on the bamboo cot inside the dugout. A kerosene lamp flickered in the middle. In the play of light and shade, a sense of mystery enveloped the boys. The caps cast a shadow on their eyes; the slanting light threw one half of their faces into darkness. Conversation continued in low voices.

'We would like to thank you for accepting our invitation,' Bharat Hazarika said, and proceeded to speak in detail about their aims, ambitions, and ideals. A beautiful propaganda speech which said a lot yet gave little away, thought Partha. It was spoken with sincerity, yet the tone of political propaganda was hard to miss; so was the use of certain clichés, like flags. At certain intervals, Partha tried to clarify things with a question or two. Routine.

Now it was his turn to ask questions.

'What is this camp for?'

'A temporary camp for purposes of work,' Bharat Hazarika answered.

'What sort of work?'

'Organizational activity and training.

'What sort of training?'

'Training in endurance and self-discipline and skills to face one's enemies.'

'What about political training?'

'That too; there are classes for that too.'

A feeble, lukewarm reply, Partha thought.

'What sort of political training?' he probed.

'All that is needed.'

Another lukewarm reply. Partha looked at him expectantly. He wanted to hear what else Hazarika had to say.

'You see, we are most interested in creating a skilled soldier; we essentially give a lot of importance to preparing a soldier. We need a disciplined soldier, somebody who can bravely take on the enemy's unlimited might.'

Is there a lack of interest in political training? But that is very important, perhaps far more important than military training. It's a fundamental question. The main conflict, anyway, is between two ideas, two thoughts. Its expression is different in different times—non-violent and democratic at times, violent and armed at others. But these are all methods. The main war is always at the level of ideas. That means politics, and so the need for political training. But your lack of interest...

**(Italicized text such as above from hereon are Partha's quiet thoughts within his head)*

He looked at all the boys sitting in the dark dugout. They sat with bowed heads. Were they unwilling to let on about their political training? That should not be the case. What was there to hide anyway? Partha could not help but think about armed struggle uninformed by politics. Weren't they wrong to confuse the means with the end? He wanted to question them about it, but he found it difficult to pester them for answers. Finally, unable to control himself, he spoke up,

'I remember a quote by a famous guerilla leader; I forget exactly who. As far as I can remember, the quote went something like this: Without political ideas and training, military training is useless, like a gun loaded with damp gunpowder. A powerful stick is all you need to combat such a gun.'

There was no reply. Bharat Hazarika fidgeted slightly; he sat with his head lowered, the cap covering his face. Rondip's unwavering gaze was fixed on Partha. The flickering lamp in the dugout was smoking. Drawn by the ray of light sneaking out of the dugout, insects and grasshoppers flew in to settle down on the chimney and the lamp, followed by a swarm of mosquitos. A buzzing sound filled the air.

'Alok, what happened to the mosquito repellant?'

At Bharat Hazarika's words, Alok leapt to his feet. Fishing out something from a corner, he lit it with a matchstick. The dugout was filled with smoke and the smell of burnt rags. Partha was racked by a fit of coughing. Rondip quickly carried the smoking tin outside and wrapped Partha's bare feet with a cloth. The drone of the mosquitoes subsided somewhat.

'Do you really think you can genuinely bring about a change in society, a revolution, by remaining alienated from the mass of people?' Partha asked.

'Why not?'

There was a challenging note in the question.

'And we do not intend to remain alienated from the people always. Who is going to take part in the revolution, if not the people?' Bharat Hazarika argued.

So, you do admit that you are currently alienated from the people.

'We have discussed this among ourselves for long. Sir must have let you know, too. We cannot imagine a revolution without people. They are our main driving force.'

Would slogan and clichés obscure reality? What is reality? Isn't setting up camp in jungles far away from people the reality today?

Rondip was trying to conceal the truth.

'And this is a nascent stage. Is it possible to be connected to the people at this stage? What do you think?' Rondip questioned Partha.

Partha smiled in answer to Rondip's question.

'What do you have to say?' Rondip asked again, defiantly.

What had he got himself into? That had been a most avoidable remark. An interview cannot be the site for a political argument.

'Highly unprofessional, my boy, highly unprofessional', he seemed to hear Choudhury's mocking comment.

'My role is that of an interrogator,' Partha tried to change the topic,' adding, 'and you are going to give the answers. I am asking you this question only because I am not convinced by the idea of an armed struggle that ignores the political aspect. Let us assume that you are not alienated from the mass of humanity, and that you have the respect and support of people. But is it possible for a tiny armed unit, however well-trained, to take on the might of a nation?'

There was silence again. Rondip fished out a diary and began flipping through its pages. There was neat handwriting on the pages. 'Let me show you something. A quotation. Here it is. I had translated it into Assamese,' he started to read aloud: ' "A small group of determined men with the support of the public can challenge a regular, disciplined army." This is a fundamental lesson. So...'

'Whose quote is that?' Partha enquired.

'Che Guevara… He is the greatest revolutionary of all time. Is there any sense in not following his teachings? We try to accept what we think is common to our situation, or important for us.'

But how were they responding to Guevara's teachings? Was it not a very mechanical response? As far as he could remember, Guevara had called the armed guerilla movement in Latin America the true form of war under some very special circumstances. He had dreamt of a revolution against American imperialism spanning a continent. Cuba, Guatemala, Peru, Bolivia—small countries, all of them. Weak, despotic governments without public support, dependent on the army, governments that would not survive without help from America. Small populations too. That was the background to Guevara's guerilla war. But here? Could the freedom of a tiny region be won by taking on a powerful central government and its military strength? It all seemed so shallow and complicated.

But I need not concern myself with these things. My job is to understand as much as I can by asking questions, not to enter into ideological arguments with them. My report will carry my analysis and opinion. But the reference to Guevara was interesting.

Two boys entered the dugout carrying a few covered dishes. They laid a dish down in front of each man present.

'We are sorry we cannot serve very tasty food here…this is all we have.'

'That's fine. When you are hungry, you don't think about taste!' Partha joked.

'We have food twice a day, particularly in the camps—in the morning and in the evening before it gets dark. But we are a little late today. Why don't you start? I have no idea what the boys have prepared.' Bharat Hazarika turned into a concerned host.

Coarse, yet tasty, grains of rice. Lentils prepared with vegetables and small pieces of chicken. Salt and chillies. Partha was hungry. He started eating with relish.

'At the time of training—especially on long marches which take us across borders—we eat before sunrise, since we have to march without interruption. We halt about twice on the way, for 10 to 15 minutes. We cook our meals before nightfall. Those are dangerous routes, with the Indian Army on one side and the Burmese on the other. We can't light fires after it gets dark; at night, the fires can be seen from a distance.'

'How far are the borders from here?'

'Depends. It might take us a month or a month and a half to march; sometimes it can take about four to six months.'

It was raining now, and he could hear thunder—a long, ominous sound that rolled over the open space. Alok began clearing the plates.

'Any more questions?' Bharat Hazarika smiled.

'I have a world of questions left,' Partha replied.

They laughed out loud.

'Let me ask you about the controversies associated with your work.'

'What controversies?'

'Robbing banks, extorting huge sums of money...what do you have to say about them?'

There was a brief silence; that was certainly an uncomfortable subject.

But I have to ask these questions. They cannot evade them.

The boy had a well thought-out answer. A brilliant propagandist speech.

'The banks are instruments of government exploitation; a means of giving loans to the capitalist class out of the savings of common people. The common people are never given loans, are they? So, the money hoarded by cheating people is collected and spent in the interest of the people, in the interest of revolution,' Rondip said animatedly.

That was old, familiar logic. So-called revolutionaries in different times had made the same claims. Nothing new, no substance in it either. But Rondip spoke well.

It was raining furiously outside by now. Water was pouring into the dugout; over the lid on the door, like a small waterfall. The sound of thunder was growing louder, too.

'Who told you that we have collected crores of rupees? That's an exaggeration; I certainly wish we could have collected that much money! Whatever money we have collected so far is for the national military fund. Haven't you heard of the national military fund? The enemy we are up against is very advanced, with a lot of armed power. We need plenty of funds and weapons to fight that.'

'Your opponents can spend in a week what it takes you a year to collect. *('Son, a war cannot be fought with money and arms alone, if people are not awakened,' he could hear Choudhury's cynical remark echoing in his head.)* But more importantly, unlimited funds and arms without political control can create problems within the organization, don't you think?'

'We are aware of that, completely aware. Only responsible members with authority are allowed to collect funds.'

Partha did not pursue the topic anymore. But he would have liked to argue *if all the young men, speeding on their bikes and Marutis and extorting money in various towns and villages, were responsible members? Or had the organization lost its control over them?* But, as a journalist, he could not ask them such questions. He had already asked quite a few uncomfortable ones.

The storm outside was fierce. There were frequent flashes of lightning and the sound of the thunder seemed to rip the world apart. The rain showed no signs of abating. Partha prepared to ask a few last questions.

'Finally…'

'Please go ahead.'

'I would like to ask you about the killings. There have been allegations against you of silencing voices that oppose you. Do you want to say anything about this politics of murder?' Partha worded his question carefully.

'Some people have been murdered. We don't deny that. On the contrary, we openly admit it. These killings are sometimes necessary in the interest of the revolution.'

'But random killings? Such killings are called acts of terrorism. What do you have to say about these killings which obviously do not have the support of the people?'

An uncomfortable silence descended on the dugout. The cloth burnt to get rid of the mosquitos and the smoke from the lamp had created a suffocating atmosphere. Darkness was deepening, and in the dark, the boys sat in silence on the bamboo cot.

Bharat Hazarika shifted in his seat. He was preparing to speak.

Had he crossed his limits? Partha was worried. The underground leaders are very insecure, he seemed to hear Choudhury say. Let's see what happens.

'I do see your point,' Bharat Hazarika said, choosing his words carefully. 'We do not believe in acts of terrorism,' he looked steadily at Partha, 'but sometimes you cannot do everything properly even if you want to. There is no need to show mercy to the enemies of the revolution. It is also not possible to involve the public in everything...and perhaps it is not necessary either.' The last words were spoken in a low voice, and after a pause.

Partha noticed that Rondip had taken out his diary once again. He opened a page and it seemed like he wanted to read from it but stopped. What had he wanted to say? Partha really wanted to know.

There was silence once again. There were many things that Partha wanted to say.

About the politics of murder, the necessity of murder, about the moral rights of human beings to kill other human beings. But he reminded himself that he was not here to participate in ideological debates. Murder was growing so common that people had even stopped thinking about it. It had turned into lifeless statistics. Such killings might create momentary ripples of sorrow among the friends and families of the victim, but death is always a hard reality. What remained after death was the overwhelming burden of scorching memories.

For every murder, one could erect a wall of justification.

All killings are in the name of the people, in the name of humanity! Men are killed in the interest of freedom, in the interest of mankind, in the interest of the country and society, in the interest of revolution or in the name of love or—best of them all—*God. Each murder is real yet unreal. Meaningful yet meaningless. But every death is the irredeemable end to a life.*

Behind every death, every murder, lies self-interest—an individual's, an organization's, a nation's, the mighty who rule the nation or politicians who oppose them. But the news of every death ripped off a piece of the soul of humanity, of society's morality, of the collective soul. Murder had never helped in the progress of any individual, group, society, or ideals. Murder had never conferred greatness on the killer... Do people who offer logic in support of murder actually use the weapons of logic to murder humanity and the human soul?

Partha looked at Bharat, and then at Rondip and Alok. Nobody was looking at him. A sense of suppressed excitement and unease filled the dugout. It was easy to see that the leader was not happy with his own answer. But what else could he say?

What more could I ask? What new question could I ask to which a new answer could be given?

Partha shook his head, as if to shake off a heavy load. He smiled at everybody and thanked them for taking part in the long interview. The air immediately lightened. The men relaxed. Closing his notebook, Partha got to his feet; they were numb.

Standing at the door of the dugout, he looked outside. Water was streaming down the corrugated iron sheet on four pillars that was used to conceal the door. It was raining incessantly. The sky was descending on the earth like a wet and heavy veil. The sound of thunder was deafening. Lightning ripped the sky to shreds. In the flashes of light, the world lit up briefly like the white fires of phosphorus.

Partha suddenly noticed the strange misshapen tree he had noticed earlier. With every flash of lightning that spread its long fingers over the bosom of the sky, the tree seemed to come alive, glowing in a mysterious light.

Partha shuddered. There was something frightening about the scene. Suddenly, the sky exploded, there was a terrible sound as lightning struck. Where did it strike? The misshapen tree. Yes, that's right, that tree. For a moment, white and blue flames engulfed the tree. The earth quivered and the wind blew furiously. To Partha, standing at the door of the dugout, the sound of the wind was like a disembodied, dreadful wail. Now he was really scared. He retreated from the door and sat down hurriedly on the cot.

The boys were sitting in silence, like shadows. Partha lit a cigarette and held the packet out. With slight hesitation, Bharat and Rondip took a cigarette each. In the dark, they sat for a long time, smoking in silence.

The rumbles of thunder subsided. Gradually, they started talking again. 'We had planned to talk to you in the village itself. We have really caused you a lot of trouble,' said Ron. 'But now, you will have direct experience of how we battle the elements.'

'Why don't you sleep here? Ron will be here with you,' suggested Bharat Hazarika.

'What about you?'

'We will sleep on the shacks outside,' said Bharat, adding, 'don't you worry. We are used to such situations.'

III

The world had transformed overnight.

When he woke up in the morning, Partha had the strange sensation of floating. It was dark inside and peeping through the mosquito net, he could not see a thing. Lifting the net, he realized that Ron, who had slept next to him on a folding bed, was not there. It was 8 am—it was really late. Where were the others? Partha lowered his feet on the ground.

'God! What is this?' he shouted.

There was water on the floor. Water till his ankles.

Partha stumbled out of the dugout.

There was water everywhere. What had happened? Only the mounds were visible, there was muddy water everywhere.

Across a stream of water, several boys were hard at work. They were bare-chested, dressed only in shorts—their fit bodies glistening in the pouring rain. A couple of them were tying bamboos together. They were building a raft—that's right, a raft. They climbed on it and tried to row it, but the raft slid under the water, like a submarine.

'Partha-da (short for dada*)*, stay where you are. I am coming,' Ron shouted from the other side. Treading water, he moved up to the dugout.

Flash flood. The water had risen in the night because of the rains.

'This is unheard of. We have never encountered anything like it. The water is rising continuously. You will not be able to leave today. We cannot use this raft to ferry you. Hazarika sir is going to take a few of the boys and leave; he will find a boat to get you out of here. Don't worry, I will stay with you. There's no danger here. I will build a *sang-ghar* (house on stilts) in the tree. We might need it.'

Partha was astounded. 'Not on that tree struck by lightning?' he asked, quite worried.

'No, of course not. Didn't you know that you get floods like these here? Last year...'

'There was no camp here last year,' said Bharat Hazarika; Partha did not even know when he had come and stood next to him. 'We knew there would be floods here, but we didn't know that the water would rise like this within a night. It must be raining heavily in the mountains.'

Water was dripping off Bharat Hazarika's muscular bare back. His wet hair was plastered to his forehead.

'I will be leaving for the village now. Let me see what I can get to take you out of here—boats or rafts. It's difficult to say how much the water will rise from here. Don't you worry, Ron will be here with you.'

'I can leave with you.'

'No, we cannot take that risk. Do you know how to swim?'

'Not very well.'

'There may be more water ahead. And the raft that we have built sinks two feet under water if anyone climbs on it. We can't possibly use that for you. There's nothing to fear here, even if the water rises. I will take you out of here as soon as I can. Ron, take good care of our guest.'

'Yes, sir.'

'I will contact you on the wireless after three hours. Match your watch with mine.'

Hazarika and eight other boys waded chest-deep through the water, pulling the raft, sunk in water, behind them. A boy tied the wireless set high on his back. Partha gazed after them till they could not be seen anymore.

'You are going to have a really hard time now,' Ron told him, half-teasingly. 'Why don't I show you the bathroom?'

There was a sentry post near the stream—more than half of it covered with black plastic. One could still get there from the dugout without having to wade through the water. On entering, Partha saw that it held water, soap, towels, and even a makeshift toilet.

'This is what the boys built for you in the morning. We don't need these rooms.'

Partha gave him a look of gratitude.

The mound on which the dugout stood was fairly big, though it was not evident at a first glance. The nearest mound held the blighted tree. How strange it looked now…it seemed to have turned a deep red in colour.

Ron led Partha through the thicket to the other side of the dugout. To Partha's surprise, he found himself in front of another shelter, covered with black plastic. This house was not visible from the dugout.

'We will stay here. The floor of the dugout is flooded and we can't stay there anymore.'

There was a spacious bed on one end of the shelter and a stove on the other. A boy sat on the bed, holding a wireless set. Another sat at the stove, making tea. Hot tea was served in aluminum mugs. Sending the boys away to have their tea, Ron sat down on the bed, wireless in hand. It was drizzling now.

'I am really grateful to you for the interview you gave me yesterday,' Partha said, adding, 'I have a clear idea about the situation now. I am unsure about a couple of things. I would like to ask you about them—only if you don't mind...'

'No, not at all. But I might not be able to answer all your questions.'

'I understand. I will try not to ask you such questions, and you can always let me know if you do not want to answer something. And I won't consider this a part of my interview. It won't be published. I am only asking you because I want to know.'

'Then there is no problem. Please go ahead.'

'I am a little doubtful about something. Why have you set up camps in such thick forest, as if you are in hiding? In uniforms and with guns. It is said about armed guerilla warfare that the guerillas should mingle with the public like fish take to water. You would probably need such a camp only in case of a big war,' Partha said, gesturing at the camp—the mounds surrounded by water, houses covered with plastic in the middle of thickets and a tree struck by lightning. 'Are you planning a military expedition very soon?'

'I won't be able to answer your last question. But let me tell you about the camp. All our members do not live in camps. But the military members, who have trained outside the country, are kept in camps to help sustain their sense of discipline, self-control, and willpower. The civilians are sometimes brought to the camps, too, for training. Our leaders believe that if the trained members are allowed to go into the towns and villages and mix with just about anybody, they would be corrupted.'

'That means your members are being kept in isolation.'

Ron did not reply.

'What do you think, shouldn't the trained, armed guerillas politically educate the people, and perhaps organize them?'

'Our leaders must have a reason for doing what they do. And as I said yesterday, our soldiers do not have adequate political knowledge. I doubt if they would be able to organize the public politically; perhaps if they were trained, they might.'

'Would they be able to resist an army attack?'

Ron slowly shook his head.

'Have you been trained outside the country?'

'Yes.'

Partha did not pursue the matter. He would, some other time. 'Do you remember me asking you about your modes of operation yesterday? In particular, about your reluctance to involve the public. You had taken your diary out and had wanted to read something out. What was that?'

'That was just a quote.'

'Whose quote?'

Ron took out his diary. 'Che Guevara,' he said. 'Here it is: "If you have a genuine desire to fight from a remote or a foreign land, clearly this battle has to begin as a small clandestine movement of members committed to secrecy and such an act should be carried out without the knowledge or support of the public."'

Partha was shocked. *Were they simply trying to legitimize what they had begun by quoting from what Guevara had written 40 years ago? Nowhere in the world had clandestine revolutions succeeded without the involvement of the public.* Of course, he did not feel like starting this argument now. But he decided to find out more about Guevara. *What a link—from the jungles of Bolivia to the forests of*

Assam. Quite a long link to find a shortcut for difficult political organizational activity.

Ron asked Partha a few things about his profession. Partha narrated some stories about Choudhury and then told him about Prabhat, how he had become a victim of the blind system, just because he had happened to study with a current leader of the underground.

'Do you know who that underground leader is?'

'His name is Subrata, he is Arindam Phukan now.'

Ron laughed when he heard the name. 'You should tell the story to our Hazarika sir.'

'Does this mean that Hazarika is Phukan?'

'He might know,' Ron answered briefly. 'Just a moment, it's time for our wireless contact.' He switched on the wireless and it crackled to life. A few minutes later, Hazarika's voice floated towards them, 'I haven't been able to make much progress. We are neck-deep in water. I can't make out till how far the water's risen. Is the water rising there too? Over.'

'Yes, it is, but gradually. Over.'

'Be careful. Keep a watch. How is our guest? Over.'

'All's well. Over.'

'Will contact you after two hours. Over.'

Partha was worried. If the water was rising, there was no chance of him getting out. There was no possibility of a boat arriving today. Wonder what would happen tomorrow. There had been a burst of rain when they were talking; now, of course, it was drizzling.

'I would like to check the situation myself. I will be back in two hours. You should rest. Here, Suren, stay with our guest always. See that he is comfortable,' said Ron, stripping off his clothes and dressed only in shorts. Accompanied by three other boys who carried long staves, he went out and swiftly moved through the water in the opposite direction.

Partha settled down comfortably on the bed. The boy called Suren stood in the rain, in attention, holding a 303 rifle, a scrap of plastic wrapped round his cap. He kept stealing glances at Partha, quickly looking away when caught.

'Please come inside. You are getting wet.'

Despite Partha's invitation, Suren would not sit on the bed. In the shelter, too, he stood in attention, clutching his gun.

Suren was a village boy. He had appeared for matric twice; he had failed the first time, but scraped through the second. He was sitting at home without work—farming was not an option as he had no land. He had met the underground leaders and joined the armed struggle without much thought. No, he had not been sent outside the country; he had been locally trained. He liked what he did—he approved of the armed struggle. But it was a lot of hard work. No, he had no problems with physical work, he thought little of physical hardship. But he hated it when he had to go without food—that was hardship. No, he had not been involved in any organizational activity among people. He had no idea about such work, and the 'sirs' had never talked about it.

A sigh escaped Partha. He got to his feet and told Suren, 'I need to use the bathroom.'

Suren, gun in hand, almost marched ahead of him to the bathroom. 'Please,' he said, showing him the door to the toilet.

Partha emerged after a few minutes. He looked at the sky, which was still clouded.

'Let us go and have a look at that tree—the one struck by lightning.'

'All right.' Suren marched ahead again.

The water between the mounds had risen somewhat. Jumping across the sheet of water, Partha and Suren climbed on the mound. Partha moved toward the blighted tree. The tree had turned black, the leaves, now a muddy red in colour, hung torn in places. The lightning had cleaved the tree into two; its bosom had split, burnt red and black, like blood. The protrusions had been ripped apart.

And what was that on the protrusions? Two fat nails that stuck out about one and a half inches. A nail above, like a hook.

'Who put the nails here?' Partha asked.

'We did.'

'Why?'

'We hang the villains here, especially the rapists, the drug dealers, and the spies. Our sirs interrogate them.'

'Which one of your sirs does that?'

'Hazarika sir.'

'Your camp commander?'

'Sometimes.'

'And then?'

'The innocent are set free, the guilty are killed. We bury the dead there in the forest.'

A shiver ran up Partha's spine. His feet felt heavy. After a pause, he hurried back to the camp. Suren marched after him. Back in the camp, he stretched out on the bed. A thousand insects seemed to be buzzing inside his head. Closing his eyes tightly, he tried to sleep.

Partha had a dream. He was standing in front of the blighted tree with its bosom split open. A number of small birds had flown down to its branches. When he looked at them, they spoke in human voices. A gust of wind blew about the tree, moaning in grief. The branches, like fingers, began to grope. In his sleep, Partha was frightened. He started to perspire, and then woke up with a start.

He saw Ron looking at him with a smile.

IV

In the evening, Partha and Ron stretched out side by side on the bed. They lay in silence beneath a huge nylon mosquito net. Neither felt like sleeping. No boats or rafts had been found today. Water had almost reached the village. It was raining furiously, incessantly. In the cloudy weather, the dark had been quick to descend.

Partha was experiencing a lot of inner tumult. He did not feel like talking at all. Yet he was aware that as a journalist he would not have a better opportunity than this to understand the situation. Pulling himself together with an effort, he prepared to talk. *No, I won't give any value judgements. I am a journalist; it is not my job to judge others but to record what I see and publish it accordingly. My conscience would rebel, but as a professional journalist, I should not allow it to—at least not now. It was merciless and cruel, this world of clandestine politics, but I am not going to justify it. I am going to talk now.*

He started to talk, beginning with light conversation. Ron was probably dying to talk himself. He joined in enthusiastically.

'Why don't you tell me about yourself? I really want to know what attracted you to such politics. Tell me about your family, your background, and don't worry. Everything is off the record.'

Ron laughed out loud. 'I have nothing much to say. Nothing interesting. I will tell you about it, but first, why don't you tell me about yourself? I know you are a rich man's son...why did you become a journalist? To tell you the truth, I am, like most people, very curious about journalists. How did you become one?'

Partha was amused. He had never talked about himself. In fact, he had not given it much thought himself. Telling his own story struck him like a game.

'What's wrong, dada? Why are you laughing?'

'You had me there. What do I say about myself? And where do I start? I was born on X day of X year...'

'Start from your schooldays.'

In the dark, Partha began to reminisce.

'Our schooldays are supposed to be among our best memories. I am sorry to say I don't have any such wonderful memories of school. I was sent to a very famous public school when I was young. An ancient palace housed our school. Huge rooms with high ceilings, long verandahs with thick pillars; on the other side of the playground full of red pebbles were the hostels, like barracks. When I think of school, I think of that palace, the houses of brick and stone, long verandahs, playground, and the barracks-like hostel and also of a bunch of wild teenagers, with acne on their faces, voices breaking in the transition to adulthood, nattily dressed-us!

I don't remember anything about the lower classes. Our seniors always bullied us, ragged us and dealt with us severely if the rules and traditions of the school were violated in any way. The youngsters had to stand up and greet a senior whenever they met him, on the school roads or in the verandahs.

Things changed slightly after the 7th standard, and in the 8th standard, the boys had the authority to bully the juniors. What else did they do? What else—apart from following the strict study schedules, they talked about girls and learnt to masturbate. Their world of fantasy revolved around the act of ejaculation.

In our school functions, we would tie turbans. The school lay a lot of emphasis on the teaching of Indian traditions. Of course, I realized much later that those traditions were based on the British models approved by feudal rulers.

Our school was no army school, but we were taught to respect the army and army traditions. We were taught with great care about the military traditions in our history. But I noticed that the heroes, whose exploits we were taught about with great pride, were all Hindu braves, who had fought courageously against Muslim invaders. Our drill teacher, Shiromani Sharma, would often make us chant on the playground: "Jai Chhatrapati Shivaji ki Jai, Jai Veer Rana Pratap ki Jai." I understood then that a clever attempt was being made to indoctrinate our young minds with a form of Hindu fundamentalism.

Although Indian on the surface, our private world was quite distinct—they adored "foreign" goods; soap, powder, razor, English music, pictures of Hollywood stars, pop singers, and foreign cricketers. Do you know what our prized possession was? Coloured photographs of naked white women shaped like cards, and small, illustrated foreign pornographic books.'

Partha looked pensive, and after a moment's pause, said, 'Really, we lived in such an artificial world. I have been blabbering, haven't I? Now tell me about yourself, we can talk about me later.'

'I don't really have anything to say about myself, dada. Things turn out very differently from what we expect, don't they?'

'Why do you say that?'

'Take yourself for example, the kind of background you come from. You could have taken up any profession. But you chose to be a journalist—and that, too, without much thought. Isn't it surprising?'

'Well, you're right.'

'I sometimes think, dada, whether we have any control over our lives. Or are we always the victim of circumstances? Or does some power beyond our perception control our lives? Do you believe in God?'

'Not particularly. I would like to think that I don't. But I would be wrong if I say no completely. I suppose, something between yes and no.'

'I had, once, tried consciously not to believe in God. I had shut him out of my soul. But once on our way to Kachin, after leaving the camp at Nagaland behind, one of our companions had fallen violently sick. The other three were unwell too. The sick one was in such a bad shape that he had to be carried. And in that state, we narrowly missed an ambush by the Burmese Army. I suddenly fell sick myself, shaking with fever. In that valley of death in Hukong, fever spelt death. I was mortally scared—the fear of fever, of death. It was a strange, debilitating fear. And that day I prayed, an age after I had prayed in school. Throwing all my reservations aside, I prayed to God. All the gods I could think of, even spirits, demons, witches; in that dense forest that day, under a few somber trees, my prayers, filled with fear and plea, invoked many gods. Inwardly genuflecting, I prayed for my life and health...have you ever felt like this?'

'No, nothing so momentous has happened to me. But, maybe yesterday, in that night of storm and devastation...for a moment, perhaps, I sought God too.'

It was pitch black everywhere. The rain had subsided. Sleeping on either side of the bamboo cot, Partha and Ron could hardly see each other. They could only hear each other in the dark; the words seemed to come to them from a distance. A mild smell floated from their bodies. In the silence between their words, they could hear each other breathe. In the dark, they spoke but not to each other; in the privacy of the night, they were baring their souls to themselves. A lonely journey prompted by lonely memories.

'You came home in the holidays; you probably saw what society was like then…'

'I came home twice a year, in the summer and winter holidays. My parents would wait at the airport at Borjhar to receive me. There would be a number of people, my parents and my sister, sometimes my aunts, sometimes a friend of Ma; the driver and Ramukai to carry my luggage; and in a supervisory capacity, a couple of Deuta's junior lawyers.

As soon as I landed, there would be a riot. My sister would run up and hug me. Deuta would light a cigarette and smile in satisfaction.

I would bask in their love and affection for a week, you see, at the most a week. They would want to compensate me for all those days spent away from home in those seven. And then Deuta would bury himself in his practice. All day long, he would be busy with his cases and clients or with his friends, clandestinely administering the politics of the ruling group. We sometimes saw him at the breakfast table only.

Ma did not have Deuta's British habits, but she was involved in a number of social activities. She had always kept away from direct politics. After a week, Ma, too, would not know what to do with me. I loved my parents very much. But perhaps because I had lived away from them since I was a child, I could not grow very close to them. You know, this was a very uncomfortable and lonely situation. I am telling you, within just a week, all of us grew very uncomfortable with one another.'

'And what did your Ma do?'

'"Partha, son, why don't you visit your Koka (grandfather in Assamese) once? Koka had written last month; had asked me to take you to see him when you came. He is not keeping very well. I think you should go and visit him", she would say to me.'

'Our Koka lived in the village in a huge house. He ran a *mouja* (a revenue area) and also a small tea garden that sold green leaves. As per Ma's plans, I would turn up at Koka's house in the holidays. I'd drive there in the family car, under Ramukai and the driver's care. Ma accompanied me a couple of times. Though Koka lived in a village, his house had all the urban facilities, a European-style commode, for example. A lot of people lived in his palatial house. The green fields I saw on my way to the village, the sugarcane crops in the fields, the flock of children running after the car—that was all my experience of a village; once I entered Koka's house, it was difficult for me to set foot outside it, so swamped was I by their warmth and love.

The few times I could not go to Koka's, especially in the long summer holidays, Ma sent me to my Mahi's (stepmother in Assamese) house in Shillong. I loved going to Shillong since I had many friends there. Mahi lived in a huge bungalow. Moha was a big businessman. But of course, he had passed away long ago. Mahi lived alone with her children. Her son, Nibir, was several years older than me, but the two girls were just a couple of years younger to me, Swati and Swaha. They were my real friends; we were the best of friends, we had a lot of fun. You know, Ron, I belonged neither here nor there. I grew up into a man without roots.'

Partha fell silent. After some time, he said, 'I have been talking my head off for quite some time. You have said nothing at all. Now, you tell me about your family.'

'Our house was in a small town,' Ron began, slowly, 'It would be fair to call it a village rather than a town. It was difficult to say where the village ended and the town began; a number of closely situated villages covered a huge area. There, a few stores, a few offices, and a few pukka houses offered evidence of township. Our old house was in a remote village in that area. It isn't there anymore…the floods washed it away long ago. Deuta was the first matriculate and the first graduate from that village. Like most of the educated men of his time, he considered teaching to be the only means of livelihood and the only ideal in life, and worked with great sincerity. He is retired today, but still tries to keep his ideals alive. He has suffered a lot because of that...'

A picture floated up to Partha's eyes—a small town, quiet and organized; in a spacious yard, an Assam-type house with a long verandah and rows of pillars; in the scorching heat of May and June, from the pukka road in the distance, the house would glow just like a mirage.

V

'The place I was born in was actually a huge village,' Ron continued. 'It had no hint of urbanity. Lives revolved around work, play, and, prayers. We have a huge garden, Deuta has planted a variety of trees there. Behind the garden, we have our fields.'

'How much land do you have?'

'Not much, about eight puras (460,800 sq.ft.). But it's very fertile.'

'Who does the farming? Your Deuta?'

'No, not Deuta. He employs farmhands. But he does some work himself daily as well. In the planting season, he makes it a point to go to the fields early in the morning—he lends a hand when the land is ploughed or crops are planted. At about 7 am, he comes back to the house and potters about in the vegetable garden before he has his bath. Then he reads a little and at about 9 am, he eats his breakfast and leaves for school. He reaches school at a 9:45 am. With Deuta around, we did not need to check our watches.'

'Did you work in the fields too?'

'We did, after our examinations—during the holidays—we had to work in the fields too.'

'What did your father teach?'

'History and literature.'

'Was he very strict?'

'Strict, but affectionate. He paid a lot of attention to our studies. He was very particular about us reading books, particularly books in English. He bought us many books too.'

They fell silent again. A conscientious teacher who lived by the clock. Such people were hard to come by—an endangered species. Only the factory workers and the factory owners lived by the clock nowadays, the former because of their bellies, and the latter, because of their greed for profit.

'What was your school like?'

'An ordinary rural school. A primary school initially, a high school later. What do I tell you about our school? An ordinary building, old desks and benches, but our teachers were very nice. Most of them taught us well. Deuta used to work there. Please tell me more about your school. That's what I like listening to…'

'I would wait eagerly for my holidays,' Partha responded. 'And when the holidays came, I would wait for school to start. I never developed a special bond with the school or with any of my classmates, perhaps that is why I am not nostalgic about my schooldays. On the contrary, I only have some irritating memories.'

'What sort?'

'For example, memories of bathing. We had to bathe in a long hall, without any partitions, naked. When I think of those rows of boys, bathing naked under the showers, I feel like throwing up.'

'Were you very lonely in school?'

'No, I wasn't lonely or anti-social. I would take part in sports, but I was never popular. I have to admit that I was never good at studies; I never tried hard enough. I was lucky enough to do well in my final examinations. I got a 1st division. Everybody in my family was thrilled. Deuta had taken all of us out that day.'

'Assamese was not taught in your school, was it?'

'No, but I knew to read and write Assamese. I studied Assamese before I went to that school. Of course, later I found it difficult, as I was out of practice. But after my high school examinations, I was at home for a long time. That stood me in good stead. Ma had a cupboard full of Assamese books—stories, novels, etc. During the holidays, I started reading them. No, I did not begin reading Assamese books because of any great love for my language. I began without thinking about it too much, and gradually grew to like what I read. That is all. But I gained a lot from all that reading. I mastered the language and, above all, formed an idea about my state and my people.'

After what seemed like a minute, Partha started again, 'After school, I went to Delhi to study. Deuta was really hopeful that after college, I would appear for the Indian Administrative Services (IAS) examinations. But I was not particularly interested in that; I was not serious about anything, you see. I went to college, studied regularly and became a graduate. My results were average, neither good nor bad. Then, on Deuta's advice, I enrolled myself at Jawaharlal Nehru University. It's convenient to train for the IAS exams there. I got letter after letter from my father, heaps of advice. I did attend coaching classes for the IAS on Deuta's advice. I never thought about what I wanted to do with my future. Somehow, nothing seemed to matter, though it wasn't that I was wild or bohemian. What did you study in college?'

'I appeared for matric from a local school. Pre-university from a nearby college, and I enrolled for my BA degree at a college in Guwahati. I must have studied for one and a half, no, almost two years before I dropped out,' Ron replied.

'Any siblings?'

'There are three of us. I am the oldest, my brother is three years younger than me. He is studying engineering; he should be out this year. My sister's the youngest. She's the darling of the house.'

'Your brother, does he believe in revolutionary politics?'

'He does. He's a Marxist.'

'I suppose he does not approve of your path.'

'No, Marxists have completely different views on revolution.'

'Interesting. Have you two ever discussed this?'

'Many times.'

Rondip tried to remember the many conversations he had had with his brother. About four years ago, when he had walked out of his house, leaving everything behind, his brother had just enrolled himself in engineering college. He himself was in Guwahati then, helping his brother settle down in the hostel. At that time, the armed rebels had begun their activities in earnest. Of course, then there was no publicity. The leaders would visit the hostels under cover of the darkness at night. Discussions would last through the night; there were hushed conversations in the hostel rooms, the verandahs, or on the benches outside. The police and spies were not particularly alert then. Rondip had met most of the main leaders. How inspiring were those days! The glow of freedom and revolution in their eyes! The frequent visits of the leaders had woven new thoughts and dreams. His exposure to clandestine politics, and his proximity to the leaders had earned him respect and fame within the college and the hostel. A new enthusiasm was born. Gradually, he had been sucked into the orbit of the clandestine politics of armed struggle.

He remembered that day very well.

Seated on a bench outside the hostel, he was talking to a leader one night. He was making some observations most enthusiastically about what should and should not be done. At a point, the leader spoke up, almost throwing a challenge at him, 'If you want revolution, stop living and dreaming in your cushioned urban comfort. Come with me to the village, to the forest. Come with me to where the struggle is seeding. A true soldier is one who participates in the actual act of war, not one who sits in the safe distance of the city and talks about revolution. Revolution does not mean mere talk, a couple of "wallings" (practice of writing political slogans in wall), distributing a few letters, or picking up a gun for the first time and experiencing a rush of adrenalin. If you want to be a revolutionary, you have to join in the act.'

A young man with dreams in his eyes had, on that day, plunged into the revolution.

'So, you consider yourself revolutionaries?' Ron's brother asked him.

'Yes, we have started the process. Do you doubt it?'

'Without the active support of the people? Without any mass-based political activity?'

He had once met his brother at the engineering college hostel. They had met after a long gap, probably three years. They had tried hard to control their emotions, and had discussed politics. In search of revolution, his brother had adopted Marxism.

'We have begun our armed struggle and have been preparing for it for the last 10 years. We haven't started it randomly. We are still at a preliminary stage. We have never said that we wouldn't have a mass uprising, but I have seen that the so-called mass uprisings are sometimes the graveyard of armed struggle.'

'That's completely wrong.'

'Perhaps, but I have come to the conclusion that—and not by living in the city, mind you, but by living in villages, jungles, and hills—mass uprising and armed struggle are not totally indissoluble, like oil and water. Success lies in the ability to weld them together, using them in the right proportion and ensuring a parallel development. And I suppose that's what we are trying to do.'

'You have my heartiest congratulations,' Rondip's brother said sarcastically.

Rondip suddenly lost his temper; his brother continued talking though.

'You communists always talk about armed struggle, but barring a few Naxalites, I haven't seen a single communist take part in it. It is only the communists who have such romantic and unreal ideas about armed struggle; you fantasize about it always, and probably masturbate at night too. You talk about revolutionary change—about seizing power, the abolition of the ruling classes and their violence, but you never translate your words into reality.'

A cold, damp wind cut through the darkness, seeping in through the net and washing over their bodies.

'You are right, dada. It's interesting that my brother is a Marxist,' Rondip broke the silence, 'But dada, sometimes I lose patience. Our Marxists have their heads full of ideas, and it's really irritating how they are so quick to offer "prescribed" solutions to problems. I know there are flaws in our ideas and our work, but we are really serious about armed struggle. And you know what, the important thing is that we have been successful in launching it. If we have any ideological flaws, we will be able to correct them in practice. But dada, when the Marxists make fun of our efforts as if they are the only ones with the right to armed revolution, I feel really bad. We might not have the support of the Marxist ideas and organization...' Ron said, his voice lost in the moaning of the wind.

'Tell you what, I believe all the so-called revolutionaries are a little envious of you.'

'Envious, Partha-da?'

'You are living the lives they had always dreamt about.'

'Ha, ha, ha, they should come here once. All their dreams would be shattered.'

Ron and Partha laughed out loud, and their laughter punctured the darkness around them.

'But you did not complete your story. What happened to your plans of appearing for the IAS?' Ron asked, changing the subject.

'I was never serious about that. I had appeared for the preliminaries after my Master's degree. Strangely, I had cleared it too. I am sure there must have been some mistake in correction of the answer sheets. But that was my last attempt. I never appeared for my Mains.'

'So, what did you do after that?'

'Practically nothing. Meanwhile I had a circle of friends in Delhi—scions of rich families who believed in Marxism. We were all involved in campaigning for human rights and the rights of citizens, the environment, politics, social service... Then it was fashionable to talk about the environment in Delhi. We visited several places, like Himachal, Tehri Garhwal, the Narmada; demonstrated in the boat club. My entry into this circle had terminated my studies, and I felt no strong desire to return home. I enrolled in a Mass Communication program to kill time, but I didn't dislike it. This is the story of my academic life. What about you? What were your subjects in college?'

'I studied a combination. I was not very good at studies; I was an average student. And sometimes, I wrote poetry.'

'Really!'

'Not a lot of it. A few have been published though; it was not actually poetry...'

'Do you still write?'

'Sometimes.'

There was a long silence. Each was immersed in his own thoughts. They could hear the sound of the water flowing and the sounds of some insects. And the sound of mild breathing, like a gentle wind rustling the sails of a boat in the ocean. A boat sailing on a journey of introspection, outward and inward, uncertain...

'How many poems have you written in this period of hiding?'

'Not many, five or six.'

'Do you remember any of them?'

'Not at all. Many poets don't remember their own writing. I will show you my work sometime.'

'I had a few poetry-crazy friends in Delhi. Once upon a time, I was in love with poetry, too. Not anymore. Today, I have met a poet after a long time.'

'A poet? I had wanted to be one someday, like most adolescents. That memory has faded into oblivion now. How can a man, who spends his life in the shadow of guns, think about poetry?'

'All poets are revolutionaries,' Partha said as if to himself. 'Revolutionaries, soldiers, human beings…'

'Poetry is such a useless thing, dada…'

'Of what use is life then?'

Finally, they fell silent. It had gotten late; sleep descended on their eyes. Ron's breathing grew regular. He had fallen asleep. Partha slept too...a sleep burdened with wild and meaningless dreams though...

He woke up frequently. In his sleep, Ron was fidgeting too. Drifting between sleep and wakefulness, Partha thought to himself: *how shaky was the ideological foundation to the boys' struggle. That was the root of all problems. They were challenging the might of the nation with guns, bereft of any ideals or principles. That was a great tragedy.* He remembered Choudhury's sarcastic remarks, 'Your friends are yet to realize the reality of the Indian nation, Partha. Its integration grew out of a unified struggle against British colonialism. You can't just wish it away and find a replacement that encompasses its essence... India is a historical compromise, my boy, and so she has sustained. When this character suffers from political chicanery, the idea of India suffers—so it has.'

Had that thought ever crossed these boys' minds? Surely not. A sigh escaped Partha. There was a huge question mark over their activities.

I hope I am wrong. An individual's mistake does not lead to huge losses. But if they are wrong, what a heavy price they would have to pay for it.

It was still raining, sometimes it would let up and at others, descend like a wet sheet. The air was heavy with damp vapour. Partha was aware of a change in guard even in that stormy, rain-drenched night. In the morning, the sky cleared like a fan gradually unfolding, and there was a burst of light.

In the morning, they had their meal sitting on the cot, their first real meal in two days. Ron's eyes were bloodshot and swollen. He had had a bad night.

'Wasn't last night an unusual experience? I am sure very few people have such experiences. I feel as if my heart has been washed clean.'

Partha laughed. 'I gained a new friend.' He was touched by his own words; he felt lighter. But his professional instinct seemed to tell him, no, not friends. Don't burden yourself with this friendship. But his heart rejected the warning. He held out his hand to Ron.

'We are generally wary of making friends with journalists.' There was a sparkle of mischief in Ron's eyes.

'And why is that?' Partha asked.

'Journalists are hand-in-glove with the police, the intelligence, the government—there is no lack of double crossers.'

They burst out laughing. None of them had said anything original but words, unspoken yet ineffable, hung in the air.

'I don't know if we will ever see each other again, Partha-da. But I will try to meet you if I get a chance...'

'You have to show me your poems.'

'Not poems, verse. You would be disappointed. But dada, you still haven't told me how you became a journalist.'

'All of a sudden. After I completed the Mass Communication course, I answered an advertisement from a publishing house that was launching a newspaper in Delhi. I was selected, to my surprise. My friends encouraged me to take it up. We had delusions about the power and glamour of the profession after witnessing the attention lavished on journalists in Delhi. I was not a bad writer. A serial report on drugs and prostitution in the colleges of the Delhi University won me some fame. In a year, I had a confirmed job. In the meantime, insurgency had gripped Assam; my editor called me one day and asked me how I would like to be based in Guwahati and cover insurgency in the North-East. I had no problems. So, in a month I was in Guwahati, armed with a promotion to special correspondent.'

'Yes, our lives are uncertain...It's difficult to say where we may end up.'

A raft was on its way to pick up the guest, a message floated over the wireless. There was a flurry of activity in the camp. In the afternoon, the raft rowed in, bearing three young men, rice, dal, and sacks of potatoes and vegetables.

'Groceries? But aren't you leaving, too?'

'I will see you off to the village. But I will have to return at night. The camp will be here and we will have to stay in the camp, regardless of the floods. This is a test, and it will go on till we have orders to break the camp. God knows how long it will last.'

A raft built out of banana trunks. A soapbox provided a seat for Partha. With a bamboo stave in hand, Ron stood in the middle of the raft. *I am not going to write about these incidents and create a sensation out of fantastic details of the journey; these are my memories, intimate and personal.* He waved goodbye to the boys in the camp. Ron issued instructions. The raft bobbed over the rising waters of the flood, slowly, like a dream, like reality...

VI

Partha was reading a published report in a newspaper against a manuscript. That was the newspaper he worked for, and the report was his.

After returning from the camp, he had sent a detailed report to his newspaper. His interview with the insurgent leaders, a few personal experiences, and the sudden flood had all served to make his report immensely readable. It was published serially for three days. It created a sensation in the world of journalism in the

Capital. A number of national newspapers quoted him. His editor, colleagues, and even the owner of the newspaper congratulated him. In Assam, the sales of his paper shot up 200 copies to 700.

Partha was elated. 'Excellent scoop,' the cynic Choudhury said.

The top police officials had wanted to speak to him, too. Following Choudhury's advice, he rephrased what he had written in his report. He could not make out if his answers satisfied or disappointed them.

Within a month, he thought of writing an analytical piece on his experiences in the camp. He called his news editor and editor-in-chief to speak about it. They encouraged him and told him it would be a centre page article. Partha was excited—such articles were generally written by experienced journalists or famous intellectuals.

The article required a lot of research. He felt as if he was appearing for exams all over again. He met a number of people, but few seemed to know much about his topic. After a month of hard work, the article was ready. A few days after he had dispatched it to his editor, he called him up, with some trepidation, to ask what he had decided to do with it.

'I have got it, Partha. It is a great piece, and will surely be published. We will place it well. Give me a couple of days. Keep up the good work, my boy,' he assured Partha.

The Armed Struggle and Che Guevara

Parthasarathi Choudhury, Special Correspondent, Guwahati

Behind every serious attempt at armed movement, there is a particular philosophy and ideology. The philosophy might not be present in its original form, disallowed by the changes in time and circumstances, but one cannot overlook its relevance.

The influence of one of the leaders of the Cuban revolution—the founder of the guerilla movement in Latin America, Ernesto Che Guevara—on the insurgents in Assam is incredible. Perhaps this dimension has not been emphasized enough in any discussion on insurgency.

What is the evidence of this influence?

Plenty of books by Guevara have been discovered in raids on the houses of the underground leaders. These are not banned books, though. Frequent mention of Guevara and his translated quotations are to be found in their diaries. In the publications sympathetic to such politics, there is abundant writing on Guevara's guerilla war. Finally, in his meeting with the leaders, this writer observed them frequently quoting from Guevara in support of their decisions and activities. This has been mentioned in the earlier report.

One can observe the influence of Guevara in the tactical, rather than ideological, dimension of the insurgents' work. But it has to be pointed out that the insurgents' tactics have also been influenced by the long-lasting armed struggle in the neighbouring states of the North-East and in Myanmar. However, one cannot ignore the importance of Guevara's influence. It is interesting that his influences have been detected in the 90s of the 20th century, thousands of miles away from Latin America. But the more important question is how the insurgents have interpreted Guevara for themselves.

One gets the impression that their understanding of Guevara is rather superficial. They have not been able to assess him with a political totality. Without their political aspect, Guevara's teachings are hollow. All strategies or methods of struggle are born from a particular political thought or line. Che Guevara's guerilla warfare is the result of a particular political perspective and understanding. The two cannot be separated.

What was the background to the development of Che Guevara's guerilla warfare? Why had he advocated armed guerilla warfare—

both in operation and tactics, aided by a handful of armed soldiers, isolated from the people, and secretly, in an almost clandestine fashion? This trend was distinct from that of the communist groups all over the world, even from the mass movement and armed struggle supported by communist groups in Latin America.

His reasons for adverting the guerilla movement were a series of evaluations he had made on the social and political conditions of the world and Latin America. Looking back, one realized that his evaluations were far from correct, and he had had to pay for them with his life. This was the ultimate tragedy in the life of a great revolutionary. The world of politics is unforgiving, sometimes exacting a terrible price for a single mistake.

What determined these evaluations? Guevara was under the impression that the countries of Latin America were ready for revolution. The common man, suffering tremendous poverty and discrimination, was disillusioned with the ruling class. The ruling and corrupt bourgeoise governments were debilitated in the absence of public support. The public was also exasperated with the army because of its frequent coups to overthrow the democratically-elected governments and establishment of autocracy. Rigged elections administered by the army to legitimize such autocracies had turned the entire democratic system into a farce. The system no longer held any charm. Under such circumstances, the public would certainly support armed revolution. A potent revolutionary situation brewed, but the communist groups were deluded by the false promises offered by the bourgeoise parliamentary system or, for that matter, other mass movements. Hence, starting an armed revolution was imperative.

But what were the real circumstances like? The democratic hopes of the people were, to an extent, still represented by the bourgeoise democratic groups; the occasional elections were proof of that. Of course, the army never allowed the winners of the elections to assume power, or soon overthrew such governments by coups. The faith of the people in parliamentary politics had declined, but they had not completely rejected it.

Exploitation and neglect may compel the downtrodden to rebel. But in the absence of a lasting and demanding political and organizational agenda, they cannot automatically be a part of a social revolution. Or for that matter, a part of the process of the establishment of a socialistic society. An unorganized public would, at the most, be neutral spectator to such attempts launched by others; they would not spontaneously turn into active soldiers.

There were flaws in Guevara's political evaluations, as well as in his evaluations of the possible role of American imperialism. In the presence of a neutral and inactive public, a weak ruling group, aided by imperialist economic and military power, can fight and scatter the guerillas. In Guevara's flawed conclusion—that in most of the countries in Latin America, the situation was conducive to revolution—lay the seeds of his failure. Guevara had even said that not all the necessary conditions needed to be met in society for revolution to occur; by its beginning, armed guerilla war would create these conditions. Keeping in mind the successful revolutions in Cuba, he had developed the principles and strategies of guerilla warfare.

Che Guevara's idealistic and ideological foundation was Marxism-Leninism. To establish socialism in Latin America on the basis of this philosophy, he had adopted guerilla war as his method—based on the previously mentioned political evaluation. It is a dangerous error to confuse the means with the ends. One should remember that Guevara was in the truest sense an orthodox Marxist-Leninist; he had been incredibly original in its practice though. Moreover, Guevara was an internationalist to the core, he had never been swayed by nationalist sentiments. A son of Argentina, he had joined forces with Mexico's Fidel Castro to organize a revolution in Cuba. And after its success, he had consciously rejected the Ministry of Finance and selected Bolivia to continue his project of a continental revolution. To exploit the ideas of such a man in the interest of a nationalistic and separatist movement is actually an insult to him.

Currently, we notice the imprints of Guevara's thoughts among the followers of insurgency in Assam. These essentially nationalistic forces (though many claim to follow the ideals of scientific socialism) ignore Guevara's Marxist-Leninist history and merely adopt his tactics—and it is doubtful how effective that is going to be. Particularly in a powerful nation with a strong democratic and parliamentary tradition, in a small corner of such a country, it is doubtful how effective or logical would the implementation of Guevara's model of armed struggle be without ensuring the active participation of a conscious and organized people. The true test of their strategies and methods would occur only when they declare a war in the real sense or face the armed might of the nation's army.

Till then, all we can do is wait.

It had been a month since he had sent the report. Partha was filled with anxiety. Every report he sent had been published pretty instantaneously, with the exception of this particular piece.

Finally, it was published. Not as a special article on the editorial page as promised, but as a feature in the Sunday supplement; it had been heavily edited too. Che Guevara's Marxist-Leninist politics had been expunged, barring a couple of lines. Two illustrated boxes had been added—one carried the story of Guevara's execution in the forests of Bolivia and a picture of his dead body. But the role of the CIA in his murder had been excluded. The second box was even more fantastic. In Bolivia, among the members of Guevara's guerilla army was a beautiful woman called Tamar Bank, or Tanya. This brave young woman had died a heroine's death in the war in Bolivia. The Western capitalist press was rife with stories of a romance between Guevara and Tamar. Partha's newspaper carried a similar hint. There was no end to attempts to reduce Guevara's political importance by painting him as a romantic, lovelorn guerilla hiding in the jungles.

Partha was filled with disgust. The article he had laboured over had been reduced to cheap entertainment by his own newspaper. From his table, he looked out of the window towards the sky. A blue sky captured by a window frame, from which he could see a few vultures circling above.

What could he do? He could protest. Would it be of any use? On the contrary, that would be provoking the management and the editor. The sense of repressed resentment was stifling.

So, this is the system. You can fight it, but at serious risk to yourself.

Picking up the manuscript and the published report, he hurled them on the floor.

THE EPIC OF BABULA

I

When he heard the news, Partha was momentarily shocked.

The call had come in the morning. He had answered while he was still half asleep, and sat up shocked as he heard the voice on the phone: Do you know what's happening? Military operations have started! Central rule has been imposed, the state government has been suspended.

Actually, there was nothing to be surprised about. People had been dreading that something of that sort would happen. The army had already whisked away a few top officers of some well-known multinational tea companies. A number of officers had secretly begun sending their families out of the state—like plump rats scurrying for safety when a ship is about to sink.

Partha's news editor had rung him up from Delhi and said, 'There's possibility of something happening over there soon. Certain circles in Delhi have become very active.'

'Have you been able to guess what?'

'Anything might happen. Stay in contact with the top rung of the police and army.'

So, the developments were not totally unexpected for Partha. Not for anybody else, for that matter, but...

'But what, bhai? Now the interests of the multinational companies have been genuinely hurt. Occasional donations are fine but asking them to participate in developmental work is a different matter altogether. They have been functioning smoothly for so long like insulated colonies—why on earth would they agree to that? Why would they submit to the demand of investment? If they accepted it here, what would happen if the same demand cropped up in other parts of the world? They can't let that happen, can they? Money, yes, investment, no—never on demand. Our boys don't understand this simple thing,' Choudhury said, looking desolately at Partha. Today, there were no traces of his characteristic cynicism.

'We are silent witnesses to the march of history. We have no other choice. But do you know what I would like to see at my age, Partha? The birth of a leader or an organization who would, with courage and foresight, revolutionize the movement of history. But there only seem to be thieves and robbers around,' Choudhury shook his head sadly, and continued, 'Forget about it. Let's talk about work. We journalists are the recorders of emergencies. That's our job. Tomorrow, a group of select journalists have been invited to witness the army's operations. Are you thinking of going?'

'Yes. I will leave today itself...after some time. I am only waiting for some communication. Would you like to come along? I will be driving there. Pradhan's going too—that freelance photographer? You have met him.'

'Go ahead, don't delay. You're young, this is the age to act. I will go by helicopter...that's better for my old bones!'

A bright, cold morning. Mist in the air. A soft veil floated over the ripening paddy like smoke. A few betel nut trees reared their heads over the veil of fog; they looked as if they were floating in water. In the first golden rays of the morning, the tops of those trees sparkled. Dewdrops clung to the grass on either side of the roads. The air was cool, with just a hint of chill. In the presence of such life and freshness, anybody would experience the unadulterated joy of living. These were scenes that cheered the heart and lightened the soul. After driving for nearly the whole day yesterday and a night spent in a shoddy, smelly hotel, the bright morning seemed brilliant.

The car sped through a region full of tea gardens. It was stopped en route by an army patrol. The men surrounded the car, brandishing automatic rifles. In harsh voices, they ordered Partha and Pradhan out of the car, with their hands held above their heads. As they searched the car extensively, Partha tried showing the captain his papers—his permits and press card. After almost 30 minutes of questioning, they were allowed to go. By that time, Partha and Pradhan were perspiring.

Branching away from the main road, Partha's car drove on an unpaved road that wound its way through a field of paddy. In the distance, one could see a military camp and a number of cars. Partha's car was stopped again by a patrol unit, but they were allowed to go when they said that they were on their way to the camp ahead. The car leapt and flew over the bumpy road. The camp gradually rose into view—rows of tents, with a huge tent in front. Military cars were parked on the side. One could see many uniformed men, miniscule in size because of the distance. Suddenly, a helicopter roared to life from behind the camp and rose to the skies. Hovering in the air for a couple of minutes, it tilted and flew with tremendous speed towards the west. Gradually, it faded into a dot in the sky.

'We are almost there,' said Partha, adding 'Now what's that?'

A heavy vehicle had apparently mowed a trail through a chest-high field of uncut paddy. The paddy, flattened by its wheels, lay prone on the ground. The trail curved its way across the field and dipped into the jungle. 'Pradhan,' Partha shouted, 'the camera!'

Pradhan hurriedly took a few snaps. 'Look at those people. Who are they?'

A group of people were moving silently on the trail created by the vehicle—women, children, old men, and a young man or two… fear and suspicion writ large on their faces; there was terror in the eyes of the children.

Partha tried to question them. 'Who are you? Where are you coming from?'

The group of 11 paid no attention to Partha. Crossing the car in mute silence, they advanced on the trail carved by the heavy vehicle and descended into the field on the other side. Only a young man whispered, 'There has been firing on the other side of the village.'

Refugees! The thought crossed Partha's mind with lightning speed. An eternal tragedy. Common people who were fleeing the scene of conflict in search of safety and shelter.

A group of three appeared on the trail—an old woman bent with age, a girl, and a woman carrying a baby. Partha looked at the camp. A motorcycle was speeding furiously towards them. He quickly got into the car and started it.

At the camp, Partha met the officer-in-charge, introduced himself and produced his papers. The officer did not look particularly satisfied. In the meanwhile, one could hear the whirring of helicopters in the distance. The officer reluctantly asked them to sit down and ignored all of Partha's questions.

Three helicopters descended on the field, like three plump, ugly birds. The wind from their fans swept over the field—the force of the wind flattened the paddy to the ground. A few top-ranking army officers and distinguished citizens got down from the first copter. The officers of the camp almost ran up to greet them. The wide bellies of the other two copters disgorged the journalists like a swarm of locusts, Choudhury leading from the front. Partha and Pradhan walked up to him.

Tea and refreshments followed, after which the military officials offered detailed explanations of the situation. They also informed the visitors about their success in controlling terrorism. Then the journalists were asked to board open jeeps and driven to the forest—for a conducted tour of the encounter sites.

And what a forest it was!

Few had seen such a forest before, so natural and untamed—a virgin forest, thousands of years old.

A forest of Holong trees, where each tree towered several dozen feet into the air. The tops of the trees seemed to invade the skies; they could barely be seen. The thick bushes and trees cast long shadows on the ground. The world of the forest, layered with dead leaves, was soft and squishy. Sunshine was denied entry into this world. In its bosom grew huge ferns, the stalks of which were the size of a man's thigh; wild creepers curled around the trees. It was difficult to believe that outside the forest, the sun shone in all its glory. The womb of the forest was dark and mysterious. Like the other journalists, Partha, too, gazed spellbound, on the ancient and terrifying mystery of this forest.

The jeeps stopped at a point. The journalists were shown a few deep holes on the road-mines. A little ahead stood an abandoned camp. With its bamboo cots and black plastic roofs, it was a familiar sight for Partha. The camp was empty, save for a pressure cooker lying in a corner.

'What do the boys think they are doing?' Choudhury panted by his side. Partha shrugged. 'It's not as if I haven't seen such scenes before. I have seen them in Nagaland, Manipur,' Choudhury continued, as if to himself, 'but I never imagined I would see them here. Camps in forests, away from the people. Even before the beginning of an operation!'

After two hours in the forest, the exhausted journalists turned to leave. A lanky, young journalist fished out a small bottle of liquor from his pocket and gulped it down with obvious relief. The army officer laughed encouragingly, '*Chaliye saheb. Bahut kuch intezaam hain aap logon ke liye* (Let's go, sirs, we have made a lot of arrangements for you all).'

Emerging from the forest, the jeeps took a new roundabout way. The vehicles moved by the side of the forest.

'This is a dangerous area,' said the officer, adding, 'There may be mines along the road. You might hear firing a little ahead too.'

As if on cue, after he had finished speaking, one could hear the sound of gunshots at a distance—the rhythmic sound of gunshots fired from automatic rifles...

The journalists were speechless. Secretly, they were all terrified. Their frightened gazes were riveted on the forest. As if at any moment somebody, dressed in military fatigues, might pop out from behind a bush and let loose a hail of bullets on them.

It seemed to Partha that the army officer was quite amused. If it was such a dangerous area, how come there were no armed guards on the jeeps? There was not a single armed guard on any of the three jeeps.

Catching his eye, the officer took out a pistol from his holster. Pistol in hand, he started to address the journalists theatrically.

A single pistol against a forest!

An empty space inside the forest; a car and a couple of soldiers stood there. 'Now what was that?'

A dead body wrapped in a military blanket; its muddy feet stuck out from under the blanket.

A collective shudder ran through the journalists.

A famous journalist from a well-known Delhi-based newspaper was sitting next to Partha. Indicating at the dead body with his goatee, he asked the officer, 'And who's that?'

'That's the dead body of a dangerous extremist. He was killed in an encounter yesterday. Sirs, please do not take any photographs. I actually should not have brought you here. But I thought you ought to know the truth. You ought to understand what hardship we have to experience in these dense forests in the pursuit of the terrorists, the uncomfortable situations our brave jawans have to battle to safeguard our country. I promise you that I will give you the photographs and facts about this terrorist today, before you leave.'

One by one, the cars drove past the covered body of the dangerous extremist.

While the journalists were busy relishing food brought from the Capital by helicopters and chatting with the officers at the camp, Partha hurriedly prepared his report. Pradhan was to return to Guwahati by the helicopter; Partha had already arranged that. He would fax the reports and photographs to Delhi. After so many years of working with Partha, he could handle these responsibilities smoothly. Partha had his own car, so he would stay back. He wanted to meet the people who had had to abandon their homes.

The helicopters flew away, the journalists loaded their bellies. Taking leave of the officers, Partha walked towards his car. Against his will, he had to take along a couple of jawans as escorts for some distance. But he found out that that worked to his advantage—he was let off easily by four patrol units.

No, the jawans did not know anything about the encounters; they had taken no part in them. Their unit had arrived yesterday and they had all been appointed as guards.

A group of people mute with fear; conflicting viewpoints; a variety of visitors to the crumbling primary school building that served as a shelter for the bunch of people. Local journalists, political leaders, pimps, social workers—each had his own self-interest, his own agenda. This must be the reality in its naked form. That is why Partha, too, was here. Wasn't he motivated by the ambition to write a sensational report?

Sitting in a corner of the verandah, an old woman sobbed inconsolably, beating her brow. She would sometimes mutter to herself, scold, and curse, and occasionally look expectantly at the road; her eyes, swollen with sleeplessness, uncertainty and tears, seemed to be looking for someone on the road. Partha failed to speak to her. A middle-aged man told him that the old woman had an idiot grandson. When the firing began, he had apparently rushed into the forest.

Later in the day, a local journalist he knew told him that her grandson must have been killed in the firing inside the forest; that he had heard that the army had the corpse with them in the camp. But who was going to tell the old woman that?

The old woman's idiot grandson? Killed in firing inside the forest? That corpse wrapped with a blanket. The feet sticking out from under it, covered with mud. The dangerous terrorist.

Suspicion and a terrible dread gripped Partha's heart.

II

The setting sun, looking like an enormous *borkahi* (large brass plate), slid over the bent end of the *bholuka* bamboo bushes.

The paddy in the fields were ripening, and the fields were a wonderful golden-green. The birds, feasting on paddy throughout the day, were now returning noisily to their nests. The smell of ripe paddy filled the air. The fragrance of the paddy and the birdsongs filled the heart with an unknown bliss.

Ahini Burhi (old woman) emptied a handful of masoor dal in a plate and stepped out of the house to clean the dal in the fading light. In a corner of the yard, wrinkling her brow, she started to divest the dal of stones and pebbles. The lengthening shadows made as if to enter her small, two-room hut. It was already dark inside the house. Peering at the dal in the fading light made Ahini's eyes ache. In the golden light from the setting sun, the old woman's wrinkled face glistened like a well-scrubbed pot. Her *mekhela* (traditional Assamese attire) was tied over her chest, an old *gamosa* (a rectangular cloth, typically red and white in colour), was thrown over her shoulders. As she worked, she grumbled, 'More pebbles than dal, the rogue. The cheat of a shopkeeper has poured all the pebbles in the world into the dal. Am I making dal or pebble curry? They have mixed whatever they can think of with the dal, only because these old eyes can't see very well. You rogue, let me feed you pebble curry, let all of that stick in your throat and may you gag to death!'

A boy stomped into the yard from a corner of the garden behind the hut. He carried a *khaloi* (a fishing accessory that is a cone-shaped pitcher), and a bunch of fishing rods were slung over his shoulders. He wore a muddy red, holey vest and a pair of khaki shorts, which had turned almost black with repeated soapless washes. Gaping at the old woman briefly, the boy put the *khaloi* down in the middle of the yard. Wiping his wet hand on his shorts, he hung the fishing rods on the nails hammered under the roof. He squatted before the *khaloi* in the yard. Lifting his head, he looked at the old woman. His eyes fell on the piercings in the old woman's ears, widened by the use of heavy *thuriyas* (traditional Assamese earrings). It seemed to the boy that one could see the red sun through the wide piercings in the old woman's ears; shutting an eye and opening the other, he tried to see the sun through them. Suddenly the sun slid down from the edge of the *bholuka*'s end and dove behind the thicket. It seemed to the boy that the sun had slipped into the old woman's ears. He began to giggle.

The old woman looked back. When she saw him sitting in the middle of the yard, hugging his *khaloi*, she opened her mouth and let loose a stream of abuses, 'You good-for-nothing, so here you are! Where were you the whole day? You do not have a care in the world if this old woman is alive or dead! These old bones have to do all the work in the house. Don't you feel sorry for this old woman at all? May the spirit of the *hola* (marshy waterbody) finish you off and bury your head upside down in the mud. That will teach you a lesson!'

The boy continued giggling. The old woman's temper rose when she heard his giggles, and she cursed him with renewed vigour. Saliva dribbled out of the boy's mouth. Spitting into a corner, he rubbed his face against his vest, his body shaking with laughter. Stumbling up to the old woman, he emptied the *khaloi* before her.

Fish—*kawoi* and *magur*—fell on the floor in a heap. Thrashing *kawoi* slipped all over the place; some wriggled near the old woman's feet. When she saw the fish, the old woman flew into a worse temper. 'You good for nothing, got the pests from water, didn't you? Where do I keep all this now?'

The boy laughed in reply, spreading his legs on the floor. A *kawoi* fish wriggled up to him and slid into his shorts. Grabbing hold of the fish, he brought it to the old woman and made some indistinct sound—aa-aa-aa. His laughter continued.

'Laughing, are you? I will give you something to laugh about. What are you gaping at? Those will crawl their way to some other part of the earth now. Catch them and put them in the *khaloi*. Put them in the tin at the *dhekixal* (place for keeping the rice pounder) with some water.'

The boy went to where the *dheki* (husking treadle) was kept to store the fishes in a tin. The old woman entered her hut and lit the kerosene lamp. Then she poured some country liquor in a bowl and put some rice and pieces of fried fish on a plate. Placing the plate and the bowl before a *pira* (a low stool), she called out, 'Babula, here, come here. Come and have something to eat.'

Washing his hands, the boy sat down on the *pira*.

'You roam about in the forest the whole day with not a care about your meals. The last thing you ate today was the morning rice; and now, you turn up at dusk. Do you know how much work needs to be done in this house? The geese need to be herded into their pens, water needs to be fetched, and I have to do everything alone! Don't you feel sorry for this old woman? You are away the whole day and, sometimes, you don't even come back at nights. One day, you will come back to find this old woman lying dead on the ground... someday she might be carried away by a tiger.'

The boy now started thrashing about on the floor. He started shaking his head violently, whining.

'Now, now, that's all right. I won't die. Tigers won't carry me away. Son, I will always be there to look after you. I can't possibly leave you alone, can I?'

Ahini wiped her eyes with the corner of her *gamosa*. The boy calmed down. He stopped thrashing about, but kept whining. The old woman held out a piece of fried fish to him. She got up from the hearth, shuffled up to him and stroked his head. He started eating in silence. Two tears rolled down the old woman's wrinkled cheeks.

Away from the warmth of the hearth, Ahini felt a little cold. Entering the bedroom, she took a sheet from the shelf on which the clothes hung, and wrapped it around the boy's shoulders. She hurriedly increased the fire in the hearth.

There was a sound of someone approaching.

'Who's that?' asked the old woman.

'It's us, Aita (grandmother).'

Shuffling to the door, the old woman held up the lamp. It was quite dark outside.

'Bhadreswar? Come in, come in. Looks like you have brought a guest. Where is he from?'

'He's from my grandfather's village. A kinsman,' Bhadreswar said as he walked in, shining his torch. They got themselves two *piras* standing against the wall and sat down. Babula had finished eating. He got to his feet, bowl in hand.

'You're lucky Babula. You have Aita's nectar for free every day,' Bhadreswar said.

They cackled. Babula hung the lamp on an iron hook on the verandah. A pale-yellow glow filled the room. Then he placed two glasses before them. The old woman poured them some country liquor that looked like thick starch. 'Would you like some fried fish as well?'

'Please, Aita. Your nectar tastes so much better with fried fish.'

The old woman smiled sweetly. She placed a pan over the fire, and poured a drop of mustard oil in it. When the oil crackled, she heated two previously fried fish in it and then held them out to the guests on a broken plate, along with green chillies and salt. Dabbing a chilly with salt, Bhadreswar took a huge bite from it and sipped his liquor, 'Aita, your liquor doesn't have its old fire. I think you don't brew it very well nowadays.'

'Good-for-nothing, you,' the old woman snapped at him, 'I dare you to find a better brewer than me in this region. Do you think your mothers and your wives can do it? Shameless. I don't brew it well, he says. I comb the shops for the best rice, best ingredients, and this good-for-nothing says I don't brew it well!'

'Don't be angry, Aita,' Bhadreswar laughed, 'You have no competition in this state, forget about the region. Everybody flocks to you, don't they? Your box must be stuffed with money.'

His friend joined in the laughter.

'Don't you have any shame? Me, a poor widow, I brew liquor to fill my belly. And here you go talking about money!'

'No, Aita, we were only joking.'

'Well, don't crack silly jokes with your grandmother! I will teach you a lesson.'

Slowly, the old woman's hut filled with people. From her *pira* near the hearth, the old woman served liquor and fried fish as per demand. Babula helped her, handing out the glasses and running small errands. Warming themselves near the hearth, the men chatted about a number of things—from the paddy in the fields to the boys in the jungle.

'Times are bad, you know,' said somebody.

'And they are going to get worse,' Bhadreswar's friend put his glass down with a thud. The man had had several glasses of liquor, and it seemed to be having its effect. 'Here, Aita, I will have one more. In our place, you can forget about having a drink in peace. I must say you are lucky,' he said, glaring at Bhadreswar.

Pouring him another glass, the old woman strained to hear what he had to say about her liquor.

'What's happening at your place?'

'All right, if you really want to know,' taking a long sip from his glass, the man began, '...not very long ago, we were looking for somebody to reap the paddy. It took us the whole day but we couldn't find anybody. We were a little upset about it, and tried to make things up for ourselves in the evening with a bottle and some duck meat. We had had barely a sip when a few boys turned up. Really young boys, you know, the milk not yet dry on their lips. We have seen those boys running about in bare bottoms. And you know what they had to say to us?'

'What?' There was a chorus of voices.

'They said "kokai, we don't like this at all".'

'I wanted to say "...and what don't you like, you pests?" But, of course, I didn't say that; times are bad, you know.'

'Were they carrying guns?'

'No; I wouldn't know if they had them tucked under their clothes though.'

'What did you say?'

'We said, but what is the problem? What is our fault? We are just trying to have a good time with friends.'

'And then?'

'Would you believe it? The snoot nosed told me, "Kokai, liquor is proving to be the undoing of our society. People are growing poorer. Characters are being corrupted. Liquor today, opium tomorrow, and the next one after that? Liquor's making it difficult for our people, especially our women, to venture out after dusk. It is like a disease for our society. We have to stop it. We plan to stop the consumption of liquor in our area. And we will do it, so please co-operate".'

The others clucked their tongues in sympathy.

'What else? Those words cast a pall of gloom over us. One of us asked, "We were having it inside our house. How did you find out?"'

'Oh yes, how did they find out? Somebody must have tattled. Some spy or loose mouth,' one of the men said.

'No, no, nothing like that. Do you know what he said? "When we were crossing your house, we smelt fried duck. So, we thought of dropping in and finding out for ourselves."'

'Ah, I see, the smell of fried duck had pulled them in!'

'Right. We felt like asking them to sit down. I said, "It's all right if you don't want to have liquor, you can have some fried duck." But of course, none of us had the courage to do that. Our tongues were frozen.'

'What happened next?'

'What else? The little scoundrel said, "Kokai, I hope after today this thing is not seen in your house, or anywhere else, for that matter. We only have your best interests at heart. Goodbye." And then, he marched out with his friends who were standing near the door.'

'So, what did you do?'

'What could we do? For a long time, we sat with the fried duck and the liquor before us. Then one of us said, "Didn't he say after today? So, we can have it today. Come on, let's have it." But the taste was bitter, you see. Liquor, duck, they all lost their taste. The words spoilt their taste forever. Here, Aita, I will have some more; I will have my fill today! So they haven't got here yet, have they? Well, they will...very soon. They have spread their tentacles everywhere.'

Ahini was listening to them with attention. Fear swept over her.

'I think that the boys are doing the right thing. In some places, liquor has actually created a lot of mayhem. Stinking drunkards in every house. These boys are trying to reform society,' said one of the men called Puna.

Ahini could not tolerate that. She lashed out at the speaker, 'So you have joined them too, have you, Puna? Big words in your mouth. You rogue, if liquor is so bad, what are you doing here? Don't come here. I don't want such ungrateful customers such as yourself in my house!'

The men burst into laughter. Puna could not help smiling, either. The old woman kept grumbling. For a long time, the men sat there, talking over liquor and fried fish. After a point, they paid the old woman and left in one after the other.

Another day ended in the life of Ahini Burhi and Babula.

III

'Where have you disappeared, you good-for-nothing, you? Have you set out with your fishing rods already? I will teach you a lesson today. You are not to go out today, do you hear me? There is a lot to be done.'

From behind the bushes in the yard, with odd sounds, Babula let her know that he was there.

'We have to get rice today. And firewood. Get the rice from Keya's shop. I had told him about it yesterday,' she ordered, and then went inside the house. After some time, Babula followed her. The old woman and her grandson started putting the earthen pots on the shelf in order; the pots inside the dark room stored country liquor. The sweet smell of fermented rice from the pots filled the room.

Finishing the work, Babula wolfed down the food his grandmother served him and made to leave. Pulling out the rice sack from under the bed, he set off at a run. His grandmother screamed instructions after him, but he paid no heed to them. He sped out of the corner of the yard towards Keya's shop. At the shop, he threw the sack on the shopkeeper's seat. The shopkeeper knew why he was there; he quickly measured rice into his sack. Babula did not wait a second after the rice was measured. Slinging the sack over his shoulders, he hurried home. Shoving the sack under the bed, he changed into some fresh clothes.

The old woman was observing him. When she saw him put on his neat pair of shorts and his white shirt, she understood that he was not going fishing today. When he slid his feet inside his brown canvas shoes, the old woman knew that he was going out on a different errand.

She squatted on the floor, and beating her brow, let out a long wail. When Babula needed to be stopped or made to do something against his wishes, her tears were her arsenal.

'He wants to leave me, fine, but don't expect to find me alive when you come back. You will find my dead body.' Her tears had no response; Babula turned a deaf ear to her cries. Making some indistinct sounds, he took up the bamboo stave that hung on the wall. At the door, he turned to look at the wailing old woman, and then stomped across the yard. In a flash, he had stepped on the road by the fields.

Pushing against the floor with her hands, the old woman rose to her feet. Knotting her *mekhela* tightly around her bosom, she shuffled out of the house and putting her hand on her waist, hurled abuses at her grandson.

Babula stomped across the field, into the grove near the cemetery, and headed straight for the swampy water body. The swamp marked the beginning of the reserve forest. He cast a glance at the fishing spots near the banks of the swamp, trying to see if any rods were lying there. There were none, he noted with a sense of relief.

He walked through the forest, past the clusters of wild *keteki* bush. Whenever he reached this spot, a strange sensation gripped him; a nameless feeling swept through his mind. Here, right here, under those trees, he had met them for the first time. The girl from his village, Seuti, and the boy, Maneshwar. They had lain, intertwined like snakes, under that tree. When he had seen them for the first time, he had been amazed. He had stopped in his tracks, and had understood with some primitive instinct that they were in no trouble. From behind the bushes, he had gazed—mesmerized—at the incredible, rhythmic union of the two sweat-soaked bodies.

Gradually, a sensual excitement spread through his muscular, 24-year-old body. He stood, thunderstruck. Eventually, the couple had got up and were cleaning themselves, which is when Seuti had caught sight of him and screamed.

Maneshwar was startled too. Then, collecting his wits, he had lunged at him. Seuti had grabbed him from behind, 'It's all right, it's only Babula. He cannot even speak; he won't tell on us.'

Maneshwar had stopped. 'But he can hear us, can't he? He understands too. He might have seen us.'

'That's all right. That half-wit cannot speak; some severe illness in childhood, you see. Come on, let's go.'

After they hurried away, he had slowly made his way to the tree under which they had lain. The warmth of their bodies lingered in the flattened leaves scattered under the tree, in the outlines of their bodies on the grass. A mild, heady scent filled the air—like the scent of wild flowers, like that of wet earth after the rains... His ears burned with a mysterious shame.

Henceforth, whenever at nights he experienced a strange fire in his body, felt an excruciating yet pleasurable sensation between his thighs, he thought of that tree in the forest, and that couple wrapped around each other like snakes. That scent assailed his nostrils like wild flowers, like the scent of wet earth...

Whenever he approached that particular spot, he would feel uncomfortable and would hurry past it. Today was no exception. Mumbling, he crossed that spot.

He came upon the narrow path leading to the reserve. The path, only traces of which remained, forked out of the Forest Department road curving through the forest. Towering trees lined both sides of the path. Creepers wound up the trees and dangled from their tops. Thick bushes and huge ferns grew on the ground beneath. Some way into the reserve, he hurried into the stretch of forest by the side of a huge *hollong* tree.

A little later, he saw them. They had caught sight of him long back. A broad smile creased his face; the boys were there.

Smiling, he moved forward. The boys were wearing camouflaged uniforms, and carried guns. They stood in attention by the small shelters built out of bamboo and plastic sheets. A couple of them were boiling rice in a huge vessel, perched atop a fire. Babula looked around; spotting a trowel, he took it up and began clearing the weeds near the shelters.

Babula had been here several times. The first time, his visit had created a commotion. For a few days, while fishing at the pond, he had seen several figures darting in and out of the forest. Hidden by the tall grass, he had been able to figure out the road used by these young men. One day, out of curiosity, he had followed the road.

When he had suddenly appeared in their midst, a few gun-wielding boys had surrounded him. Startled, he had made incoherent sounds—aa-aa-oo—like he did when upset or stressed. The boys had struck him a few times, and then confused by his reactions, had tied him to a tree. Although he kept whining, nobody paid him any attention.

A little later, a boy had come to take a good look at him and, seeing his face, had burst out laughing. Babula had met that boy in his village several times; but he had never seen the other boys before.

Laughing, the boy said to other boys, 'Let him go. I know him. this is Babula Benga; he's the liquor-selling Ahini's grandson. He is no spy. He spends the whole day looking for fish in ditches and ponds. Come on, let him go.' Turning to Babula, he said, 'Babula, don't ever come here again or you will get yourself in trouble.'

The boys had untied him, given him a good meal, and sent him on his way back.

Another day, when Babula was fishing, he had seen the boy who had rescued him from the predicament at the camp. Dropping his fishing rod, he had picked up his catch and followed him to the camp. He had emptied the fish before them.

That was the beginning. He took to visiting them—sometimes carrying fish, at others, empty-handed. In the camp, he would take up some chore or the other. In a few days, he had become one of them; if he did not turn up for several days, the boys would wonder at his absence. The boy he knew had told his friends to let Babula do whatever he wanted there, but not to let him go beyond this camp.

IV

It was a cloudy day, with occasional bursts of rain. The rain had brought along a numbing cold. Babula and Ahini had been sitting by the fireplace since evening, warming themselves with its leaping flames. Today, there had not been a single customer. In such weather, people did not generally venture out for a drink.

'No sales today, I gather. And what are you trying to build in that light? Aren't you ashamed? Look at yourself, a young man building bird traps. When one of those twigs hits you in the face, you will know,' Ahini said to Babula.

Lost in his work, Babula paid no attention to her. The old woman went on grumbling. 'Look at the rain, no signs of letting up. I suppose when they get bored at home, they will take out their umbrellas and covers, and set off for our house.'

There was a knock on the door.

Ahini grew alert. 'Who's that? Come right in, the door's not locked.'

Pushing open the door, a young man walked in. Babula recognized him immediately—that boy whom he regularly met in the village in the evenings, the boy who had set him free.

Walking towards the fireplace, the boy sat down on a *pira* without waiting to be asked. Like other days, Babula took down a glass from the shelf and hospitably placed it before him. The boy, however, pushed it away. Looking at Ahini, he asked, 'Aita, how long have you been selling liquor?'

'I wonder. Quite some time, I think. It's been two decades since Babula's father passed away. His mother had left us early too. Since then, I think.'

'Aita, do you know that this isn't the right thing to do?'

The old woman was taken aback. Her temper rose. About to let loose a stream of abuses, she stopped, and took a good look at the well-built young man sitting in front of her.

'What can I do, my son? Do you think I like doing this? I am only trying to fill our bellies. Not one, but two. I have to take care of this half-wit. I have no fields which I can till for rice. Now these old bones cannot even pound rice or toil in the fields for a few paisas. And I cannot beg, my son. It's better to die than to beg for money. As for working for other people...people these days have no money to get work out of others. Even if they had money to spare, this old body would not allow it. What do I do, if not sell liquor?'

Seeing that the boy was silent, the old woman went on, 'And I use the best of rice, no mixing ever. I have heard that people mix tobacco and stuff—you won't find me committing such crimes, my son. I make the purest liquor, and am somehow surviving without having to beg for alms. By the grace of God, I have been able to pay for my own medicines. My body aches all over, my son, I have to treat it with opium.'

'Do you sell opium, too?'

'No, my son, not at all. I only use it when the pain gets too much for me.'

'Opium, bhang, liquor...your business is flourishing, Aita.'

'No, no bhang here. I don't sell such rotten stuff. And no opium either—where would I get it? It's all I can do to get that bit for my aches. And not for long either. I do sell liquor. Why would I lie, my son? I do brew liquor and sell it, too.'

'Aita, you will have to stop doing that.'

'Stop selling liquor?' The old woman was thunderstruck. Now Ahini found it hard to restrain herself and flew into a rage, 'You swine, stop selling liquor! And how do I fill my belly then? And this half-wit, who is going to feed him? Would you feed us, you good-for-nothing?'

The boy raised his hand and cut her off.

The old woman was a little scared. So those pests Bhadreswar's kin had warned them about had turned up here too. She had heard that the boys were out to stop the sale of liquor. In a village nearby, apparently after the liquor business had been terminated, a regular drunkard had died of shaking fits. The old woman cast a frightened look at the boy. He carried on, 'Aita, your liquor business has to stop. We can't let the youth go to seed. We have thought about your livelihood...you can open a store at your house. The villagers will be duly informed. They will buy all their stuff from you. Here's some money. From tomorrow, stop selling liquor and open a shop.'

Stuffing several notes in the old woman's hand, the boy left. For a long time after that, the old woman and Babula sat near the fireplace, immobile. At times, the old woman slapped her brow, heaved deep sighs and repeated 'I am done for' a couple of times.

A couple of days passed. The old woman could not muster up the courage to touch the money the young man had left her. On the other hand, she did not know how to go about opening a store. She was stunned. She dared not talk to anybody about it; the sale of liquor had stopped too. She had had to turn away quite a few customers. She had served a few old-timers on the sly, but had faked indisposition to most.

'All my joints are aching, my son, all of them. I can't even move; how do I brew liquor with this body of mine?'

Her savings were depleting too.

One day, after much thought, Ahini set out for the city with Babula. No one knew what they looked for in the city, but on their way back, the old woman stopped at the market and bought several new glasses, a few plates of stainless steel, plastic jugs with coloured lids, and a dazzling aluminum kettle. From the Bhutanese street market near the court, after considerable haggling, she bought a baggy sweater for Babula and a woollen blouse for herself.

Getting down from the bus, as they walked through the fields, the old woman kept talking, 'And how do I start a store? Easier said than done! Nobody in my family has ever done it; we are not businessmen. Let him come, that swine, I will give him an earful—I can't run a store, he can do what he likes!'

Babula walked in silence, dressed in his new sweater, shaking the bag carrying the glasses, plates, and jugs. When she heard them rattling, the old woman lost her temper, 'Why are you rattling them? Good-for-nothing, you, you will smash them all!'

From the next day, the old woman took to selling liquor with renewed enthusiasm. The brand-new glasses, plates, and jugs shone in the light of the fire by her hearth.

A couple of weeks later, the boy paid them another visit.

The old woman was frying fish that day. 'How is the shop doing, Aita?' the boy asked. He was wearing camouflage uniform; he held a black, iron gun. Casting a fearful look at the gun, the old woman said, 'Hard to run a store, my son.'

'Why?'

'If the world asks for credit, how is a store supposed to run?'

'Who has been asking you for credit, Aita? Come on, tell me.' The old woman was trapped. Finally, she confessed, 'There's no shop, my son.'

'No shop? What did you do with the money I gave you?'

Babula now picked up the new glasses and plates and put them down in front of the boy. The boy stared at them in silence for a few minutes and then said, 'I had given you money to stop your sale of liquor, but you used that to increase your sales. Now what do I do with you?'

The old woman kept quiet. The boy felt helpless; truly, what could be done with that old woman? After some time, he opened his bag, and took out a couple of boxes. From the boxes he took out two locks, and unlocked them. In a flash, he slipped the locks into the wide holes in the old woman's ears and locked them. Ahini sat, stunned, holding onto the huge locks dangling from her ears.

'I will keep the keys until you stop selling liquor and open a store.' Throwing the keys into his bag, the boy left.

Before he had crossed the yard, the old woman regained her senses. Two giant locks swung from her ears and she had to hold onto them. When she let go, the locks threatened to rip her ears apart. Holding on to her ears, the old woman collapsed near the fireplace. Terrified, she screamed, 'Look at what the swine has done to me! He has killed me! Let the cholera take him! Oh, he has skinned me alive—come, all of you, and see what the ruffian has done! Oh, let the tiger take him!'

Unable to move with the locks in her ears, her screams rang through the village. People gathered in her yard. When they saw her state, they did not have the heart to laugh. They clucked with sympathy in her presence, but out of earshot, they dissolved with laughter. A few women sat down next to the old lady and tried, in vain, to take the locks off.

Babula flew into a rage when he saw his grandmother's state. All night, he paced up and down his house like a raging bull. At dawn, he carried the pots of liquor resting on the shelves out of the house and threw them away; the sweet smell of liquor filled the air. The men who had assembled in the house in the morning to enquire after the old woman's health fretted. Bhadreswar could not but speak up, 'Here, Babula, it's a crime to waste that bit of nectar. Don't do it! Don't do such impious things. If you don't want it, give it to me, I will take the pots away.'

A few men agreed with Bhadreswar, but nobody had the courage to stop Babula.

Inside the house, Ahini, racked with pain, heard the sounds of the pots smashing. She began to cry and lament over her fate.

V

Throwing the pots away, Babula broke into a run through the yard. He did not stop till he found himself at the camp in the middle of the reserve. Panting, he flopped down on the ground and started tugging at his ears and slapping himself on the cheeks, hard. The boys at the camp were astonished. The more they asked him what was wrong, the more he pulled at his ears and slapped his cheeks. Soon, his cheeks and ears turned scarlet from the blows.

Sometime later, the boy who had put the locks on Ahini's ears arrived at the camp. Babula still sat on the ground, mumbling incoherently, slapping himself, tugging at his ears. When the boy saw him, he knew what to do. With some of his companions, he went to the village and—with the help of the villagers—cleared Ahini's house of all signs of liquor and set up a shop in her hut. Towards evening, the boys had filled the shop with necessary goods bought from the city, and had taught

Babula to use the scales. Purchasing a few things from the shop, they departed.

That was the beginning of Babula and Ahini's shop. Babula grew so fond of working at the shop that he stopped going out to fish. Initially, Ahini struggled with the calculations, but later, she found that she could run the shop quite well. Once when he was buying a pack of cigarettes from her, Bhadreswar told her, 'Aita, you are doing this so well. You must have been a shopkeeper in a previous birth!'

'You wretch, nothing of that sort—nobody in my family has ever made a living peddling grocery! It's my ill luck…'

'Ill luck, is it? You could peddle that garbage, that rotten water though. And now, look at you, cribbing about having to sell groceries!'

Bhadreswar could not even finish his words... The old woman flared up, 'Rotten water! Garbage indeed. Have you forgotten how many times you came to my place to have that rotten water? It's my misfortune to mingle with ungrateful wretches like you…'

Fearing that the old woman would start wailing again, Bhadreswar quickly paid her and left. Bhadreswar was now at the forefront of the villagers who were out to eliminate the liquor business from the village. He heaped praises on the boys who had started this mission. Not only in his village, he was also trying to stop the sale of liquor in the Nepali village nearby. He stood to gain—the boys recognized his efforts, and he could always smuggle a glass of strong liquor, which he would relish in the privacy of his room with the door securely bolted. A trustworthy Nepali acquaintance from that village would meet him in the forest and furtively slip a bottle into the bag dangling from his bicycle. In public, however, he would generously praise the efforts of the boys and lecture the villagers about the dangers of alcohol consumption.

'Here, Kokai, don't I myself know what a rotten thing liquor is? You know how fond of it I was once upon a time. I feel so much better after giving it up. I feel younger too. Of course, I won't deny that it was hard to give it up initially…it was tough on my body. But I realize now what poison I have been having all along. I can't thank those boys enough. Kokai, we have to stop the brewing of liquor in every house—we should bring this up in the *namghar*,' Bhadreswar would say to people.

'Well, yes. I suppose you are right.' Nobody had the courage to oppose Bhadreswar now.

Ahini took up the broom and tried to clean the hut. 'Look at the clutter in my room…one cannot even turn around. There is so much dust!' The room held sacks of rice, flour, potatoes, and onions. Biscuit tins lined a plank supported by bamboo sections. The plank also held tea leaves, toffees, and sweets in glass jars, candles, matchboxes, coconut oil, and soap. The basket with the areca nuts and betel leaves was also placed nearby.

Ahini suddenly remembered the locks, and a shiver ran up her spine. She remembered the weight of the locks on her ears, and the pain that racked her body from top to toe. Like other days, when Ahini remembered that incident, she burst into tears.

As she swept the room, a huge rat sprinted out of a sack of rice and disappeared under the floor. Ahini was startled; her anger was now directed towards those boys.

'Those wretches have turned my house into a den for rats and mice. Let the tiger drag them away! Earlier you couldn't find a single rat here, not even one the size of a jackfruit seed. Go on, you; finish off all that rice and dal...come and take a good bite out of my chest! Look at him now, hiding in that corner, gnashing his saw-like teeth. Get out of here, you pest, go outside and perish!' the old woman grumbled bitterly as she swept.

At that very moment, an explosion rent the sky, followed closely by another, and another—the world shook as if in the grip of an earthquake. Shrieking birds flew into the air. The geese swimming in the ditch at a corner of the yard cackled with fear. Hurrying out of her hut, Ahini saw Maneshwar's cow sprint past, tail upraised. The monkeys on the tall tree near the *namghar* screeched and bounded from one branch to the other. Deafening reports followed the pause; something seemed to be exploding in a distance.

Ahini was frightened; her heart pounded. She understood dimly that something terrible had happened. Straining her ears, she tried to find out where the noise was coming from. Yes, it was coming from the forest, from the reserve.

'Babula, where are you? Can't you hear that sound? Don't go near that, don't...'

Babula stepped into the yard. The old woman and her grandson stood in silence, trying to figure out where the sounds were coming from. In between the reports like cannon shots, something else was exploding too. They craned their necks for a look. Screams reached them from one end of the village. Now what had happened there? There was the sudden sound of running footsteps behind them. Startled, they turned around. Why, that was Maneshwar, running for his life; and that was Bhadreswar behind him. What was wrong? When he saw Ahini and Babula standing near the gate, unable to move, Maneshwar yelled, 'The soldiers are here, they have filled the village...there has been shooting in the reserve.'

Neither of them had time to pause. They were running for their lives. In his haste, Maneshwar's *gamosa* slipped off his shoulders.

Babula and the old woman stood rooted to the spot; they did not know what to do.

Suddenly Babula seemed to remember something. In the reserve, there was the camp, and the boys, too—the boys who had come to their house. That boy was there, too—the one who had locked his grandmother's ears. That boy had been so nice to him. With a choked cry, Babula ran across the yard towards the reserve, with the small knife he had been carrying, and without so much as a look at his grandmother.

The old woman was stunned. When she realized what had happened, she tried to follow him; then she changed her mind and ran towards the village.

There was pandemonium in the village; people were running helter-skelter. The men, the boys, and a few women were running towards the shelter of the fields, carrying whatever they could lay their hands on. Screams and sobs filled the air. Before Ahini could collect her wits, several huge jeeps roared to a stop in front of the *namghar*. A crowd of army soldiers disembarked—fearsome, wearing camouflage uniforms, black scarves tied around their heads. They fired into the air and shouted instructions. They surrounded the frightened villagers and herded them towards the primary school building, shoving and hitting them. Pushing the women and children inside a room, they made the men stand in the field in front of the building—their hands held above their heads.

The voices of the army men rose above the clamour. Their '*Chup raho, daro mat, kuch nahin hoga!*' (stay quiet, don't be afraid, nothing will happen) did little to calm the terrified villagers. They clammed up in fear, but the muffled sobs of the children could still be heard.

There were screams, and the sounds of gunshots, all around the village. The army men now looked in houses for people whom they might have missed the first time, kicking and beating whoever they came upon. At times, one could hear the frightened cries of women too. The people trapped inside the school building had their hearts in their mouths. The soldiers drove another lot towards the building. The sight of their friends standing with their hands held high was of little comfort to the newcomers.

Two soldiers were leading a man towards the building, hitting him with the barrels of their guns. The people saw that the man did not seem cowed; on the contrary, he was shaking himself violently.

An old woman followed them, beating her brow and crying hard.

Wasn't that Bhadreswar? And the old woman was the liquor-selling Ahini. What was Bhadreswar telling the soldier? They would tear him to pieces. A hum throbbed through the crowd of men, waiting with their hands held above their heads.

A jeep was parked in front of the building. A young officer stood near it, smoking a cigarette and carrying a pistol. The soldiers shoved Bhadreswar towards him. The officer looked at him, the cigarette sitting between his lips. With surprise and wonder, the villagers noticed that far from shrinking, Bhadreswar had drawn himself to his full height and addressed the officer in a clear voice, 'My name is Bhadreswar Samua, *main ye school ka shikshak hoon. Aapke sipahilog ne is buddhi ko peeta. Main dekh kar daur aaya. Kyon peeta is buddhi ko? Bahut kharaaab, anyay hain, adharm hain!*' (I am a teacher at this school. Your soldiers beat this old lady up. I saw and came running. Why beat an old lady up? It's deplorable, it's unjust, it's immoral!)

The villagers were struck by his courage. How that man rattled off words in Hindi and English. Was he delirious in the presence of death?

A soldier said, '*Ye budhiya jungle ki taraf bhaag rahi thi.*' (This old lady was running towards the jungle.)

The officer said something. The cigarette on his lips dipped; he made a sign. Suddenly, one of the soldiers hit Bhadreswar hard in the stomach with his gun; he collapsed on the ground. A suppressed cry rang through the crowd. Ahini threw herself on Bhadreswar and wept, 'You sinners, don't beat him...'

The officer said something in a stern voice; nobody knew what. But the soldiers lifted Ahini and Bhadreswar from the ground and pushed them towards the building. Bhadreswar was made to stand with his hands above his head. Flinging herself down on the steps, Ahini began to cry. 'Babula,' she wept, 'where have you gone?'

On the door hung a portrait framed in glass—black ink on white paper, discoloured by the sun and dust. It was a portrait of Mahatma Gandhi, proceeding with long steps on his Dandi March. It was under that portrait that Ahini sobbed bitterly.

For a day and a night, the villagers huddled in the building on empty stomachs. The next day, the soldiers drove off in their jeeps.

After a long time, the villagers began to gauge the situation. The soldiers were nowhere to be seen; they must have left. There was not a sound to be heard…it was as silent as death all around. When they realized that the soldiers had left, the villagers began to move. They did not dare go back to the village. Slowly, they made their way towards the city—an uncertain journey that began through the paddy fields. They moved in small groups. In the middle of the field, they saw that a huge vehicle had trampled a way through the paddy. Moving on that route through chest-high paddy, they would not be seen from a distance. They felt safer taking that route rather than the open road. Now, the people moved on that route, through the paddy. The groups were led by Bhadreswar, who had by now become their unofficial leader.

The traumatized city-bound crowd had Ahini in its midst.

VI

Trampling over bushes and thickets like a raging bull, Babula leapt on to the road winding through the reserve and immediately fell into the soldiers' hands. A group of soldiers, their cars parked on the road, were busy with some work. When Babula tore into their midst, a soldier cried out, 'Catch him! Catch him!' Before Babula knew it, four well-built soldiers had pounced on him. They tied his hands behind his back, flung him on the ground, and tied his feet. Trussed, Babula lay like a dead frog on the pukka road. Somebody kicked him hard on his butt. He moaned in pain. The man turned him over with his foot; it was the man who had seen him first.

Lying on his back on the road, Babula saw the sky. He saw the leaves of the towering *hollongs*, and the sky shining bright through those leaves. The man who had kicked him was staring at him. Turning to his companions, he gestured towards Babula and said something. A few soldiers immediately picked him up and heaved him bodily into the back of an army jeep. Babula fell with a thud, like a sack, among a pile of things. He yelled in pain.

Time passed. Babula could make out that the soldiers were digging by the side of the road. He could hear the sounds of shovels and axes. The joints of his shoulders and his hands hurt; they had tied the knots too tight. His fingers were numb too. He tried to move his hands, but a bolt of pain gripped his body. Moving his legs, he tried to find a comfortable place among the iron and sacks.

After a long time, the soldiers leapt into the jeeps. Trampling on Babula, they made themselves comfortable on the seats on either side inside the jeep. So far, his head had been lying on a sack; somebody nudged the sack aside with his foot and Babula's head hit the floor. The jeep started, and with each jerk, his head thudded against the floor. With each blow, his head swam, his teeth clattered; after some time, Babula nearly passed out.

When the jerking stopped, Babula opened his eyes. He saw that the sky was darkening. He felt a little cold. His shoulder hurt, and he could not feel his hands anymore. After some time, a few soldiers sat him up. They untied his feet and lifted him out. When they propped him up, his head throbbed violently and he almost collapsed. The soldiers pushed and shoved him into a tent where several other soldiers stood, wielding guns. A man sat behind a table. Babula was made to stand in front of him. His head spun, and so, he swayed like a drunk. The man started asking him something. At first, he could not understand a single word he was saying. Then somebody spoke to him in Assamese. He understood that they were asking him about the boys in the reserve. He started making some strange sounds.

The soldiers talked among themselves.

'Is he dumb?'

'He seems to hear quite well. So, he is not deaf, only dumb.'

'He might be a scoundrel. He might be faking it.'

Suddenly, one of them took out a whip. Babula screamed in pain as the whip fell across his body—his hands, his feet, and his shoulders. Saliva dribbled from his lips.

'I think he really is dumb. He can't speak.'

'Is he trying to act smart? We have an answer for that too.'

Babula lay groaning on the ground, like a scared, wounded beast. The soldiers were talking agitatedly now, their backs to him. Babula understood very well that the soldiers were getting angry because he had not spoken. But how could he speak? All he could utter was some useless sounds. Few could understand him; but he understood everything. He could not speak—he felt utterly helpless. Tears streamed out of his eyes. Through his moans, he tried to convey to the soldiers that he could not speak. But would they understand?

Now the soldiers lifted him onto a wooden table. They tied his hands and feet, removed all his clothes and tied a few wires to his chest and penis. Leaning over him, a soldier asked him in Assamese about the boys in the forest. He could only groan in reply.

Suddenly, he felt an excruciating pain in his chest and between his thighs. The pain, intense and shocking, racked his body. The repeated electric shocks drove him wild; he began to scream. When the wave of pain receded, mumbles—incoherent and endless—poured out of his mouth.

The soldiers were now convinced that he was dumb. They untied his hands and feet, and stood him up. Babula's head seemed empty of all sensations; a haze descended before his eyes. He drifted in and out of consciousness. He could sense that he was being pushed out of the tent. He felt a wave of cold, dewy air wash over him; it made him feel a little better. He dimly sensed that he was being taken into another house and pushed into a dark room. Babula did not know what happened next.

He only woke up when two soldiers pulled him to his feet. It was bright outside. He was dragged into another room. Stumbling into the room, he saw a table—the memory of the agonizing pain of the previous night swept up within him. He shrunk with fear. But the soldiers did not torture him today. On the contrary, they gave him food and water. They removed his dirty, tattered shirt and handed him a khaki-coloured army shirt as well as an old pair of khaki pants. After he had finished eating, he was dragged into another jeep. A number of soldiers sat there, holding guns. The jeep started as soon as he got in. One, two, three, four—four cars made their way slowly towards the reserve. Near the forest, the cars stopped. The men disembarked. Babula's hands were tied tightly behind his back again.

A soldier told him that he had to show them the way. He had to show them where the boys with guns were hiding inside the forest. If he did not, they would...the man grabbed his penis and squeezed it hard. Babula yelped in agony.

The soldier saluted somebody sitting inside a jeep and spoke to him. The man sitting inside the jeep sternly said that it had been quite a few days; they hadn't been able to catch a single militant, and had not been able to recover a single piece of arms. He ordered his subordinate to destroy all the militants hiding inside the forest somehow. They were hiding inside the forest—one could still hear gunshots.

Babula, of course, did not understand what was being said. With Babula leading the way, the group made its way into the forest. Babula knew what they wanted him to do. But what could he do?

His hands were tied behind his back, and he could not speak—how could he show anything to anybody?

Prodding him with the butts of their guns, the men entered the forest. At the slightest sound, they would lie down on the ground. They moved like alert hunters. Babula watched them, amazed.

All day long, the soldiers moved in the forest—prodding Babula in front of them, ducking behind the *hollongs*, and crawling under bushes. At the sight of a stream or a piece of thick forest, a soldier would prod Babula with his gun and ask him to show them the way. Out of fear of being beaten, Babula would lead them through bushes and thickets. He noticed that the soldiers were reluctant to enter the thick part of the forest. Actually, they were going around in circles. Gradually, it grew dark. The darkness clustered in corners of the *hollong* forest; the sky peeping through the leaves was turning blue, then crimson. At one time, the group found itself on the road in the middle of the reserve. Now, its leader confronted Babula, grinding his teeth. He started abusing Babula in an obvious temper. Babula did not understand his words, but he could make out that the man was angry because he had not found what he was looking for. What could he do? He did not know this stretch of the forest at all. He had never been here. The camp he had been to was not here. What could he do? A few incoherent sounds and saliva dribbled out of his mouth.

Now the soldier started hitting him with his fists. Warm, salty blood streamed out of his brows and nose, and seeped into his mouth. Screaming with pain, he looked at the other soldiers. The naked violence on their faces made him quake. The day-long, fruitless hunt in the forest had turned each of them into a dangerous beast, ready to pounce on him.

Somebody barked an order. The soldiers leapt a few steps back. In the deep forest, Babula stood, alone and unarmed, before a row of loaded guns…

Babula knew what was going to happen next.

He flew into a terrible rage. He lifted his face, smeared with blood. He felt as if his eyes would spring out of their sockets. Angry and disgusted, he raised himself, swaying like a madman and spat at them—spittle mixed with blood.

The silent forest reverberated with the sound of gunshots.

It had been a busy day. Trucks loaded with soldiers frequently arrived or departed. Helicopters whirred. Important officials had arrived, so had top leaders. And there were the people from the press—top journalists. The helicopters carried food from the Capital, served in the tents erected in the open fields. The journalists would be given visual proof of the fight against terrorism. They were taken on a conducted tour of the forest in jeeps. On their way back, after sporadic glimpses of deserted camps, a few single-barreled guns, waste paper, and a few drill wooden guns, at a certain spot they saw a dead body!

Two muddy feet protruded from beneath the blanket that was draping the dead body. A shudder ran down the journalists' spines. The man sitting next to Partha, a famous journalist who worked for a well-known newspaper in the Capital, pointed towards the dead body with his goatee and seemed to ask the officer who it was.

'That's the dead body of a dangerous extremist,' the officer spoke with pride, adding, 'He was killed in an encounter yesterday.' He then launched a speech about the anti-insurgency operations...

Babula, the half-wit, had turned into a dangerous extremist.

In that thick dark forest of *hollongs*—between the tall trees wrapped with wild creepers, by the huge ferns in their midst, near the thorny thickets of cane and the stinging nettle bushes, on the bank of the swamp deep enough to swallow an elephant with its mahout—it is said that a spectre roams. It searches for something under the trees. Apparently, many people from the village had caught a glimpse of that spectre, and it's said that he wears a tattered army shirt and carries a bunch of fishing rods…

STAR-STUDDED NIGHTS

I

How boring, he thought to himself.

He found no interest in his work; there was nothing new to report. Military operations were going on in full swing—villages surrounded, arrests; widespread atrocities had become common. Leave aside headlines, these incidents did not even find two inches of space in the newspapers. He did not feel like writing anything besides his routine reports. His office had not asked for anything either. An inexplicable fatigue enveloped him. He did not feel like meeting any of his friends.

Why don't I go to Shillong? Spend some time with Mahi (aunt) and have some fun with Swati and Swaha. Looking out of the window from his room on the upper floor, Partha's thoughts were scattered. Let me call up the editor. There had been news of a foreign link to the insurgents in Shillong; I can carry out an investigation. All the important people were in Shillong now. Picking up the phone, Partha put through a long-distance call. 'Hello, Mrs Verma! Looking beautiful as always, I hope.'

'Partha, you naughty boy,' chimed the editor's personal secretary—an efficient robot. Partha was one of the few people who could crack a joke with the robot. He told her about his plans to tour Shillong; he knew that the old woman liked it when he told her anything before he talked to the editor.

'This can be a big scoop, Partha. Like your other one. Hold on for a second, let me see if the editor is free.'

After a few moments, the editor came on the line. Partha told him about his plans. The editor approved immediately; the old man swallowed the bait. How could he not, once Mrs Verma had primed him? After he had hung up, Mrs Verma told him, 'Be careful, Partha.' So the old woman was still on the line.

'There's nothing to worry about, except that I might turn into a hostage. Somebody might kidnap me.'

'Oh, you will be able to charm your way out of that.'

He decided to leave for Shillong the next morning. He would take his father's car and driver. But nobody was answering the phone in Shillong. Was Mahi not at home? But he would have known if they were out of town; Ma would have known for sure. He decided to go anyway.

At night, he received a few government press releases. He decided to send them to the office before he left. In the morning, he went to Fancy Bazar to type out his report and fax it; there were several private faxing centres there.

After faxing his reports, he stood on the footpath and lit a cigarette. He looked back when he felt a tap on his shoulder. 'Hey!' he almost shouted.

Following the newcomer's gaze, Partha looked around too. There were hardly any people on the road in Fancy Bazar in the morning. Lowering his voice, he looked at the newcomer who was smiling at him.

'Ron! And where have you come from?'

The newcomer merely smiled.

'What's the matter with you? You have lost a lot of weight.'

Truly, Ron had lost considerable weight. His skin was tanned, his strong chin and cheekbones stood out. Only his eyes sparkled, touched by his impish smile.

'I was sick.'

'What happened?'

'A severe case of malaria. Also, eczema.'

'What are you doing here now?'

'Nothing in particular.'

'Nothing?'

'I am on medical leave. I have been asked to take rest.'

'Where?'

'I have no idea... I will have to think of some place.'

'I have an idea...why don't you come with me?' said Partha suddenly.

'Where?'

'Shillong.'

'To Shillong?'

'Yes, I am going there for a couple of days for a break. I don't feel like working anymore. Come with me if you think you can.'

'I can, but...'

'No buts if you want to come along. Where's your luggage?'

'Here,' Ron said, pointing to a huge bag on his shoulders.

'Come along,' Partha said, taking him by the hand. Walking up to the car, they got into the back seat. The driver turned the car round.

Partha felt very happy. The meeting was a great co-incidence... and now, this trip to Shillong together. They could really talk—they had a lot to talk about. His journalist's curiosity was stoked, but Partha controlled himself. This was a time for leisure, not work. But he could not help thinking about what he had told his editor about the foreign link. He thought about Swati and Swaha. He was going to take a dangerous guerilla to meet them—in living flesh and blood. What fun. He was amused; this was also a way to thank Ron for the hospitality shown to him at the camp.

'What happened? Why are you smiling?'

'Nothing in particular. I thought of something. Isn't this a strange coincidence? So sudden and surprising...'

'Nothing surprises me anymore.'

The car sped past Khanapara on the road to Shillong. 'I hope you don't have any arms with you.'

'No.'

'What about documents?'

'Nothing at all.'

'There might be checking on the road.'

'I am on leave nowadays.'

'From the revolution or from yourself?'

'Both.' They burst out laughing. The car now rode uphill. Driven by expert hands, the car ate up the winding roads.

'Is the camp still there?'

'No. We discarded it when the military operations started.'

'And the boys?'

'They have been scattered. I have no idea where they are at this moment. Some are hiding in villages, some are absconding—maybe they are in the cities.'

'Have the operations smashed the organization?'

'This is a real setback,' Ron said. He did not seem keen on pursuing the topic. Partha got the cue, and did not press him. Interesting, Partha thought; had the organization ever thought about how it would react when confronted by the State's repressive forces? The rules and structure of an organization determine to a large degree its reactions to varying situations. In this context, it was imperative to look at the situation in its entirety analytically…

'Tell me about your illness.'

'I had malaria, but I am much better now. I do feel a little weak sometimes. This is an old ailment. I have been having it on and off for the last couple of years. The only difference was that I had eczema very severely this time. It was awful...' Partha nodded, and then both fell silent and looked out of the car's window. Pines could be seen on either side of the road now. There was a slight chill in the air. Pine seedlings throve on the slopes; earlier, there were huge pines on these slopes, but now they had all been cut down. The hills had been denuded too. The old charm of driving to Shillong, through pine-filled roads, was not there anymore.

Near Umiam lake, it began to rain. The sun peeped through the clouds. In the rain and the sunshine, the lake looked glorious. Looking at Ron, Partha saw that he was fast asleep, leaning against the seat. His head lolled against his chest; his soft, curly hair fell over his forehead. Partha did not feel like waking him up.

The car stopped in front of his aunt's house. The house stood upon a small hillock. There were several other houses, rented out to banks and offices—a legacy of his uncle. The rent supported the family.

Partha shook Ron awake. 'Wake up, we have arrived.'

Ron woke up with a start. 'What? Where?'

'Shillong...my aunt's house. We will stay here.'

'You never told me that we were going to visit your aunt.'

'I thought I would surprise you. Come on, get down. It's a very comfortable house—spacious, safe, and scenic,' Partha said, pointing at the pretty bungalow surrounded by pine and deodars.

They walked up to the wide verandah and Partha rang the bell. Pushing the door, he walked in; Ron waited outside. He saw a girl walk out of the inner room—a tall girl with a caramel complexion and large eyes, and a carefully styled mop of hair made to look unruly. She wore an old baggy sweater over a long, frilly cotton frock that had small flowers on it.

'Partha!' she screamed joyfully and flew into Partha's arms, and hugged him. She let him go when she realized that there was somebody else at the door. Partha introduced them to each other, 'Swaha, my cousin. Ron, my very good friend.'

Swaha stepped back gracefully and ushered them inside. 'You will stay I hope, both of you? You will have to. I won't hear anything else. Where are your bags?'

'Come on, Swaha, of course, we are staying.'

'Really? How nice! *Kancha, gaadi se bags lao aur guest room mein rakh do. Didi, khaabar ready kor, Partha-da asheche* (Kancha, bring the bags out of the car and keep them in the guest room. Didi, get the food ready, Partha-da has come). And now, Partha-da, where did you spring from?'

'From Guwahati, where else? Where's Mahi? And Swati?' Partha asked, sitting in the tastefully decorated drawing room.

'Ma and Swati are in Kolkata. My cousin is getting married. It happened suddenly. Today's the wedding; they left in a hurry yesterday. They will be back after a week.'

'Which means you are on your own…'

'I am used to it. Didi's here, so is Kancha, and also the night watchman. No problems. Didi, get some tea. Now tell me about your plans.'

An elderly woman served tea—a shining teapot, cups, sugar, and milk on a lace-covered tray, and plum cake on a plate. She put the tray down on the glass table near Swaha.

Ron noticed that she sat with her knees close to each other, her feet to one side. The frilly frock fell over her knees and across most of the sofa. Pouring the tea with expert hands, she held out a cup to Partha, and another to Ron. 'I don't think we have met.'

Ron looked at Partha. 'My name is Ron…Rondeep. I-I am Partha's…'

'Swaha, I will tell you something.'

Swaha looked at him questioningly. Ron realized what Partha wanted to do. He grew cautious.

'Partha,' Ron said, slightly confused.

'Don't worry. There's nothing to fear, believe me. Swaha, you have heard about the revolutionaries, haven't you? The underground guerillas? Ron is one of the top leaders of that organization,' Partha explained matter-of-factly.

Swaha's eyes widened in wonder; she stared at Ron unblinkingly. Was there a shadow of fear in her eyes? She got up, moved up to Ron, sat down next to him and asked, looking him in the eye. 'Really?'

Ron felt uncomfortable. But his discomfort melted because of the ease and spontaneity of her manner. He smiled, 'Partha is fibbing. I am not a top leader.'

'I need to ask you a lot of things, that is, if you are all right with it.'

Ron threw up his hands in a gesture of surrender. 'I have no problems in facing interrogation.'

They burst into laughter.

II

I had sensed the electric current that had passed between them, silently, in the first meeting. I could feel the current in the air, all around them. It was certain that they were drawn to each other. This might have happened without their knowledge initially; the environment was conducive to their mutual attraction.

After a late lunch, we sat in the drawing room for a long time, listening to music. Swaha was very fond of piano concerts, and had a number of cassettes in her collection. The sound of piano filled the air. After some time, I started feeling sleepy. It was a cloudy day; the evening was colder than the day. I snuggled into a blanket and dozed off immediately.

When I woke up, it was quite dark. I walked into the drawing room—the music was still playing softly. Sitting in the settee near the window, they were rapt in conversation; they did not hear me come in.

'Did you spend the whole evening listening to music?'

Ron jumped up. Swaha laughed, 'Let me offer you a cup of tea. I hope you had a nice nap.'

She poured me a cup.

'What about you?'

'We have had tea twice already! I kept yours warm for you, but it must have gone cold by now.'

'No, it's fine.'

I sat down near them. We talked randomly for a long time.

'I am going out for a walk.'

'Why don't we all go together?' Swaha said.

Ron hesitated.

'I don't think Ron should go out too much.'

'Okay,' Swaha seemed to understand,' we will stay back. Can you get me a few things? I will give you a list.' Swaha went inside. Partha and Ron sat in silence for some time. Then Partha asked Ron, 'How do you like it?'

'Very much.'

'And Swaha? Do you like her?'

'I am not sure.' He thought for some time, then said, 'I have never talked to anybody like this, particularly a woman. I don't think I know the answer to your question.'

'Here's the list, you'll get all the stuff nearby,' Swaha said, handing Partha a list. Partha walked out of the house. It was quite cold. There was a gentle breeze, and a light veil of clouds on the moon. Partha had many friends in Shillong—old classmates and people he knew from Delhi. But he did not feel like meeting any of them. He peeped into a few well-known hang-outs. No, there was nobody he knew; only a crowd of strange faces. Partha felt a little lonely. He walked a long way. On the way, he bought the stuff that Swaha had asked for. Bag in hand, he reached Police Bazar. The newspaper vendors had their shops open, so he bought several newspapers—including the one he worked for. There, he bumped into Chinmoy; he was a freelancer, and his work was published in many newspapers. He asked Partha, 'On an assignment, I presume?'

'Assignment of rest.'

Chinmoy laughed. Talking, they entered a bar. Partha thought of pumping him a little for information.

'Shillong has become a hotbed of insurgency. I have heard that most of the important meetings take place here, whether with the government or with foreign countries. I am sure you can do a good story on that.'

Partha thought his reactions would be significant, but he suddenly resorted to pleas, 'You keep meeting these leaders, don't you? Can't you give me a link? I have been trying hard, but in vain. If we freelancers cannot do anything exclusive, nobody is going to read us. How long can we make up stories?'

'Well, I am looking for a reliable link myself.'

'Take me into confidence, brother. You have nothing to worry about…you have a job. All you need to do is submit a routine report. We have such problems in our lives. I do my bit, but nobody wants to give interviews to a freelancer. Please let me in if you have any "foreign link" stories, brother. I promise I will tell you if I come across any clues.' Both men were a little tipsy. Partha promised to help him all he could. Then he thought of Ron—what would Chinmoy do if he met him? Partha stifled a laugh.

Paying the bill, they walked out of the bar. Partha felt more cheerful after having had the pegs. Talking, they walked on the empty road. Chinmoy lived Swaha's part of the town.

'I feel sorry when I think of them, Partha—all those young boys who have taken that arduous road with dreams in their hearts. Insurgency has no future in the North East.'

'Why do you think so?'

'It doesn't look as if they have understood the character of the Indian State. They think the State is very repressive. But its biggest distinction is that it is highly accommodative—of course, on its own terms though. But these terms aren't very strict. It hasn't been able to harm the movement through repression as much as through agreements and baits. I don't think any organization has the theoretical and ideological stuffing to take on the Indian State.'

'And what if we do have such an organization in future?'

'Perhaps. But I am not hopeful, because such an organization would have to have a very modern, tolerant frame with a broad outlook.'

They walked in silence for some time. Chinmoy's words could not be shrugged off; they were, to a large extent, correct. When Partha walked into the house, it was late. Those two were still in conversation. 'What kept you? We were getting tired waiting for you.'

Partha stopped himself from asking if they liked or disliked the fact that he had been late. Thankfully, I did not...such a remark would surely have spoilt the environment, he thought to himself.

They had a cheerful dinner, following which, Ron and Partha stretched out on the two beds in the guest room.

'I am feeling sleepy in spite of my afternoon nap.'

'I feel sleepy too,' Ron said.

'Let us go to sleep then.'

Partha heard Ron heave a gentle sigh. Why did he sigh? Partha wanted to know, but could not bring himself to ask him.

The next day was no different from the previous day. They woke up late and had a late breakfast. Then Partha went out, while they stayed back. He also napped after lunch. When he woke up, it was evening; the dark had been quick to descend because of the clouds and a light rain. They were seated near the window, deep in conversation. Ron was talking and Swaha was listening, entranced. They were oblivious to Partha's presence. Without saying a word to them, he went out. He looked for Chinmoy, but didn't find him. Then he called him, and got him to come out of his house; they met and talked for a long time. Partha's evening went off very well, and he got home late. The rain had stopped, the moon was pale in the sky, and the cold wind stung Partha.

There was nobody in the drawing room when he got back. The table was laid and the dishes covered. Where were they? Had they gone out? On the way to his room, Partha noticed that the door of the room near the corridor was shut; faint sounds floated out to him. Yes, that was Nibir's room; Mahi used it as an extra guest room nowadays. Partha pushed against the handle. The door was locked from inside; a faint light streamed out of the chink below.

Partha walked out to the drawing room. A balcony overlooked that room. It was accessible from the drawing room also. Carefully opening the door, he stepped on to the balcony. The curtains of that room were drawn and there was some light inside. He peeped through the window, through a slit in the curtains.

The room glowed in the soft light of the shaded bedside lamp. They were lying on the bed, their eyes closed in satiated fatigue, whispering in each other's ears out of some deep affection. Their clothes lay scattered on the carpet; the blanket on their bodies had slipped off the bed on to the floor.

Partha felt as if he was watching a movie in slow motion. They seemed to float in a magical, unreal world, bathed in soft light. Partha did not know how long he stood there looking at them. At one time, he could hear his heart beat—each excited heartbeat drummed against his ears. Life swept through them again. He withdrew from the window and walked to his room in silence. His feelings were mixed. In the couch in his bedroom, he sat in the dark puffing a cigarette, trying to marshal his scattered thoughts.

He felt a strange restlessness in his heart. Was that anger? Pique? Or envy? Between flashes of his adolescent memories, he was seared by a nameless fire—Swaha, Ron!

I must have been in the 9th or 10th standard. Yes, that was after the annual exam of my 9th standard. I would be promoted to the 10th. Swaha must have been in the 7th or 8th standard. The first stirrings of youth had stoked our awareness of sex. On a visit to Shillong that year, Swaha and I, behind the pines and the forget-me-nots in the garden, had touched and felt each other. We had felt each other's sexual organs, shuddering with excitement. But that was the end of our sexual adventure. After a little while, Swaha had run indoors and I had emerged from behind the trees.

Moral questions flowed through my mind. But who had made me a judge of morality? Who had given me the right to sit in judgement on Ron and Swaha? But Swaha was my sister, my aunt was not home, and it was my responsibility to ensure her well-being. I had got Ron here; a man who roamed wild in the jungles—what if there was a serious love story here? He had betrayed me. I suddenly felt angry with Ron.

But this might not be love after all, perhaps a tender moment in their lives, a beautiful memory they would cherish forever...something that would enrich the experience of life.

Was that the fire of envy in my heart? Yes, that was the scourge of envy, nothing else. Unbearable. But I should have been happy. I was neither envious of Swaha, nor of Ron. Perhaps the envy was on account of the beautiful moment they had shared which I lacked in my life.

Partha sat for a long time in the dark room blowing rings of smoke, with many thoughts crowding his mind. But how long could he sit there like that? He got up. The door to their room was open now. It was empty. He walked out on to the verandah.

The lawn outside glistened in the pale moonlight. A sweet fragrance wafted from the flowers. Partha saw them on the grass, in the light and shadows thrown by the moonlight and the pines. In the distance, one could see the lights of a sleeping Shillong twinkling like glowworms in the impenetrable darkness, somewhat misted by the light fog.

They talked randomly for some time; none of them was in the mood to talk though. They were lost in their own thoughts. They gazed at the lights in the bosom of the distant hill in silence. There was a sudden gust of cold wind. Swaha shivered. She looked up at the sky. Partha and Ron followed her gaze. A bunch of stars shone in the dark blue sky. It was a clear sky; there were no signs of rain. In the round, bowl-shaped sky framed by the tips of pines and mountains, the stars sparkled—like bits of diamond, like tears.

A star-studded blue night!

III

Swaha and Ron now lived in a world of their own—a transformation that took place within a single night. The shining stars seemed to have transported them to another world. In the morning, Partha noticed their bright faces and their lively conversation—he felt the silent electric current flowing between them. Was the change a result of the chemical reaction brought about by this electricity? It was clear that they were lost to the world, in spite of their normal behaviour. Was that love? No, that wasn't love… It wasn't lust either. They did not mind his presence. Truly, they did not. But they were not particularly aware of him either.

And yes, that attitude miffed Partha. He felt an inexplicable envy scorch him. But he did not want to admit the presence of this mental torment; which is why he felt it all the more acutely. After breakfast in the morning, he announced, 'I am going to be very busy today.'

'And you were planning to take a break?' Ron asked.

'Well, rest through work. One can't exclude work from rest. I have to send a report to the office. I will meet some of the local journalists today. Don't wait on me, I will have something to eat outside.'

Swaha did not say a word; she did not even look up from her food. It seemed to Partha that Swaha could sense his envy. Female intuition? Damn! Women can strip you off your clothes without uttering a single word. He left the house. Actually, he had nothing to do. Now, he would have to look for something to occupy himself with. Partha had actually planned to relax in Shillong. One could find good English books here. One could spend time reading a good thriller and discussing it. Browsing in bookstores and buying a book had a charm of its own, but he was no longer in the mood for it. Mahi was not around, neither was Swati. And Swaha and Ron lived in a world of their own…

No, that wasn't love. Love did not mean merely physical and emotional attraction. This was a momentary spark; it had its own sweetness though. Yes, it was sweet. All sweet moments were welcome in life, which is so uncertain. I won't blame them. If they had not made use of such an opportunity that would leave behind sweet memories, I would have laughed at them. I should be happy for them. Do not such coincidences and events make the world more meaningful, more livable—even if only for a minute?

Partha tried to look at the whole incident philosophically. But no, the attempt failed. Far from comforting him, it generated a self-destructive urge in his mind. Restless, he proceeded on the wet roads of Shillong. He reached Police Bazar, entered a bookstore and began to browse.

'Hi, Partha, what are you doing here?' somebody said, clapping him on the back. Partha was startled.

'Lemon Star, old boy, what are you doing here?' the joy was evident in his voice.

'I asked you the question first!'

A brown tweed coat, with leather patches on its sleeves and elbows. A colourful shirt, silk handkerchief around his neck, faded stonewashed jeans, and lanky hair—Lemon Star had not changed at all. The creases on his face winked at Partha. Lemon Star was his close friend from his days in Delhi; his companion in many an experience of forbidden pleasures.

'What are you doing nowadays?' Lemon Star asked, leading Partha out of the shop.

'Journalism.' Partha answered, mentioning the name of his newspaper.

'Are you serious? And what happened to the civil services?'

'Forget it. What about you?'

Lemon Star guffawed. 'I am currently a bloody professor!'

'You, a professor?'

'Why not. Do you think I am not good enough to teach?'

Partha remembered how Lemon Star had bunked classes in college and had given the professors various nicknames.

'I feel sorry for your students—poor fellows! But why a fucking professor?'

Lemon Star stopped in his tracks and collapsed with laughter. Holding Partha by the hand, he said, 'I like it, Partha! Original!'

Suddenly, two boys greeted him; they must have been his students. Lemon Star waved at them, then suddenly gesturing towards Partha, he told the surprised boys, 'Do you know what my friend has to say? He is calling me a fucking professor, and that I fuck your careers with my lectures.' The boys smiled weakly. People turned to look at them.

The narrow road glistened in the sunshine after the rain. People clad in raincoats were closing their colourful umbrellas. Partha's spirits rose. So far, he had nothing to do; but now, he looked forward to having a good time.

'Today is Saturday and I am free. If you have time, why don't we celebrate, for old time's sake?'

'Sure! Where are we going?' Partha said enthusiastically.

'To my place. I will treat you to *kakiyat* (locally brewed beer)—you were so fond of it!'

'No, no *kakiyat*. I would like some wine…some chilled wine. I am feeling a little low.'

'Sure. Will get you something out of this world.'

They walked up a winding road to Lemon Star's cottage in the mountains. It was a small wooden house, with a red roof and a pine floor. The long verandah held a number of orchid tubs. They made themselves comfortable on the verandah, with glasses of chilled wine.

'How do you like my bachelor's pad?'

'Beautiful.'

'Aren't you in the mood today…a really creative mood?'

'What do you teach your unfortunate students?'

'Political theory.'

'What?' Partha almost spilt his wine.

'Why not? I have a degree in political science and international relations.'

'But you hated politics.'

'I still do.'

'Do you remember? You used to say that all politicians were villains—irredeemable villains…'

'Yes, and criminals, too. Politics…and people involved with politics complicate our lives unnecessarily. It is probably in their interest, but what about the people? Do the people they purport to help benefit from their kind of work? No. They are the real criminals—they fuck the whole world! All the political leaders and parties ought to be exterminated.' He stopped for breath, and took a long sip from his glass.

'And when did you become a nihilist?' Partha asked, bemused.

'I have always been a nihilist. And an anarchist.'

'But nihilism carries the seed of its own negation—it annihilates itself.'

Lemon Star was silent for a little while. Then he spoke up, 'That's right. Many have sought to transcend anarchy through anarchy. This is not the right path—a wrong path does not lead to a right goal. Partha, these are illusions, but I feel good when I wonder if anarchy can destroy all the unwanted elements before destroying itself—like the State, dictatorship, or slavery.'

'The world? Civilization?'

'What's wrong with that?'

'We would all turn into primitive man, sinless and innocent.'

They were silent for some time. Then Partha said, 'Really, anarchist thoughts are growing in expression. There has been an attempt to make militant activities more acceptable by parading them in the robes of anarchism. Is voluntary anarchism the natural instinct of people or the way out for a rootless middle class?'

He did not feel like thinking about it any longer. Raising his glass, he said, 'Come on, Lemon, lets raise a toast. This is for life and the joys of living!'

'Amen,' said Lemon Star solemnly. Partha joined him in laughter.

'Forget about politics, Partha. Things are getting progressively complicated. But interesting as well. Marxism as we knew it is finished. Anarchist thought would try to fill this vacuum, especially in the minds of the middle classes. But after the fall of the Soviet model, Marxism has been liberated from its traditional confines. Have you noticed, Partha, nobody can claim what Marxism stands for nowadays… Have you noticed how this has created room for many imaginative possibilities?'

'Do you really believe in that?'

'As a student of political science, I do.'

They kept quiet for a little while.

'Where are you putting up? Why, of course, with your gorgeous cousins! What are they up to nowadays? I see the younger one on campus sometimes.'

'The younger one's doing her PhD.'

'What's her area of research?'

'A comparative study of the sexual prowess of middle-class, hypocritical youths—us dare I say—and revolutionary young men.'

They collapsed with laughter, spilling their wine. Partha found a perverse pleasure in making an uncharitable remark about Swaha that was lost on Lemon Star.

Partha and Lemon Star, after all these years, embarked on an endless drinking session. At one point, they felt hungry; they had not had anything to eat all evening. Locking the door, they stepped outside. Partha felt cold; it was drizzling, so he wrapped his jacket closer around himself. They entered a small restaurant.

'What will you have?' Partha asked.

'Hot and sour soup, and brown bread. If I have anything else, I will have a blasting hangover in the morning. Plum wine is real poison!' Lemon Star said jokingly.

The dinner sobered them and they stepped out of the restaurant. The cold breeze outside was refreshing.

'Where to now? Home? Let's take a walk. Night is a long way off.'

It was growing dark. Rain pattered down. They walked on the damp roads lit by the pale light from the street lamps.

Suddenly, Partha spoke up, 'I need a woman, Lemon, now.' Lemon was quiet for a while. Then he said, 'All right, come along. I feel something, too, thanks to what you had to say. We can go to Martha's. It's a decent place, we might get lucky.'

They climbed down a fleet of moss-grown steps.

'Our first joint adventure since Delhi!' Lemon laughed.

Partha nodded. They reached a pukka road. Lemon Star ushered Partha into a well-appointed wooden bungalow, with flowering begonia tubs in the verandah. At the gate, he whispered, 'We will have to spend some money.'

Partha whispered back, 'Don't worry. I have plenty of cash. Only make sure it lasts us the whole night.'

Martha answered the bell. 'Are we welcome today, Martha?' Lemon asked with a smile.

'Come in, come in, both of you!' Martha answered.

It was a homely environment. A warm, comfortable room, where music played softly. Two girls with straight hair who looked like sisters entered with dinner—chicken fried rice. And hot brandy afterwards. An evening spent in pleasurable anticipation. Martha withdrew after dinner. A little later, Lemon said, 'Let us go to bed, too, Partha.' Partha nodded.

Partha accompanied the girl called Lisa into the bedroom. A long, narrow bed covered with a floral bedspread lay on a jute carpet; frilly curtains covered the windows, an almirah with a looking glass, a shaded bedside lamp, a vase, and a glass of water was placed on a small table. Closing the door, Partha took off his clothes and flung them on the floor. Lisa asked him if she should switch off the light. Partha shook his head. Lisa, with her experience, was quick to turn him on. Under the warm quilt, their bodies fused.

Partha quickly realized that the experience stopped at a mechanical, physical stage. But what else did he expect? He suddenly thought of Swaha and Ron. His breath quickened, his blood pulsed, he felt the hot flush of sexual urge. In a strange fantasy he started believing that he was Ron, and in the heat of excitement, the words poured out of him, 'Swaha. Swaha...'

A mental fatigue enveloped him. Was he looking for catharsis? It did not work. His mind did not feel unburdened. Finally, Partha fell asleep—a deep, dreamless sleep.

He returned home in the rain. Swaha and Ron were sitting in the drawing room, and got to their feet when they saw him.

'Where were you?' they asked together.

Partha tried to joke, 'Pussy cat, pussy cat where have you been? I have been to London to visit the Queen.' Swaha walked up to him.

Feeling his wet jacket, she said, 'What a mess you are in. You are stinking. Freshen up, we will have breakfast together.'

The scent from her body reached his nostrils. A fresh scent. Was that wild rose? Or eucalyptus? It was a feminine scent.

In the bathroom, he could smell his own body—the mingled smells of wet clothes, rain, stale wine, and semen. His face contorted.

IV

The room was dark. Through the window, one could see the bright February moon. A bunch of red lights twinkled on the panel of the tape recorder; soft strains of piano filled the room with a rhythmic silence—the silence of the piano, perhaps.

Swaha was seated on a couch in the room, her shapely legs curled beneath her. A light, expensive pashmina shawl draped her shoulders. She was gazing in silence at the play of moonlight on the top of the pines.

Was the young woman in the dark room reminiscing about a star-filled night? She had felt an intense attraction towards Ron—on the very first meeting, after a few words with him. Swaha had no hesitation in admitting that. He was so different from the men she knew. He was without the cultivated manners of the educated, rich young men one came across. His politeness, humility, and chivalry seemed natural to him. Oh, he was so natural—no awkwardness in his behaviour! This was not the English-speaking culture she was familiar with. It's strange how little we know about the tiny world we live in, she thought to herself.

The refined values that she had cultivated seemed artificial when set against Ron's characteristic naturalness. Before him, she felt stripped.

He was surely tall, dark, and handsome—the owner of a trim physique, like the rich hero of a Mills and Boon novel. But the rich and poor valuations did not apply to Ron. He was, after all, a guerilla on the run.

She had gradually been drawn to Ron in the course of their conversation. When the maid had placed the lace-covered tea tray in front of them—which held a teapot, sugar container, hot milk, and a pair of cups—she had coquettishly asked him to help himself. With a pleasant smile, he had said, 'I have never been offered tea like this. You will have to help me.'

She had made the tea with all the art at her disposal and had handed him the cup. He had offered, 'Let me pour you a cup of tea.' He had proceeded to pour her a cup gracefully; he was so natural. No that was not love… Swaha had felt an unusual attraction towards him. There were moments in the course of their conversation when the educated young men she knew would have made an interesting remark to flatter her or give broad hints. Ron, however, handled these moments gracefully. There was attraction, romance, and interest in an unusual acquaintance. She knew Assamese, but a lot of words he used were unfamiliar to her. Yet she knew their import. She also knew that he was deeply attracted to her too—but the attraction was never cheaply evident in his behaviour.

She felt like holding his hand once.

'Let me have a look at your hand,' she stretched out her hand.

'Do you read palms?'

'No, not at all. I just felt like holding your hand.'

A powerful and hard, masculine hand, but not coarse. When she let go, Ron's hand did not linger in hers. He must have been delighted with the fact that a beautiful girl had taken his hand; that was evident from the glow on his face. For a long time, he sat looking at his hand. Then he had looked at her and laughed.

None of Swaha's previous conceptions applied to Ron. He was a boy from a village, but unlike most village boys in English novels, he did not have tea from his plate, nor did he noisily gulp it down. Were the Assamese village boys more civilized than those in England? Or were all civilized men—and the invented signs of civilization—meaningless?

It seemed as if a light veil rippled over the pine leaves, and moonlight scattered in the yard. A cloud must have floated across the moon.

On the second day, Swaha realized that she desired Ron—deeply, passionately. She attached no value to virginity; she was not a virgin either. Through many bodily experiences, happy and sad, she understood that this experience might be a flash of joy—like the experience of listening to some incredibly beautiful music. It might be an ineffable sensation. The essence of fulfillment beyond physical experience. Alternately, it might collapse into repulsive bestiality.

She told him clearly, 'I want you very much, Ron.'

After a few moments silence, he had taken her hands in his and said, 'Me too.'

After that, there were no obstacles left to her surrender.

Totally inexperienced, it must have been his life's first experience. Swaha had no doubts that Ron was about to lose his virginity, but his self-control struck her. He was never oblivious to her, even in the most intimate moments. On the contrary, she had become like the frothy waves of a turbulent sea, and had embraced his whole world. Her eyes had closed in the scent of his hair, as if drunk. The next time, she had felt as if she was floating rhythmically on a sea of music…

The memory of a rhythmic movement was supreme in her mind even today. The young man who had lost his virginity was a real man, somebody every woman wanted a man to be like. Also, his behaviour after that evening was very normal. But the whole atmosphere inside the house had changed; an invisible, bright cloud had closed on the two of them. The cloudy, moist sky had changed as well. It had dazzled with bright stars.

Partha had kept away from the house for a whole day and night. The next day when he had turned up—wild, filthy, wet, and smelling of cheap wine—Swaha's sixth sense had told her that he had spent the night with some cheap whore. She was certain that he knew about the intimate moments that she and Ron had shared.

Pity for him wrung her heart. Later, of course, that memory of Partha would annoy her a little.

She remembered how Partha had attacked Ron the next day; how he had tried to hurt him, and had attacked him in harsh political language. From the next room she had overheard Partha's cynical comments. She walked out; she knew how to handle Partha. Standing behind his chair, she had held him by the hair and pulled his head to her bosom. Placing her cheek against his, she had said, tenderly, 'You don't have to try to be a journalist all the time, dada, life and happiness are more important than journalism.' Then she had whispered to him, out of Ron's earshot, 'Why are you torturing yourself unnecessarily?' Partha had calmed down like a little boy. Ron was highly amused by the whole incident. Partha had become the old Partha he had known—cheerful, friendly, and calm. The memories would still leave a bad taste in Swaha's mouth. He had almost spoilt one of the sweetest moments of her life, a moment which, in her imagination, had been transformed into a charming unreality—more attractive than any reality.

For a long time, perhaps even today, she hoped that a letter from Ron would arrive. But she also knew that if such a letter arrived, she would have never opened it. She would have preserved the essence of her happiest memories. She had wanted to bear his child. Today, she intensely recalled the decision she had made that day. The thought occurred to her a couple of days after he had left. A shudder of excitement had racked her body. She would have reared his child alone, she would have borne the stigma of unwed motherhood.

After Ron had left, she gradually realized that her attraction for him was different; with every passing moment, it deepened. Was that love? No, she was not ready to admit that initially. She had no idea what love was. She had thought of all the intimate relationships she had forged so far in life as infatuations. Those encounters had turned into blurred memories.

But why did she want to keep these memories private, her very own? Why had she wanted motherhood?

Her family would have been shocked and hurt. But she would never have disclosed the father's identity. Regardless of whether Ron came back or not, she would have secretly preserved in her heart every memory, every happiness and sorrow.

Swaha had really hoped to be a mother. When the particular date had passed, her heart had thudded with a nameless anxiety. She was filled with a deep sense of anticipation. She did not know where Ron was then. Nobody knew who he actually was; nobody knew if they would ever see him again. She wondered what he thought—did a sapling take root in his heart as well? Did his attraction for Swaha mature into something deeper? She had no way of knowing. But was it important to know? The coming of the child would be the beginning of a new life for her, hard but fulfilled. In that life, Ron's presence would be welcome but not indispensable.

When motherhood eluded her, tears streamed out of her eyes. A hollowness seized her heart… Wasn't she prepared to bear all this pain for Ron, in spite of knowing that she would probably never see him again? Wasn't that love? Had she discovered the wonderful valley of love—the valley of happiness and tears? Of sacrifice?

The realization had shocked her, and filled her mind with a strange, welcome sensation.

Swaha slowly rose to her feet and walked to the window. Shillong slept in the bright moonlit night. The tips of the pines trembled in the gentle breeze. In the waves of moonlight, the world seemed deserted. She leant against the window and closed her eyes.

The music from Dr Zhivago played on the tape; the immortal Lara's song on piano. The land mass that was Russia—huge and naked—floated before her eyes. Snow-covered parts of the black earth; snow levelling the pits in the land of that world. The barren trees stretched out their dark branches to the heavens in supplication. A lonely railway line lay in that deserted nook. A few ravens flew overhead. On the line a small train, like a toy train, moved in slow-motion, billowing smoke. On a small mount some distance away, Swaha stood looking at the moving train. She wore a heavy and warm coat, and a fur cap on her head. Snowflakes dusted her shoulders and her cap, and her scarf fluttered like a flag in the wild breeze.

Was Ron riding away in the train billowing smoke?

The haunting music of Dr Zhivago played on—a sense of loneliness, pain, and anticipation filled the room.

Swaha had not seen the narrow railway line winding through a sea of grass at the foot of the Himalayas to Murkokseleng in Assam. She had not seen the train, where the endearing Mising (a tribe) boys hawked peanuts. How could she think of the other lonely train?

Switching off the deck, Swaha moved to the empty bed with fatigued steps. She switched on the light and prepared to greet the long night with an English novel.

Many days had passed. She had begun to teach literature. In the meanwhile, she had met Partha several times, but she had never asked him about Ron.

THE BALANCE SHEET OF JUSTICE

I

A dusty evening had enveloped the city. The wintry sky hastily soaked the setting sun. The buses were crowded; the number of homebound pedestrians and vehicles were dwindling. At times, a military jeep would thunder past, leaving its reflection lingering for long in the terror-struck gazes of the passers-by. There was a checkpoint at every main square. With nightfall, checking would intensify; these checkpoints—made of empty tar drums, iron flats, and sandbags—would be there till morning.

Cigarette smoke smothered the evening get-together at Choudhury's house—it hung like a veil of fog overhead. There weren't many people at the gathering; the invitees did not stay for long either. Delays inevitably resulted in unnecessary harassment at the checkpoints.

At one time, there was only Partha and Jagdish left.

Partha threw open the window. The cold wind scattered the layer of smoke; the curling smoke blew out of the open window and the heavy air inside the room lightened. Sitting by the window, Partha breathed deeply. In the light from the streetlamp, his Maruti seemed to have changed in colour; the words 'PRESS' on his windshield stood out boldly in the halogen light.

'Well, lots of arrests these days,' Jagdish said.

A car sped by.

'The police have become very active,' said Partha, to nobody in particular.

'Rubbish, Partha, rubbish!' Choudhury said suddenly.

So far, he had been sitting in silence, fondling his glass, his eyes closed.

'You have never seen the Special Armed Force Acts and Disturbed Areas Acts in practice before, have you? You will see that now. The role of the police will be determined by the army. Practically powerless, the local police are an orderly, nothing more and nothing less! Ha! Ha! Ha!'

Two cars roared up to Prabhat's house and screeched to a stop. The cars blocked the narrow road completely. A number of men leapt out of the cars. Dressed in civil clothes, they carried guns. Banging the doors shut, they ran noisily into Prabhat's yard, as if they had no intentions of keeping their arrival a secret. Some of them surrounded the house, and the rest ran up to the door and pounded on it.

Prabhat's father was not at home—only Prabhat, his mother, and his sister were home. His mother and sister ran up to the door the moment they heard the noise. A young boy who was riding his cycle in the dark started ringing his bell because of the cars blocking his way. The men waiting near the gate immediately pounced on him and started beating him. They threw his cycle into the ditch and forced him to kneel down in Prabhat's yard.

The commotion in front of Prabhat's house warned the neighbourhood. The people seemed to understand that the police were here without any words being exchanged. The lights in every house went off, doors were quietly bolted; from their dark rooms, people peered out. The television sets playing in every house were switched off, too. One could no longer see the reflection of the screens in the windows. An unnatural, artificial darkness and silence descended in the neighbourhood. The hibiscus and deodars clustered in front of the houses seemed to draw their leaves into themselves; the darkening houses began to tremble gradually—like men experiencing the winter cold.

'The real fun begins after arrests, you see—interrogation,' Partha's friend Jagdish quipped.

'You human rights people are a bit too interested in torture, Jagdish,' Choudhury interjected.

The old man was in the mood today, thought Partha. Withdrawing from the window, Partha sat down next to Choudhury to hear him talk.

'Torture doesn't begin on the interrogation table, under bright lights or in a closed room, Jagdish. That is what people think. It's naïve, simplistic, if you ask me. Actually, torture begins from the time of arrest, or perhaps earlier. You doubt it, do you? Is it so planned and deliberate? Yes, it is, ever since the modern State started using torture in implementing governance.'

The moment Prabhat's mother opened the door, the three men barged in and shoved the women out of the way. The girl screamed.

'*Ladka kaha hain?* (Where is the boy?) Prabhat?' The men pushed their way in. Prabhat was at his study table. Two men grabbed him by the arm. '*Kya naam*? (What is the name?) Prabhat? *Theek hai, yaheen hain* (Alright, he's here).' Twisting his arms behind his back, they pushed him to stand before the third man. From the corner of his eyes, he could see the pale faces of his mother and sister. He was afraid. Helplessly, he looked at the man in front of him.

The man suddenly started slapping him mercilessly before his mother and sister. The sounds exploded inside his head; with blurred eyes, he could see the windows and doors swing open and shut violently and quickly. With a fearful cry, Prabhat's mother ran towards her son but the man pushed her aside. '*Hat jao!* (move away!),' he swore at her obscenely.

Meanwhile, his brother Paresh had reached the house. Two jeeps in the yard? What was wrong? Who was it at this hour? When he entered, two men jumped on him. Before he could collect his wits, they had pushed him inside.

'*Ye kaun hai*?' (Who is this?)

'My younger son…' the mother cried out in anguish.

'*Andar jao.*' (Go inside) The man pushed Paresh towards his mother. He stumbled; his mother pulled him into her arms. His sister suddenly burst into tears.

'*Chup raho ladki*! (Keep quiet girl!),' the man hissed at her. They combed the house looking for something. Prabhat saw a few apparitions digging the floor of his house to the sounds of his sister's muffled weeping. The men picked up a few books from Prabhat's table.

'*Apni padhaai mein dhyaan nahi hai, ganda novel padhta hai sala.*' (No concentration on your studies, scoundrel reads dirty novels) The men threw the novel *Jeebonor Batot* into a corner. The book struck the wall and disappeared into thin air. Now Prabhat's hands were twisted behind his back and cuffed. He was led away before the terrorized gazes of his mother, sister, and brother, and shoved into a car.

'Where are you taking him? Where are you taking him?' Prabhat's mother, hysterical, ran up to the cars with her children. The cars sped out of the yard.

Prabhat's mother crumpled onto the ground.

Only now did the deodars unfurl their leaves.

With a loud shriek, Prabhat's sister threw her arms around her mother. Somebody was kneeling in the dark. The trees saw the man; their leaves began to close again.

Prabhat's mother saw a ghost rise out of the earth. Trembling, the ghost picked up a bicycle from the ditch and disappeared into the darkness…

'Arrests are generally made in the presence of the family, and that's deliberate, you see,' Choudhury said, opening his eyes. 'It's a common practice now to humiliate the victim and his family at the time of arrests. Do you know why?'

'To scare them,' said Jagdish.

'Exactly. To scare, to create terror. Creating terror is an integral part of arrests. The days of the freedom struggle are gone. A police officer you knew would come to your house, and say, "Sir, there is an order for your arrest. This is the warrant. Please come to the station," his voice dripped with sarcasm. He added, "Oh yes, do finish your lunch. I can wait. And do take some warm clothes, it is cold in prison." Gone forever, Partha. In today's time, the arrests aim to terrorize…so the methods are violent. When a particular family in an area is terrorized, the terror contaminates the entire area…'

Hoarse, foxy laughter echoed in the room.

'You see, Partha, the idea is to break a person's will. So the abuse, the humiliation…the family is the victim as well; they are not told what is going to happen or what is happening. That is how a person's will breaks in uncertainty and terror—they are helpless, they suffer from low self-esteem. Such people can no longer protest against injustice, forget about resistance.'

The environment had become stifling—from the dull light from the lamp, cigarette smoke, the taste of tobacco and cheap whisky.

There was a nerve-wracking awareness that something was amiss in the darkness of the night. Yet he did not feel like leaving. Partha cast his gaze out of the window, at the bit of ashy sky framed in the glass of the window. The discussion continued…

Prabhat was made to kneel on the floor of the car, behind one of the seats. A man held his head down. A smelly rag covered his eyes; it covered part of his nose, too. He found it hard to breathe. Boots were planted on his thighs. Each jerk of the car caused him incredible pain—the boots were being pressed down on him deliberately.

'Torture has an ancient history, Partha,' said Choudhury. The man was in a talkative mood today. He continued, 'It is probably the third-oldest profession in the world, after the army and prostitution. The pharaohs and priests of ancient Egypt would regularly torture thieves and criminals, besides prisoners of war. In Greece, that seat of your Western civilization, confessions in court—particularly, confessions from slaves and the common man—were extracted through torture. It was thought that people could not lie when confronted with such extreme physical pain; torture was sought to be rationalized.'

'In the courts of law too?'

'Torture had become a part of law, Jagdish.'

'What do you mean had become?' Jagdish snapped, adding, 'Isn't it the case today? Don't the courts accept that the police have to resort to torture to get the ordinary criminals to confess? Why else are they handed over to the police? Of course, in ancient Greece this was done openly, not so in today's legal system. The "civilized" men of today are nothing but hypocrites!'

'You are right, Jagdish. I sometimes suspect that hypocrisy is an indispensable part of civilization. Do you know that torture was almost a festival in Rome—a public spectacle for which holidays were declared?'

Prabhat was kicked out of the car. His feet were numb from having knelt too long. When he was asked to get down, he could not move. Somebody nudged him with his boots. His knees gave way under him.

'*Gir gaya, sala, pakdo* (Fell down, scoundrel, get him). Hey, *uth, uth* (Hey, get up, get up).'

They pulled Prabhat, still blindfolded, to his feet and pushed him onward. His steps were unsteady, like a drunk. His head seemed emptied of all sensation; he could not even feel his joints hurting. He could sense that he had been pushed up a few stairs and into a verandah. All men withdrew, but one stood holding onto his handcuffs.

Scraps of conversation floated up to him. The sounds of whispers were punctuated by silence. The pungent smell of urine hung in the air. Suddenly, a terrible cry rent the air; Prabhat's blood froze. Whose cry was that? The man holding his handcuffs said softly, '*Daro mat.*' (Don't be scared.) He suddenly felt the man's hands stroking his buttocks. A shudder ran up his spine.

'Do you know where exactly torture originated as a political tool in the interests of the church and the State? In medieval Europe, where the church and State were inseparable. In that age, torture was developed into something of an art. The interests of the fathers of the church and the royalty were protected in the name of preserving the purity of religion. The torture was the means of the ruling classes for squelching rebellion. They really invented some unique instruments of torture…'

'Torture existed in China too,' Jagdish quipped.

'Water drop treatment,' Partha chuckled, then continued, 'A man's head was first shaved, then he was strapped to a chair. Drops of water were then allowed to fall on his bald head, one after the other, for hours on end. At one point, the man would scream in unbearable agony.'

'Wasn't torture defined as a tool of State administration following the French Revolution?'

'Exactly, Jagadish. It was after the French Revolution that terror and torture were accepted by the modern State as an instrument of State policy to control the anti-government elements.'

'Did we have it in our country too?'

'That's a good question. Let me show you something,' Choudhury pulled out a book from the untidy heap on his table. Flipping through a few pages, he said, 'Look at what Kautilya had to say in his Arthashastra. There are about 18 methods prescribed to get the guilty to confess. In Chapter 83, investigation through interrogation and punishment! Do you understand? This is not to punish the guilty, but to get the accused to confess.'

'Is this the rule of the shastras?' Jagdish asked incredulously.

'Look at the list of penalties—beating, whipping, hanging with a rope from high places, pouring salty water through the nostrils… these are forms of mild punishment. And here are the others: tying the head tightly against the thighs, giving 32 slaps, trussing the man like a bow, inserting needles under the nails, making him sleep on a bed of thorns on cold nights, feeding him fat and letting him roast in the sun or heat…'

'And gouging out eyes and knee caps, don't forget that…' Jagdish interjected.

'That's enough,' Partha said, suddenly feeling sick.

'Well, this is life, Partha. This is the beginning of the age of torture. We will have to witness that daily. There will be a torture factory almost daily to extract confessions.'

'What sort of confession?'

'Information. But remember, Partha and Jagdish, the aims of torture do not stop here, its main intention is far more serious and widespread. As I said, it is to break a human being completely, make him and his families submit to the State and the people in power—to make him conform Partha, to conform.'

II

Prabhat was pushed into a room. Wooden benches and desks were piled in a corner of the spacious room. A solitary bulb hung from the ceiling and a few sacks lay on the cracking floor. A blackboard lay in a corner. The windows with iron bars were closed. When he entered the cold, damp room, Prabhat shivered; the smell of urine hit his nostrils. He could not see anything because of the blindfold; he could only smell the urine.

'But it's not easy to make people conform, they might conform externally but…in their hearts…' Partha expressed.

'And so, Partha, torture aims to bring about the inner conformation. That is why the modern State has developed torture into such a fine psychological tool. Its primary intention is the psychological transformation. If a prisoner is taken to a deserted spot, blindfolded, physically abused and kept in suspense as to what is coming next, his willpower and confidence are bound to crumble…'

The handcuff was unlocked from one of his hands. He was now asked to take off his clothes. He stripped down to his underwear, still blindfolded. He shivered violently in the cold and tried to moisten his dry lips with his tongue. A man rolled up his clothes and threw them on the blackboard. Now, Prabhat was cuffed to a window bar. The men left the room. Trembling with fear and shame, Prabhat stood in front of the closed window.

'A man's personality is sought to be crushed by crushing his sense of personal dignity. If your personality is crushed, you have no willpower left. That is done systematically—by stripping him naked, by abusing him, trussing him like a beast, and treating him like one. Only after that is he taken to the interrogators, so that by that time all signs of shame and human dignity have been wiped out. He becomes an animal, Jagdish, not a member of civilized society—when you are stripped off your personal dignity, you become an animal. An animal, Partha…' the words poured endlessly out of Choudhury's mouth.

For a long time, Prabhat stood in front of the window, shivering in the cold. Scraps of conversation floated up to him—incomprehensible, rough instructions, the sounds of cars, and patches of silence. A long time passed. Perhaps several hours.

As the night deepened, it grew colder. There must have been a slit in the window, the cold air would occasionally drift up to him. Prabhat would shiver violently. He felt the urge to urinate, but he tried not to think about it; the urge grew stronger. At times, he felt cramps in his abdomen. In spite of the cold, beads of sweat formed on his brows. His hands were tied to something. What could he do now? He felt very helpless. He thought of the moments when he had been picked up, of the tearful faces of his mother and sister. He hoped they had not hurt his brother. His father—what was his father doing now? Why was he blindfolded? He suddenly felt like crying loudly, that intensely did his abdomen hurt. What could he do? And suddenly that terrible, agonized cry ranted through the air. Was that a human cry? Was it possible for any man to cry like that? Something exploded inside his head. Closing his eyes, he gritted his teeth and suddenly found that he had lost control over himself. A warm stream poured over his calves and his feet, drenching his underwear. Along with a deep sense of shame and confusion, Prabhat felt a huge sense of relief. He relaxed his thighs, released the pressure on his body and urinated on the floor, just like an animal.

'You seem to have conducted plenty of research on torture.'

'I know it's unpalatable. But that's reality, Partha.' Choudhury sounded morose.

Their glasses were empty, but they did not feel like having another peg. The liquor had had no effect on them; on the contrary, they felt restless and uncomfortable. Choudhury's glass was only half-empty; he was turning it in his hands.

'As a journalist, you ought to know what torture is and why it is carried out. Or else in this environment of terror, your analysis would not be correct.' He gulped down the contents of his glass and looked at the other men. They showed no interest in helping themselves. He lit a cigarette. Blowing out smoke from his nose and mouth, he said, 'Now, what was I saying? Oh yes, softening up. This is like Kautilya's prescription—abuse the victim physically and mentally before interrogation and attempt to crush his willpower and self-respect, so that at the time of interrogation, he is unable to react like a human being. He can only react instinctively, like an animal.'

A few men marched into the room. In spite of his blindfold, Prabhat tried to turn and look at them in fear. One of them gripped his hair. '*Iska paani chut gaya sala.*' (The water in the scoundrel has released.)

Somebody slapped him hard on his right ear and cheek; if he had not been tied to the window, the force of the blow would have sent him flying. His ears rang.

Blows rained on him, on his shoulders, arms, back, and waist. Prabhat screamed in pain. After some time, he could only feel the blows—the sensation of pain seemed beyond his experience. He shrank against the wall in order to protect himself from the blows. He did not know where the blows were coming from; he started to moan helplessly, like an animal. The men dragged him from the wall by the hair. 'Who are your friends? Give us the names.' But they did not wait for his replies...the torrent of blows continued.

Finally, Prabhat lost all consciousness. His body, in a half-sitting position, hung from the window.

'The first aim of the torturer is to turn the victim into a mass of fear. Only then is he ready for official interrogation.'

'It's so organized, like a factory,' Jagdish said, sounding dejected.

'When there is large-scale terror, torture is a travesty of a factory. It comes in many forms—detention camps, interrogation centre, et al. I saw all those in my 20 years as a reporter in the North East.'

Prabhat slowly regained consciousness. Mingled sounds floated to his ears—cars came and went, the sound of a sharp whistle, a machine creaked. He tried to recall where he was; his head swam and his hands were numb. He tried to stand up, unsteadily. His whole body hurt and his limbs were stiff with cold and pain. Somebody barged into the room. Was he going to be beaten again?

Somebody unlocked him from the window and pulled him out of the room. He stumbled and would have fallen if somebody had not gripped his arm. He felt very cold when he stepped out of the room—his teeth chattered. They took him into another room, pushed him into a chair and handcuffed him again. Now, his blindfold was removed.

It was very bright; he was blinded by the glare. In the bright light, he could make out a table in front of him, and a shadow across the table.

'Give us the names of the people you know. Don't lie. We know—we have proof that you have contacts with the insurgents. We have no time to waste, give us the names like a good boy. Or else, you will be in trouble. Fast, if you want to go back home. Where do you keep the guns? And the bombs? Where are bombs made? What are you staring at like an idiot? Tell us, fast.'

The voice grew harsh. The questioner suddenly yawned, as if he was very bored.

'You won't answer us if we ask politely. You bastard, we know how to get the likes of you to sing.'

The touch of two thin wires on his shoulders and then excruciating pain—once, twice, and thrice. He was almost flung out of his chair. And then the same questions all over again—a softer voice trying to reason with him, abuses and threats, a hard slap. Prabhat gradually began to moan. At one time, his hands were untied. He was made to sign on two blank sheets of paper. The interrogation continued.

'The idea behind interrogation is not only to pump for information—the idea is to break the victim's mind completely. The aim of interrogation is to ensure that he never raises his head again,' Jagdish said.

'You are right. A repressed individual does not, or shall I say cannot, protest against the authorities, the State. Such individuals are cowed forever. They meekly follow all rules and orders; they can never muster the courage to protest against injustice. They become submissive like domestic, trained animals,' Choudhury explained.

'And vested interests are secure.' Jagdish added.

'But why is it necessary to treat individuals like this?' Partha asked.

Choudhury closed his eyes, as if meditating. Then taking a long sip from his glass, he said, 'Partha, the issue is easy to understand in certain situations. For example, during a dictator's rule. A class of people creates a dictator and enjoys all its fruits. They exploit the country and make use of terror to suppress the resentment of common people. This is quite straightforward, isn't it? Democracy is more complicated. When the moral foundation of those in power weakens, they try to protect their interests by terrorizing the opposition and the public through different laws. Like Emergency of 1975—terror is the handmaiden of autocracy. Sometimes terror is necessary to make people swallow a certain idea, a theory, Partha.'

Partha walked up to the window again; there was light fog outside. Terror was necessary to plant a theory in the public—interesting! Partha had never looked at it like that. The theory that Indian was a nationality, that India was a nation State? Was not a class of people enjoying all the powers and opportunities with the aid of this theory? It was not important whether the idea was historically true or untrue. The idea, which protected their interests, had to be true—and that was sought to be planted among people, with all the skill at their disposal. Those who challenged this idea, and the vested interests, would be sought, to be dominated with the State's naked power—with terror.

A shudder ran up Partha's spine. He suddenly seemed to have stumbled upon an important discovery. He looked at Choudhury, who was talking to Jagdish in low tones.

The roaring fires of the gases, and that disembodied voice from the core of the earth. The dancing fires. Partha could never forget it.

What would the checks and balances of the decades yield? The fires that painted the night's sky an angry red? Or the hundreds of trucks bound westward carrying raw material? The annual floods? The endless migrations that unbalanced the population? Not to resist or protest against them? A cipher on the balance sheet. Would not men one day calculate their gains and losses? Was not the North East telling the same old story? Was an implanted idea sought to be imposed through calculations? And hence the torture, the terror? Really—or am I being carried away? What is the truth? Partha thought to himself.

It was growing late—it was actually not safe to be out so late in the night. He felt uneasy...should he call up his parents? Forget it. He would go back soon. But he did not feel like leaving the discussion. He felt an unhealthy attraction towards the conversation. He looked at Choudhury.

'When terror—and torture—begin at a large scale, Partha, it slips out of the control of the initiator. It becomes autonomous in its own right with a momentum of its own, and finally gains ascendancy over the situation. Sometimes, it creates new situations. We will probably see something like this happening here, too, Jagdish. This is the reality—and the tragedy. I am beginning to feel that the history of contemporary time is the history of injustice and abuse inflicted by man on man.'

Two soldiers dragged Prabhat's unconscious body across the verandah by the arms. He was taken to the old room. They dumped his limp body on the canvas on the floor and handcuffed him again. A soldier picked a sack lying in a corner and threw it over his body. One could glimpse the sun in the eastern sky. Prabhat's interrogation was complete for the day.

III

Partha was sitting in front of the typewriter, with confused thoughts. He could not bring himself to type; he repeatedly withdrew his fingers from the keys. Thoughts played in his mind...scattered ideas, but he found himself unable to organize them well enough to type something cogent. Memories of two boys haunted him. When he thought about them, an indescribable feeling weighed on his mind.

He wondered why, perhaps because he was inseparably involved with their lives. Perhaps, he had not been able to be as professional and detached as Choudhury had instructed him to be; he had not been able to control his emotions.

Sometimes the memories irritated him. But most of the time they left him with a feeling of sadness. When he thought of Ron, he thought of a bright-faced handsome young man, dressed in camouflage, rowing a raft on swelling floodwaters. And when he thought of Prabhat, he only remembered his father's agitated expression. We probably remember things the way we want to. Memories are selective, perhaps.

He knew intuitively that there were some serious errors in Ron, and his companions' activities. He was aware of the limits inherent in the absence of political maturity, and violence and mechanical killings in the name of armed struggle. Yet, somewhere in his blood—in the marrow of his bones—he could feel the tremendous potential of the process exploding with volcanic force. In a secret corner of his heart, didn't Partha have support, sympathy, some appreciation even, for their activities? And a nameless dread, mingled with the fear of total failure of their project?

And Prabhat? Was he not a victim of this terrible and potent process? And wasn't he a victim himself? Ron, Prabhat, and he were all victims of a powerful and unstoppable process.

He had once brought up the topic before Choudhury.

'Your sentiments are so useless,' Choudhury had almost barked at him, 'A generation is going to seed before our eyes, do you understand? An armed struggle, do you know what it is?' When he saw that Partha was silent, he answered the question himself, 'Armed struggle is politics of the highest order. Once it gets to that stage, all other roads are closed for a long time, if not forever. One needs immense maturity for it.' Choudhury was saying nothing new; he was repeating a commonly-held belief.

'Partha, it's not as if I have never thought about the things you have brought up. But I have seen a lot. I have seen that if political training and foundation are not sound enough, the participants are soon demoralized. And then they are easily sucked into the vicious circle of crime. Don't you see how the ethnic insurgencies are involved in drug and heroin businesses now? In society, they have all been marginalized. And why? Because they have no faith in their ideology; and in order to maintain discipline in their organization as well as to acquire public cooperation, they use fear instead of ideals, Partha, fear. They resort to barbarism. Ruthless killings and violence, and finally, they drift away from the common man, far away. How do I have confidence in such a process, Partha?'

His last question seemed more to himself than anybody else.

'This is a very negative analysis,' Partha said, not convinced.

'Perhaps,' said Choudhury, indifferently, 'but I have been forced to offer this analysis. We are the old-timers. When we talk about movements, we mean serious political movements.'

His voice was full of sarcasm. 'You are younger, Partha,' his voice softened. 'Those who have taken up arms must be closer to your age. It's natural for you to be emotionally drawn towards them. But if I reacted similarly, I would think that something was wrong with me. This is the drama of your generation; my role in it is that of a spectator.'

'Then what should be done? the words escaped from his mouth, against his own wishes.

Choudhury snapped at him, 'How would I know? I have not joined politics. Don't ask me such questions. You are here for journalism, Partha, carry on with that. We are the spectators of a play with plenty of action—bloodier the action, the better it is for us. That's our bread and butter.' The hoarse, foxy laughter rang in the room.

The memory of Choudhury's words left a bad taste in his mouth. He could not avoid talking to Choudhury, otherwise there would be nobody left to talk with. He had met a number of people in a short span of time—teachers, intellectuals, editors. But when it came to the burning issues of the nation, they all seemed to have taken a vow of silence. He often felt as if he hit a blank wall, a moss-grown wall without a single slogan on it, or a single graffiti. A poverty of ideas? Perhaps. And fear... We live in an intellectual void, full of dishonesty. This was reality, this was a curse. We are the haunted race in a cursed time.

He felt suffocated. And uncomfortable—very uncomfortable. And the armed expedition against the armed struggle had led to a tragic procession, filled with dishonesty and untruth...

Prabhat's father had come looking for him, wild and incoherent.

'Please do something, please,' he almost begged Partha. 'They have taken him away. It has been six days! There's no news of the boy.'

'I understand. Please calm down. Who has taken him away?'

'We do not know. It might be the police; it might be the military. They had come in civil clothes. Please do something. Where is he? Is he alive?' Hazarika answered, bursting into tears.

Partha put an arm round the man's shoulders and led him inside. He took him to his office and helped him into a chair.

'I can't understand anything...what has happened?'

'His mother's in a very bad shape. She has been laid in bed. She has been crying continuously, and often faints. Please do something. Or else...' the man said, covering his face with his hands. After some time, he controlled himself. 'I know I am irritating you. I am sorry. I don't have anywhere else to go.'

'What about the police?'

'I have already been there.'

'And what did they have to say?'

'Same old "Your son's not here. We don't know anything about it. It must be the military" line. I asked them why they had picked him up, that they had told me that there was no case against him, that he was innocent. But the man just said, "Haven't I told you that we haven't taken him? Go away, don't bother me anymore. I already have plenty on my plate." They almost drove me away from the station. I don't know what to do, or where to go...'

Partha took Narayan Hazarika to meet his father. He generally refrained from involving his father in his work; he always felt that his father would not like to be involved. Of course, he never had a chance to put his theory into practice. But today, Narayan Hazarika's state compelled him to change his stance.

In his chambers, Partha's father listened attentively to what they had to say. He asked them a few questions. After some thought, he said, 'Straight case for habeas corpus. We will have to appeal in the high court.'

'High court?' Hazarika's voice broke.

Partha's father looked at the man—a man broken by a nameless fear and uncertainty. He also looked at his son. Then he said, 'Don't worry, Hazarika. I will take care of everything. Partha, take him to meet Arup. I will call him up and ask him to start work on the case.'

'High court? The expenses...'

'Don't worry about that. I will appear myself. The costs of paper and typing are minimal, Partha will take care of that. You need not worry—it's not as if there are no laws left in the country. The police and military cannot just pick up anybody they want. The country has its laws, let them work accordingly. They can't simply do whatever they want.'

The senior lawyer reached for the phone. Partha helped Hazarika outside. The man was mumbling something about the high court. Partha was secretly elated by his father's response. When helping Hazarika into his car, he said, 'Please don't worry, Hazarika. The government will be forced to produce your son, wherever he is.'

Sitting hunched in the seat next to him, Hazarika heaved a long sigh, 'Provided he is alive…'

IV

A judge sat on his high seat in the court, dark-faced and sullen. There was a slight sense of boredom in his expression. Partha was not particularly reassured; he could hear his heart pounding with a nameless uncertainty and dread. He looked at Narayan Hazarika—who seemed to have shrunk into himself—was clearly devastated; his responses seemed blunted. Like a child seeking reassurance from adults, he followed Partha—his eyes, wild and aggrieved, clung to the black-clad lawyers moving in and out of the courtroom.

In the long corridor outside the courtroom sat Partha's father with Arup and several young lawyers, flipping through papers. Partha and Hazarika stood in the other corner. The acrid smell of urine wafted up to them. Grimacing, Partha walked up to a corner of the verandah and spat. Hazarika followed him, but he stopped and swallowed his saliva. He refrained from spitting in the premises of the court.

Through the door, the courtroom was visible. A lawyer stood in front of the judge, talking, fat books open in front of him. Partha could not hear him…his voice sounded like a hum. The lawyer looked like a fat hen pecking at the earth. After some time, the hum stopped; the lawyer dramatically ended his petition. Partha was startled by his dramatic gesture.

It was perhaps time for Prabhat's petition. Yes, it was time for Prabhat's petition.

When the judge saw a senior and respected lawyer like Partha's father walk in, a tired smile flitted across his face. The smile seemed to say 'now let us hear what you have to say'. In a low yet clear and grave voice, Partha's father began to present the petition for habeas corpus. Partha was privately elated, because he suddenly realized that he had never seen his father in court before.

Narayan Hazarika sat next to him, his eyes wide open and his jaws dropping.

I would like to present a petition for habeas corpus in front of the court today. The appeal for producing a person physically testifies strongly to today's disturbed times. Briefly, your honour, the facts of the case are as follows:

> Shri Narayan Hazarika is a middle-ranking government employee. Prabhat Hazarika is the eldest among his three children, a BA student in a local college. For quite some time, the police had been calling him to the station, forcing him to present himself in connection with an investigation regarding the whereabouts of certain insurgents and harassing the family unnecessarily. I have brought up the issue of unnecessary harassment because, at one point, the officers had stated that the boy was above suspicion and had stopped calling him to the station. Some time passed without any disturbance and the boy restarted his studies. But a few days after the army operation was launched, a group of armed men visited Hazarika and asked for his son. They pulled the boy away from his study table, abused him physically as well as verbally before his family, whisked him into a car and took him away to some unknown destination. From that day onwards, there has been no trace of Prabhat. The officers are unable to say who

> has taken the boy, let alone what the charges against him are. The local police officers have denied having the boy in their custody, and the district administration has no information either. We suspect that the army has picked up the boy, but we have no evidence. We are all in the dark as to where the young boy is at the moment, whether he is even alive or not. There is no need to mention before Your Honour that the laws and the constitution have not authorized any powers to arrest and secret away anybody without concrete proof. I pray to Your Honour to consider this matter seriously and pass the orders for 'habeas corpus' at once, keeping the welfare of the young boy in mind.

The judge looked over the papers in his hands for some time. Then, looking at the government advocate, he said something briefly. He looked at Partha's father and nodded in greeting; Partha's father reciprocated and walked out. Another lawyer took his place to present his case.

Partha was stunned at the speed at which things had been conducted.

His father had reached the end of the corridor. 'Let's go,' Partha said, taking Hazarika by the hand, and hurried after his father.

'What happened? What did the judge say?'

'He has ordered for Prabhat to be produced before the magistrate within 24 hours. He has also asked us to inform the court tomorrow.'

'What, 24 hours?' There was panic in Hazarika's voice. 'What if something happens to him in the next 24 hours?'

Partha's father looked at Hazarika with compassion, and said 'Don't worry, Hazarika. Everything's going to be all right. The court has given the right orders. This is the rule.' Partha led Hazarika out of the court; Hazarika kept mumbling 'God, 24 hours! Another 24 hours!' to himself.

The next day, the respected journalist Choudhury visited the court too. 'I am coming here after a long time, Partha. I have an instinctive distaste for courts and lawyers, you know. Please don't mind, I am not being rude about your father,' he said with a mischievous smile. He then became grave, and added, 'In the coming days, the courts are going to occupy a more central role in our lives.'

'Why do you say so?'

'The longer the anti-insurgency expeditions last, the more habeas corpus petitions are we going to have. There will be more violations of human rights, forcing the courts to take a more active role.'

Partha recalled the judge's sullen face, then asked, 'What do you think the courts can do?'

Choudhury thoughtfully rubbed his chin. 'I look at it a little differently, you see. This is also a kind of political movement, and the use of this particular platform is determined by how effectively it is used. When senior, well-known lawyers like your father take up such cases, it gives the movement a certain direction. Prabhat's case is not only important for the boy or for his family; I believe it will have far-reaching influences.'

Partha felt a thrill of happiness; he felt proud of his father, and proud of himself for getting involved in Prabhat's case.

They were seated on the wide field in front of the court, soaking in the sun—the warmth of the soft winter sun was nourishing indeed. Before the clock struck 12 pm, they entered the court; Narayan Hazarika joined them too. He looked worse today, thought Partha. He surely had got no sleep all night; there were dark circles of anxiety and dread round his eyes. He had made an attempt to make himself presentable for the court by shaving and ironing his clothes, but Partha could not bring himself to look at his face for long. He looked away.

An employee at the court held out a piece of paper to the judge, who then read it attentively. The judge looked at the government advocate, and the latter rose to his feet. He wore a grave expression. Today, a high-ranking police officer stood behind him; an army officer entered and sat down in one of the front benches.

Partha looked at Narayan Hazarika. The man sat at the edge of the bench, staring fixedly at the judge and the lawyers.

'Your Honor,' began the advocate, 'the boy called Prabhat Hazarika, about whom the court had issued orders yesterday, has already been presented before the magistrate and, at this moment, he is in the police station.' He mentioned a police station on the city's outskirts.

An incoherent moaning sound interrupted the pin-drop silence in the courtroom. Partha saw that Hazarika had risen to his feet. He pulled him down.

Now Partha's father stood up. He first thanked the court, thanked the judge for his magnanimity and then requested the court to return Prabhat Hazarika to his family and stop harassing them. He knew that he had crossed his limits in making that appeal—such appeals were not part of these cases. The habeas corpus petitions ended as soon as the individual's whereabouts were located. But in the contemporary situation, he felt that there was nothing wrong in making such an appeal.

He was right. The judge looked enquiringly at the government advocate. Partha observed that a lot of things were carried out in the court through glances and signs. The advocate now stood up. Casting a grave look at Partha's father and then at the judge, he said, 'Your Honor, it is my duty to let the honourable court know a little more about the case. The boy called Prabhat Hazarika has been arrested under the TADA (Terrorist and Disruptive Activities [Prevention]) Act.'

'TADA…' Choudhury muttered incoherently.

Partha could feel his mouth dry up. He felt a strange anxiety.

The advocate continued, 'I would also like the honourable

court to know that there has been clear evidence of Prabhat Hazarika's contacts with the insurgents. He, and his father, have confessed to that effect before the police. Under the TADA Act, such confessions are taken as evidence. The responsibility for this case would now be given to the designated court, which is beyond the area of the high court.'

The judge looked grave. So did Partha's father. The former shifted a little in his seat. He had at least determined that Prabhat was alive; now, they would know what was going to happen to him. However, it seemed to Partha that the judge was not very happy with the outcome.

'Now, the designated court is going to decide Prabhat's case,' the judge said, looking at Partha's father. There was a trace of defeat in his voice.

Partha left the court with mixed feelings. People crowded the corridor. He saw his father talking to Hazarika and moved towards them. His father was telling Arup to make an appeal in the designated court, so that the father could meet his son.

'First class first,' commented Choudhury. Partha was quiet; uncertainty veiled his heart, yet again.

V

'I still can't believe it.'

'Believe what?'

'That the high court has no more power.'

'Arre bhai, that is the marvel of the TADA Act. All special powers are with the designated court. You could move the Supreme Court if you are not happy with that. But no high court.'

Partha, Choudhury, and Arup were talking in Choudhury's house.

Choudhury was sitting in his favourite armchair, cradling his glass of whiskey in his hands. Eyes closed, he spoke in hushed tones like a conspirator. Often, he would let loose a cynical statement. But he was in a good mood; he had asked Partha and Arup over for a Sunday chat.

'What news of the boy?' Choudhury asked.

'He is in a special jail now,' Partha replied.

'Has his family met him?'

'They have got permission to meet him once a week—or in a fortnight.'

'The poor man! I feel sorry for the family.'

'There are many families like that dada—special families, special courts, special jail...' remarked Arup.

'I haven't met them for long,' Partha said, sounding guilty.

'These are routine matters, Partha,' said Choudhury, adding, 'Jail visits on such and such date, legal advice on another date, hearings on yet another—all a matter of routine. And between that, you have your meals, sleep, shopping, sex... Ha! Ha! Ha! What is the position of his case, Arup?'

'There was no news for a long time. Then we had the police report—I was actually surprised by the promptness at which it arrived. Perhaps because of the habeas corpus. If the police do not send reports, there is no way out except to request them. I would call this case an exception... You know, it is interesting. Prabhat's father has been named as an accuser in the case.'

Choudhury opened an eye and looked at him.

'Well, briefly—you do know that the police kept calling him to the police station, right? They were conducting investigations on one of his old school friends, who is now a top insurgent leader. I wonder why they thought Prabhat was involved... Initially, Prabhat and his father had no idea why he was being called to the station. Later, the father found out why and in order to prove his son's innocence, he went to the police station and told the police officer what he knew about the matter. Prabhat had had no contact with the other fellow for the last few years, but the police entered the information in a file and made him sign on it; Partha knows about it. The police have entered that as evidence against Prabhat in his case now.'

'But would that count as evidence?' Partha asked.

'It does in TADA. Under the TADA Act, confessions made before the police or the magistrate are considered evidence.'

'So, you see, Partha, any confession extracted through considerable torture from an individual can be used as evidence against him, under TADA,' Choudhury said sarcastically.

'Exactly. But do you know what is more important, dada?' said Arup, '...it is Prabhat, or as his lawyer, my responsibility to prove Prabhat's innocence. The government does not have to provide evidence of his crime. So, in case you are arrested, Partha, under a false accusation, it is your responsibility to prove that it is false. There, you have that Act!'

'I never knew that there could be such an Act!'

'There are some terrible clauses under that Act. You can be jailed for a year without trial; the trial can be carried out in secret, and without the presence of the accused; the trial can be conducted instantaneously...you get my drift.'

'How could this Act have been passed?' Partha asked incredulously.

'Well, the parliament passed it,' Choudhury said, adding, 'That must have been in 1985; many innocent lives had been lost in terrorist bomb attacks, so it was then that the bill was passed. Later, the Act came into operation throughout the country—its duration extended under some pretext or the other. I remember something else...five men were arrested in this bomb case. However, none of them were tried under the new Act. Do you know why? They all died in police custody.'

'So Prabhat might never receive a trial?' Partha asked, visibly shocked.

'Yes, he can be under arrest for a whole year,' Arup informed.

'What about bail?'

'We are going to try to get him bail, but bail is only going to be granted if the designated court is convinced that the accused is innocent, and is not going to be involved in any illegal activities when he is released. This is a very difficult task for the judge,' replied Arup.

They all fell silent, each feeling a sudden depression. The weather was gloomy, laden with the winter cold. It had been drizzling since evening…the ashy sky was enough to dampen their spirits. In the evening's dim light, the bushes in the garden seemed to hunch; it seemed to Partha as if the rain-drenched shrubs were drawing their leaves closer to them.

'How is the boy now? Have you met his father?' Choudhury asked Arup, breaking the depressive silence. They could not but return to the topic, however uncomfortable.

'Yes. Both his parents had come to meet me.'

'What did they have to say?'

'The mother said, "The boy is in very bad shape. He just won't talk. When we met him, he showed no enthusiasm. He seems scared all the time. He kept looking at the guard in the distance throughout our meeting. How can I, his mother, look on? He is such a harmless, innocent boy." I tried to console her and asked her not to cry, that we were trying our best. I then asked after his health, and the father said, "Very bad. He has lost a lot of weight. They tortured him a lot after picking him up. Beatings, shocks… Of course, none of that has happened in jail."'

'Was Hazarika saying all those things in front of the mother?' asked Partha.

'He is a very simple man. He said whatever came to his mind. But you should have seen the mother after that,' replied Arup.

'What else did he have to say?'

'He said that the other prisoners were very kind to his boy; that they try to cheer him up, but Prabhat's spirits always remain low.'

'Poor boy. The innocent suffers the most,' Choudhury sighed.

'You know, dada, Narayan Hazarika had something strange to say in the end.'

'What was that?'

'He said "Did not the government accuse him of having links with the underground?" in a bitter voice, then added, "Now he stays 24 hours with them in the jail. It's good, isn't it? The government's accusation has at least come true!"'

There was silence once again, each got immersed in his own thoughts.

'Man is helpless before the modern, all-consuming State. Truly. Mice and mountain—the mountain would not be eroded, no matter how much the mouse burrowed. The story from *Panchatantra*: the mountain said that the mouse is greater than me, because he can erode me by digging holes in my body. False, utterly false illusions we believe in. In the modern State, the individual is not only insignificant, he has no existence.' Partha felt extremely disturbed at Choudhury's words.

'Where is your revolutionary friend now, Partha? He is not going to surrender, is he?'

Choudhury pronounced surrender as 'soorrender'. Damn Choudhury. He had probably learnt to wear an armour of cynicism in order to live. Yes, to live—the primeval urge of man.

Sometimes, Choudhury impressed with his words. The other day he had a nice poem to recite about the TADA Act.

'Do you know what the TADA is, Partha? A naked weapon to protect the interests of those in power. A terrible weapon for the group in power—a law for the rulers, only for the rulers. Let me recite a poem for you. Have you read Alice in Wonderland? There is a wonderful poem in it about the laws of the rulers.' He began to sing:

Fury said to a mouse,
That he met in the house,
'Let us both go to law:
I will prosecute YOU.
Come, I'll take no denial;
We must have a trial:
For really this morning I've nothing to do.'
Said the mouse
to the cur,
'Such a trial,
dear Sir,
With no jury or judge,
would be wasting
our breath.'
'I'll be judge,
I'll be jury,'
Said cunning old Fury:
'I'll try the whole case,
and condemn you to death.'

Ludicrous, but this was reality!

THE CHILDREN OF THE IMMORTALS

I

Suddenly a pack of foxes started howling.

First it was one.

A sound, like a moan in pain, tore through the night sky. Others joined in. In reply, the village dogs started barking, shattering the silence of the wintry night. In a hut in a corner of the village, Sombori and her old father-in-law squatted in the kitchen; on the fire a curry made out of a handful of masoor dal, with pieces of gourds and some herbs thrown in it, bubbled.

'The foxes must be feeling really cold,' said Arjun Volunteer, wrapping an old frayed shawl around his body. 'Can't you hear them howl?' he added.

It was a night bright with moonlight, and bitingly cold.

The air from the hills of the North seemed to have carried in the cold to the village. By sunset, the fog had hung like wisps of smoke over the fields. When the moon rose, it looked like the fields were filled with water—the tops of the trees floated on the sea of fog as if on a flood. It was a full moon night. The sand-coloured moon dominated the sky. Moonlight streaked the yard.

There was the comfort of the fire, darkness, and warmth inside the hut.

'The scoundrels are calling for misfortune to hail on our heads—nothing else.' Grumbling, Sombori put some twigs into the fire, which instantly leapt into flames. Taking the curry pan down, Sombori placed the pot of rice on the fire. She poked in the fire with a twig for a few roasted berries. Shaking a drop of oil and some salt over the berries, she mashed them. The sweet smell of roasted berries filled the atmosphere.

Sitting with his back to the pillar near the fire, Arjun Volunteer began to cough; his was a chronic cough. He coughed for a long time, and then feeling the phlegm rise in his chest, shuffled out. It felt good to get rid of the phlegm. He shambled in from the cold, wrapped the shawl closer to him and settled down by the fire. He fished in his pocket for a beedi, lit it, and blew rings of smoke out his mouth and nose. He coughed again.

'Why do you have to smoke a beedi again?' Sombori said, softly, 'As if you are not coughing enough. You cannot sleep at night because of it—there must be no lungs left inside your chest. Someday, this habit of yours will carry you to the other world.'

Pressing the beedi between his thumb and forefinger, the old man took a short puff and said, 'That will be good. Yama's guards will know me from my cough for the beedi-smoker that I am. He will say, "Here, Arjun Volunteer, let me have a puff, too!" ' Sombori kept quiet. Pleased with his own wit, the old man chuckled, and was racked by cough again.

The rice pot started to bubble. Sombori put a twig in the fire.

The foxes howled again; this time the howls seemed to come from very near. They must be in the headman's sugarcane patch, Sombori thought, and shuddered.

'They are somewhere near the yard, those pests,' Volunteer muttered, and added, 'Get lost! You won't find anything here, no ducks or pigeons.'

Suddenly, the old man remembered something. 'The boys haven't been here for a long time,' he spoke as if to himself. 'Why? They could have shown their faces once…'

Decanting the starch water out of the cooked rice, Sombori asked, 'But how will they come?'

'You are right. The police-military are everywhere,' he paused. He remembered something again, and said, 'But I have seen them in the village; they seem to be visiting other houses. The other day I had run into one of them. He had greeted me and asked me how I was. Of course they could have come to see us!'

Sombori kept quiet. There was no point in arguing with her father-in-law.

'And how long haven't you cooked for them?' the old man asked himself rather than his daughter-in-law, '…must be over a month now, or maybe more, maybe more.' He persisted, 'They could have come if they wanted to. And they always get rice for us, don't they? I think they had come empty-handed only once… but then, they had left us money—they always get something for us. Sometimes a little rice, a little masoor dal, sometimes a pair of pigeons or a duck. You could have cooked them some nice duck curry.'

'You seem more interested in the duck curry than the boys,' Sombori said softly, then jokingly added, 'They are getting ready to sacrifice their lives for the country, and here somebody is lusting for duck curry!'

'What do you mean? Ah, may you have the pox!' the old man retorted, wrapping his shawl tightly, and sat straight. 'They can work well only if their bellies are full. And don't talk to me about sacrificing… How hard I have worked for this country...' Volunteer's memories floated around the kitchen like smoke and the warmth of the fire.

'Without a care for cold and heat, without a care for my body, how hard I worked. I have taken part in so many movements—opium prohibition, alcohol prohibition, Swaraj, *Bharat Tyag*. There is not a single village in this region that Arjun Volunteer has not been to during the Congress movements. I had been in them as my duty for my country. Setting aside the fear of tigers, I had carried food and letters for the underground leaders hiding in buffalo farms in the forest, and guided the leaders in pitch-dark.'

The old man rambled on. Sombori directed her attention to the hearth. The cooking was over; she got ready to serve the meal. Arjun Volunteer went on…

'Have collected money for the Congress fund. Do you know how? I would leave a pot in every house and people would drop whatever they could spare in it—a paisa, a handful of rice or dal. At the end of the month, I would carry the stuff to the Congress fund and return the pot to the owners the next day. Not even a grain of rice was misplaced. We drove the British out on the strength of a handful of rice and those coins. All those people have now become leaders, contractors, or businessmen…but Arjun Volunteer remained a pauper all his life.'

The old man took Sombori's silence to imply that he had taken part in these movements out of greed for power and wealth. She had mentioned it to the old man once. He growled at her, 'If I had such dreams, we would not be living in a hut today—we would have had a pukka house to ourselves. That Sarupai Satola also got the freedom fighter's pension. The rascal opportunist who collapses at the feet of the leaders when they come from town. He's useless, but what a smooth talker he is. A scoundrel like him gets a pension, but nobody thinks of Arjun Volunteer. Thank God that this piece of land was not confiscated and auctioned off by the British; we have at least a hut to shelter ourselves.'

'Let's not think about these things. Whatever God has given us...'

The old man almost snapped at her, 'And what has He given us? I don't need money or land. But He took my son away, made you a widow. I don't even remember my old woman's face anymore. How I worked for this country, and I never asked for anything in return. The communists came after Independence to fight for the rights of the farmers. I have believed in non-violence all my life, but worked with them also for some time.

'The meal is ready,' Sombori said quietly.

'Well, serve the rice. It is very cold. Let us go to bed early—times are bad. One never knows when the police-military will turn up. But I still think it would have been nice if the boys could have dropped in to say a few words. In old times, the leaders came—the Congress or the communists, they would round up the villagers and talk about the condition of the country. We would crowd around them and ask them a few questions, and they'd find out about the place from us. But now, those boys…'

'What about the boys?'

'They don't ask us any questions, and they don't tell us anything either. They come, speak a little, eat and then sleep...'

'They might be asking the others some questions,' offered Sambori.

'Yes, perhaps the headman, they might ask Budu Mahajan too—those are the two people they visit the most. When they visited us the first time, I thought they had come to talk about what they are doing and what we are supposed to do. But no, they don't talk much…have you noticed that?'

'They will probably tell you if you ask them.'

'How many times have I asked them? They say they are fighting for independence, but nothing in detail. They stroke their guns like stroking a baby. And I stopped asking them—and I told them not to think I lust after their duck meat. When I worked for my country, I went hungry for days and ruined my health. Yes, they have been feeding us ducks and pigeons, but they need not bring these here anymore; yes, they can visit us though.'

Sombori served the rice to her father-in-law. The old man ate the hot rice with great relish. Clearing up after him, she helped herself to some food. While she ate, the old man took beetle nut and pan, lit a beedi, and stepped out to shut the gate.

What was that? Yes, that was the sound of cars. Cars were driving up to the village through the road amidst the paddy fields. The lights danced over the unpaved roads. Arjun Volunteer hurried into the house.

'They are here, they are here. Can't you hear them? Quick, wrap up everything!'

Sombori quickly gulped down the rice and threw the waste away. She stepped inside and bolted the door; the old man blew out the lamp. Throwing a fistful of water into the hearth, she got into bed. The old man had already lain down. She shivered as she drew the cold quilt about her. She could hear the old man singing something in a muffled voice.

It took some time for the warmth to seep through the patched quilt. She did not know how long she lay there. There was silence all around—the foxes were quiet, so were the dogs. A horn blared. Sombori shuddered. Was that the sound of running feet? She could not make out where the sounds were coming from. There was a sudden loud sound, then silence. She strained her ears from under the quilt.

The moonlight filtering through the chinks in the wall filled the room. In the dark, Sombori's eyes glowed like those of a cat. Somewhere, a dog barked, and then there was a sudden blast. The dog yelped and fell silent.

What was that? Sombori shuddered.

Somebody was coming. She could hear boots pounding—the sound reached their yard. No, it passed. Was that somebody running towards the distance? Towards the fields? Thank God they had left. What were they doing here at this time of the night? But...were they coming back? Yes, they were... God, they were in the yard. They were opening the gate. God, have mercy on us. They were advancing. Sombori's heart started to thud painfully.

Somebody kicked open the bamboo door. Sombori yelped.

The bolt flew out of its hinges. The light from several torches flooded the hut. Terror-struck, Sombori sat up on the bed.

The light from the torches flew about the other room. Sombori could hear her old father-in-law's voice—Hari, Hari—and could sense him quake. Somebody was asking him in a harsh voice '*ladka log kaha hain*? (where are the boys)'; they were also abusing him in Hindi. Somebody pushed open the door between the two rooms; the light licked at her body. She did not see the smirk on the face of the shadow that advanced towards her.

A trembling Arjun Volunteer wanted to say something, but what could he say? Would they even understand Assamese? During the freedom movement, he had learnt to say a few words in Hindi. He tried to recall them, but his mind seemed to go blank.

'*Ladka log kaha hain, batao mujhe*! (Where are the boys, tell me!)' Somebody prodded him with the butt of his gun in the stomach. The sharp prod brought back broken Hindi from the freedom movement. The old man screamed aloud, 'Mahatma Gandhi ki jai! (Let Mahatma Gandhi's victory prevail!)'

The man was near Sombori's bed. He suddenly walked up to the door and said something to his companions. Placing the shining torch on the bed, he pulled Sombori—who was crouching near the wall—towards him. She felt as if a huge snake had wrapped itself around her body and was squeezing her. The dark mass behind the torch forcefully invaded her body. Releasing a scream, she went limp. The moonlight from the chinks in the wall fell on her eyes.

When the two men led the old man out of the house, he kept up his slogans. They must have been surprised. '*Kya kaha*? (What did you say?)' one of them asked him. Arjun Volunteer thought they had not understood his Hindi. He cast about his mind for a few more words; then he remembered something. He started shouting as if in a procession, '*Vande Mataram*! (I praise thee, Mother India!)'

The light from the torch, and the dark mass, left Sombori's limp body and moved out of the room. One of the gun-bearing men shouted at the old man, '*Buddhe, chup kar*! (Shut up, old man!)'

A horn blared—long and loud. '*Chal tem ho gaya*. (Let's go, time is up.)' Leaving Arjun Volunteer and Sombori, the three men jogged away.

II

The morning light filled the village.

The bright crimson sun shone in the foggy eastern sky like a rotating *borkahi* (large brass plate).

Arjun Volunteer stood near the fence where the soldiers had left him, trembling violently; he was rooted to the spot. It was not sure if his daughter-in-law's moans had reached him from the hut; if they had, he did not have the courage to step inside.

When the morning sun shone on him, Volunteer seemed to regain his senses. Shaking himself, he felt the spot on his stomach where the gun had prodded him. It still felt sore. With unsteady steps, he walked into the yard. But he could not go very far—when he reached the middle of the yard, his head swam. Shaking, he sat down on the yard. The old man sat very still, the daylight washing over him.

As day broke, men stirred from their houses; a few women stepped out too. That night, the soldiers had entered several huts. The men, cowed in terror all night, now began to talk.

'They have taken Konmoina away.'

'For the third time. What will be left of his body if they keep doing that? Every time he comes back, he is in bed for two weeks at least.'

'They have taken Buduram, too. His wife and children are crying their eyes out.'

'But why him? Oh, what times are these?'

The men stepped out on to the road. A black, furry animal lay in their path.

'Hari, Hari, what is that?'

'That's a dog...why, that's Buduram's Bhaluka. What a good pet he was... He must have chased after them when they took his master away, so they shot him. Look, he is splattered with blood.'

Surrounding the dead animal, the men clicked their tongues with sympathy. The crowd swelled; a few schoolboys came up with their shovels. They dug a hole under the bamboos near the road, buried Bhaluka in it, and pushed some bamboos round the grave to keep out the foxes.

It was the school mistress, Menaka Mastarni, who rallied them around.

'We cannot sit idle. We will have to see how many houses they entered at night, and what damage they have caused. We need to find out who all they have taken away.'

She did not wait. She walked ahead with the other women; a few men and children followed her. At one point, the crowd reached Sombori's yard. Arjun was still sitting in the middle of the yard.

'What are you doing, Volunteer Dadai?' somebody called out.

'Dadai, what are you doing?' another asked.

The old man lifted his head to look at the crowd. Tears streamed out of his eyes. He tried to stand up, but felt so dizzy that he had to sit down again.

'Hey, catch him! Look at Daiti (uncle), how he is behaving!'

The men leapt over the gate and ran inside. They took the old man by the arms and gently helped him up. Volunteer started mumbling, 'So you have come, o, raij (o, people). We have lost everything, everything...'

When she heard his words, Mastarni hurried inside. In the dark room, few things could be made out in the sunlight that filtered through the holes in the wall. She saw Sombori sitting on the floor—disheveled, with barely any clothes on her body. Her face was streaked with tears. Mastarni embraced her in anguish.

'I have lost everything, Baideu (older sister),' whispered Sombori, bursting into sobs.

People started whispering among themselves in small groups. The ground seemed to sway under their feet. If such things happen, how will people stay in the village—and with what assurance? Anxiety clouded their faces. The senior members started to assemble at the headman's house in twos and threes.

'It seems as if the Burmese are back,' the village headman told his audience. He continued, 'Walking into somebody's house and molesting a woman—this had not happened even in the days of the British in these areas. They could have just as well shot her.'

He suddenly remembered something and hurried inside. His wife, who was in the kitchen, said, 'We have to do something about Majoni. We can't keep her here any longer.'

Majoni was his oldest granddaughter; a student of 10th standard. She walked a couple of miles to school every day. His son and daughter-in-law stayed in Halflong with their other children.

'A tiger that has tasted blood will be back. Don't you remember how they ogled at her the last time they searched our house? They will be back in force,' the headman said.

His wife clutched at a pillar for support as her feet quivered. 'What will happen now?' she asked her husband in a whisper.

'We will have to send her away to her uncle's house in Guwahati as soon as possible. Nobody needs to be told. Pack her stuff; only make sure that she can leave at a moment's notice.'

The headman walked back to the crowd again.

'Gaoburha (headman), aren't you supposed to be informed when they search the village? Aren't you supposed to accompany them when they search the houses?' asked Budu Mahajan.

'That's the rule,' the headman answered heatedly, 'but who cares for rules nowadays? The last time they were here, they ransacked my house. All these rules are useless—they are all lies.'

A heated discussion was in progress at Sombori's house too; Menaka Mastarni and a few women sat around Sombori.

'Don't worry Sombori,' Mastarni said, trying to console her. She continued, 'We are all here for you...you have our support, the people support you. And the scriptures say that if somebody soils your body against your will, your soul isn't soiled. We will protest against this crime. We have to find a remedy for this heinous act. Don't you worry.'

Sombori sat with her head buried between her knees, like a stone. Although the women pressed her to extract more information about the incident, she only replied in monosyllables. The tea somebody had left near her had cooled down. Mastarni could not, try as she might, persuade her to have the tea.

In another corner of the yard, a few young men stood, discussing the incident heatedly. Arjun Volunteer still sat in his original spot, trying to imbibe the warmth of the sun, and slowly dipping biscuit into a cup of tea somebody had offered him; he strained his ears to listen to the conversation of the young man.

'We can't let it go...something has to be done.'

'Can't we inform somebody?'

'Of course, we can, but what do we do right now?'

'Whatever you do, remember that it's the question of a woman's reputation.'

'But how do you keep it a secret? And it's not correct to keep it a secret. The whole village knows! We have to protest against this atrocity.'

'I am not saying it has to be hidden.'

'That's right, my son. We have to redress it,' Arjun Volunteer spoke up with determination.

The discussion grew more intense.

'But for any redressal, won't we need something first?'

'What?'

'Won't we need proof? Proof that the incident has occurred. Nobody is going to believe us otherwise.'

'But how are we going to prove it?'

'As far as I know, there has to be official evidence. There should be a medical examination. Think about it carefully. Remember that incident in Lakhimpur that had appeared in the newspapers? That was proved by a medical examination.'

'The government…the government should be told!' the old man almost screamed.

The boys were startled.

'Which government, Dadai?' somebody asked, a little lightly, 'Dispur or Delhi?'

'Don't you make fun of him. He is right, the government should be informed. The Sub-Divisional Officer (SDO) should be informed in writing.'

A young man left the group, went up to Mastarni and whispered something. Mastarni nodded her consent. The young man told her, 'See that she doesn't have a bath, Baideu. That will be the end of all proof. We will try to do something as soon as we can.'

Before a final decision could be taken, the village was in uproar. Many people agreed to what had been proposed—something had to be done; the perpetrators must not be allowed to get away with it. But a few people were confused. There was a heated discussion in Budu Mahajan's grocery store as well. Mukheshwar Satola, Ghanakanta Sarkar, Lambu Bayan, and a few others were present; they got excited.

'What are our boys about to do, Mahajan? They listen to you… Talk to them. Are they going to town about this scandal, spreading the scandal of our village all over?' asked Satola, one of the men.

'That's not a nice thing to say, Satola,' said Mahajan, adding, 'Don't talk about it as if it is a scandal. You and your family may be in trouble in future too. People must speak up. An innocent woman has been tortured—this can happen to anybody, in any house of the village.'

'What are you saying? All right, let us not call it a scandal, but this is shameful. It is one thing to say she has been touched or pulled by the hand, but once you let a doctor examine her, it will be public knowledge. Think about it carefully, Mahajan. Everybody should not be carried away by what a few youngsters say. Well, I have done my bit, so don't blame me later,' Satola spoke as if with great sadness and walked out. The rest were silent.

'Satola said something really serious,' Budu said to the rest, 'and we can't ignore him altogether. What if you go and report to the government and those monsters come the next night and shoot us all like dogs? Even if we keep quiet, the underground boys will catch hold of us. Either way, we are trapped.'

'Do you know what Sombori has become?' asked Nareshwar. He walked up to Budu and whispered in his ears, 'She has got a promotion, Mahajan. She has become a martyr—a living martyr.'

'Shut up, what rubbish! Don't bring all these things to your foul mouth,' Budu bristled.

Gunaram Pathak, who used to read Bhagavad Gita after the prayers at the *namghar*, entered the store to buy masoor dal and oil. Budu told him everything, and then asked, 'Now tell me, Pathak, what should we do?'

Pathak thought for a while and said slowly, 'You have got me into real trouble. A sin does not stay hidden. A sin's a sin, regardless of the intention. But a sin is lighter when it is committed without your knowledge or against your will. I think she should atone, because as of now she is a fallen woman. She should undergo a *prayachitta* (atonement) and, after that, atone by prostrating before the villagers; the villagers will take her back. She is our daughter-in-law, and nobody has ever had a bad word to say about her. You have seen how devotedly she has been serving her old father-in-law after her husband's death. She is a good, pure woman. We will take her back into the fold.'

The men present exchanged glances.

'That's for later, Pathak. We will consider that in time. But what do we do now? The question now is whether we ought to report it to the government...'

'Don't drag me into those matters... I know little of government work. I have given you suggestions about lifting her from her fallen state and taking her back to the fold. Now it is up to you.'

Discussions continued in small groups. Finally, it was decided to inform the government in writing and request for corrective measures. But since it was already night, the trip to the city was postponed to the next day.

III

To get to the Subdivisional Headquarters, one had to walk for two miles and catch a bus near the high school.

The crowd of villagers walked through the field, enveloped in fog—a few young men, Menaka Mastarni, two of her friends and in the middle, Sombori, with her veil drawn over her face, walked amidst them. The headman was supposed to come too, but, apparently, since last night he had been throwing up and having loose motions.

They came pressed into each other in the crowded bus; there was not a place to sit. The young man got two of the boys known to them to vacate their seats in the bus and managed to sit Menaka Mastarni and Sombori.

The crowded bus reached the headquarters a little before 10 am.

Now the small crowd walked towards the SDO's office. An inexplicable embarrassment preyed on their minds; they were eager to avoid familiar faces. They were also frightened, though they did not know it themselves why they were frightened. An inexplicable apprehension pressed over them; they felt as if they would be saved if they could avoid someone they knew. Sombori's heart was racked by mixed feelings of agitation, resignation, and a deep fatigue. Surrounded by the villagers, she moved mechanically amidst them. When they reached the SDO's office, the people were shocked.

Two military vehicles were parked in front of the office. Several gun-wielding soldiers stood on the verandah and near the car in attention. There were signs of fear on the faces of the employees; a few clerks would not even look up from their work. The door to the SDO's office was closed. Outside the door, Dharmakanta, the old peon, was standing. He, too, looked frightened.

Uncertainty descended on the small group. They retreated to a tea stall a little distance away and ordered tea. A young man walked up to the men standing in front of the nearby paan shop and asked, 'What's wrong? Why so many soldiers here?'

He returned with the information. 'An officer's here to meet the SDO. Apparently, these are routine visits.'

'It looks as if they are quite thick,' Menaka commented.

Sombori fiddled with her glass of tea; she sat with the veil covering her face near Menaka Mastarni. Her mind was blank, emptied of all thought. She felt no interest in what the others were saying, nor did she feel any apprehension.

Half an hour later, the officer walked out of the office. The waiting soldiers jumped up on the vehicles. The cars roared away. The office now burst into life; a hum of conversations could be heard. Menaka walked up to the office, gesturing to the others to follow her. In front of the door, the group hesitated slightly. The old clerk and the peon, carrying files into the office, tried to stop them, but Menaka pushed them aside.

The SDO looked up in surprise at the group marching into his office.

'We have come to submit a complaint in writing,' Menaka was the first to speak, '...We want an injustice to be redressed.'

'Just a minute. Where have you come from?'

'We are from Napam.'

'Napam? You mean the village. Okay, what is your complaint?'

'Day before yesterday the army entered our village,' a young man began, 'They have been there a few times. They picked up quite a few of our villagers.'

'That's happening everywhere,' the SDO interrupted, 'The laws are in the hands of the Armed Forces. The law has given them the power of searching, for catching the insurgents.'

'That's not why we are here; we have come here to complain that the day before yesterday, in the course of the search, they raped our widowed sister, Sombori.'

'What?' the SDO sat up straight in his chair.

'Yes, sir. The victim's here too; she is present herself before you. We went through a lot of trouble to get her here. Here's the written complaint.' A young man held out a folded sheet of paper towards him.

The SDO slowly read it. Then he looked at Sombori and the others. 'What do you want me to do?' he asked.

The young man looked at each other.

Menaka began, 'We want you to investigate the incident and inform the government. We want the injustice to be redressed.' The rest nodded their heads in agreement.

The head clerk spoke up from behind the group, 'This is a police case, sir. A report should be lodged with the police.'

'What did you say, Barthakur?' the SDO asked at once. He looked at Menaka gravely and said, 'That's right. You should go to the police first. Please have a seat.' Turning to the clerk, he said, 'Barthakur, ask for a few more chairs and don't let anyone enter.'

Looking at Menaka, he started, 'Now, Baideu, let me explain the situation to you. I might be the SDO, but I cannot act according to my wishes. I have to obey the law, too. You have brought a very serious complaint. If it is proved, it is going to have very serious consequences. The law permits the soldiers to use their guns if necessary, but it does not permit anybody to molest a woman, or rape her. This is a serious offence. The government will surely punish the offenders. But first, you must inform the police about this crime. They will record the case, send a report after investigation, and order a medical examination. You did a good thing by coming here, because I can advise you on how to act. Please go to the police and file a complaint. Don't worry; I will keep the information in writing too. You tell me about the incident in short. Give me all your names and addresses. I shall note down everything in my diary. I will personally send the report to my higher-ups. But you should not delay in filing a police report.'

After about an hour, the group walked out of the SDO's office. One of the group members said, 'Will we come to any harm if we go the police? They have recorded our names and addresses here. What if the police lock us up when we go to them?'

'When we have come this far, we shall only go back with some result. Come, let us start, we have to go to the police station,' Menaka said.

They made their way to the police station; it was quite crowded. When they shuffled up to the verandah, a constable rudely asked them what they wanted.

Menaka moved forward. 'We have been sent here by the SDO. We would like to meet the OC.'

'The OC isn't in. But the second officer is here,' the constable's voice softened, and he took them to meet the second officer.

Menaka immediately held out the piece of paper towards him. The officer began to read; his eyes almost started to bulge out of their sockets. 'Where are you from? What's all this? Who's Sombori? You have obviously made a mistake. Napam village does not fall under this station's jurisdiction. You will have to go to Ghilamara. Now, please leave, you are wasting your time here.'

Taken aback, the group filed out. They came out through the people crowding the front of the police station silently.

'We will have to go to Ghilamara. There's no other way.'

'Come let's move. We have to rush. Will have to catch the bus to Ghilamara,' Menaka Mastarni rushed everyone.

They waited for the bus to Ghilamara at the bus station. The bus going there only came late in the afternoon.

It was too late to go to Ghilamara on that day. So, deciding to go to Ghilamara the next day, they took the return bus home. The following morning, the group began its journey again—but without two of its members, who backed out at the last minute. This time, Arjun Volunteer joined them. The headman was still unwell. Apparently, he had been laid up in bed. The group reached Ghilamara police station early in the morning. It was a small station with fewer policemen. Several tents had been set up next to the building; this was a military camp.

'Those fellows are here too,' someone warned.

Their footsteps slowed down.

'That's none of our business. Let us do our work,' Menaka said.

The veil drawn over her face, Sombori moved as if by clockwork. The policemen turned to look at the group. Now, Arjun Volunteer stepped forward. A policeman called out to him, 'Isn't that Volunteer Daiti? What brings you here?'

'Gajen,' Arjun obviously knew the man, 'Is the OC in?'

'He has gone home for some time, Daiti. Do sit down. What brings you here? And these people with you...'

'It's a serious matter, Gajen. We can only tell your boss about it.'

The women sat down on the bench in the verandah, and the man stood nearby. Volunteer started pacing the verandah impatiently; he would crane his neck to look at the OC's quarters. Suddenly, there was a terrible scream. The men looked at each other, a nameless dread in their eyes.

'This is getting unbearable,' said Gajen, '...these screams, day and night...'

'Who's screaming?'

'Who else,' there was no feeling in his voice, 'They are interrogating the boys they had picked up from the village. I can't take it anymore.' He moved away rapidly.

The people cowered in the verandah—their hearts started thudding with fear and suspense. Even Volunteer's steps slowed down.

Finally, the OC arrived. Arjun, Menaka, and a few others moved hesitantly towards his office.

'And what do you want?' the OC shouted.

'Daroga sahib, where is our country heading to?' Arjun spoke up emotionally, 'I gave my life to the country. We did not have such injustice even in the days of the British. In my house, Daroga sahib, in my own house! They stole into my house like thieves and raped my widowed daughter-in-law, and hit me in the stomach...'

'Just a minute. Who raped whom?'

The old man's voice rose, quavering. 'My daughter-in-law, in my own house. We have come to you for justice. Catch the offenders, punish them.'

A young man tried to explain things to the OC, and offered him the written complaint. The OC did not even look at the piece of paper. He looked out of his window at the camp—one could still hear the screams coming from there. Then, without looking at anybody, he said, 'I can't take such cases.'

'Why not?' Menaka tried to argue with him. But the OC was obdurate; he would not even look at the paper. He told them in no uncertain terms that he would not accept their complaint till he received instructions from higher quarters. The group felt very helpless. As they quarrelled, one could hear Volunteer's deep sighs: 'Ramkrishna, Ramkrishna.' Finally, Menaka asked the OC, 'Then tell us what to do.'

'Go to a doctor... Do what you want, but don't come here. The situation is bad, in any case...' he did not complete his words.

Helpless, the group filed out from the OC's room.

'What now?' someone asked.

'Our country has gone to the dogs. Such injustice, and no punishment. Forget about catching the criminals, the police are afraid to accept complaints,' Volunteer was grumbling to himself.

Sombori gently tugged at Menaka's arm and said, 'Let us go, Baideu, let us go back home.'

'Don't lose heart, Sombori. It will help to go to the doctor. One has to fight for one's honour, you see,' Menaka tried to console her.

'Honor won't come back even if you fight, Baideu.'

'Why are you talking like that? If you don't fight, you will be left with nothing. Now, you don't say a word. We are here for you. Let's go to the hospital.'

The hospital was a couple of miles away from the police station. The group moved on the road leading to the hospital. There were no buses to be found at that time of the day. They marched on foot and reached the hospital before noon. The premises were near-deserted—the doctor had left to see some patient somewhere; the nurse was in her quarters. Only the chowkidar was moving around. Hungry and thirsty, they had to wait till afternoon.

When the doctor came, they surrounded him.

'Don't crowd around me. I will look at you one by one,' he said.

'We have not come to consult you; this is a far more serious matter,' Menaka spoke with force, 'You have to examine this young woman and write a report. The military has raped her…'

'What?' the doctor was stunned. A young man proceeded to tell him the whole story.

'Please sit down,' the doctor said. Looking at Menaka and the young man, he said, 'Ask the young woman to sit down too. And this is...her father-in-law? Please sit down, Deuta. The rest can leave. Shut the door behind you.'

When they had left, the doctor said, 'I want the paper.'

The young man held out the written complaint.

'No, not this one. You can leave this with the SDO. I want the paper given to you by the police.'

'What paper? The police have given us no papers, police said…'

'Has there been no case entry? Haven't they given a requisition? Well, yes, no policeman is accompanying you. Is the OC coming?' the doctor now asked hesitantly.

The young man told him about their experiences at the police station.

'You are our last hope,' he told the doctor.

The doctor suddenly looked very helpless. 'Now, this is a problem,' he cleared his throat and was silent for some time. Then, he spoke up, 'You see, these are MLCs, meaning, medical-legal cases—a part of the Criminal Act. I cannot examine her and give my report unless instructed by the police or law. This is the rule… I hope you understand. My hands are tied. Tell me if you have any other problems? Any pain or wounds? I can give you all the medicine for that.'

'The wound is in her soul, what medicines can you give for that, doctor?' the young man asked, and got to his feet.

IV

The next morning Sombori took a long bath and came inside the house in her wet clothes. She changed and entered the kitchen. The fire had not been lit for three days. They had eaten only when somebody had brought them food; otherwise, not at all. The kitchen was in a mess. Sombori quietly put things in order, then scrubbed and layered the whole earthen floor of the kitchen with a rug soaked in cow dung and earth. Lighting a fire, she made some black tea and poured a cup for her father-in-law. Taking out some pieces of black molasses from an earthen pot, she called out to him. The old man sat hunched in the verandah, warming himself in the morning sun. Like a child, he scrambled up and tottered in. He sat silently near the hearth, and dipping a piece of biscuit that somebody had brought, slowly sipped his tea.

The sight of his daughter-in-law's face, wiped of all expression, wrung the old man's heart. He quickly dabbed at his eyes with his wrist.

'Finish your tea, I will be back soon.' Picking up his bag and staff, he stomped out of the hut.

For a long time, Sombori sat near the fire warming herself. Then she began checking the tin jars; there was a little bit of rice, a handful of masoor and a handful of black dal in the house, and only a few drops of cooking oil left in the bottle. Sombori rose to her feet. She picked some leaves and herbs from the tiny kitchen garden, and keeping these in a bamboo *dala* (husking tray), she straightened her clothes with a resolve. She remembered that the headman had asked her to pound rice for him many days ago; that was before the incident had occurred. She started for his house.

Without looking at anybody, Sombori reached the headman's house. She noticed that the headman was sitting outside.

'Isn't that Sombori?' the headman called. Drawing her veil over her head, she stood in the verandah.

'I have heard that your work could not be done. I wish I could have come along, too, but I fell so sick. I though it may be the cholera itself. Tell me, what brings you here?'

His wife joined and asked Sombori, 'What's wrong, Sombori?'

'I thought I would pound some rice for you.'

'Really? But are you feeling well enough?' The headman's wife stepped inside. She made a bundle of rice, dal, flour, and potatoes, walked out, and held it out to her, 'Not today, my dear, go home and take some rest. You are not well. You don't have to go around looking for work.'

Clutching the bundle, Sombori moved away diffidently.

Cooking a meal, she waited for her father-in-law. The old man was nowhere to be seen. It was evening when he set foot inside the house. Putting his bag and staff down, he said, 'It's no use, no use at all. I personally met all of them: the SDO, Daroga…nobody wants to take your complaint down. They won't even write a report for a doctor's test. The Daroga yelled at me. I asked them what they were doing here, and what kind of officers they were that they can't even protect us from the evil of the demons, but nothing happened.'

'The rice is done. I have heated some water for you…wash up. You don't have to go there anymore,' Sombori said quietly.

For a couple of days, she stayed indoors, but how long could she do that? What would she eat if she did not work? What would the old man eat? She made for Mahajan's house. He always needed some help with pounding the rice and with other chores. She made her way to his back door instead of the store in front. Mahajan's wife was sitting in the verandah, working on something. Sombori went straight to her and asked for work.

'Work?' The woman seemed thunderstruck, and asked, 'How are you going to work in our house? No, no, you don't need to work here.'

Sombori's words froze; she understood clearly. They would not let her work anymore. She was…she was…

She suddenly felt dizzy and abruptly turned around to leave. Without looking at anybody, she made her way home.

'Sombori, here, Sombori look here.'

Who was that? Was that Mahajan? Yes, that was him. When she did not stop, Mahajan called out brusquely, 'Here, haven't you heard me? Come here for a moment.'

Sombori stopped. Then she went to Mahajan, dragging her feet.

'What has happened has happened. That can't be undone,' his voice softened. 'Now we…all of us…will have to take you back into the fold. The elders in the *namghar* have discussed it. You are, after all, our daughter…our daughter-in-law. In your days of misfortune, the village will not abandon you. They all say that you should atone, undergo a *prayachitta* and arrange a meal for the village so you can get lifted up to the fold from your present situation. The public will forgive you totally. I thought of letting you know. I will tell Daiti myself.'

Sombori did not wait to hear him anymore. She did not know how she reached home. Opening the door, she collapsed on the bed and clutching the old, stained pillow, burst into tears.

Sometime later, Menaka Mastarni arrived; she got Sombori to talk only after a lot of persuasion. When she found out why Sombori was crying, far from losing her temper, she hugged Sombori and broke down herself.

Arjun Volunteer visibly changed. His speech and actions were not very normal in the past either, now they took a turn for the worse. He would be out of the house most of the time, and he would go without his meals. For a couple of days, Sombori waited for him at mealtimes. But when she found that she could not persuade him otherwise, she stopped talking to him about it. She took to having her meals by herself and kept the old man's food covered in the hearth.

The old man would set out in the morning with his staff and his bag. He would roam around the whole day; sometimes, he would take the bus to the sub divisional office. A couple of days, he was given a ride by military vehicles. Most of the time, he would mumble to himself. At others, he would sit quietly, hunched in a corner. Only sometimes would he behave normally, as in the old days. Sometimes, he would sing revolutionary songs at the top of his voice. Once, he sang these songs while riding a military jeep:

> 'O! Welcome
> With songs and music
> The people have arisen
> The Gods have arisen with the people
> O! Welcome
>
> We have come to your door
> We who are ready to die
> We who travel the extreme path!'

The soldiers moving about on the village paths—in cars or on foot, hiding guns in their shopping bags or shawls—became a familiar sight to the old man. He came to know the men also.

He started frequenting their temporary camps.

One day the old man came back from the military camp wearing a huge overcoat. When he marched through the village wearing the warm coat—carrying his staff in one hand, and carrying a bag full of stuff that the army men had given him—the villagers stared.

When Sombori saw him, she began to cry. What had happened to the old man in such a short time? She began cursing her fate. Now, Volunteer would not take off his coat even when having his meals; he sometimes fell asleep with the coat on, or would place the great coat atop his tattered quilt. He would fall asleep the moment his head touched the pillow.

One day, two unknown young men paid Sombori an unexpected visit. They were accompanied by Pradip and Haren from the village. One could make out from their clothes and their behaviour that they were from the city. Pradip approached Sombori, 'Bai, they are journalists from Guwahati. They work in newspapers. Please tell them what happened. I have already told them what happened to us in our search for justice. Now, they are our only hope. Everybody should know about these atrocities...'

'Will everybody know?' Volunteer sat up on his bed and called out from the other room. 'What will happen if everybody knows? As if I will get a new coat!' he added, and then hugged his coat.

'Keep quiet, Daiti. Bai, please come out. Menaka Baideu is on her way, too. Haren, here, get the stool out in the sun. They will take her pictures.'

One of the young men asked her to sit on the stool and clicked several pictures of her. She turned her face away, and in spite of repeated requests, would not look at the camera. The other young man switched on the tape recorder and asked her numerous questions. She answered as shortly as possible. When she talked about the incident, her voice faltered. Menaka encouraged her to speak. With her encouragement, Sombori somehow managed to complete her narration. The young journalist named Partha noticed that when she talked, her eyes were not only dry but also lifeless.

'It is necessary to tell your story yourself, or else, there is no point in recording,' he said, as if to himself.

'Record it, record it,' Arjun Volunteer, squatting on the threshold, suddenly spoke up loudly. They were startled, 'Record the news that they raped me!'

'Daiti, do keep quiet.'

'Yes son, this is the time to keep quiet. People will keep quiet, either out of fear of blows or because of the rumble in their bellies.'

Arjun Volunteer then started singing:

'O, o, we have become free
Ram Rajya has come
O o, seeing the state of the Rajya
Ran away did Ram.
O o o, Ran Ran away…'

The journalists wrapped up their instruments and loaded them on their Maruti van. They left with the promise that they would publish this news of army atrocities from Guwahati as well as other places.

On her way back, Menaka ran into Budu Mahajan. She did not even see him coming; she was jolted out of her thoughts only when he called out to her.

'Mastarni Baideu, are you coming from Volunteer Daiti's house?

Menaka nodded.

'It seems that some people from the newspaper had visited them.'

'You are right.'

'Will they write about Sombori?'

'They will; they have also taken her pictures,' Menaka said enthusiastically.

'That wasn't a good thing to do, Baideu. This should not have happened in the presence of wise people like you,' Budu spoke with great sorrow. He continued, 'The family's shame should be kept to the family. We did not have a medical examination, and we do not have any evidence either. What is the point in going to town about the scandal?'

'Scandal?' Menaka was thunderstruck.

Budu did not wait to hear her words; he nearly ran away from the place. For a long time, Menaka stood rooted to the spot. Then she slowly made her way home.

V

Arjun Volunteer's mental state deteriorated. On some nights, he did not come home. Now, he simply refused to take his coat off. The coat was so long that it covered his dhoti entirely. Only his thin, bare legs showed below. He also got himself a hooded cap from one of the camps. Now he did not need his bag—the coat had so many pockets that a bag was not necessary. In his cap and coat, barefoot and staff-wielding, the old man was a peculiar sight indeed.

He started doing some strange things as well.

Once, he turned up at the SDO's office on a Sunday. Standing in the verandah, he stared at the locked door for some time. Then he suddenly and noisily urinated in front of the door; looking at the stream seeping in under the door, he muttered, 'Go, you bastard, go!' Without a care for the passers-by, the old man took to lifting his coat and pissing by the roadside, anywhere he liked.

His not staying home at night became a regular occurrence. He won't say where he had been or where he had stayed, even after repeated asking.

A few days after the journalists had visited them, the old man returned home at noon in an obvious hurry. 'Here, take a look,' he shouted, 'a newspaper from Guwahati. It has your photograph. Can you see? That's me on the threshold. They have written everything! I will read it out to you.'

'No, don't.' Sombori's voice was loud.

The old man was taken aback. 'Okay, if you don't want me to…' Stuffing the newspaper into his pocket, he left the hut in a huff.

Sombori sat very still in the kitchen. The curry bubbled in the pan; after sometime the twigs burnt out, and finally, the pan started to cool. Sombori sat silently before the heath, oblivious to everything. Soon, the day ended and dusk descended on the open fields.Soaking in the smoke floating on the roofs of the huts, the darkness clustered in the yards. In the cold and dark, the trees drew their leaves about them like a quilt. In the distance, the foxes could be heard howling.

Sombori sat by the dying fire. Her mind was empty of all thought…a sense of huge emptiness seemed to engulf her. The howling foxes seemed to draw closer; they must be in the marsh now…now, in the sugarcane patch. A knock on the door brought her back to her senses.

'Who's that?'

'It's us, Baideu.'

'Come in, the door's not bolted.'

Two boys entered the room in darkness. They came in and stood by the hearth.

'Who are you?' Sombori had asked.

Blowing at a stick of firewood, Sombori lit it. Light and shadow danced in the room. The boys brought two *pira*s in the light and sat down facing her.

'Don't you remember us, Baideu? You had cooked food for us,' they said.

She looked at their faces; they did look familiar. Yes, she knew them. They had brought a duck for her once.

'Why have you come?'

'We came to enquire about you. We did not know about the incident until yesterday. You know, we haven't been here for a long time. We thought of coming to meet you today. We know everything, Baideu.'

'You do, do you?' Sombori's voice was hard, 'And what do you propose to do about it? Can you do anything? Can you punish the one who laid his hands on my body? Can you? You have guns. Can you find him and punish him? Answer me, why don't you answer me?'

Her sudden outburst caught the boys by surprise. They kept silent.

'Why are you silent? So, you can't do it! Why do you take up guns if you cannot protect the helpless widows? Why did you get all of us in danger? You think it's a game? Your childish doings have brought us doom.'

Sombori grew agitated. The light and shadows played across her face, and those of the two boys. Her eyes, wide open, glowed with the light from the fire. She had never used this tone before; today, something seemed to have possessed her.

The boys did not know what to say. Finally, one of them spoke up, courteous yet awkward, 'We will do what we can, Bai, but we don't know what. Your sacrifice will not go in vain. We had brought something for you, please make use of it. Goodbye.'

They stood up suddenly; so did Sombori. The boys disappeared into the darkness. Sombori did not even turn to look at them. She stood near the fireplace, as unmoving as a statue.

The night deepened. Sombori did no more cooking that day. She did not put the rice to boil. Drinking a bowl full of already cooked curry, she kept the rest for the old man. Hugging the dying warmth of the fire, Sombori sat very still. After some time, she heard somebody clearing his throat outside.

'Who's that?'

'Is Daiti home? Well, I thought he wouldn't be. How are you Sombori?'

It was Budu Mahajan. He helped himself to a *pira*.

'Had your food?'

'You haven't made it very easy for me to have my food, Mahajan.'

Mahajan looked at her face in surprise. What had come over this woman, who always kept her head lowered and spoke in quiet tones, he thought to himself. Even Sombori was surprised by her own words.

'Yes, that is what I have come to talk to you about.'

'The public feast? If I die, only then will somebody get to eat the dead's feast. How do I atone and feed you now? I will have to cut my head off and cook it for you.'

'Don't lose your temper, Sombori,' Mahajan said, gently, 'You have reason to be angry, I know. I understand what misfortune has hit you. But what can we do? Some people have narrow minds. But you need not worry about that. I have come to talk about something else.'

Sombori did not say a word.

'Sombori, I am your well-wisher,' Mahajan's voice was sad, 'I speak only for your good. I know how you must be feeling. I know what is true and what is false. But think about it, there has been no medical examination, so there is no official proof. Now, if you write on this paper that no atrocity was committed towards you, we will be able to find some employment for yourself.'

'So, I have to say what is true is false and what is false is true.' Sombori said, calmly. 'Is that why you came, Mahajan? Aren't you sorry? Ashamed?' she asked, her voice shaking.

'Sombori,' Mahajan's voice was hard, 'I have no self-interest here. You cannot use that incident as your capital all your life. Remember my words. Think over them, and let me know your decision. But don't delay it too much.'

That night, Sombori could not even shed any tears.

From the next day, it began to drizzle. The sky was ashy in colour, and gloomy. The cold thickly enveloped the earth. The last traces of winter threatened to freeze the limbs of the people.

Arjun Volunteer had not returned home for two days. On the first day, Sombori was not very worried. But when he did not return home for the third night, she was seized with panic. Where was the old man? Should she inform Menaka Baideu? Or Pradip or Haren? What would they do? How can they go out in this drizzle to look for the old man on this bone-breaking cold night? She lit the fireplace, but made no attempt to cook. Strange fears crowded her mind; weird premonitions of evil flashed through it. She sat near the hearth silently with her disjointed thoughts. Why, those foxes had started howling before nightfall…

Somebody was cycling up to the yard. She could hear him throw the gate open and walk in. Who was that? Her heart thudded. 'Sombori Bai, Sombori Bai,' ringing his bell, Pradip called out. With the kerosene lamp in her hand, Sombori hurriedly walked out. 'Bai, Daiti has been taken to the hospital.'

'What happened?'

'What else, he was lying in the rain all night; he must have fainted. His coat and cap were soaking wet, and he had almost frozen in the cold. Somebody saw him in the morning and took him to the dispensary. He was given a few shots and taken to town in a car. They immediately admitted him to the hospital.'

Sombori clung to the pillar for support and slid down to sit on the floor.

'Bai, are you all right?'

'No, no, I just felt a little dizzy. How is he? How is he now?'

'He has come around. Don't worry, he will live. The doctor says that the cold has entered his bones. Menaka Baideu was in town; when she heard about it, she said that she would go to the hospital and come back tomorrow night with all the news. She asked me to tell you not to worry. I will go there myself in the morning. Don't worry, Baiti, he will be fine.'

Sombori was silent for a little while, then she said, 'Come in, Pradip.' She walked in, picked up an envelope kept amidst the bamboo planking of the wall, and handed it to Pradip—who had followed her in and was standing near the hearth.

'There's some money here. The boys had left it for me. I thought I wouldn't touch it. But take it, buy the old man whatever medicines or injections he needs. Should I...should I come along too?'

'Perhaps later, Baiti. Baideu will be back tomorrow…she will tell you everything.'

Pradip left. Sombori sat by the fireside. It began to rain again. Random thoughts played in her mind. What was wrong with her father-in-law? He had never fainted before. He was lying in the rain all night? Her heart trembled with an unknown dread.

The foxes began to howl again. Their howls were short, and then gradually, they became longer. There was an urgency in their cries… she tried to shut her ears. A hundred howling foxes seemed to have surrounded her. It was an ill omen, an ill omen for sure. No, no, there might be a leopard around, Sombori tried to assure herself.

The night deepened. Sombori did not know how late it had grown. She mechanically kept on putting one or two twigs into the fire, and kept it going.

Was that a car? She seemed to hear a car. Who was it at this time of the night? Yes, yes, that was a car. It seemed to be heading her way. Was it…them again? Let them come. She had nothing to lose now. Would they kill her? That would be a good thing. She would be free.

Has the car passed their gate? It seemed to have. She tried not to pay attention to the sound of the car. Was that the sound of footsteps? Somebody was coming, slowly, cautiously. She got to her feet and moved to the door.

Somebody was forcing the door. She tried to make out what was happening. Somebody had pressed on the door and, through the gap, put in a hand to open the bolt. It opened; the bolt opened up! Should she scream? But who would listen to her?

Somebody entered. Her eyes closed in the glare of a torch. The light from the torch danced in the room.

'*Buddha nahin hai*? (the old man isn't here?)'

A familiar voice. At the sound of that voice, Sombori's blood froze.

The man said a few words to somebody standing outside the door. Then closing the door behind him, he moved towards her.

'*Kya khabar hain*? (What's the news?)'

In the light of the torch shining on the ground, Sombori saw that the man, with a torch in one hand and a gun in another, was laughing. She remained silent.

The man advanced towards her. He then pushed her to the inner room. Leaning his gun against the wall, he placed the torch on the ground. In the dull glow of the fire and the scattered light from the torch, Sombori saw a shadow reaching out for her. She tightly closed her eyes. She did not resist. When the man pushed her on the bed, she lay like a log of wood. Anger, grief, pain, fear —her mind was wiped of all sensations. At one point, the man stood up and picked up his torch and gun. He took something out of his pocket and put it near the fire.

'*Phir kabhi aunga*. (I will come another time.)'

The man walked out. The car started. Lying on the bed, Sombori could hear the vehicle's fading sounds.

It was morning when she got up from her bed. A surprising indifference filled her mind.

She mechanically lit the fire and made herself some tea. Pouring the tea into the brass bowl, she started to sip it. There was a 10 rupee note on the floor. Sombori looked at it for a long time; there was no interest in her gaze. That gaze was as lifeless as that of a dead fish. She was unable to make out anything of that note. Without thinking of anything in particular, she slid the note into the fire. There was a flame of green and the note crumbled into ashes.

She got up, had a bath and then closing the door behind her, set out.

Mahajan was in his store; his account books open in front of him. He was calculating the interest on the money he had advanced as loans. When he saw Sombori, he said, 'Come in, come in, Sombori. Do you need anything? How is Daiti? You don't know, do you? You will surely get some news today. Mastarni is supposed to come back today. And a couple of other people too. I will let you know as soon as I hear from them. Don't worry, there are good doctors in town. He will be fine.'

'I have come for a different reason today', Sombori said.

'I see, tell me about it.'

'Do you remember that you had asked me to write something on a piece of paper? Will you write it for me? I will sign.'

'Really? Good, good,' Mahajan spoke enthusiastically. 'Okay, I will write it for you, and then you can sign it. I shall personally go to get it. But be careful, nobody should find out. Once I get the paper, I will see to your employment. With a little education, you could have become a teacher. Perhaps you can be an ayah now, or a gram sevika—but consider yourself employed. And forget about the feast; the people will bless you and take you back to the fold in the *namghar*.'

Sombori did not reply. She proceeded with slow steps to her house.

There was sound of running feet behind her. Panting, a boy ran up to her. She looked at his face; her heart missed a beat.

'He's dead, isn't he, Punakan?' she asked.

The boy somehow nodded, gasping for breath.

'When?' she asked, with a startling calm in her voice.

'Yesterday night.'

'Somebody had come on a motorcycle to Mahajan's shop. Apparently, Menaka Baideu and a few others are bringing him home.'

Once inside her hut, Sombori made straight for the fireplace. Absent-mindedly, she lit a fire. She sat immobile for some time.

Then she suddenly got to her feet and picked up a bottle from the shelf. Long ago, she had borrowed a bottle of rat poison from the headman; half of it was left. Taking the cap off, she poured some hot water into it. Shaking it, she swallowed the contents of the bottle.

But Sombori did not die. The rat poison could not kill her. She lived...she is still living. It is not known if the soldier came looking for her again. It is not known if the public took her back, or if she ever found employment. All we knew about her was that she was alive. She lived.

Partha, the journalist, looked at the boy sitting in front of him.

'Sombori is alive,' Partha's words sounded like a monologue. Pradip nodded his head. 'I remembered your address. It's been some time since I left the village. The police had made it impossible for us to stay. Please write about this in your paper.'

Partha bade him goodbye.

'Sombori is alive.' The words haunted him like the refrain of a song.

When he had sent Sombori's report to the newspaper, he had not expected it to appear on the front page in a bold headline. When he next spoke to his editor, he thanked him.

'It was an excellent piece, Partha,' his Harvard-returned editor spoke in clipped English. 'The senior editorial staff discussed your report; we decided that we could not keep quiet. A few stray incidents can actually erode the whole system of the country, and bring a bad name to our carefully-built democratic edifice. So, we decided to publish it prominently. We also contacted the military bosses. They have assured us that within three months they would identify the offender and court-martial him. You have done a very good job. You could perhaps expect an award for this.'

When he remembered his words, Partha had mixed feelings. Three months? Why? Three months had passed! He had not heard of any offender being punished. Perhaps, he had been punished. The system could not be so dumb. It will surely punish the culprit to keep its moral image intact, but it would be done discretely—without much publicity. The politics of power were truly sophisticated.

Would his paper publish the following chapters of Sombori's life? It would, if it helped protect the interests of the system. That was the truth.

What was Sombori doing now? Pradip had told him that the women of his village had begun a non-violent campaign against the military for picking up their husbands, sons, and brothers indiscriminately. Hundreds of women had surrounded the camps, and had blocked the passage of the military vehicles. The military had been forced to release the innocent men. Was Sombori there too? Surrounding the camp? Blocking army vehicles?

Drums and cymbals sounded when the cars made their way into the village. The women would start ululating; they dropped their work and rushed out…it felt good to think of Sombori as one of the leaders of this non-violent movement.

Forget it, Partha thought, Sombori is alive... That was the most important thing. Sombori is alive.

A JOURNALIST'S DIARY

I

Partha was sitting at the table, with a diary open before him. Sometimes he would idly scribble something, then cross it out and start again. He had been doing it for a long time. The page of the diary was filled with random sentences. On the unlocked typewriter on the table, there was a report yet to be completed. He had not been able to complete it despite struggling for a long, long time.

The fan overhead was whirling. Sitting like an owl on the chair, Partha absent-mindedly drew a series of crosses on the paper. Then, he abruptly wrote: Who am I?

The words swelled and rushed towards him.

'I am Sri Partha Choudhury,' Partha wrote in a tearing hurry, and continued, 'Today, I shall examine myself. Analyze and assess myself. To hell with it, such big words…'

He stopped writing and began to think. *I am a confused Assamese youth. Confused and timid. I don't have the courage to call something right boldly, or state that something is wrong for that matter. I am frightened by the danger that my secure position is due to my social status.*

Partha felt that the line marking off good from bad, justice from injustice, and right from wrong had become blurred lately. Days mired within everyday routine and triviality passed endlessly once he stood like a helpless spectator. He had no role to play. None whatsoever. What role could an individual have in such a situation?

He thought about the boys who had given up their homes and the familiar world; maybe they are immature and romantic, but the attraction towards such romanticism is, after all, the most natural thing in the world. Are you not attracted to it? Partha asked himself. *Could you really say with your hand on your heart that you are not attracted? No. You do feel the attraction, but you lack the courage. People like us can only imagine taking up guns, but lack the willpower to do so in actual life. Then what are we to do?*

People like us, therefore, try to prove how wrong, how mistaken it is to take to arms, and rationalize our unwillingness. And sometimes, from the opposite end, try to persuade someone else, that taking to arms in an unavoidable and a historical necessity.

The realization slowly pervaded his mind and he felt depressed. Recently, Partha had met a lady who was a former revolutionary. Nowadays, she was quite established in academic circles. While discussing the role of armed struggle, sparks of the past seemed to flare up again in her bright brown eyes. 'We always prattled about armed struggle,' her voice became thick with chagrin. She continued, 'Does an armed struggle take place in a vacuum? Without arms? It is not enough to chatter idly about guerilla wars. In order to build up a guerilla force, should there not be a disciplined, well-trained organization, training in arms and modern methods of waging war? We did nothing of that sort. We failed to build up the wide network of links within society that were so necessary. If someone amongst us spoke of procuring arms, we condemned him. No, we even regarded him as an enemy agent. Not arms, but the awakened consciousness of the people is the main force of the revolution—we believed in such slogans with such naiveté, and so mechanically, that we did not realize the importance of arms and training even while organizing an armed struggle. As if all problems were solved with the awakening of the masses…we instigated them to face the bullets of the army and the police with machetes, choppers, axes, and bamboo staves.'

'Well now, look at the Tamil rebels of Sri Lanka,' the lady's eyes and voice now seemed to catch fire, 'What an efficient armed force! Look how long they have been at war. Every act, every matter has certain laws. You will wage armed struggle without arms—how can that be possible?'

The lady stopped short of saying 'bullshit', Partha felt.

'Then why do you criticize the underground organization as militarist, as obsessed with arms?' Partha asked.

'There are only arms, but no politics,' the lady's voice grew sad, as though burdened with tormented memories. 'And we, the communist revolutionaries, had people on our side—the situation was appropriate. But we had no arms to take advantage of the situation. We did not appreciate the importance of arms while preparing for an armed struggle. Partha, there must be a combination of politics and arms, bullets and ballot. We failed. For armed struggle, an arsenal of arms is a must.'

Partha was impressed. That's why he had a vivid memory of it. 'Red Salute, Comrade, Red Salute,' he uttered in his mind.

Hell, am I becoming a cynic like that old blighter, Choudhury? Cynic! What is its Assamese equivalent? Is there any? What's the need for an equivalent, Partha thought to himself.

Partha had mentioned the former revolutionary before Choudhury.

Choudhury had closed his eyes. Contracting his eyebrows and making a face, he had burst out, 'There are few creatures as useless as Indian communists, what do you know? One group thinks that they have monopoly rights to armed struggle. Another group finds revolutionary elements even among gun-toting lumpen and go ga-ga. All crap!'

Partha had protested vehemently, 'You make light of everything. One can't stand such cynicism all the time.'

Choudhury had stared at him. Then he kept silent for a long time, as if he was lost in thought. I have touched a raw nerve today, Partha had thought.

Then Choudhury had turned towards him and spoken slowly, 'You might think my cynicism is a defence mechanism. That's not true. My cynicism, my jest, and quips—these are my protests. Do you follow, my protests?'

Choudhury was panting and looking at Partha with a questioning gaze: 'Is not the world heartless and treacherous? Only crooks qualify to enjoy it, isn't it? Do not thieves rule this world? And toadies who prostitute their intellect—aren't they recognized as true scholars? And can one man take a stand against it alone? Is he not helpless? Against the callousness of the world and my own helplessness, my indifference and cynicism are my kind of protests.'

He had then taken the glass of whisky and gulped all of it down at one go. Partha felt like shouting 'Bravo' at the end of the emotional lecture, but had kept quiet.

Snapping out of memories of this conversation with Choudhury, Partha's pondering came to a conclusion: Choudhury's outlook is utterly individualistic. There must have been a time when many people would have found it modern. But today, it would be greeted with laughter. And rightly so. Today, the most modern of men have come to realize that the true way lies through the man. Curtailing one's private hopes and aspirations, even one's freedom to some extent: therein lies the true way to life. Man has found the promise of fulfillment in the mass in search of security and solace.

II

Partha was seated in a temporary military camp. For the last three days he had been in the area of armed operation. How long could he prepare news on the basis of government press notes, half-truths, rumours, and interviews? The real events were taking place in the field that was the countryside. That's why he came out with the consent of the office.

Within the tarpaulin tent facing him sat the army captain. A young man with a lean, well-built figure. His chiseled chin was split by a dent, and the upper lip showcased brown whiskers. He had kept his goggles on. He was sipping his morning cup of black coffee. In a corner of the tent could be heard static from the wireless set. An operator was glued to it in a posture of rapt attention.

Partha looked out through a gap in the tent. The army had pegged the tents on the raised front yard of a rural office. There were paddy fields all around. Planting was over. The paddy fields had spread a carpet of green stretching all the way to the horizon. The bamboo grove and the lonely trees floating on the sea of green appeared to be like a mirage.

A bird cried raucously in the air. Following Partha's gaze, the captain's eyes also rested on the orderly rows of military vehicles, the tents of tarpaulin, and sentries at attention. Then he began to speak slowly, 'You are right. The insurgency is a political problem and it requires a political solution. The military should not be used to solve such problems. Our work is to guard the frontiers and meet the threat of external enemies. But we are bound to follow orders, and orders have come from above to quell disturbances. And we shall accomplish that work with as much sincerity as we can.'

'How?'

'What do you mean how? We shall search and catch every insurgent and crush their organization!'

'That's what I wanted to know. How are you going to search them out?'

The captain looked embarrassed. Then, he smiled and said, 'We have our methods.'

Partha did not go any further. He knew they had been briefed about the enemy before the campaign. What kind of enemy? The enemy was from 18 to 25 years of age—mostly half-educated, definitely unemployed, trained abroad, armed with deadly small arms, and ideologically driven to rebellion. Partha heaved a deep sigh. Where will they find such an enemy? They will naturally round up all the young men in the villages and try to squeeze information out of them. Choudhury had himself disclosed that information to him based on his experience. And it was the truth, as recent incidents proved.

'If you do come upon an insurgent, what are you going to do?'

The captain smiled, as if he had expected this question. 'We will use all the strength and wile at our disposal to catch him alive. He is more valuable alive to us. And if we cannot catch him alive, we shall surely kill him,' he said non-chalantly.

Partha shuddered. How easy it is to put out a man's life.

There was a hum from the wireless set. The operator with the earphone grew alert. He gestured to the captain to come over. The captain came with one stride to the wireless set and started speaking excitedly. Short, coded messages were exchanged, spreading excitement throughout the tent. A while later, the captain took off the ear phone and made as if to leave after telling the operator something.

'Please excuse me. I have to go somewhere.'

Partha's suspicions were aroused at once. He replied, 'Something must have happened. May I come with you?'

The captain thought for a moment and then said, 'OK, please come. But you won't write that you had accompanied us, right?'

Partha nodded his consent.

'Come, there has been an encounter,' the captain announced and hurried out. Within a couple of minutes, one jeep and two army vehicles began speeding along the rugged, potholed country roads.

On both sides of the road were rice fields with sweet Aijong rice in luxuriant growth. Sunlight sparkled in the water at the root of the plants. There was not a soul around. Partha was sandwiched between the driver and the captain, holding on desperately to the bar in front with one hand and the bottom of the seat with the other as the car rushed over the uneven ground with terrific speed. The jeep was followed by two other vehicles full of soldiers with cocked rifles and wireless sets switched on.

Suddenly, the captain tensed. Next moment, Partha also heard the sound—the sound of shots at a distance. The jeep was halted and messages were exchanged on the wireless. After covering some distance, the convoy came to a full stop and everybody jumped down. At the captain's signal, the soldiers bent double as they ran into the rice fields and took positions. Then they began to run in a single file. Partha was momentarily stunned at the rapid happenings, and then he, too, started following the soldiers.

There was the sound of gunfire in the distance again. And then, there was a village on one side and a jungle on the other. In the middle, there was a swamp bordered by clumps of bushes and plants. The soldiers ran on under cover of the bushes on both sides of the swamp. Not far from them was a clump of bamboos and thorny bushes. Suddenly, two young men dashed out of the bushes in the distance and tore into the jungle. This time, from all sides, the guns exploded. The jungle appeared to quake with the sound of guns. From the jungle, too, there was a burst of gunfire; the youths were returning the fire. The soldiers lay flat on the ground and kept shooting. Partha, too, lay flat. It was high ground, from which he could see both the paddy fields and the jungle.

He could now hear his own heartbeat. The race through the fields had tired him out; he was sweating too. He saw a few soldiers advancing through the fields on the farther side of the jungle. There was a sound of gunfire again from the jungle, and the soldiers at once became invisible; perhaps, they had ducked.

A terrible silence seemed to descend on the scene. Not a sound was heard anywhere. Then he realized that some soldiers had crept into the cover of the bushes close to the jungle. At once, there was a burst of gunfire from the jungle—a deafening roar of guns in return. The jungle started shuddering. Soldiers from fields on both sides advanced with tremendous speed towards the jungle, crouching low.

Partha felt his throat turn into a dry piece of wood. He longed for a little water, a few drops even, to wet his throat.

Suddenly, someone stood up near the base of the bamboo grove and threw something into the distance. Another youth materialized from behind the thorn bushes and hurled something again. There was a deafening explosion. The jungle was covered in a fog of dense white smoke.

Some people were scurrying away under cover of the smoke. The soldiers rushed into the fog, and there was a scattering of shots. The blue sky now had a streak of light-yellow smoke. The crows were flying helter-skelter in the sky.

When Partha neared the jungle, silence prevailed again. The soldiers stood here and there in groups.

The green shirt of the boy was drenched black; he appeared to be sleeping near the thorn bushes. One hand on his chest, the other hand flat on his side. In the hand on his chest, he still clutched a blue-green revolver firmly. He was very young; his unshaven beard was soft like fur. On his face there was an unknown, incomprehensible expression.

Partha stared at the boy as if mesmerized. A short while ago, he was a lively young lad; now, an inert dead body. Many random thoughts crowded his mind. His own paper—and others too—would most certainly portray a scene of romantic heroism. Well, not entirely untrue. Practically, a fight with the powerful army. They tried to break the cordon with intelligent tactics and did not run away like cowards. This young man had stood up to throw a grenade, and fired from a prostrate position again. It was then that the bullet struck him. Truly, a heroic death. But this corpse? This corpse lying without any sign of life with a strange expression on his face, the body that had been driven by adrenalin now lying like a log. No, there was nothing romantic about a dead body.

Someone nudged at his elbow. It was the captain. He brought him to another spot a little farther away. What was that? Another body sprawled there. The other one lay face down on the mud-and-water of the rice fields. Dead.

Oh God! One more dead body, Partha felt like shouting like a mad man. He suppressed the urge with great effort. He walked towards the dead body in a trance. The bullet had pierced the skull near the ear. Blood poured into the field, tinting the water red. The man lay on the riffle still in his hand.

At the captain's gesture, the soldiers came near and lifted the body from the field onto the dry land. This time, Partha had a good look at the face of the dead man.

Partha was thunderstruck. Bharat—it was Bharat Hazarika.

When he had met him for the first time, he had appeared so tall and robust. And now, he looked puny. His face had lost its glow. It was covered with dust and fatigue. His powerful arms had shrunken. The man looked so helpless in his casual attire of shirt and trousers. The man? It was a dead body!

And there was no question of a dead body appearing helpless. Suffering, pain, and age make a man helpless; love and dreams too. Now, Bharat Hazarika had left all of them far behind. A dead body has no such problems…

A series of pictures flashed through his mind like a movie. That blighted tree, the flooded camp. The handsome, confident youth standing erect on the raft that moved like a submarine under the surface of the water. Then he suddenly remembered another face—Prabhat's. Had he not suffered so much because of his past acquaintance with Bharat?

'They fought very bravely.' At the captain's words, Partha's mind reverted at once to the present. 'They died like heroes too,' the captain spoke in a grave voice. 'But there was no heroism in killing them,' he said, as if to himself.

Partha bade his goodbyes. The captain's jeep would take him to the camp, from where he would take his own car. But where would he go? He had to return to the village. As a journalist, it was his duty to collect all the available information. The captain nodded. 'We must perform our own duties,' he said.

Partha noticed two soldiers hauling Bharat Hazarika's body by the hands, probably for post-mortem. The vehicles had come close to the patch of jungle.

The captain shook Partha's hand as he said goodbye. 'You witnessed an encounter today,' he was trying to smile, 'You saw that not all encounters are fake.'

'True enough,' Partha tried to appear normal, then added, 'No encounter with death can ever be fake.'

III

After an hour, Partha returned to the village; it was sunk in an eerie silence. The sky, not long ago torn into shreds by gunfire, now appeared grimly quiet. There were knots of people here and there, under trees or in front of the houses; they appeared silent. If they spoke at all, it must have been in low, terrified whispers, not heard from a distance. Military and police vehicles were parked here and there on the road going through the village. Two dead bodies had been put in the back of a truck. Most of the assembled people were intently staring at the truck.

Two soldiers with automatic rifles were guarding the dead bodies. A little farther away from the dead bodies, a few military and police officers were talking earnestly. They were surrounded by armed guards. Partha parked his car a little distance away and came out. He looked around briefly. A few villagers were being questioned in a corner.

The huts in the village were all built with bamboo and thatch. Two or three huts, covered with two thatched roofs, met at an angle around a clean yard. Some had a small granary, a cowshed, and a small orchard. Near the gate, there were a couple of trees—grapefruit, Bokul, and Gulanch. There were areca nut trees with bunches of nuts and with withered leaves hanging on them. It was clear that the village was far from prosperous.

Partha approached the officers. They stopped talking and looked at him with undue hostility. The captain he had met earlier was also in the group, and he behaved as though Partha were a total stranger. As a journalist, Partha was used to such behaviour—rudeness, even insults. He could shrug these off casually. He asked, 'You have made a thorough search in the village. Could you find anything?'

A military officer advanced towards him. 'And who may you be?' he barked at him.

Partha identified himself and also showed him his identity card. From a corner of his eye, he saw two soldiers take their positions on either side of him. But the officer appeared mollified. 'You work with a very good newspaper. One of my relatives also works there.'

'Who is it?' Partha asked with genuine eagerness.

'Ravi Kapoor. He oversees the economy page.'

'Oh yes, I know him. In fact, we are close friends. I have been to his house in Defence Colony in New Delhi several times. He has a great collection of African music discs.'

A smile appeared on the officer's face. 'An odd character. I have often wondered why his wife has not left him yet,' he offered his hand to Partha, 'I am Lieutenant-Colonel Kapoor. Pleased to meet you. Please repeat your question, but all must be strictly off the record.'

'Off the record,' Partha grinned, and said, 'It is a wonder how a little personal acquaintance works like magic.' He remembered Choudhury. He used to say, 'Everything depends on links and acquaintances, you see. The personal touch is the most important factor.'

'This time, we had absolutely reliable information,' the colonel said, adding, 'We came to know that the leaders were going to hold a meeting here. It was correct information. We surrounded the area within one night, and you can see we have been quite successful.' He stretched out his hand and made a peculiar gesture, then said, 'But I would have been personally happier if they were caught alive.'

'Only two men held the meeting?' Partha asked with just a little touch of irony.

'There were more. Certainly, there were more. But they fled.'

'Fled?' Partha asked, with disbelief in his voice.

'Such things happen. But we found the two main leaders.'

Two corpses, Partha thought to himself. Turning towards the interrogation of some villagers at a distance, he asked the officers, 'What do you plan to do now?'

The officer followed his gaze. 'They are being questioned.'

'Will they be taken to the camp?'

'No. We have no hope of learning from them more than what we have already learnt,' the man said, with a mischievous smile on his lips.

Partha felt relieved; the officers were about to leave. The waiting vehicles roared into life together. The officer moved towards the jeep to climb into it. Shaking Partha by his hand, he said. 'Please do visit my camp. It's only a field camp.'

He mentioned the name of the place, then added, 'Not many amenities. We shall have a little chat. If chance permits, we shall have a drink together in the evening.'

The jeep rolled away.

Momentarily, he had a fleeting glimpse of a third person seated in civil dress between two armed guards. He had a black cloth around his head; only the eyes were visible. Their eyes met. Those eyes in the veiled head glinted suddenly. Partha felt as though the two eyes had recognized him. Whose eyes were those, like those of a cat? Partha had no way of finding out. But the expression in the eyes changed in a trice to a challenge. Partha was sure it was a challenge, and the impression stayed with him even as the jeep sped away.

Whose were those two eyes?

Those of a traitor. Yes, those of a turncoat—the informer who provided the 'reliable information'. That meant that the process of betrayal had already started. Otherwise a military campaign in such a remote village would hardly have been possible. A shiver ran down Partha's spine.

So, the process of corruption had already started. This is the tragedy of any serious revolutionary movement. Partha felt a bitter taste in his mouth. He stood looking at the departing vehicles. At the back of one of them were two dead bodies, the relics of exuberant youth… And at the back seat of one of the cars, there was a traitor seated in the darkness.

What am I feeling now? Contempt? Contempt for treachery? Is it justified? It is justified, to be sure. Although I don't support the principles and mode of action of the underground organization, my contempt for such cold, calculating treachery is quite apt. This is the natural and human response. But as a professional journalist, is it proper to entertain such emotions? I must be careful. My work is to disseminate neutral information—what is known as hard news. And in its interest, I must speak even to that bastard of a traitor. I must learn from him what prompted his slide down the slippery slope of treachery. What is it that drives people towards treachery? Is that also a human problem?

Partha had turned back towards the village. The scattered crowds of people stood in the same spots. Two youths stood among the middle-aged men. All of them had a grave expression on their faces. Partha introduced himself. The elderly people nodded.

'Was there a meeting in the village?'

'Who told you?'

'Well, the military officers.'

The people kept silent; their faces, expressionless. After a little while, one of them broke the silence. He spoke slowly, 'We came to know about the meeting only later. After all, such things take place secretly.'

'It seems some succeeded in making off?'

This time, many people nodded. A youth began to speak, 'They probably became aware of the army's arrival early in the morning. They at once split into two groups and moved off in two different directions. One group went off. The other took position behind a clump of bamboos.'

'They fought for a long time,' another added. The people were becoming more open now. 'From the morning till this afternoon.'

'And the other group?'

'They left long ago. Must be quite far away by now.'

'This group covered their retreat by fighting the military, and allowing them to get away.'

'Those two could have run away too, if they had so wished. But they did not do so in order to save their comrades. They are martyrs,' the speaker's voice became heavy with sorrow.

'Nobody knows where they held the meeting; it was not held in the village. They held it in the patch of jungle yonder. If some insider had not informed the army, nobody would have known.'

'Some insider?' Partha pretended surprise.

There was a subdued hum in the crowd. A little later, one of them said, 'Yes, one of their own fellows. He was with them until sometime back. He became a top leader even. He suddenly disappeared a few days before the military campaigns. Then we heard he had surrendered. It's only today that we came to know what he was up to.'

Someone shouted a warning and the voice broke off. 'He came with his head bound with black cloth?' Partha asked, then informed, 'I had a glimpse of him at the back seat.'

'Yes, it was the scoundrel himself,' one of the villagers said; others nodded their consent.

'What is there to say, they will fight among themselves and massacre one another now,' someone remarked in a bereaved voice. The elderly people slowly made their way home. A few young men lingered. Partha continued talking with them.

'Have you any idea who that young man with the black cloth around his head was?'

The young men fell silent. One of them said softly, 'He moved around in this region before. Some time back, he was promoted to a leading position. Today nobody could, at first, identify him behind his black hood. But when he started questioning some people, we knew who he was. His name is Alok. We don't know if it is his real name. He was a decent chap at one time.'

The young man sighed. Partha could not help but sigh either. He did not remember having met anybody with that name. But he was sure he knew the boy, and the latter also knew him well enough. He had a vivid memory of the glittering cat-like eyes, and the sense of recognition and the challenge in those eyes.

Yes, I certainly know him, Partha thought to himself, but he did not disclose it to the young men.

'Do you have any idea who the leaders were who escaped?' he asked the young boys.

'No. How could we? But the way their escape was covered, they must have been among the top leaders…those at the very top.'

'Why, the boy who guarded their retreat was Deep. Yes, I am sure it was Rondeep. Don't I know him?'

Partha was stunned.

Rondeep? Handsome, tall? With a mole on his chin? About six feet in height?'

'Yes, he was Rondeep. He did have a mole on his chin. Must be Ron. He is one of the very big leaders. Very brave,' One young man remarked.

Partha felt a sudden thrill. Rondeep! That could only be Ron, no doubt about it. Ever since returning from Shillong, he was totally absorbed in working for the outfit. Partha felt a lump in his throat; he seemed to have lost his voice. And Bharat Hazarika! Look at the coincidence! Whom did Ron guard in penetrating the siege of hundreds of soldiers? Bharat Hazarika and his companion had also lain down their lives in covering the retreat of those very leaders. Partha's heart began thumping in his chest. And like the scenes of a movie, hundreds of pictures flashed across his mind.

Bharat Hazarika must have been in charge of the meeting. He had chosen the site and made all the arrangements. And Ron was there with him. And the dead boy. The meeting started after all careful, secret arrangements. But there must have been a gap. Through that gap, the boy with his head covered with black cloth had come to know those things.

Suddenly came the news of the arrival of the soldiers. Someone on guard duty must have come rushing with the news to Bharat Hazarika; he must have then taken a quick decision in military style. The meeting was cancelled. The leaders must leave at once. His command must be obeyed by everyone, for it was his responsibility to ensure the safety of all. There was no time to waste.

'Ron, you take our leaders out through the patch of that jungle. It has no road running through it. Nobody could approach it quickly. And take a short cut through the village. Don't delay; you have to leave at once,' he must have ordered, thought Partha.

Ron must have followed the command without a word. With an automatic rifle in his hand and a few other youths, he had succeeded in taking the leaders out of the encirclement.

And Bharat Hazarika?

'We shall remain here. Do not stop even if you hear gunshots. You step out carefully and quickly. We shall soon follow you', Hazarika would have said, and bade goodbye to all. He had, in the meantime, made up his mind. He would not leave. He would try to arrest the progress of the military within the patch of jungle. Two of them against hundreds of soldiers. Not even two men—one adult and one teenager. Time, he must rob the military of time. He must delay them until Ron and his party moved away. He took the decision with a cool mind.

And that indomitably brave teenager? Did his heart feel a wrench when he looked at him while taking that decision? What a hard, rough reality.

Partha shook his head. The young men around him were saying something, but nothing registered in his mind. That young man with his head covered in black? Alok? Did I meet him along with Ron and Bharat Hazarika in the camp? Yes, yes. When I first entered the village on the way to the camp on that night of calamity; it was the same Alok who had first played host to me. It was he who had taken me along the sandy bed of the stream flowing through the swamp to the camp. When I was interviewing Hazarika and Ron, he was there too. And the day after, he had left the camp with

Hazarika over the flooded plains. Yes, it was the very same Alok who had come today with his head covered in black.

Partha broke into a sweat. His ears began to buzz with the excitement of the discovery. Hurriedly bidding goodbye to the boys, he got into his car.

He was returning along the bumpy road through the Aijong fields. It was evening; the sky had turned a golden colour as the sun set behind the distant bamboo groves. Like the colour of golden wine. Partha could no longer contain himself. In the midst of the vast solitude of the rice fields, under the golden skies, he suddenly started shouting 'Ron, Ron!' frantically.

A RIVER

I

Partha was returning again. The red Maruti, speeding over the smooth highway, seemed to quiver at times with a nameless dread. Trees, meadows, hills, and the sky flew past its windows. The harmony from a piece of Western music played inside the car. From the chaos of sounds, a tune was born—a wonderful harmony that rose out of the bosom of that chaos, uncertain at first, gradually clearer... The ascending tunes flooded the world... A tune born out of chaos, a tune born out of sound and fury... A tune that filtered through a chink and flooded one's consciousness. The awareness sent a shiver up his spine.

He suddenly remembered a shoal of fish he had seen in a clear river bank. The little brown fish with black stripes on their back that had suddenly become agitated by their slow swim, and how they had start darting back and forth in their small world, creating a nervous energy filled with anarchy. And from that mess, suddenly two or three fish had started swimming in one direction and soon, at the bat of an eyelid, the whole shoal reformed after them and darted off like an arrow. The shapeless anarchy got transformed into a pointed triangle...

An aim, an intention, was born. Scattered incidents occurred—bereft of sense, bereft of logic. They had spun out of all control. One could do nothing but watch helplessly... Strange! Uncomfortable! The military operations were on. Guns exploded. People died. Meaningless, tragic, and heroic deaths. A travesty of regulated laws—clever words defeated the purpose of the law. Encounter killings; kill an innocent half-wit and pass him off as a dangerous militant, and parade the body before a 'conducted tour' of the country's leading journalists. Theory sought to be created out of discredited debris of ideology. Rape. Tortures. Betrayal. A compounded anarchy that gained an unreasonable and unstoppable momentum of its own.

Obscene. He wanted to utter an obscene cry.

And in that collective anarchy was his journey of today, like that tune born out of sound and fury? Or, perhaps, like that school of fish? He was a mute spectator of a tragedy enacted all around him—the spectator as well as the scribe. Right, he was no more than that. And both the roles were passive.

'Can't you do anything? You are a journalist, you have medium, facilities. You can influence people; you can contain any situation!'—when she had first put the question to him, Partha had provided her with a readymade answer with a characteristic pleasant smile. He had several answers to this question; he chose his favourite, the one he considered the most intelligent:

'India is really two nations,' he had said. 'Two nations with two different people. The language of one is English, of the other is the different vernaculars. It is from this second India that the protests, resistances, and revolts are always born. But I work with the first India. That India considers all protests, all new thoughts as anti-national. If I have any role at all, it is really very small.'

'Your mental apathy has only limited it—your role is getting limited because you have not thought and reflected,' she had responded calmly.

Partha was taken aback by the girl's words. Lots of other people had asked him similar questions, and he had given his stock answers and grown accustomed to people accepting his answers. The girl's reaction startled him.

She was cleaning the glass chimney of an oil lamp. Dusk was falling fast; they were in the verandah outside. Darkness had started to gather under the leaves of the trees around. The crows had finished their flight towards the bamboo thickets in the distance. The fruit bats had started to appear. Somewhere, the petals of some night-blooming flower were opening, and the verandah was awash with their sweet scent.

They sat silently for some time. Her chimney-cleaning was over; she lit a match and touched it to the wick of the lamp. All her attention was engaged in the work she was doing. The wick sputtered to life and the flame of the lamp stabilized after some time. She reduced the flame of the wick and placed the glass chimney on the lamp. Slowly, a golden glow spread around. Flickering golden light and shade started to dance on her face.

'Did you try?' she asked without lifting her head. Then she added, as if to herself, 'consciously…'

Partha looked at her; she was looking at him intently. Many thoughts passed through his mind. He wanted to say yes, he had tried; that the country had come to know properly about the underground from his reports. That he had exposed the attempt to pass of the dead body of the village idiot as that of a dreaded underground leader; that he had exposed rape. That there were desired effects from his reports. But was it all that he could have done? Was it sufficient?

Partha held her gaze steadily, and slowly said, 'No.'

She looked at him for a long time. Then her eyes suddenly brimmed over, and two teardrops rolled down her cheeks. She lowered her eyes.

'No, no, please don't cry,' Partha said softly.

She wiped her eyes with the end of her chador.

Both of them sat in silence. It had become dark. The flowering shrubs at the end of the lawn had already dissolved into darkness. The trees had turned into statues of shadow.

'I don't know where my elder brother is, what he is doing,' she had started to speak. 'Have not seen him for such a long time; no communication whatsoever. Don't know whether I will meet him again. And because of my eldest brother, my younger brother is also unable to stay at home. Who knows, he may be picked up from home by the authorities randomly. Such things have happened, you know. The dead body of brothers picked up from home in the dead of the night were found lying in some isolated roads.

Partha looked at the girl. Her eyes shone with tears in the light of the lamp. Could he, could he really have done something, he asked himself repeatedly. He had done so before; he really wanted to do something. He constantly suffered from contradictions—he did not want any division of his country, yet, he wanted justice for his state; wanted utilization of the natural resources of the area for its rapid development; wanted the people to be able to chart their own destinies, and yes, within India. Without even going to the reasons and arguments of Chaudhury, he wanted all these from the bottom of his heart. So, he could never support secessionism from his heart. Yet, he had seen the mindless savagery of the anti-insurgency operations—the tortures, the denial of human justice and freedom—these, he could not support. And he saw no solutions to the problems.

What would he do? What should he do? It is so easy to take a side, whether right or wrong. This middle path is always so troublesome.

He had talked about this with Ron's father, too.

'That is the most difficult problem,' the old man had replied after thinking for some time. 'I always think about these things, too. You have seen the condition of our home. The eldest son left for armed struggle and we heard no more from him; the younger one also cannot stay at home. Then, our daughter also left for her post-graduate studies, and we, the old ones, are left alone at home.

The house has been raided many times already. When the soldiers saw the empty beds of the children, they asked, "Only you two old people stay here, then who are all these empty beds for? Surely, some people come here to sleep at night. " They do not like to believe when we tell the truth. So, I removed all the beds. Only after you came did we put on one of the beds. Ah, look at this… what you had asked and what I am saying. Words have lost their reason it seems'.

That was during Partha's first visit to Ron's house. He had met Ron suddenly a few days back then. That, too, was for a little time. From Ron, he came to know about his father's illness. He had not been able to go home, even after learning that. He did not know what his father's problem was. He was really morose when he had told Partha about it. Partha had then offered to go to enquire about his father's health. Ron's eyes shone with happiness. Unable to say anything, he had only clasped Partha's hand.

'Don't worry. I, myself, will go and enquire about his health. If something needs to be done for his treatment, I will see to it that it is done.'

Giving a hurriedly scribbled note to Partha for home, Ron had said, 'I don't know what to say, Dada. You have taken a load off my heart. Please do whatever needs to be done. Someone from us would meet you in Guwahati.'

Partha went to visit Ron's home a few days after that. He had a mental picture of Ron's home after hearing from him on different occasions; it was exactly like the picture he had imagined. Stepping on the verandah, he had the feeling that he had been here before… an uncanny feeling of déjàvu.

A girl came out; he could make out that she was Ron's sister. Slim, tall, and well-proportioned. A beautiful face, oozing freshness as if recently out from a bath. Large, magnetic black eyes. Partha asked about her father. The girl told him that he was not at home;

and that the mother had gone to *namghar* for prayers. She then asked him to sit in the living room and brought him a glass of sherbet. He sat there glancing around the room for quite some time. The girl did not come out again; though he could make out her talking to some women inside the house. The simple furniture pieces in the spacious room were tastefully arranged. A corner vase had a bunch of fresh flowers.

Ron's father hurriedly came in while he was sitting alone in the room; he was exactly like what Partha thought he would be. Finding Partha in the living room, he stopped short. He looked at Partha, and then to the red Maruti car parked outside the gate. With great civility, mixed with a tinge of doubt, he had asked, 'I am not able to place you.'

Partha introduced himself and held out the little scribbled note from Ron. In the meantime, the mother had also come and stood by the door. The father read the letter and silently gave it to his wife. It was nearly evening by then. The mother peered at the letter and read it in the weak light. She then looked at Partha with a strange look. Both father and mother remained silent. It was clear that they were buffeted by waves of emotions; they had nearly forgotten that Partha was standing before them. When the girl took the letter from her mother's hand, read it, and raised a hue and cry, only then did they came to their senses.

The whole household immediately made him a part of itself. They had forced him to stay the night with them. Partha told them about Ron, how he had first met him, how they went to Shillong together, and how, by pure chance, he had met Ron a few days back.

'My son, I can't express how happy you have made us with your visit,' she told Partha through her tears, adding, 'That he is well… how can I tell you how important that news is to us!'

Partha stayed with them for two nights. And that was the first time he had met Ron's sister.

She was called Bakul. With large, dark, and expressive eyes, with the thick truss of hair, with the freshness like that of dew on a wet flower—she was Bakul. She must have had another name, a ceremonial name; Partha forgot to ask it. For him, she was now only Bakul.

Today, he is coming back again...he is returning to Bakul.

While he drove on the highway, the memories of the first meeting came back to him like disjointed images.

II

'I cannot support their actions from my heart,' Ron's father had told Partha firmly.

Partha looked at the man—a tall man with a straight bearing, his words carried the convictions of a principled man. When Partha was talking about Ron the day before, he had heard every word with great attention. He had not uttered a single word, had not shown any kind of reaction, and had not asked not a single question. He occasionally tried to say something in favour of the struggle Ron and his friends were waging; he told him about his own experiences, and described the ghostly fire blazing near the oil wells. Occasionally, he had become a little emotional too. Even then, Ron's father did not say anything. Sitting cross-legged on the bed, he had hung on to every word.

The next morning, he had called Partha out to show him the garden. He started talking amidst his carefully laid garden, as if he was replying to yesterday's conversation, 'I want to live with some beliefs, Partha, even in the present difficult times.' He went on speaking, as if to himself... 'Young people like you would probably say these are old, outdated, and unnecessary sentiments. But after thinking long and hard, I have realized that if one gives up these beliefs, there would be no anchor in life. Life would cease to have any meaning too.'

They talked amidst the lemon bushes planted in neat rows. Partha suddenly felt that in that fresh morning, he had been transported into a silent and peaceful island. A few beetles were flying amidst the lemon bushes. Ron's father plucked out a lemon from one of the trees and gave it to him. 'Smell the fragrance,' he said.

The sweet smell of the fragrant lemon spread all around.

'I have searched many places for this sapling,' he said with pride. 'Nowadays, I am busy with this garden. Both the boys are not at home. There is no school after my retirement. This garden is my solace now.'

Partha looked at the man. He went on talking and, at the same time, tended to his plants—plucking a dead leaf here, straightening a supporting pole there. His voice did not have anxiety, and it did not lack the natural warmth. It was as if he had come to an understanding with his own soul.

'Why do you not support your son's path?' Partha had suddenly asked.

'I have no support for either their aims nor their objectives,' he had said, straightening up from bent position. 'There may be two reasons. First, I believe in unity and not in division; and secondly, I have faith in non-violence, obviously.' Pausing for a while, he spoke firmly again, 'I have no faith, no faith in violence at all. I cannot support it under any pretext.'

'What if the opponents take to violence, what then?' Partha had asked, a question which was only too familiar in these violent times.

The old man had replied with conviction, 'I am not a khadi-wearing salesman of Gandhism. I have not taken part in the freedom movement. We were quite small at that time. We have never done anything except shouting "Vande Mataram" in our village roads; I have but read few books of Mahatma Gandhi—

that, too, is negligible. But like the Mahatma, I also believe that in any given situation, active non-violence is more effective and powerful than violence.'

'Still? Even now? After so much has happened, you would still say that?'

'My belief has been strengthened, Partha,' the old man said. Before Partha's questioning gaze, he continued, 'When you speak about non-violence, the first impression is that it is the refuge of the meek, the weak, and the passive—at least for your generation. It is really not that way. Gandhiji never spoke about passivity, or about passive non-violence. That is where he differed from Tolstoy.'

Partha looked at the retired teacher with genuine surprise. His eldest son had left home to wage a war against the State. The other son could not stay at home for fear of reprisal either. Yet, the man, with his calm gaze on the green trees and shrubs in the distance, could clearly say, 'Have we ever tried to seize the initiative, to move forward with proactive non-violence? Haven't we taken violence as a short cut? But is there any short cut in society, Partha?'

They strolled through the garden. As they reached the end of the garden, bushy *Bijuli* bamboos that were planted on the edge greeted them. Beyond them, there was a very tall *Chatiana* tree. A pair of drongos were sitting in its tall branch.

The old man started talking in a firm voice.

'Partha, violence is not our tradition, non-violence; you know, non-violence makes people more courageous.' He remained silent for some time, then started again, 'One thing I acknowledge, Partha. I may not support but I respect one who could go on courageously in the path my son has chosen.' He then came to stand before Partha and, holding his gaze steadily, asked in a calm tone, 'I have not seen him for a long time. You have only met him recently. Does he have it in him—the faith?'

'How can you say doubts and suspicious don't arise, Partha-da. These are there, and is it not natural to have them? Everything is new,' Ron had told Partha once.

He had then met Ron after a long, long time. The contact had come from Ron's side. It was not that he had not tried to establish contact with Ron, but all his efforts had bounced back from a dead wall. After meeting him in Shillong the last time, a long time had passed without any news.

After hearing from Ron, Partha had gone out to meet him carefully on the outskirts of the city, changing buses several times on the way.

A small house atop a hillock. A government accommodation. From the window of the house, one could see the winding, busy highway below—day and night cars, buses, and loaded trucks plied continuously on that serpentine road. One could see a police check post, some empty coal tar drums, and sandbags kept on the edge of the road. The edge of the bamboo pole used as a drawbridge to stop the vehicular traffic was pointing upward to the sky; a sad khaki-uniformed constable stood near it. One could also see the rows and rows of long, tin-roofed houses of the Nepali dairymen. If the wind flowed this way, it carried the smell of cow dung and milch cow.

At the time Partha arrived, Ron was looking out through the window. They had embraced each other.

Partha had made many plans of what he would do after meeting Ron, but nothing came of these plans. Both of them inexplicably remained stiff for a long time. Ron had changed markedly in the meantime. He had become thin; the skin of the cheeks had stretched out thin over the bones. The lively, warm, and enquiring gaze of the past had been replaced with a cautious, restless look in his eyes. In place of spontaneity, there was measured and somewhat mechanical smile and bearing.

How must have Ron passed all this time? What had he been doing and where? Partha had heard that he was now a very important leader. He'd also heard that he had been outside the country, that he had received training—and himself had raised a new batch of trained soldiers. Partha has heard many rumours; how much of it was true and how much made up, there was no way of knowing. And Partha could ask, sitting in front of Ron, all of these questions.

'On the day of the encounter, I had just arrived at that place,' Partha started to tell Ron the whole story, who continued to listen to it silently. 'I came to know at that time that you had been able to come out of it successfully. After that, I had never even dreamed that we would be meeting like this again.'

Ron had simply smiled and nodded.

'Why did Alok turn out to be like that, Ron?'

'People do change, Partha-da,' Ron had replied briefly. After a moment of silence, he had continued, 'He had changed much before it actually happened. There were some troubles too. At the beginning we heard that he had been caught. For a long time, there was no news of him. Now, he has emerged in this new avatar... We had studied in the same school. He was two years my junior. He was really a good boy...'

There was a tinge of sadness in Ron's voice.

What could Partha ask Ron? What other questions? This was not an interview.

He looked at Ron again. He was looking out of the window intently. Was he thinking about Alok?

Alok—is he also not a result of this particular path, Partha thought to himself. A product of this secretive, dangerous, uncertain, and unfathomable journey? Once one steps on this path, there is no way to exit. Overcoming all the dangers, doubts, and suspicious on the way, can everybody complete this journey? People do change. If one does not want to travel anymore on this path, the only way one could go was the opposite way. If one wants to quit, does it automatically make one into a dangerous opponent? Does violence, counter violence, treachery, and tragedy always remain woven in the same thread?

A deep sigh came out of Partha's chest.

'Even when something is successful with violence, that success itself carries the seeds of further violence...do you understand that, Partha?'

When they were returning home after seeing the luxuriant kitchen garden, Ron's father kept on talking to Partha. 'Even when a new society is born through violence, violent repression becomes necessary within that society too. A society born out of violence is not much difference from a fascist dictatorship; there may be difference of degrees, but the essence is no different.'

After hearing the old man, Partha stopped for a moment. The eloquent words spoken by an old, retired teacher who had passed his entire life in teaching! Had they been spoken by some political leader or an intellectual, Partha would have heard them with one ear and expelled them through the other. But the heartfelt words of this unknown yet principled school teacher, who spoke them out of his studies and realizations, made Partha pause and reflect on whether it was such a principled stand that had helped him to withstand the storms in his life.

'Look here, Partha,' the old man had spoken again, 'With non-violence, there is always a moral force. Therefore, it touches the heart of the poorest of the poor in the society—it can awaken him, and so, at the end it always gives good results. Come, come, you don't have to take off your shoes, come.'

The old man nearly pulled up Partha into the verandah. In the back verandah near the kitchen, breakfast was being served; Bakul was carrying it out.

'You start my boy,' he had said.

'What about you?'

'I will take a cup of tea. I do not eat anything in the morning. I will have an early meal of rice. The habit of school days is still there. You start, please. Bakul, have you given him boiled sticky rice? Do you take that stuff?'

'I do,' Partha said. He was little worried though. He gave the fragrant lemon to Bakul. She smiled shyly.

Hearing Partha's loud sigh, Ron had turned back to him.

'What is the matter Partha-da?' he had asked.

'No, it is really nothing, I was just thinking about you,' he had replied.

'Don't think too much Partha-da, what is the use?' Ron tried to lighten the moment with a jocular tone, and continued, 'A chapter has ended, a new one is starting. Everything is new...have not I told you? Every small thing, we had to learn through trials and tribulations.'

'Abductions, kidnappings...these are also new things to be learnt, aren't they?' Partha suddenly assumed a sarcastic tone.

Ron just smiled. 'I won't argue with you about that Partha-da,' he had brushed aside Partha's sarcasm. 'There is no need for an argument. But have you noticed one small aspect Partha-da? Even a properly planned and executed small deed sometimes exposes the weakness, the vulnerability, and the helplessness of the government and the State so beautifully, no?' Ron's naughty joviality manifested in his tone.

'Are you joking?'

'Why?'

'You cannot hold innocent people's life in ransom and play cops and robbers with the government or the State.'

Ron remained silent for some time. His gaze had also become cloudy. He possibly did not see Partha sitting before him. After a pause, he had smiled again and said, 'Tell me one thing truthfully, Partha-da. When those kidnappings occurred…at that time, as a journalist, you had met many people, and must have come to know about people's reactions. Tell me, what was the private reaction of the intellectuals of Assam? Don't tell me everybody had unreservedly condemned it. Even if you tell me that, I won't believe it.'

A few days after the abductions, at journalist Chaudhury's house, and at his initiative, a few notable writers, journalists, and intellectuals had gathered. Partha was also present there. They had decided to issue an appeal to the underground through the newspapers to release the kidnapped persons. An appeal was drafted, approved, typed, and signed. After the signatures were over, everybody talked freely. Partha had then observed, with great surprise, the real feelings of many. They were secretly elated that the kidnapping incident had really exposed the hollow character of the State.

'If the captives are released now, the whole advantage would be lost,' one of them had commented, and the others had nodded.

That whole evening, Partha had sat silently.

Now, he replied to Ron, 'Is there any dearth of double-speaking people, Ron? People nowadays seem to have great enthusiasm for doing anything in the name of politics. Tell me, do you really think your actions are right? You are also into politics... How long will it continue this way? How long will you keep moving from country to country? Without building organization among the people, and without taking part in elections from time to time, do you think you can be a major political force?

'What other ways are open to us Partha-da, can you tell me?' Ron asked after a deep thought. 'Please tell me what you yourself think about it.'

'Do you know what I feel?' Partha asked, then continued, 'And these feelings have not come from observing your work alone, but also from watching the neighbouring underground organizations and from reading about such situations on a global scale...'

'What do you feel, dada?' Ron had asked.

'If you remain in the present way, you would always stay as a marginal force in the political scene of the country. You may be able to pull off a spectacular action from time to time, and may be able to help this or that political party to win or lose in the elections when they come, but you would never be able to lead and show the way to the society; you cannot guide the destiny of our people,' Partha spoke emotionally.

'And... What more, Partha-da?' Ron had asked.

'And because of your preset overpowering presence, no new leadership will emerge in our society in a normal way.'

Ron suddenly looked at Partha sharply. His eyes glistened.

'Partha-da, I can make out from your words that you have deeply thought about the problems, no doubt. But I also have a feeling that you are accusing us for all that is happening at the present.'

'That is not true, Ron,' Partha had replied equally firmly. 'I am not being judgmental about you. Who am I to do so? Your present work shall be evaluated and judged by time, by history. I am trying to think about all these things quite deeply the best way I can, so I am telling you all these. Look here, Ron, each generation probably gets only one chance to work for the betterment, for the transformation of the society, in its lifetime. In our generation, it is you who has come out to do something. You have vowed to make the supreme sacrifice for your convictions. And you have also paid a price for it already. I do not support your ways or aims but, from my heart, I don't want you to fail in your effort of transformation of the society for good. I ask you to think everything in a new way and find out new ways of acting. I have become quite emotional, you see, which is quite unlike me,' Partha laughed nervously.

'One can use these same arguments to get bogged down in the mud of parliamentary politics. Is it not so, Partha-da?' Ron asked casually, looking out of the open window.

'I do not know,' Partha said. 'My own feeling is that one has to work amongst the people, organize them, and lead them in a mass non-violent struggle to get justice. It may sound like a political cliché—no doubt, it is the toughest way, but its results would be long lasting.' Partha added, paused, and then continued, 'Is it as tough as it is made out to be? Is it really as difficult if you have a group of dedicated people?'

Both of them remained silent for a long time.

The long hand of the quartz clock on the wall jumped over the minutes with jerky movements. Partha possibly didn't have much time left to talk to Ron since much of the time passed in small, insignificant talk...silly enquiries about home, and lots of it passed in some abstract arguments. What else could he talk about with Ron? He became agitated looking at Ron, and said softly, 'So what after this, Ron?'

'I don't know Partha-da. We possibly will have to go forward like this. We hope that good times will come. We shall wait and prepare for that. What else can I tell you Partha-da? I can't say I have understood everything myself,' Ron's voice became quite sharp with honesty. 'I am telling you all this because I can speak to you. I feel like speaking to someone openly; I cannot talk about all these things with the boys who look up to me. They must not see my doubts and suspicious. See what a burden I have to carry?'

Partha nodded. It was as if they had understood each other anew.

The roar of the trucks rumbling by on the road below floated up to the silent room. Through the open window, the red earth path winding up to the hilltop could be seen.

Ron suddenly got up, stood before Partha, and said, 'I must leave this place now. After half an hour, you should walk out leisurely. We would definitely be meeting again, just like today. Yes, we shall definitely meet again.' Ron clasped Partha's hands tightly, smiled, and walked out.

III

'When you had met him, Partha,' sipping his tea, Ron's father had asked slowly, 'did you have the impression that they themselves have fully understood what they are doing? You have been meeting him for quite a long time…' His eyes glistened with the unstated desire of meeting his son once. 'I have not understood it, Partha, so much anarchy, this fratricidal war, these unnecessary deaths, this atmosphere of friends becoming enemies!'

'Who amongst us can claim to have understood it completely? When I think I am beginning to understand something, it appears as if it was false. The reality is that all of us are confused. What forces are driving us, and to where, we do not know,' Partha said, his words sounding like a confession.

Bakul brought a cup of tea. When she gave him the cup, she suddenly said, 'He once came to our house.'

'Who?' Partha asked, his curiosity aroused.

'Leave aside those things,' the father had said.

After breakfast, Partha had come out of the house. He was to return to Guwahati today; he had thought of leaving in the morning, but was forced to stay until lunch. Ron's father had improved considerably after treatment. He had had a bad attack of gastric, but now, he had recovered. Partha asked him to come to Guwahati for a check-up. He had merely smiled and said 'we would see'. Partha came outside and started cleaning the car. He thought about the conversation he had had at the breakfast table. He somehow did not want to leave this house today; he felt a strange attraction towards this home...

Bakul came out with some mouth fresheners in a bowl.

Wiping away the small fallen leaves of the Amla tree from the car, he started talking with Bakul.

'What did your father stop you from telling me?'

'He came to our house a few days back, Alok.'

'What did he have to say?'

Bakul proceeded to tell Partha of Alok's visit:

'Have you heard about Dada?'Bakul had asked upon seeing him.

'No. Dada is well. I have recently come to know about it. I just came to enquire how you are,' Alok had answered.

Bakul had remained silent. Her heart had started fluttering violently and her breathing had become distressed. A strange fear had descended over her.

'If you establish any contact or get any opportunity to communicate with Dada, tell him not come to these areas for some time; intense military operations are going on right now. And know one thing, no harm would ever come to him from my side,' Alok had said.

Bakul remained rooted to the ground like a person struck by lightning. There was nobody at home that afternoon.

'Bakul, I want to tell you a very important thing, hear me out,' Alok's voice seemed to quiver; that unrest transmitted itself to Bakul's heart and body...

'If Dada ever wants to return back to normal life or if he has to come back, then you just have to inform me. I would do everything that is required for Dada's return, Bakul... I would make arrangements for his safe and honourable return. Don't ignore these words, Bakul. Convey them to Dada, please.'

'What did you say then?' Partha asked Bakul.

'I froze like a stone. I could not even utter a single word. Tears started to flow out of my eyes. But, he had possibly misunderstood me. While leaving, he told me that he will definitely do this for Dada, that I should rest assured about it. He also added that if Dada himself didn't start anything against him, he will try to protect him as much as he can.'

Partha also became speechless after hearing this. He looked at Bakul; his eyes shone with a strange glitter. She was trying to hold back her tears by biting on her lower lip.

Trying to be normal, she smiled and said, 'I was very much worried at first, afraid even. Nowadays, I try not to worry much. And I can do it too; I am only worried about my father. He does not know how to speak, he just says whatever comes to his mind openly. When you tell him so, he would just say that his whole life he has spoken up, and clearly. That he has never harmed anyone, and that at this late age, he doesn't think he can change.'

Partha looked at Bakul; she looked like a fresh flower. Something gripped inside Partha's heart. Oh, what must have passed through this family, this girl. Their days have surely passed through uncertainty and unspoken terror. He suddenly felt a wave of compassion for her. She was standing before him with the bowl in hand, her long hair flowing down on both sides, framing her shapely face. In the light breeze, a lock of hair near her right ear was trembling from time to time. Partha suddenly had a feeling of a river starting to flow out from some deep recess within her heart...

You feel, sometimes, that a particular river is very beautiful. The river may not be very large. It may not have strong currents in it; still, in a calm, languorous way, it flows on the earth carrying the promise of peace. You then feel like speaking out 'this, this is my river'.

He wanted to extend his hand and touch Bakul's hair.

'Partha-da...' Bakul hesitated, 'Can't you stay back tonight?'

Partha started stammering...

'All of us feel so good that you are here. It is as if we are able to breath freely. Even though my father wants it very much, he will never be able to ask you to stay. Mother has told me to ask you.'

Partha casually patted Bakul's back, and said, 'Ok, I will stay. Let us go inside.'

The day passed in simple easiness, but some charge had come to the atmosphere. They were surrounded by a web of invisible electric current, and they became more talkative to be at ease. He talked the whole day with Ron's father and mother. And in the evening—when the mother had entered her kitchen to cook and the father entered his prayer room—they continued to talk alone in the front verandah. Bakul started her chimney cleaning exercise.

'When will you leave for hostel?' Partha asked.

'In about a fortnight, or maybe a month.'

'I will come again before you leave.'

Bakul had looked at him with her large eyes. She did not say anything. In her eyes, Partha saw the reflection of the lighted lamp.

His red Maruti was now gliding over the smooth highway. The music from his car's tape recorder no longer penetrated his consciousness. In his mind, he saw the image of a river.

After Partha had left, a turbulent river raged through Bakul's mind. One moment, her mind would fill up with an inexplicable happiness, only to become vacant in the next moment. Did she get something or did she lose something? Was it a dream or reality ?

Her family was no longer on her mind—every moment was filled with remembrance of Partha…his way of talking, his mannerism, the small nuances, the inaudible deflections in his voice…

She entered the room where Partha had stayed to make up the bed. In the morning, he had raised the mosquito net and tried to pull the bed sheet straight. The pillow still held the indentation where he slept. She started to make up the bed. Whose shirt was that in the cloth hanger? Partha's? Yes, it was Partha's—the shirt he wore the first day! Ah, he had forgotten to take it. Bakul stretched her hand and brought down the shirt from the clothes hanger. She lifted the shirt before her eyes with both hands. She gathered the shirt in her hands, brought it to her bosom and buried her face into it. A strong, unknown smell immediately flooded her nerves, her whole being. Partha's fragrance... Partha's.

In her cheeks and behind her ears, in her bosom and over her thighs, an unknown pleasurable warmth started to spread. She felt weak in her knees... She hurriedly folded the shirt. She then brought out a plastic bag from under the mattress and put the tightly rolled shirt in it. She took the packet and placed it between the layers of clothes in her wardrobe. She will preserve it, she will preserve that smell.

Partha and Bakul were sitting on the backside verandah. Mother had already entered the kitchen nearby for the evening meal. When in the evening Partha had suddenly appeared, everybody was happy and surprised at the same time. Partha talked about something that had brought him again to these parts, something to do with his job, but he himself was not convinced that his lie did not show through.

He had bought some stuff too. Near a bridge, the village folk were selling their catch; they would hold up the fresh fish to the gaze of the passing cars to entice them. When he had come laden with fish and vegetables, there was no other way but to ask him to stay. Although he had weakly said that his friend in the nearby town would be expecting him, nobody was ready to hear that.

When Bakul brought him a cup of tea, she said, 'I never thought that you would really come.' Before he could say anything, she had moved away.

'Your younger brother has not come home in between?' he had asked her.

'No, but he may in a day or two.'

The atmosphere gradually became easy.

In the evening, they were talking in the back verandah. Mother brought out a lighted lamp to them; in the evening, power was always out. Partha told Bakul about Prabhat.

'He was arrested under TADA Act and sent to a special jail,' Partha told Bakul, and continued, 'I was involved actively as long as the case was in court, and would meet his father frequently and enquired about his family. But after he was sent to the special jail, my connection got cut off.' Partha made a gesture of helplessness, then added, 'I failed to go to his home, failed to visit him in jail, too. I could have done that easily. Now whenever I remember it, I feel bad.'

'After doing so much for him, why didn't you go even once to meet him?' Bakul asked softly.

'I honestly can't say why I didn't. Really, I can't say. Now, I think there were probably two reasons for not going. The first may be that I, myself, was very busy at that time; events kept occurring in rapid succession then. And I also kept meeting his lawyer, Arup, who happened to be my father's junior, so I kept getting scraps of news from him. And the second reason may be that I knew Prabhat would be safe in jail, that he would not come to any physical harm and there would be no more torture... But all these are reasons that I have thought up now. It is a real bad thing that I have not enquired about the family at all. I feel really bad now.'

Bakul lifted her eyes. In the faint light of the dusk, her eyes looked like two deep green pools. She was touched by Partha's sincere tone, his open confession of his failings. Possibly, he is trying to lighten his own conscience by admitting all this so candidly before me, she thought to herself. She wanted to reach out and touch his hand, but she also knew she would not be able to do it. She just asked, 'Then, what happened?'

'For a long time, there was no news; I had not met his lawyer, Arup, either. Narayan Hazarika, his father, also did not come. One day, while I was sitting in my room at office, Narayan Hazarika came to meet me in an agitated mood.'

'What did he have to say?' Bakul asked.

Partha recounted the tale to Bakul:

'I have come to disturb you again,' Narayan Hazarika's voice was quite hesitant.

'Oh, hello! Please come, have a seat. What is the news? Please feel free and tell me,' Partha tried to cover his guilt with his jocularity. 'How is Prabhat? What news from the jail?'

'He is in jail same as before. But today, I have come for a different matter, I need your help...'

'What is the matter, please feel free...'

'You are a journalist; you must know lots of senior police officers.'

'Yes, I know some of them,' Partha said, immediately becoming cautious.

'After the declaration of general amnesty, they are releasing lots of prisoners...every day, one or two are being released... You, yourself, know about it,' Hazarika said.

Partha knew about it. After the declaration of the general amnesty, some TADA prisoners were being released. State had chosen to declare this amnesty at the same time as the intensification of military operations. There was a lot of controversy. And Partha was busy with the political aspect of the events.

'I have heard about it,' he said to Hazarika.

'You have to help me! This big help I need from you,' Hazarika nearly wailed.

'How can I help you?'

'The prisoners who will be released, their files have to be put up before the judge by the police. Only then would the judge pass the order for release, but...' Hazarika hesitated for a moment.

'Sure, sure,' Partha had said. He thought Narayan Hazarika would probably request him to ask some highly placed police officer for his son's release. Partha's reading was right.

'If you do not pay money, the police never prepare the cases for placing before the judge,' Narayan Hazarika then started to speak rapidly. 'I have come to know about it from a credible source. You know lots of people. Please help me to pay the money at the right place to put up the case before the judge, please. I have collected 5,000 rupees.'

'Wait a bit, Hazarika, don't be impatient. You don't have to think about giving money to anyone now. Wait, I know a very good officer, he is quite close to me. Let me call him.'

Partha telephoned the officer before Narayan Hazarika. The officer assured to help.

'Hazarika, you go and meet him now. He has agreed to meet you now, and he has assured to help you all he can. It will be done, it will surely be done. Don't worry,' Partha reassured Hazarika, accompanying him to the door.

'Then what happened?' Bakul asked.

'Two days after that, I had to go to Delhi. I was called from my newspaper office. I stayed there for quite a few days on this or that work. After getting back from Delhi, I got busy here. More time passed, and I forgot to enquire what had happened. I remembered Prabhat after nearly two months and, one Sunday, I went to Hazarika's house.

'Hazarika, how are you?' Partha had greeted Hazarika, who was reclining on a couch in the verandah.

On seeing Partha, Hazarika had risen to greet him with a wide smile, 'Please, come in!'

'Prabhat has been released! You never ended up giving me the good news! The police officer did help you, didn't he?'

'He did, he did,' Hazarika made Partha sit in the comfortable couch in the verandah. 'He is a very good man, a real good man. After you had spoken to him over the telephone that day, I went and met him. He patiently listened to everything. Then, before me, he phoned one of his subordinate officers and sent me to meet him. That officer was also a very good officer. After hearing me out, he himself took initiative and searched out Prabhat's file. Within a week, all necessary processing were completed and, on the 10th day, he was released. Only, it costed me a little more… 7,000 in place of 5,000.'

Narayan Hazarika brimmed looking at Partha, 'His early release was possible only because of you.'

Partha became speechless. After a while he smiled and said, 'At least, the boy came back home after such a long time!'

Narayan Hazarika slowly turned towards Partha and spoke in a strange tone, 'Did the boy really come back home?'

'What? What are you saying?'

'Come, come with me,' Narayan Hazarika nearly dragged Partha.

Between the main house and the rented house, there was a narrow courtyard about eight feet wide. In that, there was a bent guava tree and in flower posts around the wall, untended plants, clumps of weeds, and a few scattered bushes. From the outside, the courtyard was not seen.

In that courtyard, under the bent guava tree, stood Prabhat—alone. He was wearing a pyjama and a half shirt. The hair was combed tidily, but his eyes had a troubled, lost look in them. From the courtyard, through the Oleander bushes near the wall, he was looking intently at the small stretch of the front road that could be seen. There was no reaction when his father and Partha came and stood at the edge of the courtyard. No reaction, none at all.

'The whole day, he stands outside like this,' Hazarika started to whisper in Partha's ear. 'Does not want to go inside. Whether he is afraid or for what other reason, I don't know. At meal times or whenever he is called, he comes inside for sure...but after sometime, he goes out again and stands like this. He is very much frightened of the sound of a motor car. Sometimes, he does not even want to stay inside at night either. He does not sleep; he tosses and turns in bed. Only after a long time does he fall asleep.'

Partha went forward and stood before Prabhat. Looking at his expressionless face, he smiled. Then he embraced the boy, and said, 'Prabhat, we have met after such a long time. Come, let us go inside. We have lots to talk about.'

'Will you interrogate me?' Prabhat asked in a voice devoid of any human warmth.

Partha felt as if his body had turned into stone.

'No, no,' Partha blurted out in an alarmed tone, 'We will only talk.'

His mother came out through the kitchen door, 'Prabhat, come in,' she softly said. Partha guided the boy towards the kitchen door. He turned to look over his shoulders to the road outside, and then obediently went into the kitchen. His mother poured something in a glass for him. And like a young boy, he drank the milk.

Partha returned like a sleepwalker, following Narayan Hazarika to the front verandah. Hazarika was continuously speaking in a dull monotone.

'I have tried a lot, you know, but I am unable to dispel his fear. The boy is finished, you know, totally finished. He has to take medicine regularly to control his high blood pressure. Yes, I had him checked up, lots of tests were done. Shown him to many doctors. One of them really frightened us by saying that his kidneys had gone bad; he had passed blood in his urine. They say it was due to the severe beatings he was subjected to. Now, they say the kidneys are all right. Ah, what did you ask? His studies? He says whenever he opens a book, he feels a great pressure in his brain. He cannot read. Now I have given up thinking about these things…his studies. Fate—it is our fate. I have employed shamans, *ojhas*—all sorts of people. They have exorcised him. I brought him charms and talisman, but nothing seems to work. Now, we have to put on the light only when he is not aware. He seems to cower when he sees a light switch being put on; he gets startled when an electric bulb lights up. Eating? It is like he is giving up eating. His mother nearly force-feeds him. Today is Sunday, I always used to go out to buy mutton on Sundays, and I would search and buy the best meat. Now, I don't feel any urge to go to the market. The younger son goes sometimes to buy some skin and bones in the name of mutton. Lately, I have started taking him to a renowned Psychiatrist of Bharalumukh, one Dr Phookan…'

'I thought that in jail, he would not come to any physical harm... But I never even once thought about his mind...' Partha said sadly.

Bakul was looking at him with wide eyes. The deep green ponds now brimmed over. She started to sob silently. Partha also felt a choking sensation in his throat. Bakul's mother also came out from the kitchen and sat near them. In the gradually thickening darkness, all three of them sat silently for a long time.

IV

Today, I will have to go. That was the first thought that struck Partha when he woke up in the morning. He kept lying on his back for quite some time. He reached out to the window near the bed through the mosquito net and drew the curtain. The sun-washed morning leapt into his bed immediately; he blinked his eyes in the bright light. Rubbing them, he tried to listen to any sound from the kitchen. Yes, he had heard rightly. Soft clinking sounds from the kitchen indicated tea being brewed.

Bakul must have had her bath already. Drops of water must be hanging in her hair here and there like crystals.

It was so strange—what had happened to Partha so suddenly after meeting Bakul. Quite shamelessly, he had come all the way again to meet her before she left for the university hostel. Now, she said she would be leaving only after a fortnight!

And he will have to go back today.

Suddenly, there was a commotion in the house. Bakul's voice could be heard, 'Ma, ma, Dada has come!'

Partha was startled. No, it can't be Ron. Her other brother was supposed to come, might be him. Partha got up from bed and started dressing.

'You have come!' Partha heard the father speaking, 'You have brought all your luggage too. What is the matter?'

Partha did not hear what the boy answered.

He came out hurriedly from the bed room.

The boy was startled at Partha's sudden appearance. Except for the height, there was not much resemblance between the brothers. He was quite thin, and soft.

A quite long, and at times embarrassing, introduction ensued. When it was over, the boy shifted his glance from Partha to his sister; Bakul passed it off nonchalantly. The unspoken exchange did not escape Partha's notice.

'Dada, I can't express how happy I am to meet you in our home. I never imagined I would meet you like this. I have only read your articles in the papers!' Bhaity spoke warmly.

They all sat on the table in the verandah with cups of tea in their hands.

'Why did you come back with your belongings? You were supposed to come only for a day…' the father, itching to ask it for a long time, launched. Everybody looked at Bhaity.

'One cannot stay in that place any more. The fight between these two groups has reached that place too. That oil town is a very small place. Within a few days, everybody comes to know everybody,' Bhaity spoke rapidly.

'But your job?'

'That was only a private job. The person I was working with told me that I had better move out.'

Everybody became silent.

'He had given me a letter,' Bhaity continued, 'addressed to an engineering firm in Guwahati. They need civil engineers. He had talked to them the over telephone also. I will go and meet them in Guwahati…I will get the job.'

'You must leave today then. You need not stay here for even one night; trouble here is only on the increase,' the father said forcefully. 'Alok has started living in Guwahati now. From time to time, he would come down with his group and roam the villages with armed forces in tow. He creates trouble, even beats up people,' Bakul said excitedly. 'Until now, he has not killed anyone as far as I know.''So much change in such a short time?' Partha asked.

'Nobody knew before where he stayed or what he did. Only now have people come to know.'

'Father, please do not worry,' Partha suddenly said. 'Bhaity would go with me to Guwahati today. If he gets that job in the builder's firm, well and good. Otherwise, it won't be very difficult to get a job for a civil engineer in a private firm. Till then, Bhaity will stay with me in our house. We have quite a large house, so it won't be any trouble.'

Partha did not look towards Bakul, but he would never forget the look of relief and gratitude in the eyes of the parents.

The father then started hurrying, 'Finish your cooking early, they must reach Guwahati before night falls,' the old man said to his wife.

He turned to Partha and said, 'You are getting enmeshed in our problems… I feel bad about it, I am ashamed. There should not be any trouble in your home, I cannot allow that. Bhaity has said he will stay with some of his friends. You drop him there. He has studied in Guwahati; it won't be difficult for him. You please just keep an eye on him…'

Partha listened to the old man and kept smiling; he did not say anything. At one point, Bakul also came and told him, 'Let Dada stay with his friends. Do not keep him at your home. Don't force him, because if you do, he would do whatever you say to him.'

Taking leave was always difficult. Especially when lots remained unsaid. Partha was silently packing his small bag and thinking his confused thoughts. What after this? What should he do now? And Bakul?

Bakul came into the room.

'Ready to go?' she asked.

'Yes, getting ready,' Partha replied like a fool.

They stood facing each other for a moment, and in that silent period their eyes had become eloquent. Like monsoon clouds changing their colour fast, their gaze changed fast…

'Last time you forgot something.'

'What?'

'A shirt.'

'Oh, was it here I left it? I couldn't figure out where I had lost it. Where is it?'

'I will give it back on one condition.'

'What condition?'

'Give me the shirt you are wearing in exchange.'

She held out the shirt had kept tightly wrapped in a bag. Partha looked at Bakul. A river started flowing out from some secret recess of his heart. And the river started flowing through his being—his mind—a turbulent, foaming, swirling river with gulls flying over its banks.

He gazed at her hair with its parting in the middle...the thick trusses going down on both sides of the face. A faint smell of wild flowers wafted from her hair.

Partha took off his shirt, wet at places with sweat, and held it out to her. She lifted her eyes just for a moment and, after a glance filled with a mysterious electric charge, dropped them down. Leaving Partha there, she then went out of the room.

'Partha-da, I am ready,' Bhaity shouted from outside, pulling Partha out of his stupor. He hurriedly came out of the room.

Taking leave from Ron's father and mother, he went to the car waiting under the *amla* tree. Bhaity sat on the passenger's seat; the back seats were filled with his bedding and suitcases. He looked quite happy.

Bakul was standing in the verandah. Partha lifted his hand and softly gestured a goodbye. She didn't say anything. The car roared out of the compound.

V

'You are a Marxist, aren't you?'

'My brother has told you that, hasn't he!'

Partha started talking with Bhaity in the car. For a long time, he had nearly driven in silence—deep in his own world of thoughts. After a while, he saw that Bhaity had fallen asleep. He had come in a night bus, and immediately after lunch, had set out on this journey. It was natural for him to have fallen asleep. Partha was thankful for it; he wanted to be alone, so he could collect his thoughts. Images, words, memories kept floating into his mind in a disjointed way. All these seemed to be apparently without any link; yet, there was a link—a secret thread that had passed through all these ostensibly separate things. And only he was unable to uncover the link.

At one point, he reached his favourite dhaba. Parking the car under the big Peepul tree, he looked at Bhaity. Yes, there was a definite resemblance; the similarities between him and Ron came into view when Bhaity was asleep.

'Bhaity, get up. Let's have a cup of tea.'

Sitting on a bedstead in the shade of the Peepul tree, he had started talking to Bhaity.

'What do the Marxists say about your brother's insurgency? Partha asked Bhaity casually, mainly to start a conversation.

'The Marxists are divided—into different parties and groups,' Bhaity had answered. 'Every party has its own evaluation. But all of them are united in one point—that this insurgency is mainly a nationalistic movement. Whatever our Dada and his people may say about socialism, essentially, they are nationalists. But that's the extent of the common ground between the two groups, Partha-da. Some say their nationalism is ultra-nationalism—meaning, it is reactionary. But this reactionary war must be opposed in every way. This kind of theorization often leads Marxists to a position of inadvertently supporting the violence and terror used by the State to suppress the insurgents. A vicious circle of good-hearted intentions that is eventually bathed in blood, if you ask me.'

Partha was surprised to hear Bhaity's words. He had probably not expected this kind of analytical response from him.

'Well, what do the others say?' he asked.

'The second camp holds that such nationalism has a democratic aspect to it. It's not that this is only a struggle against oppression, neglect, and injustice; and so, it does have a progressive possibility. Therefore, it is necessary to work with it to a certain extent; in certain issues, for example, in the question of human rights, or, opposing state terrorism, etcetera. One has to influence such struggles in this way, and work for its progressive transformation. Then there are several other camps that are yet to come to a firm decision, so they are speaking whatever suits them at any particular moment! They swing like a clock's pendulum to this and that camp as and when it suits them. You already know these things, Dada.'

'You have put this across very clearly,' Partha said, adding, 'It is clear then, that the Marxists would not take part in this struggle.'

'The main thing is what you mean by taking part, Dada,' Bhaity said, looking at the tea in his glass. 'If by taking part you mean leading the struggle, I think no Marxist would do that. Although they are well-equipped to do so, they wouldn't provide leadership to a nationalistic struggle. Their task is to build socialism through class struggle, not to build a new Nation State. However, it's not that there are no exceptions to this rule. If a country is subjugated by a foreign power, then the Marxists lead the national liberation movement with its associates and, parallel to it, they try to effect revolutionary transformations in the society. If you put it in general terms, Marxists support the democratic and progressive national aspirations of a people.'

Partha nodded. Bhaity really could speak convincingly.

'All these are theories, Partha-da. The main problem is putting these into practice.'

'And that's what is not happening.'

Bhaity nodded.

They got into the car again and continued their journey.

Partha looked at Bhaity; he was looking out of the car window. The dark green and luxuriant tea gardens were rushing past. Suddenly, Partha had strange mixed feelings towards Bhaity. The thought that Bhaity was Ron's brother, Bakul's elder brother—a sharp and an intelligent boy, was indeed something. And if he happened to marry Bakul, then Bhaity would become his relative—he will then be called brother-in-law! Partha so liked the idea that he felt a sudden tender warmth towards Bhaity.

'Your father so firmly believes in non-violence, but both of his sons have chosen the path of armed struggle,' Partha commented.

Bhaity smiled. When he smiled, he looked more like Bakul. He started jocularly, 'Marxism automatically does not mean armed struggle. Mass organization, mass movements, workers' movements or, in one word—class struggle, is its aim. Yes, the question of armed struggle may come in at some time, it probably would, but armed struggle for its own sake? That cannot be. I think people like my brother have understood it that way only.'

Partha turned to him and asked, 'Do you really think they have understood it like that?'

'He had argued about it so much, scolded me…even hurled expletives at me! Now, he has jumped into a nationalistic armed struggle. But before that, when there was a big student agitation against the foreign nationals, he was nearly inactive. I was active then; I opposed it, and for that I had to face humiliation—got beaten up once too! But he was totally detached. Even my father was part of that agitation.

'Your whole family is really interesting,' Partha said.

'I also think about that.' Bhaity concurred. 'Our father is a Gandhite idealist; elder brother, a gun cultist; me, a Marxist; and mother, a sentimentalist,' Bhaity's humour sounded just like Ron's.

'And Bakul?' Partha asked a little hesitantly.

'Bakul? Oh, she is a worthless liberal humanist!'

Both of them laughed out loudly.

'What does she say about it?' Partha couldn't help asking.

'Do you know what she says? She says that all our ideologies will die and disappear, that only her liberal humanism will endure in this world.'

'What? She speaks like that?' Partha asked, surprised. 'Does she say that seriously or just for fun?'

'She is very serious; she reads a lot too. She does not speak without thinking, that's for sure.'

Partha was enchanted. He felt waves rising within his bosom.

'What is she majoring in at the university? I never ended up asking her...' Partha said.

'English Literature.'

Partha kept silent. He was always in awe of people studying Mathematics and English. The first was probably because he was a raw egg himself in Mathematics; and second, possibly, because many brilliant people whom he met were literature students. Now that he had discovered a new dimension of Bakul, he felt inwardly happy.

'How is your Marxist revolution taking shape right now?' Partha asked Bhaity flippantly.

'Two sons from a family like ours can't have the luxury of chasing revolutions, Partha-da,' Bhaity had suddenly become serious, and Partha, mum.

The sun was already starting to set. After driving for so long, Partha felt a little tired. There was a forest inspection bungalow a little ahead. He used to drop in there occasionally. A chowkidar lived behind it, and he made fabulous tea. He drove to the bungalow and decided to stop for rest.

'Oh, what a beautiful place,' Bhaity remarked upon arrival.

It was surrounded by plantations of tall teak trees. Through its dark shadows was the driveway to the small bungalow. The car came murmuring over a carpet of fallen teak leaves and stopped before the gate. Partha sounded the horn; he saw the old chowkidar coming out of his quarters at the back. Partha and Bhaity came out of the car and stretched their bodies. They came down the wooden steps to the wide verandah of the two-roomed bungalow. The chowkidar came and opened one of the rooms.

'Can we get tea?' Partha asked.

'Sure, I will make it right away,' the chowkidar replied.

Bhaity sat down in a comfortable cane chair in the verandah.

'Partha-da, would you mind if I have a smoke?' Bhaity asked.

'By all means, go ahead! You have your smoke, I will go and wash up,' said Partha, and left.

When Partha came back, it was Bhaity's turn to go and freshen up. Partha made himself comfortable in the other cane chair, and lit a cigarette himself. He stretched out his legs over the cane table in front, and waited for the tea to arrive.

From the verandah, one had a panoramic view of the rolling hills, shadowy teak forests, and red-earth path winding down in the distance. There was a light breeze, and the large teak leaves rustled in it. The sun had become softer. Partha was silently taking in the beautiful evening when he saw two cars coming at great speed by the forest road towards the bungalow. He immediately became alert. Without thinking, he placed his chair before the door of the room where Bhaity was in such a way that it would be difficult to enter it. He then shouted, 'Bhaity don't come out of the bathroom. Stay inside. Somebody is coming.'

Both the cars entered the compound of the bungalow at great speed. A Maruti van with tinted windows screeched to a halt just in front; the other vehicle, a gypsy, also stopped nearby. Before the doors of the van could open, three-four boys leapt out of the gypsy; they carried automatic rifles and carbines. A few police constables also got down with their guns. Before Partha's surprised eyes, the doors of the van now opened on both sides, and two armed youths got down from it. They were followed by a man who got down slowly. He carried no arms.

The old chowkidar came running from somewhere, opened the door of the other room and gave a bowing salute. The man came to the verandah and looked at Partha.

'Oh! Alok!' Partha's blood froze. He had a premonition of it when the cars had come rushing in.

The cat's eyes became alive. He came towards Partha and said very softly, 'Dada.'

Partha had stood up in the meantime.

'Meeting you after a long time, Alok!' Partha said, extending his hand. And in Partha's grip came a soft, flabby, and dead hand. There was not the slightest inclination of the other hand to grip his hand.

Partha felt a chill creeping through his back.

'In fact, I wanted to meet you, Alok,' Partha said.

'Why?'

'I want to ask you some questions. I want to know so many things, you know. I want to interview you—purely as a journalist.'

The cat's eyes became dead.

'Interview me, Partha-da? We are now no longer in a state where we can give interviews to the media. Still, you are welcome. Come, we can surely talk,' Alok said in an easy manner.

'Now, I am in business. Timber business to be precise, and I stay in Guwahati now,' Alok added.

He then brought out a small notebook, wrote down a phone number, tore the page, and gave it to Partha. 'Give me a ring when you want to come.' After a pause, he added, 'Let me freshen up a bit. You take rest, please.'

Dragging his feet on the floor lazily, Alok went in to the other room.

Partha looked out; his eyes stayed glued to the luxuriant teak trees. How old were these trees? Surely, at least 50 years. How much more life did these trees have? The armed guards were looking at him from the corner of their eyes. The barrel of their guns was hanging down, pointing to the earth. The police were looking insolently towards the verandah.

Alok came out of the room. The guards stirred a little.'Dada, I am leaving. When I come this way, I usually come down here.' When he saw the chowkidar waiting in the verandah, he said to him, 'Are you giving any tea to Dada or not?'

He saluted and informed Alok that tea was being prepared.

'OK, Dada, so long. We shall meet again,' he said, and started towards the van and got in without looking back. Two guards also leapt in from both sides; the doors closed loudly. Within a few seconds, raising a storm of dust and fallen leaves, the cars sped out of the compound.

Partha collapsed into the cane chair. Bhaity finally came out of the room; there was an anxious look on his face.

'It was Alok, wasn't it?' he asked.

Partha nodded.

Both of them sat silently in the verandah. The old chowkidar brought them two cups of steaming tea.

'This Alok fellow comes nearly every week,' the chowkidar said as if to himself. He continued, 'He usually stays the night when he comes. Today, he didn't, because you are here. Brings lots of friends, police folks, and other officers. And they bring lots of food too. They cook it themselves. He hardly takes any solid food nowadays.

Neither of the two men really wanted to hear the chowkidar's chatter. Without encouragement, he became silent. Drinking their tea in silence, Partha and Bhaity came back to their vehicle after tipping the chowkidar. While leaving the verandah, Partha looked at the tall teak trees standing proudly one last time. With the onslaught evening, darkness had started gathering under their leaves...'

THE WHIRLPOOL

I

He had not been home for a long time. Had not seen his village, enmeshed in the memories of his childhood and adolescence, for a long time.

He did not know whether he would ever be able to return to his village; he just did not see any possibility of that.

When he remembered this, he felt his mind shutting down. He felt an uneasy pressure on both sides of his forehead—it was as if an electric bolt had shattered all thoughts inside his brain.

They had caught him in a deep pit.

Yes, a deep pit—a hole in the earth about 10-foot square. It was covered with lattice made of stout, whole *bhaluka* bamboos. From the bottom of the pit, through these lattice small squares of the sky, tips of tall trees and the bright hanging stars at night could be seen. When it rained, water dripped through the cover and filled the bottom with mud and dirty water.

That pit was a prison.

Many people passed through that pit. Prisoners! They hung, as if suspended midway between the sky above and the mud below; they were not hung by any rope in the pit though. But once anybody was put in that pit, their condition was like that of a soul suspended between life and death. Once a day, salt and rice was lowered into the pit in a tin hung by a rope; in the earthen pitcher kept at the bottom, water was poured from above. From that hell, some returned to life and some vanished without a trace.

They caught him in that pit.

A spacious room, sparsely furnished. The windows had thick iron bars scaffolding it. In the centre of the room was a bed covered with an expensive foam mattress. Above it, a fan that spun at full speed all the time. There was a table and a chair on one side, a reclining couch and a clothes stand near the door to the attached bathroom, and a huge wooden wardrobe on the other side. The floor was made of black cement. His long summer days passed in that suffocating room. He passed the endless summer afternoons tossing and turning in the bed, clad only in a pair of shorts. He sometimes got aroused in that suffocating heat and became restless too. And quite frequently, this phase ended in an unsatisfying ejaculation. The tiring wait in the whirring of the electric fan started again.

Yes, that was a period of waiting.

He used to move around in a new gypsy bought from someone. Powerful engine. Tremendous speed. Four or five companions were always with him, ever ready to follow his every command. There was not much of trouble, nor need for much caution. One just had to avoid the police outposts and take another way; there was no dearth of roads. There was no lack of money, weapons, the thrill of power, conscious self-importance: nothing was lacking.

He could not forget one incidence from those days. He could not have, even if he wanted to; the incident had left a deep scar in his memory.

It was dusk; one could not even see the hairs on the forearms. They were waiting near a bend on a road in a silent forest area. Why or for whom, he could not remember now.

There was the sound of a scooter approaching. Here? Why? They waited, on full alert. The scooter came and stopped in the darkness under a large tree before the bend. He suspected something. Gesturing to his companions to remain where they were, he silently got out of the car. People did not come to these uninhabited dangerous areas. Why had a scooter come here? It was being dragged towards the tree and hidden! Suspicious.

He silently stood by the tree.

A boy and a girl. The boy was not local, but he had no accent. The girl hesitated a little; the boy was telling her something. At one point, she seemed to agree. Both of them went inside the forest and sat on the ground at a convenient spot. The boy took her in his arms. He watched the whole episode from behind two trees, transfixed. He observed the boy growing impatient, the girl silently surrendering—and their rhythmic union. His own breathing nearly stopped, and he felt a wave of increasing warmth spreading through his body…a tide of nervous excitement. Their embrace disentangled before his eyes; they gathered themselves, dusted their clothes, and stood up. The boy hurriedly looked at his watch, took out some money from his pocket, embraced the girl, and pushed the money inside her blouse.

Something seemed to explode inside his brain at that moment. He let out an animalistic cry, leapt, and caught the boy. He whipped out the revolver from under his shirt. Hearing his shout, his companions came out of the car with their guns. The boy trembled violently; the girl had turned into stone—her eyes widened in terror.

'You swine,' he swore, kicking the boy violently. 'You are spoiling everybody with your money!'

The boy and the girl were trussed up. They did not have any chance to say anything. Bound up, they were put on the floor in the back of the gypsy; they lay there all night.

In the endless summer afternoons of lying in the comfortable bed, he repeatedly remembered this incident. At that time, they had a camp—deep and inaccessible—inside the forest. Next day on his return to the camp, he took the boy and girl along with him.

There was a big commotion in the camp.

The boy confessed his wrongdoing. Yes, it was true that he had enticed the girl with lots of promises, but pleasure was his main aim.

At that time, they used to follow a very strict moral code; it was not possible to tolerate such incidents. The boy was sentenced to death. But the problem occurred with the girl; what was to be done with her? Everybody blamed him for bringing her to the camp without blindfolding her. There was the question of the breach of security. Ultimately, she was ordered to be killed.

Whenever he remembered this incident, he had mixed feelings. The memory of the boy still provoked anger in him, but sometimes—especially in the silent summer afternoons—when he remembered the copulation, he would get excited. He had forgotten the girl's face; she had become a faceless memory.

II

When he remembered the endless waiting in those summer afternoons, his blood boiled. A ceiling fan spun at full speed inside his head. His condition had then become like that of a caged animal. Sometimes, he would start panting in a nameless rage. He would leap out of the bed, and soft pillows would fly about. He would kick the pillows in rage and they would fly and hit the closed door. The old orderly deputed to look after his needs would cautiously open the door and peep inside; he would close the door immediately upon seeing him restless—pacing inside the room, completely naked.

He had not yet got up from bed in the morning. There were sounds of gunfire. And there was shouting.

He was sleeping on a high bamboo platform under a nylon mosquito net. Last night, there was a meeting in the camp which stretched well past midnight. Many accusations were levelled against him too—that he had mismanaged money and accounts was one among them. That was a lie. Yes, he had spent money freely, but all for a purpose—all for work. Sure, he had not kept accounts, but he had not spent a single rupee on any other work. His conscience was totally clear. There were accusations that he had secretly made contact with the government, with political leaders! Yes, that was true. But he had done it only after obtaining permission from the higher-ups. All done in the interest of work. He had taken advantage of the opponents' weaknesses. It had been useful, very useful. It was not treachery. Opportunism? Who does not exploit an opportunity when it presents itself? Your enemies always wait to exploit such opportunities. That he had shown brutality was also an accusation. What was the need of showing compassion to enemies though? He had endangered security by bringing the girl to the camp without a blindfold. Yes, he had committed a mistake. But tough steps had been taken to maintain security. The girl did not go back...

But he felt his arguments hitting a wall. He did not receive the support he expected to get from the leaders. He realized that the number of people who disliked him was not insignificant; there was no dearth of opportunistic companions. He was being sucked into a whirlpool of a dangerous tussle between groups within the organization. His position became shaky. After the meeting, he could not sleep for a long, long time. It was only towards dawn that he drifted into a slumber.

He heard the gunshots in his sleep. In that hazy state, he wondered if he was in for some action with Hazarika and Rondeep sirs! He woke up the next moment. There was an explosion. He jumped out of bed and threw himself flat on the ground. A few troops came running out of the forest on the other side of the camp. The automatic guns in their hands spewed fire.

He crawled away to the other side.

There were gunshots on that side too. That meant the troops had surrounded the camp.

He started to crawl like a snake through the bushes and undergrowth. Gunfire sounded quite near; there were sounds of footsteps too. What should he do? In front was the pit of the prison. It was empty. Lifting the heavy bamboo covering over the pit, he jumped inside, and landed into the dirty mud at the bottom of the pit.

When the troops discovered him, he told a strange tale: that he was imprisoned for difference in opinion, and was put in the pit. He made up this story to save himself.

There was interrogation. Without respite, it went on. At times, he nearly froze in fright. They did not believe his words. Barrel of guns came close to his head. He was tortured—unbelievable torture, hour after hour of interrogation. His identity, the accusations levelled against him—all these, he recounted truthfully. The only lie was that of his imprisonment. He could pass through that period of interrogation without changing his word.

Ultimately, he was taken away. He could breathe easy now. He was given clothes, hot food, and first-aid.

Then he was given two options: certain death or a comfortable life. The price of life would be help. He had to provide information about his comrades, his companions. He agreed after a lot of hesitation. He had to give proof of his intention too. Around the abandoned camps inside the forest, many things were hidden. Arms, ammunition, rice, and other essentials. He knew all these would go to waste anyway; his comrades would never be able to retrieve those. He showed them all those hidden stores. His conscience was quite clear till then.

He passed the first test. The officers of the armed forces were elated to find all that surplus material; they formed part of their list of success in the campaign. He was praised, and top officials talked with him.

A new journey began.

He was provided with bodyguards. They kept him under surveillance day and night. In the cantonment near the city, he was provided accommodation in a barrack and food from the mess. In the centre of the spacious room, there was the bed with the foam mattress. His house! House or prison? There was an old orderly to do odd jobs for him; he brought food and whatever else was required.

He was promised things, attractive things. But with the passage of time, nobody talked about those promises anymore.

An endless waiting started.

Sometimes he was called—his face covered with a black hood with two eye holes—and asked to identify captives. He was supposed to identify absconding rebels from a group of boys picked up at random.

How his heart had pounded on the first day.

A long line of captives. He was seeing most of them for the first time in his life. Suddenly, few known faces in the line. What should he do? Nobody would recognize him under the black hood. He passed by many known faces. Suddenly, he saw one particular face—a face which had levelled true and false allegations against him. That face was also, to some extent, responsible for his present state. His ears started ringing.

He pointed out that face.

The face exploded in terrible screams before the executioners, but he felt no remorse, no guilt.

He had stepped on the path of treachery.

He started to think that a secret plan had been hatched against him for a long time inside the organization. No, there was no solid proof. Snatches of conversation, some assumptions, some guesses… but nothing concrete.

He became restless.

He then started to interrogate the captives himself.

His anger turned into a sort of ruthlessness, a sort of inexplicable rage. At times, he had to be dragged away from interrogating…

After such an episode, the endless waiting would start again…

Lying in bed made him restless; he would press his head with both his hands. Some days when he closed his eyes after lying down, he felt his head becoming lighter and the bed becoming slippery—as if one end of the bed was rising up and, losing balance, he was starting to slip out. He would suddenly sit up in those moments, with sweat beading his forehead…

Occasionally, he was disturbed by memories of home. He had not been able to go home for a long time…had not seen his village, enmeshed in memories of his childhood and adolescence. Had not seen his family members. He did not know whether he would be able to return to his village someday. Once or twice, he thought it might be possible to do so if he sought permission, or employed some strategy. In the meantime, he had been to several places with his bodyguards. With them, it might just be possible to visit home once, at night, under cover of darkness. The possibility used to excite him. But the next moment, his enthusiasm would shrink, soon replaced by fear and doubt.

In reality, nobody knew whether he was dead or alive. That was the arrangement he had consented to—his capture would be kept a secret.

To the outside world, he was missing. His comrades, friends, family members had no idea where he was or how he was doing. He lived in anonymity and secrecy. And this anonymity was what kept him alive. But he was not a fool. He knew full well that when he ceased to be useful to his captors, they would have him removed. And this anonymity would prove very convenient then. If he went home, this anonymity would be lost—they would not let it happen.

To live this moment and to continue living. Yes, staying alive had become his main problem now.

He had sought newspapers. For several days, there was no reply to his request. That was in the beginning, when he had just come to live in the barracks. But one day the newspapers arrived, not one or two, but seven papers—including dailies and weeklies. An instruction accompanied them too. Every day, he would have to cut out the news items relating to armed operations against the insurgents, and of the underground organizations, paste them in a notebook and write a summary in English. This activity took up a considerable part of the day. Occasionally, they would ask for a full translation of a particular news item. Within a few days, he became fairly good at this job and earned praise from his captors. They were making him work; his usefulness would remain intact. It was far better than identifying people while hiding behind a black hood.

Occasionally, he read snatches of some statements issued by his erstwhile comrades in the newspapers. The armed struggle will go on—that was the gist of most of the statements. He felt a pain in his chest. Younger boys whom he had drawn into the struggle, whom he had trained, were speaking out. Though gradually he had realized that the struggle could not be continued in the old way, the pain still emerged...

He felt as if he was a fallen star...a comet that had broken away from a joyous circle of friends. He felt like turning back. He would hold hands with his comrades and dance together in a circle under a deep blue sky. The sky would have wispy cotton clouds floating in brilliant moonlight! Where, where did he see that last? In camp? Yes, in the training camp in the hills under the moonlit sky! They sang songs, revolutionary songs, and they danced the *Bihu.* Oh, if only it was possible to get back to those moments again, to go back to that moonlit, song-filled meadow.

But it was his colleagues who had made life impossible for him, who had pulled the rug from under his feet. Surely, he had committed some mistakes. But his conscience was clear; he had not done any wrong deliberately. Instead, he had done a lot of very important work and climbed the organizational ladder fast. Can't a man's achievements be turned against him as allegations to hang him with? When he thought about these things, the two veins in his temples would throb. He would then press his eyes firmly—disjointed images then started to pass through his mind... A mud-filled deep pit covered with a bamboo frame; a man with his face covered with a black hood with eye slits; a line of young men brutally worked over; and amidst them, a hooded figure searching for its prey; a procession of newspaper headlines; a bed with a comfortable mattress; masturbation in summer afternoons; and an injured heart suspended in loneliness—oh!

Faces appear in a procession—his parents, brother, sister, his comrades, enemies, and that girl who was killed in the interest of security and secrecy. It happened because of his thoughtless mistake, that unnecessary death! He was accused for that also. How was that face? No, he could not remember.

And sir! Rondeep's father—his teacher!

More than his son, he used to argue with him. The man held steadfast to his non-violent principles. 'The path is equally important, the goal is not everything, the path itself is a goal too. The path which does not offer a chance of connecting with people—where there is more danger of spiralling down than of growing in moral strength—cannot be a true path,' the old man would say. He had been angry then, and had stomped off in a huff. Ron's father only laughed. But he had not been able to forget his teacher's words.

III

One day at noon while he was lying in bed thinking about nothing in particular, the old orderly opened the door a bit and informed that the commandant was calling him. He immediately dressed and went out. His guards followed him.

Commandant was much more warm than other days.

'What? You haven't had lunch until now? Why, it is quite late! Orderly, ask the boy to bring coffee and sandwiches for sahib, and black coffee for me.' When the food came, the commandant asked him to start, and took the coffee cup himself. Sipping his black coffee, he said, 'Look, here, I have called you for a big job. Nobody knows anything about you. Whether you are dead or alive, where you are, what you are doing, whether you even exist at all—nobody knows. Things cannot go on like this. This uncertainty is intolerable…is not it? And in this situation, if you disappear altogether, nobody would be any wiser…'

He did not say anything; he went on eating with bowed head. He was not unprepared for such a threat.

'I want to give you a big chance.

I want to give you a way out of this uncertainty, and a chance to start a new life. A straight path. Surrender publicly to the government, and there would be no more problems in life for you.'

'Surrender?'

'Yes, surrender. A public function will be organized; top officials, politicians, press—everybody will come, and you shall surrender before everyone. After that, you will be a free man and nobody will disturb you again. All facilities for your personal security and rehabilitation shall be given.' He knew it was an order. At that time, he did not have the courage or any way of disobeying the order. It was a straight choice. He was given the chance to choose between life and death. Life? What kind of life? His hanging status would end for sure, but the door to another world will close forever; the possibility of sometimes being able to hold hands and sing in a moon-washed world would cease.

'Alone?' he had asked the commandant.

'No, no, not alone,' a smile played on the commandant's face. 'A lot of boys are being held captive—in this camp, and in two others.

All of them will surrender. And you will have to talk and convince them to surrender. You are a top leader, so this will be your task.'

Two poisonous insects seemed to enter his ears and started droning inside his brain. He came out of that office swaying a little. He walked slowly towards his barrack quarters. The commandant had asked him to formulate a plan immediately. There were about 20 or 22 captives in this camp. He would be provided with a car and a driver to go to the other camps. Time was short.

The moment he reached his quarters, he stretched out in bed. He didn't know how long he stayed like that. Suddenly, he got up and got ready to go out. He counted the money given to him as daily allowance and put it in his pocket. Outside, a car, a driver, and security guards, everybody was waiting. He drove to the commandant's office.

He wanted to see the captive boys immediately. He first wanted to talk to the boys of this camp, and then go to the other two tomorrow. Commandant gave out the necessary orders. He was taken to a long, barrack-like structure. The windows of the long house were barred. He was taken to a room at the farthest end; armed guards stood outside it. Just as he wanted, the inmates were brought before him one by one.

It was as if a procession passed before him.

He did not have the black hood with the eye holes on this time. He felt strange and insecure.

A silent tension floated inside the room, while he talked with the boys—as if at any moment, this tension could spark like a lightning bolt and explode. In the faces of the procession passing before him, he saw fleeting reflections of anger, hatred, pity, fear, and relief...

The same scenes were replayed in all the camps.

A process started to take shape; the commandant was happy. He fixed a date; it could not be delayed any longer.

It was quite late in the night. He was returning after doing his work in another camp, and he was tired. He leaned back on the car seat on the way back to his camp. The city roads were nearly empty at night; people did not dare to venture out of their homes because of police and military check-posts. The armed escort vehicle that was with him had gone in the front and was nearly out of sight. He was alone in the car. In front sat the driver and his security guard. His weary eyelids closed.

They were reaching a familiar area on the outskirt of the city. A large area of petty business and slums started from there—railway yard, warehouses, lines of loaded trucks, jostling of the loading and unloading done by labourers, small, shabby, and box-like shops —the whole place was aglow in the light of the halogen lamps at night. The place was still crowded.

There was an intersection in front; the way to the camp was straight ahead.

'Driver, take the left turn,' he suddenly said.

Both the driver and the security guard turned back to look at him. He was indifferent. The security guard squirmed in his seat.

'We have to go someplace,' he said calmly.

His busy schedule in the last few days, and the different treatment shown to him by the commandant and other officers of the camp, had not escaped their eyes. The driver silently turned the car to the left at his order.

A little distance, yes, his known shop was a little distance ahead.

'I will enter a shop to talk about some important matter,' he said. 'You stand on guard till I come out.'

'Yes, sir,' the guard answered, placing himself before the outer door.

A big shop of a Marwari trader. The trader was a little startled when he saw him, but then greeted him with an open smile brought about by long trading experience. 'What will you have, sir? Tea, sweets, or cold drink?' the trader asked.

He held the trader by his hand and led him to the backside of the house. There was a small door at the back, leading out from the high-walled compound. He knew the way from before, and had used it also. He told the trader he would go out to the slum for some time through this backdoor, and that he should not go out of his house till he returns.

A sprawling slum with the roofs of the houses touching each other. Day labourers thieves, con man, foreigners, Bangladeshis, whores, cheats, and small-job holders—all kinds of people stayed in that slum. Always busy and crowded, it was a different world altogether.

Through the slums with its kissing roofs by the side of the hills, there was a way to the river Brahmaputra. Near the river bank, there were the dwellings of the fisher folk. One could get boats there; he had used them before... It was only a question of money. It was only a one-hour journey to Darrang across the river. The other bank was well known to him...

Oh, freedom! That way led to freedom!

Were they there, on that path were his comrades of the moonlight-filled meadow, waiting for him? Would he be able to hold their hands and move in a circle singing together? Would they allow him to be a part of that circle? What was waiting for him on that path? A pallet of molten lead passed through his back to his chest! A deep pit covered with a heavy bamboo covering? The bite of an electric shock like a poisonous serpent? Humiliation, bad name, impotence? His heart fluttered like a caged bird.

While he was deeply immersed in his thoughts, the car had long passed the slum area and reached a bumpy bad patch of road.

'Driver!' he shouted out, 'Turn back, turn back to camp, to the camp!'

He laid his body in the rear seat and closed his eyes tightly.

Partha was engrossed in writing a letter to Bakul.

> Dear Bakul,
> I have at last met Alok in Guwahati. I wanted to interview him for the paper, but he did not agree to it. He talked for a long time though. So, I will have to write a piece based just on that. You must be wondering what was his reaction was. How shall I say it? He said he was forced to surrender. That may be true. But after his surrender, his previous colleagues started a campaign against him; there were two attacks on him. I had told you about Bharat Hazarika—the leader who died in the encounter—he had directed the campaigns against him. He said he had to counter attack in self-defence. He made many such statements, many such arguments to defend himself. One thing is certain, a fratricidal strife has started. This is a big tragedy. Where will this game of violence and counter-violence end, one cannot say. One cannot find answers to these complicated questions.
>
> Alok's health has deteriorated. That smart, bright boy I knew is no more. He's probably is intoxicated most of the time. He has undergone a huge metamorphosis; he has been transformed into a lazy, suspicious, prematurely old animal. He is also a victim. In the tides and eddies of this violent process, he is a victim too. We all are—Ron, Bhaity, you, and even me—our whole society.
>
> The letter is getting too long. It is now time to stop. I have written many things, but didn't really write what I had actually intended to. Anyway, adieu for today, I shall be coming to Dibrugarh on work soon. I am excited at the prospect of meeting you soon.

With that, Partha signed off the letter, and retired for the night.

SOJOURN IN THE KARBI HILLS

I

The sky shattered like a mirror into million pieces at the call of an unknown bird.

From the dark forests, a smell of vegetables was floating in. The topmost branches of the tall trees had coalesced, weaving a large net, and through the gaps of that net a small fragment of the sky above was visible.

A very strange silence hung on all sides, and the insects were also strangely silent.

Walking through such a forest, Ron was startled by the sudden hoarse call of a bird. He stopped in his track for a moment. Old man Ingti, who was clearing the path through the forest with his long-handled *dao* (sickle), mumbled something under his breath.

'What happened?' Ron asked.

'Not much way left to cross the forest,' the old man replied reluctantly.

Ron felt as if a wave of peace had engulfed him. He looked at Ingti with a sense of gratitude. The old man was his longtime guide—a kind but taciturn man whom he and the boys called Grandpa Ingti, or Ingti Koka.

That was the third time Ron had come to the forest-covered Karbi hills. The police and the armed forces were spreading out in all areas; like packs of hunting dogs, they were roaming day and night in civil clothes on the trail of the insurgents. The silent roads through the paddy fields frequently roared with the passage of army jeeps. A band of surrendered former colleagues were also co-operating in this open hunt now.

It was necessary to move away—at least temporarily. After some time, any campaign loses some of its steam; the hunting dog packs also get tired after a point. But before that, in the interest of self-preservation, it is necessary to retreat for some time. That eternal puzzle of how many steps backward will lead to how many steps forward...

The need of self-preservation brought him seeking shelter in the Karbi hills this time. A few temporary camps had to be built, because for a few months, some boys would have to be kept hidden here.

'We have reached,' the old man declared suddenly.

'What? Where have we reached?' Ron asked eagerly. Everywhere, the forest was the same—impenetrable even for the elephants! That had not changed. Ingti Kaka was still advancing, cutting a path through the forest.

Only when he looked a little up could Ron make out the difference. The net-like lattice of branches overhead had become less dense and, through the wider spaces, could now be seen the entrapped pieces of the blue sky. Blue sky. A net-like blue sky!

That meant the forest was ending. Sounds from a gurgling river could also be heard. Then there was only the bright blue sky in the front with a line of steep green hills. The forest actually stopped at the edge of a deep gorge. The narrow valley was filled with large rocks and strangely stunted dwarf trees. On the other side of the valley, the face of the tree-covered tall hill rose steeply.

A narrow valley filled with large rocks and dwarf trees! A long, winding, serpentine valley with a crystal-clear stream in the middle that meandered through the large rocks and dwarf trees widening at places into placid pools.

'Most suitable, Grandpa, most suitable place, Ron bubbled with enthusiasm.

There was no change of expression in the old man's face. He stood at the edge of the gorge, looked both ways, and then pointing to downstream, said, 'If one starts to walk at dawn, by sundown they will reach a large settlement. And four hours' walk from that village will led to the road where motor cars run.'

'Is there a road by the river to the settlement?' Ron asked while trying to do a rapid calculation in his mind.

'No road,' the old man shook his head, 'but one can go.'

In one place, the edge of the gorge had broken down and formed a wide, winding path to the valley below. One could easily go down by that path. It looked as if that path started right from inside the forest itself. The old man looked at Ron curiously examining that path, and commented, 'That is the path of the of wild elephants.'

From the hills beyond, crossing the valley and the river, herds of wild elephants came to the forest through that path. So, the path appeared quite wide and well-trodden. Ron, however, did not see any elephant droppings nearby.

On the other bank of the river, between the steep hill face, the rocks, and the dwarf trees, one could build camps nicely. On one side, the impenetrable dense forest, on the other, the treed high wall of hills and the silent solitary valley between with a sparking stream in it—human habitation was far off; the boys could stay here safely for quite a long period. No, helicopters could find this place easily; there were lots of hiding places in the hills and forests.

Ron took deep breaths at the edge of the steep bank of the gorge. He thought many things: that he would himself stay with the boys in this camp; that old man Ingti would be the sole link with the outside world because nobody could cross that dense forest without the old man's help.

Ron thought of exploring this valley with the boys; he would go both up and down stream; would climb the hills and go to the settlement. A system of bringing supplies from that settlement would have to be worked out.

'The settlement on that side, whose settlement is that?' Ron asked.

'Karbi people,' the old man replied.

Ron nodded his head. He felt reassured.

The old man then gathered dried twigs and leaves; he would now brew black tea in the aluminum kettle he constantly carried in his hand.

Ron came and sat nearby. He took out a plate and some food stuff from his shoulder bag—dry flaked rice, molasses, and some soggy biscuits. Ingti's tea started to boil; he took out two bamboo drinking cups from his bag and poured the tea into it.

The bright noon sky was overhead. Ingti looked at the sky and then towards the forest. Ron understood that the old man was gauging time. They would have to start back early after finishing the tea, and would have to reach old man Ingti's farm before darkness. Ron looked at Ingti anxiously; the old man was in no hurry. He slowly munched the dry flaked rice, sipped his black tea, and looked to the distance enmeshed deeply in some thought. That meant there was still time; Ron held out the packet of biscuits to the old man. Ingti liked biscuits very much. Pouring out one more bamboo mug full of tea, Ron went out to the edge of the chasm and sat there, hanging his legs down.

Staring straightforward, he could see only two colours—crystal blue of the sky above and the bottle green of the steep hills below. Only if one looked down did the narrow valley with the huge stones and dwarf trees came into view.

This was the third time he had come to the Karbi hills. Here, he was free from the daily worries and anxieties of an underground life—there was neither police or military chasing him here, nor was there any danger from ex-comrades. Everyday uncertainties and excitements were not there... It was as if he could breathe freely after coming to this place and fill up his lungs with the pure air of the hills; as if the fragrance of the virgin forest had spread to his mind, nerves, and muscles.

Hanging his legs down, Ron closed his eyes, and drawing in lung-full of air, tried to catch that elusive fragrance of the earth.

In these leisurely moments, some questions and some thoughts had risen in his mind. At first, he tried to suppress these thoughts. Then, one day, he asked himself what he was doing. Trying not to think about anything, trying to close all the doors and windows of the mind, he wondered whether it was even possible to do it. The time for questions was probably now.

Ron fidgeted a little. He saw two birds starting their flight against the backdrop of the steep hill; the birds looked like two brown dots against the green hill. One bird flew upward and, crossing the upper line of the hill, appeared against the blue sky. Ron suddenly felt as if the bird had soared into the sky from the hill itself. It then flew in circles like a black dot in the sky.

Yes, if one can avoid some thoughts, they can stay quite peaceful. Faith is much more comfortable than reason. What is the use of seeking answers to the sums you, yourself, have set up? Will a new path, a new way, emerge? It may or may not; and even if it does, what guarantee is there that the path would be the correct one?

Does that mean one shouldn't think? Why, have you forgotten the saying—'Faith leads to God, but arguments drive him away'. Such a simple explanation. But what guarantee is there of faith leading one anywhere? Is there any? No, no. So there is really no alternative to thinking, no alternative.

Ron rose from the bank. It was time to return.

There are many questions; really there are many questions, he thought. And with the questions, some doubts, some uncertainties, some worries, and some anxieties come too. Like unstoppable hiccups, these thoughts tend to come out from the depths of the bosom.

The time of self-questioning has come—and there are endless questions.

While Ron was immersed in his head, the pair of birds had disappeared from the blue sky; he could not spot the birds anymore.

Old man Ingti stood up and shook himself. Holding the long-handled *dao* in his right hand and the aluminum kettle in his left, he was ready to return. Ron also lifted his bag. He looked at old man Ingti; he was silent and his face was expressionless.

'Let us go, Koka,' Ron said, 'we must cross the forest before dark.'

There was no change in the old man's face. Holding a machete in hand, he entered the forest silently. Ron followed him with brisk steps. He felt that as soon as they entered it, the dense and mysterious forest embraced both of them and placed them in her bosom. It was as if they had entered a primitive realm; a mysterious journey had started. On the way back, Ingti walked at a brisk pace. Ron had to nearly run to keep up with him. The crystal blue sky overhead seemed to have been sucked in by the gloom of the forest, and spread only a muted sad light...

II

It was the third time Ron had come to the Karbi hills.

Yes, for the third time.

The first time he came to this green world, he was entrusted with an important task.

Yes, it was a really important job: he was given the responsibility of finding out a road. Yes, a road! From Nagaon and Shillong, he had to find a secret way through the Karbi and the North Cachar Hills to Bangladesh. The local cadres of Nagaon were talking about such a path for quite a long time. Ultimately, the idea made its way into the minds of the leaders. Yes, the path really existed! Local people were travelling from one place to another by this path; they did not go the whole way because it was not necessary for them to do so. If one could connect the pieces, the whole route will be found out.

He was given the task of finding out this path.

With a few companions from Nagaon, along with his shadow-like bodyguard Mohan, he started looking for this path. Oh, he really felt like an intrepid explorer. David Livingstone, Sir Cecil Rhodes, Drake, Cook, Amundsen—so many courageous explorers, searching for treasure-laden countries through the dense forests of Africa, charting the course of the Amazon through the impenetrable forests of South America, or trying to find new trade routes through the seas of the world! Partha felt like the heroes of yore— the intrepid sailors, the courageous explorers who did all those things. He would also try to discover a path, a forgotten mysterious route. No, he did not disclose his feelings to Mohan or any of his companions, but his heart was filled with happiness. He became elated with the thrill of the campaign, with the expectant uncertainty of a discovery!

And he found the route.

Like many small streams coming together to form a river, many small paths originating at different points joined one another to form this route. The name of the route is also quite catchy: Umpanai-Howang Khanduli path. Starting from various places of the Karbi and the Khasi Jaintia Hills, this route twisted its way down from north to south and reached the hot water springs of 'Garam Pani'. From the east, this route can be accessed from Kampur and Baithalangso, and from the north via Roha, Jagi, Khala, or Nelli of Nagaon. From the west side, one can get to it from Shillong, Nongpoh, Umpanai, Umsning, and also from Hamren. From 'Garam Pani', one can go southward to many places, to the Naga and Mizo hills, Manipur and Tripura, and crossing the international boarder, to Burma (Myanmar) and Bangladesh.

Many people do not know about this fragmented route; it is not possible to know and there is no need to know. In most of the places, there are no motorable or even properly built road sections. But people travel through every part of it, walking over long stretches at times. While travelling over these paths, Ron realized that it was an ancient and historical thoroughfare, an ancient trade route. It was the old historical way of communication and trade between Assam, Jaintia and Kachari kingdoms, Nagaland, Manipur, Tripura, and Bengal too.

During the Ahom rule in Assam, envoys, messengers, traders and, at times, armies travelled by this way. Yes, Ahom envoys Ratnakadali, Ramcharan, Bijoyram; envoys of Tripura, like Rameswar, Nyayalankar Bhattacharya, Udaynaranayan Biswas, or Jaintia envoys like Joy Visharad, Kanthabhusan, Pitambar—all travelled by this path. They came to Guwahati, to Raha, and to Kajalimukh by this route. Afterwards, as the Britishers opened up other roads, this route disappeared from memory. Only the local inhabitants knew about these paths and used them; it was also used by petty smugglers, clandestine arms merchants, and by the guerrillas.

When he entered from the Shillong side, he had to travel part of the way by a ramshackle bus. These vehicles carry vegetables, spices, poultry, and pigs put in bamboo baskets on the way to Shillong, and on the way back they take garments, flour rice, and other provisions. A part of the way has to be travelled by famous World War II vintage 'mama' jeeps pulling a trailer behind. People sit on the load of bags of rice, oil tins, and other goods. In some places, one has to walk a stretch; then again, one might get a bus or a 'mama' jeep. One the way, one finds village settlements on the side of the road—two rows of wood and tin shanties lining both sides, wherein some of the *jadohs* (cabin) sell fried pork and *kakiyat* (local brew).

When he entered the road from Nagaon side, he had his bodyguard, Mohan, a few local comrades from Nagaon and a guide—old man Ingti. How the local comrades could find this guide was surprising, really surprising.

Ron felt really strange when he embarked on the exploration. These places were so near but were so unknown; he never knew about these places before. It was strange, really strange.

It was a really strange hilly path. At all times, you feel as if you have lost your way travelling over it. Sometimes over the hills, sometimes through dark forests and sometimes, you could even travel a part of it by a motorable road. Human habitations were far from one another; one had to walk nearly half a day to go from one to another. After one crossed the villages of the Karbi people, Jayantia and Khasi villages came into view; and towards Umrangso, Dimasa villages sprang up. Old man Ingti easily guided them through this long-forgotten path. Ingti was a really strange and kind person. This thin man built like a curved knife was really quite old. The skin over his chest and abdomen had wrinkled into loose folds, and his expressionless face had a thousand wrinkles. The eyes could hardly be seen due to these. And because of these lines on his face, Ingti appeared to be always smiling. His teeth were black and had gaps; a few in between had already fallen off. The old man had a pair of carefully folded khaki trousers, a khaki shirt, and red canvas shoes without laces. On the first day when he came with them, he had put on his khaki dress and canvas shoes. But the very next day he gave up that attire. He folded them neatly and put them inside his hanging shoulder bag. He felt much more comfortable with his daily wear—the loin cloth and bare torso. Whether day or night, the old man did not leave his *jhola* (tote bag) and the long-handled *dao*. In the other hand, he would carry an aluminum kettle. Many a time on the road, he brewed tea in it and offered it to everybody. Once or twice, he even cooked rice in it. Holding his *dao* in one hand and the kettle in the other, he would walk so fast that Ron and others found it difficult to keep pace with him sometimes.

Row after row of hills, some covered with forests but some nearly bald, their hard, stony surface barely covered by a thin layer of grass and shrubs; sometimes there was a lush valley between two lines of hills, sometimes a deep chasm, with a small river or a stream flowing through them with many bends. At places, there was slash and burn type of cultivation, while in some were the regular rectangular fields of paddy. At one place, Ron observed that in the paddy fields down below the path, people were ploughing the fields with water buffaloes. But looking a little closely, he saw that the plough was missing; the man was just driving the huge buffalo in the muddy fields.

'Ingti Koka, what is that man doing with the buffaloes?' he asked.

'Ploughing the field,' the old man answered without looking there.

'Without a plough?'

'Here, they till the fields like that.'

Ron stopped to look at the spectacle below. The old man also stopped. He took two steps back towards Ron and looking at the scene of ploughing below, said,

'They build bunds and dam the water in the fields for a long time. When the land turns soft, then they bring in buffaloes and make them walk to turn the whole field into soft mud; then they plant paddy there.'

Habitation was very thin in these areas. On his way through the hills looking for the route, Ron saw newer and newer sights. They then reached the villages of the Beite people. Ron had never heard before that such a people also existed. Between the Jayantia hills district and Mizoram, a tongue of Cacher district went forward and touched the border of Bangladesh. That was the heavily-wooded Kayu valley, and the way to Bangladesh ran through it. With the help of the Beite villages, the underground insurgents, criminals, and smugglers cross the international border. The highway from Shillong to Silchar also crosses the Kayu valley at a place.

Ron found the route from Nagaon to Bangladesh with the help of his companion and Ingti. He had submitted his report about the route where he had to do so. He did not know whether his discovery had been put to any use. May be it had been; it was unlikely that it would not be used.

He also had a second task.

After finding the route, he had to find a secure place for a meeting. He did that with the help of Ingti as well; in fact, it was Ingti who found a secure spot.

The shadows inside the forest started to darken. Ingti Koka hurried. Following the old man, past memories came flooding to Ron; memories of the path-finding expedition, of the meeting—of the dead fish eyes!

Near a Karbi village, situated on the bank of a gurgling stream, there was a government rubber plantation. And the venue was chosen in the plantation bordering the dense forest. The place was very remote, but there were many ways of reaching it. His site selection was approved by the superiors.

Temporary bamboo huts were built inside the plantation for the camp, complete with a kitchen and rows of latrines. The huts covered with plastic sheets were camouflaged with branches. Ron was given the entire responsibility of setting up the camp, gathering necessary provisions, making security arrangement and escorting the main leaders to the meeting—he had to supervise everything.

Everybody attending the meeting, even the top leaders, had to deposit their personal arms to him. During the meeting—except those specifically detailed for security duty—nobody could carry arms.

He was not a participant in the meeting, but because he was the main organizer, he had to frequently go to the meeting area. It was on the third day that for some reason there was tremendous agitation in the meeting. He was so busy with the arrangement that he did not get the time to find out what it was about. Everything was alright till lunch break; everybody ate in easy camaraderie. Suddenly, in the afternoon it happened, and happened quite suddenly. The meeting was on and he had just entered the venue for some work. It was then that a death sentence was announced on a top-ranking leader, and it was executed immediately during the meeting itself.

Molten lead erupted out of a steel barrel and in the warmth of a living body, it hardened to rocks.

The sound of the shots raised echoes and then died down into a long silence.

It was Ron who had escorted the executed leader to the meeting like he had escorted all the others. Oh, how lively were his steps, his smile so bright and defiant. And his eyes? His eyes had such a joyous sparkle. And the look of surprise and disbelief that spread over his face before his death! That expression etched itself permanently in Ron's brain.

He had become rooted to the space like a thunderstruck man.

The meeting went on; he also went on working mechanically.

As he was in charge of arrangements of the meeting, the responsibility of the cremation, too, fell on him. A couple of soldiers carried the dead body in a bier after him into the deep forest. At the bank of the stream, in a patch of earth covered with green luxuriant ferns, he ordered the carriers to dig a pit.

The dead body was laid in the green grass nearby.

Not a man but a dead body was lying there. A few hours back, a man walked proudly on this earth; oh, what strength life brought to his steps. Now instead of a man, lies a body—dead! Waiting to be interred into earth. Luxurious ferns would grow over this spot.

He was ordered to cremate the body with full honours after a military discharge. After looking at the body, he thought that more than military honours, he would cremate the body with human dignity.

He would take off the bloodied military fatigues, remove the belt from his waist, cap from the head, and all undergarments; he would remove all the clothes completely.

He would collect medicinal herbs from the forest, crush them into a paste and, with that balm, cover the wounds created by the bullets.

He would line the pit with a thick layer of tender fern shoots and on that green bed, he would lay the naked body with the eyes facing the sky, He would collect a few wild flowers and place them over the closed eyes, mouth, over the heart, and genitals. He would cover the body with a layer of tender green ferns. Then the warm earth would embrace the lifeless body.

To dust would return the body of dust.

Ron was shaken out of his reverie by the harsh sound of earth being dug.

He went near the dead body.

In the pale light of the dusk, he peeped at the face.

The face still had an expression of surprise in it. He opened the lids of the closed eyes; the bright shining eyes had turned dull and cloudy—like that of a dead fish. And in them the dull, darkening sky was reflected. After a few moments, that reflection would also disappear...

They came out of the forest and reached Ingti Koka's farmhouse before the last traces of light from the sky disappeared. Sitting in the old man's stilt house, Ron constantly thought about the 'eyes of dead fish'. They floated into his memory continuously, like that of a movie, while he was walking through the forest.

It became dark soon, and a large moon like a flat disc rose into the sky behind some tree branches. And soon, it looked as if the moon was climbing from branch to branch among those trees.

Ron brought out a candle from his knapsack, lit it, and opened his notebook. It opened on a page containing one of his old incomplete poems. He did not like what he read, it seemed immature and sentimental... He blew off the candle, closed the notebook and put them both in the knapsack.

The moon had left the web of branches now, and was climbing steadily into the clear inky sky. The few twinkling stars that appeared hung in the sky.

He pulled down the mosquito netting and laid face up, looking at the unfolding night sky. Ingti Koka's bamboo platform was much stronger than anything they had built in the forest. He got immersed in the silent procession of his memories again.

He had sent his companions back; they would bring the boys to an appointed place and then he would lead them into the hiding place. After that, they would be his responsibility.

And he stayed back in Ingti Koka's orange plantation alone to swim in the uncharted seas of his memory.

III

Why did he come the second time to these hills?

The first was to search for the route, the third time to find a hiding place, but the second time? Why had he come and from where?

From Shillong, and from Swaha!

But why he came away from Swaha to these places, to Ingti Koka and his orange plantation, he did not know clearly.

Oh, Swaha! A girl like rain, like a storm!

He had never met such a girl before—such a natural, such a spontaneous girl without any artificial airs.

The world from where he had come and the world which he dwelt in were totally unknown to her. She had never been in it. She knew what he did, what he was doing. Yet her communication, her behaviour was so natural. When they felt a very strong attraction for each other, she never kept a wall of difference between them. That was also so natural, such a sweet union. Every time, her company gave him the feeling of becoming pure in mind and body—like after having a bath in a pure pool. The excitement of body also became a pure feeling.

His whole life had changed forever!

What would Swaha be doing now?

In this late afternoon, when the sun at the end of the day was sliding down the horizon, the shadows were lengthening, and the darkness of the night were starting to gather under the leaves of the forest? When all the harshness of the world was softening, the moon was starting to climb up the sharp ridges of carambola-spined hills—what would she be doing? Did she remember him even once? Just like the tides of memory that brought in an inexplicable sadness over him, did it also do the same to her?

Ron? That means you want her to suffer the same way, don't you? You want that she should also suffer with your memories; even though you don't want to admit to yourself, you do want her to suffer like you do—like the painful cramp that starts up deep inside your chest every time you remember her! Oh! Don't you sometimes also wish that she should forget you completely, expel all your memories from within her? But can you continue that for long? Don't you always want to know whether she has also started loving you as you love her? Does she still love you like you love her? Tell the truth Ron, admit it.

You want her to love you for satisfaction of your ego.

You had practically run away from her; yes, you did run away from her. Leaving an unsigned two-line note, you escaped, you ran away.

Were you afraid that she would bind you, or that you would get trapped...

And, therefore, in one of your subsequent visits to Shillong—and despite staying there for couple of days—you returned without even contacting or meeting her.

No, no it was not that, not that.

Ron came down from the bamboo bed, lifted the mosquito net and, coming out, started to pace the path below the hills in a restless way.

I know if I had gone to her she would have welcomed me with real happiness, would have greeted me most naturally. I could have put my lips on hers, and there would have been no need for words. I could have lain in her bosom and could have dreamed about the yet undreamt dreams. We could have floated into a foaming ocean just like the last time. I have that much faith in me and Swaha.

But what is the basis of such a belief? She might have changed. She might have forgotten me completely, banished my memory from her mind totally. She might have developed some other relationship with someone else.

No. No. Something screamed inside Ron. A nameless jealousy burnt inside him suddenly. He walked with a restless pace near the house on stilts.

No, I know it is not true, I know.

How do you know?

It is true I did not met her while in Shillong. I went there nine or 10 months after I had first met her. Was there for a week or so. It is true that I had not met her, but it was not that I did not see her. I went and saw here once with my own eyes—on the last day, the day before I was to leave Shillong. That day, I went towards her house. Not to meet her, but to see her once. I went and waited amongst the shops at the crossroad near her house. From there, the gate leading to their house could he seen clearly. I waited for her to come out of her house. An hour, two, three hours passed. I did not know whether she was at home, or whether she would come out or not. But I waited.

Suddenly, I saw her coming. She opened the gate and came out of the compound. Yes, she was coming, Swaha was coming! Walking slowly by the footpath on the other side of the road, she was coming towards me, towards the crossroad where I was standing.

She wore a knee length dress with pleats. Her shapely legs showed off in the heels she was wearing. A very loose and thin cardigan covered her torso. Two thin gold earrings in her ears were the only ornament on her. Her hair, like a cascading waterfall, was gathered into a high bun and covered with white net.

Exactly the way I thought I would find her! I saw her exactly the way I thought.

Carrying a white plastic shopping bag in her hand, she walked with firm, sprightly steps.

My heart fluttered like that of a 17-year-old boy; I became nervous. I immediately shifted to the inside of a shop and stood behind a decorated glass window where she would not see me. And I gazed at her without blinking…

She came and stopped for a moment before the small shops on the side of the road. She looked around as if amongst the crowd in the road, amidst the parked cars, she was searching for someone. Then she started buying small things. I kept on looking at her, at each movement of hers without batting an eyelid. She bought some vegetables, dozen ripe red tomatoes, carrots, and lettuce. I knew she liked to buy these things herself; I had also come with her to buy exactly the same things once. After buying the vegetables, she climbed some steps to go to the variety store nearby, and she moved away from my view. The time she spent inside the store, my heart nearly stopped. Then she came out of the shop, with a bag in her hand full with the articles she had bought. Standing in front of the shop, she searched the road on both sides for something again. She also looked across the road, and looked long into the shop inside which I was standing.

And then I saw her eyes. And I saw that she was grabbing the shopping bag tightly; her knuckles turning white.

Between us was the transparent glass window and the road—quite narrow, like a river.

Her large, deep, and sad eyes were focussed at some distant point, as if she was looking for some particular person amidst the crowd in the road.

Her glance was searching for a memory; amidst the busy road, she was passionately searching for someone from her memory.

I was staying at Swaha's house in those long-gone days. Thanks to Partha-da, I was staying practically like an underground there. One evening, bored by staying indoors day and night, we came out to the evening market at the crossroads. Partha-da was practically not to be seen those days. We really enjoyed our time at this market; bought many necessary, and, unnecessary things. Not that we needed them, it was only for the pleasure of buying them together. I bought her the white lac hairnet that time; yes, in that very shop. We shopped for vegetables for salad, and bread and butter for breakfast. In the main Chinese restaurant at the crossroads, we ordered wanton soup and chowmein. We crossed the road repeatedly in need and even without it. We simply forgot that in the world around us there were other people too.

She suddenly started to turn back. For a moment, her gaze came through the glass pane of the window and fell on me. But she did not see me. Not because of the glass pane. Bright lights had lit up the inside of the shop in the meantime. She did not see me because her memory had changed in the meantime; maybe the object of her memory got transformed in her mind. So, she could not recognize me even though I was standing right before her...

The statue-like man with a pale face and a pair of moist eyes looking intently at the figure on the other side of the road would be difficult to recognize indeed—that man standing like a guilty person…me.

Then she turned to return home by the footpath. My hand rose up and slowly started to extend towards her, and from the fingers fell drops of tears. I wanted to call out to her, call out 'Swaha! Swaha!'—

I was completely sure that it was me whom she was looking at unconsciously; it was me she still loved.

And, therefore, I did not call out to her.

I did not call out to her. The journey I had started on an uncertain and perilous path of no return—how could I consciously bring the girl I loved to the dangers of that path!?No, I cannot, cannot. In future, may be...

These thoughts brought a terrible headache to Ron. He pressed on his head with both his hands and sat down suddenly in the bamboo platform. A terrible physical and mental tiredness engulfed him.

Carrying the distressing emptiness of a burnt-out field in his bosom, he had rushed that time from Shillong to this place; why particularly to this place, he did not know. He came by that secret trail which he had discovered, and reached old man Ingti's village; and the next day, he had come to this farm. And while old man Ingti was not present, all alone in the bamboo platform laying prone and looking at the sky, Ron had cried loudly. Without any restraint, without any shyness, he had cried like a child.

And it echoed all around. In the ridged hills, in the orange bushes, on the wings of the birds sitting on the leafless trees, his cries echoed and returned back to him.

IV

Ron was all alone in old man Ingti's orange garden.

That was a time of waiting; the boys had not arrived till then. When they did, they would contact Grandpa Ingti—who was waiting for them in his village.

Burdened with the memories of yesterday, Ron was in a bad state. A splitting headache had started in the morning; his eyes were burning, and a chill was slowly spreading in his body. And then the fever came and along with it, shivering that crept into all his tissues, all his muscles.

Such a familiar feeling. Ah, malaria.

Ron opened his bag and took quinine and pain killers. One did not fool around with malaria of the hills.

The waiting started again on Grandpa Ingti's orange plantation.

Grandpa Ingti's orange plantation! Really, the old man had strange hobbies. This orange garden on a beautiful slope of a hill was about one hour's walk from his village; rows of shapely orange bushes on the slope, and a small house on stilts amidst them. There was a packed earthen fireplace on the bamboo platform of the house. One had to climb a wooden *dondon* (leader) to reach the platform of the house.

There was another Karbi tree house, a little distance up the hill on a large branching tree; this small bamboo thatched house also had a small packed earthen fireplace. Ron stayed in this house every time he came to the orange plantation. He had started to feel as if the small house was his own. In addition to the house he was born in, he felt this tree house was his permanent address in this world.

When he and his colleagues first came to the orange plantation, it was old man Ingti who had brought them here to stay; he had stayed in the lower house with his bodyguard Mohan, that time. That was the time for orange blossoms, so old man Ingti refused to take them out in search of the road without completing some essential work in the orange grove.

They also helped Ingti in his work. The ground below each orange bush was cleaned thoroughly like the floor of a kitchen, not leaving even one single blade of grass standing. The weeds, grass, and leaves were heaped at places to dry so they could be burned. The smoke spread through the bushes, and the wind that climbed up the sloping face of the hill scattered the ashes everywhere. All dead leaves and branches from the trees were removed; the stalk of the bushes were smeared with a thick coat of lime. Ron felt as if each orange bush was meticulously being prepared to be pregnant with fruit.

Before leaving, Ingti had entrusted one of his nephews to look after the plantation; he took him to each tree and explained something. In the meantime, the early orange blossoms had started to appear, and the hum of the bees could be heard.

'Grandpa, there is not a single orange plantation in this area. How did you start this plantation?' Ron had asked the old man.

'I have asked so many people to start, but nobody pays any attention,' the old had man replied. 'The Jaintias taught me to start this garden. They chose this land also. How to plant, how to care—they taught me everything. That was 20 years ago.'

'Do you make any profit?' Ron had asked.

'I get some money every year. You may call that profit. I just like working in the garden. The wholesale traders come every year.' Ingti had replied, explaining the mechanics of orange plantation. With his thumb and forefinger, he showed a size not larger than a marble, and continued, 'When the oranges are this big, they come and fix a price, and pay some advance too. I get some additional money for looking after the garden for them, and for weaving bamboo baskets for the fruit. When the fruit ripens, they come and take away the oranges on weekly basis. If you walk for four miles, you get the road where motor cars run. No, nobody has the inclination to start plantation. I have asked so many to plant oranges but nobody is interested.'

That was during Ron's first time. Second time, he came to cry unabashedly and the third time, he came seeking shelter for the boys; and here he was—having a bout of malaria.

He continued to take quinine tablets every eight hours for three days. The fever went down, but still continued in infrequent bouts. On the third day, his ears started ringing, and he felt unsteady like an intoxicated man. When Ingti saw him on the third day, he got worried. He started to fuss over Ron.

'Oh, for two nights you stayed alone in this state! Tonight, I shall come to stay here. Do you want me to bring you anything? Anything to eat?' Ingti asked.

'Bring a chicken and a bottle,' Ron said, and gave some money to the old man.

Late afternoon, Ingti came back carrying a chicken, a bottle of country liquor, and some dried pork.

The old man then started to cook. After slaughtering the chicken, he carefully cut every piece and cooked it with herbs and potatoes. When it was nearly done, he threw a handful of crushed sesame seeds into the pot and covered it. The aroma of chicken cooked with sesame soon wafted all around.

Ron offered the old man the bottle as a mark of respect. The old man was very amused. 'You are becoming one of us—*Arlang* (man in Karbi),' he said in jest.

With pieces of victuals and the guts cleaned and cooked, both started drinking the brew and talking; Ingti talked about many things—about himself, his life, many stories and myths of the hills. After the drinks, there was a feast of rice and chicken. Ron's malaria also disappeared from that day.

While they were drinking, Ron asked Ingti about his wife. They had been together so many times, but he had never asked the old man about his wife. He only knew that his wife had passed away.

In the comforting intoxication brought on by the arrack, Ingti started to talk about his wife, 'She belonged to a Teron family from the village across the hill.' The old man then got immersed in his memories.

When he had first met Kadom Teronpi, old man Ingti was a stripling young man. Being the youngest of the family, he had no responsibilities. He had three elder brothers and several elder sisters.

The eldest brother was more like a father; after his father's death, the eldest had ably cared for them. He was a powerful man—headman of the village and involved in local politics too. 'I used to play the flute all around that time. I stayed in a dormitory, and we used to visit the families who had daughters—either in groups or alone. I had quite a reputation then. People used to call me Bonglong Kro,' the old man said. After a pause, he continued, 'It was then that I met her.'

'What is Bonglong Kro, Koka?' asked Ron.

The old man laughed, exposing his black teeth; the folds of his face then buried his eyes completely.

'Ha, ha, ha, how would you know what is Bonglong Kro!' the old man said, sipping his arrack. 'I will tell you that later…for now, hear the story of my old missus.'

He closed his eyes and tried to remember. The cooking fire threw images of light and shadow on his lined face.

The Terons put out word that they had few sons. So if anyone wanted to marry a girl from their clan, the groom would have to stay with them and work for two years. After hearing that, I kept silent for some time. Then my mother heard something from someone and asked me, "Should we now go and ask for the hand of Teron's daughter?" When I said yes, my eldest brother prepared to go within a week to ask for the bride with all sorts of presents. Before leaving, he told me, "There would be no working in their house for two years, we will bring the girl by paying more bride price if necessary." My brother brought the girl alright; but instead of bringing her for his brother, he married her himself.'

'What?' Ron asked, surprised.

'Yes, he married her himself.'

The sky fell on old Ingti Koka's head. His smile disappeared; the flute in his hand also became silent. He started to stay away from his home and roamed around the hills after that incident. After sometime, he left home altogether. He went to the Jaintia hills, then to the Khasi hills. That was the first time he saw orange plantations. He worked in different places doing different kinds of work. He worked as a porter in many places. And it was during his roaming around in the hills that he came to know about the different routes; he also became familiar with the people of different tribes and villages. He then continued on and reached Shillong. There, he became a watchman in the house of a wealthy coal and timber merchant. He stayed there for quite a long time; the secret of his khaki uniform and red canvas shoes date from that period.

For four years he did not return home; he had no connection with anyone from home either. After four years, wearing his khaki uniform and red canvas shoes, with cigarettes and money in his pocket, he returned home. A month before his return, his elder brother had suddenly died of an illness.

After such a long period, it was a strange feeling seeing his sister-in-law Kadom Teronpi. No, he did not remember that incident; he remembered nothing of those days. But after a few days he suddenly realized that after his brother's death, Kadom Teronpi was now free!

His sister-in-law Kadom Teronpi was free! Ingti became happy suddenly.

Then, very soon, according to the prevailing customs of the tribe, he had married his dead brother's wife. After four years of waiting, he got the girl he had initially sought. His first child was from his elder brother; after that he had seven children, of which four survived.

After his marriage, Ingti led a regular life; he looked after the cultivation and all the household work. But still, he occasionally became restless, and felt suffocated within the bounds of his house. Then old man Ingti started going away from his home again. He roamed the old tracks, and did the old jobs again; after some days, he would return home to his old missus. In between, he started the orange plantation and, gradually, the plantation became an obsession with him. The old lady also came. Occasionally, both would come and stay in the small house on the plantation for days together—away from the din and bustle of the village home. They tended to the orange bushes together while talking to each other for long periods of time. They would also cook various dishes that they liked. The most beautiful memories of the old man's life were closely related with this orange plantation.

The old lady died two years ago. And old man Ingti's life became totally empty. It felt empty too; the orange plantation felt empty as well.

What happened, Koka?' Ron asked with concern.

'Cancer,' Koka replied. 'Yes, it spread over the whole stomach. I took her to the civil hospital, but nothing came of it,' the old man added, visibly emotional. 'Oh,' Ron let out a sympathetic sigh; he couldn't find any more words to say. Ingti Koka did not pay any attention to it and continued with his own story.

'I have not been able to hold the *Chamangkan* (a ritualistic colourful festival in honour of the dead, organized by a family member of the Karbi tribe) after her death. If not this year, I plan to hold it the next at least. Then she will go to heaven. After that, I shall also die. Both of us had already decided in whose house we wanted to be reborn after death. We shall take rebirth together, and we shall marry again.

Ron looked at Ingti Koka incredulously.

No, the old man was not joking. He really believed that after their deaths, he and his wife would surely be reborn as per the pre-decided plan. Faith in rebirth was centuries-old in their folk belief. The society also really believed that such and such person would really be reborn as a boy or girl in such and such person's house. From the first day when a son would be born in that household, people would start talking that so and so had been reborn in this male baby. Just like he had said he would, his soul had come and taken rebirth. From a very young age, the baby would hear those stories; everybody would tell him about the person whose reincarnation he was. The boy would gradually learn about the details of that person's life; and slowly, he, himself, would start to believe it. Centuries-old tradition of folk belief would convince him. The same thing would happen to the girl. And the circumstances would be such that they would be forced to be attracted towards one another; and if they married, then this cycle of rebirth would strengthen and continue.

Birth, death, rebirth, love, marriage…

Oh, it is such a comforting thing this belief! It felt so nice to think about this possibility.

'I may live for four five years more,' old man Ingti continued, 'and after another 10 years or so, both of us would take birth again. We have already decided where we will take birth.'

'And the people would remind you about your previous birth, won't they?' Ron asked.

'Surely, they would!' the old man laughed.

Arrack had spread its warmth over both of them. Rice and sesame-flavoured chicken was finished, and the bottle was empty.

'You spoke about Bonglong Kro?' Ron said, 'Tell me now what it means?'

The old man nearly collapsed with laughter. He began to speak about Bonglong Kro and Ron heard the story with increasing amusement: Bonglong Kro was a Casanova-like character of the myths and legends of the Karbi people. He would roam around the Karbi villages, trying to make love to the marriageable maidens. In this, Bonglong Kro was very efficient. He could not only seduce young girls with his honeyed-tongue, but could easily make love to them too. He had a power of seduction, and any damsel who fell under his spell could not come out of it.

The parents would guard their unmarried daughters to save them from Bonglong Kro. But even through such protection, even when the girls were made to sleep with their grandmothers, one could never tell when Bonglong Kro would come and make love to them—he was a real terror for the parents of unmarried daughters.

Ron looked at the old man. The narration of the myth of Bonglong Kro had brought a lively and amused expression to his face. All the lines of his face had started smiling, and the small eyes shone in mirth; his body language became very expressive. But Ron had difficulty in imagining the old man as a Casanova of myths of the yore. How was the old man when he was young? Ron had seen the youngest son of the old man. He had gone out through the backwaters to study in a missionary college in Shillong; he was very handsome. He had a well-built lean body, sculpted by practice of the martial arts. His colour was golden…yes, golden; old man Ingti, too, must have been such a golden boy in his youth. And that gold-skinned youth played his flute over the hills and dales, and the youth from the young man's dormitory became very popular among the girls—and was called 'Bonglong Kro'.

Old man Ingti's story of Bonglong Kro went on and on. It was quite late at night; Ron went to sleep in the tree house a little up on the hill slope. Walking upward through the orange bushes and finding his way with a flash light, Ron thought about the Karbi myth, and if people could really be reborn according to their own wishes. Then he and Swaha could also have decided where both of them would be reborn in their next birth! Before death, they would have declared their intentions before everyone. And after birth of a boy and a girl in those families, people would start reminding them of their previous birth—who they were, and who had taken rebirth as them! If the Karbi tribe's belief was really true, then both the heartache of unfulfillment and the fear of death would disappear. Oh, the fear of death would be no more.

But can one totally dismiss this belief of rebirth as false?

A PORT IN THE RIVER OF LIFE

I

The boys had come, they had come!

They had come in small groups and made contact with old man Ingti. Ron became busy—his work had now started. He would have to hide these boys in the Karbi hills now; he lead them across the deep forest, to that beautiful, narrow valley—of large rocks, dwarf trees, and the meandering stream he had decided beforehand where the camp would be constructed. Once the order was given, the experienced boys started to collect bamboo and other types of wood from the forest, and started to build the camp. Ron returned to the orange plantation. He would have to wait till the last of the boys arrived; there were still 20 or more boys to come.

When Ron had seen the man who was leading the first group of boys, his heart jumped. Prabin-Dul! He had run out and embraced him.

Though thin, Prabin was very powerfully built. He wore a pair of spectacles with thick lenses; he always kept a spare pair of glasses in his shirt pocket so that in case of any mishap, he wasn't devoid of proper vision. He always wore a stern expression—or maybe the glasses contributed to his stern look. He spoke in a short, clipped manner. But Ron knew well that underneath such a stern exterior was a soft, poetic heart; sometimes, before his close friends, he would hum some famous lines of poet Duara: *My heart is like the leaves of Jetuka (Henna in Assamese) Green as the grassy meadows…*

A boy with a heart like the leaves of henna, who tried to cover a sentimental heart by thick-lensed glasses and a stern exterior.Ron called Prabin to one side and exclaimed, 'Oh, we have not met in two years! Two long years!'

'It has be more than that,' Prabin replied indifferently. Ron, however, did not pay any attention to his feigned indifference, because he knew that Prabin would continue to behave like that—cold voice, stern mask, indifferent behaviour, for a long while. Slowly, the ice would melt.

'We have somehow survived these two years, Dul,' Ron's voice became quite emotional. A softness also descended in the eyes behind the thick lenses.

'You are right. Surviving two years is the main thing.'

Both of the them remained silent for some time; various emotions and memories ebbed and flowed through their minds. Ron then said, 'Come, let us make arrangements to send the boys. Then we would go to the orange plantation and wait there till the last of the boys arrive.'

Lighting a fire on the small packed earthen fireplace in the tree house, they started to talk in the evening.

'We have to hide these selected 50 boys in Karbi hills for some time,' Ron told Prabin. 'For that, I have found a very good place. After three months or so, depending on the situation, we shall decide what to do next. In the meantime, we have to protect the boys from open hunt of the military, police, and the traitors. What do you say, Dul?' Prabin remained silent. He kept looking at the dancing flames of the fireplace. Ron continued, 'You will have to help me. Oh, even in my wildest imagination I did not think that you would come this way. I did not know beforehand who all would be coming except for one or two. We must keep the boys busy, must keep them trained and fit, Dul!'

Prabin looked at Ron from across the smoking fire. Ron saw that his gaze from behind the thick glasses was penetrating. Prabin replied without warmth, 'Whatever you order, sir.'

'Oh, shut up.' Ron chided him. 'What is this "sir" now? I will give you a...' he raised his hand.

'OK! OK, sir!' for the first time, a glint of amusement appeared in Prabin's eyes. That meant his mouth will open now, and the indifferent expression from his face would fade away.

'This is our period of staying incognito,' Ron told Prabin with a smile, 'like the Pandavas who had to stay incognito for a year after their banishment to forest for 12 years.'

He laughed out loudly in jest.

Prabin did not say anything for a long time; he kept watching the smouldering fire intently. When he raised his head and looked at Ron, Ron had the feeling that a sharp, penetrating gaze pierced through him once again. Holding his gaze steadily, Prabin said, 'I have many things to talk about with you, Ron.'

'I know. Me too,' Ron replied softly. 'We won't talk about those today,' Prabin said, 'because we will have a lot of time for that later.'

'You are right. We won't talk today. Nobody knows how long this hiding period would last, so we surely have a lot of time on our hands.'

Both of them remained silent for some time. Then Prabin said, 'You have not changed in the last two years, Ron.'

'You have also not changed. You didn't learn how to put on weight! You are the same steel frame, Oh, I still remember the time you felt sick on our way to Burma. You got ready to call it a day. "Leave me here, we have enemies everywhere. If you keep on carrying an invalid like me, all will be killed. Leave me here, under this big tree." Didn't you say so? And I was thinking I could easily carry you on my back because you were, and still are, so thin! What a mistake I made. You are such a thin guy, how are you so heavy? I carried you for two days. You were nearly unconscious then and didn't know what was happening. And I am telling you the truth Dul, sometimes—specially while climbing up the hills—I felt like throwing you off to the gorges below. My, like a two-mound sack. Had I known it before, I would have left you under that tree.'

Prabin started laughing in fits.

'Now you are laughing, you rascal,' Ron also warmed up to the mood. His eyes shone in happiness. He looked at Prabin and asked, 'Do you still practice Brahmacharya? Do you still lecture others not to sin by letting the drops fall?'

Prabin's giggles increased. Leaning back and facing the sky, he said, 'No, no. I don't practice it any longer; I am a regular man now!' he said, nearly falling sideways in his laughter. The whole tree house started to creak.

The fire was dying down; Prabin poked and rekindled it. The air had a chill in it, but the warmth of the fire made it very comfortable. In the bright moonlight outside, the orange bushes looked like old men sitting on their haunches, burying their heads between their knees. The ridges of the hills shone brightly in the moonlight too. Inside the tree house, in the warmth radiated by the fire, old friends continued to talk for long.

'How long since you've gone home?' Prabin asked.

'I have really forgotten, Dul. I don't remember when I had last gone home. Now one cannot go that way, thanks to Alok. I could not go even when I got the news of my father's illness. One of my friends helped and arranged for the treatment. Communication with home is nearly impossible…'

'Have you heard about Bakul?' Prabin asked.

'Bakul? What about her?' Ron became anxious.

'Then you do not know. Nothing to worry. It is not bad news. Rather it is good. It is about her marriage.'

'Marriage!?' Ron's voice had an edge of surprise and incredulity. He became dumb. Bakul's marriage. He looked at Prabin helplessly.

'I suddenly thought that you might not be aware of this development,' Prabin said, and continued, 'You will have to be told from the beginning. A few months back I had to take shelter with a family at Dibrugarh, in my uncle's house. In a rented house near my uncle's place, there is a university with a girl's hostel. My cousin also studies in that university. She stays in that hostel most of the time during the day. I saw a handsome, young man coming in a Maruti car and talk with a girl for a longtime outside the gate of the hostel many times; occasionally, he would take her out in the car too...'

Prabin looked at Ron's face.

'Go on, Dul,' Ron said. 'Tell me everything.'

'One day, just out of curiosity, I asked my cousin who they were. Only then did I come to know that the girl was Bakul. I had seen her at your place three or four years back, so I would not have recognized her even if I had met her face-to-face. My cousin is good friends with Bakul, and they study in the same department.'

'Who is the boy?' Ron became impatient.

'The boy is supposed to be your good friend, a journalist in a big English newspaper. His name is Partha Chaudhury.'

'What?' Ron stood up in excitement. 'Are you sure?'

'Yes. I am sure. I came to know about it from my cousin.'

Ron suddenly became restless. He got down from the tree house and started to pace in the orange plantation. Bakul? Partha-da? Such a strange thing! No, it is impossible. Why? Why is it impossible? It is not impossible. It was totally possible, and quite a natural thing to happen; why are you getting so excited about it, Ron? You should be happy, he thought to himself. Various conflicting thoughts came and swirled inside his mind. He was not sure what he should do.

Prabin had come down from the tree house in the meantime.

'Dul!' he called out to Prabin. Prabin came near him.

'What did you say about the marriage, Dul?'

I heard from my sister that the boy had come to Dibrugarh about a month or so before I saw him. And it was then he had proposed marriage. And Bakul had accepted it.'

An indescribable feeling flooded Ron's mind. The news about Bakul's marriage had really affected him. A little sadness, a little inapplicable apprehension of uncertainty, all these feelings came together and crowded his mind. He looked at the moon-washed sky through the orange bushes; the moon appeared to be hanging without any support behind the web of a net.

'Then?' Ron asked Prabin.

'After that the boy is said to have talked about the marriage both in his own and also in your house. But...' Prabin paused for a moment. Then seeing the questioning look in Ron's eyes, he continued, 'It appears that there was opposition to the marriage from both families.'

Ron became speechless. He can imagine why there can be opposition from Partha-da's family. But what happened in his own home? He asked Prabin in a helpless way, 'In our family? What is there to oppose the marriage from our side?'

Prabin remained silent for some time. Then he said, 'Look Ron, I am telling you what I have heard from my cousin. Ah, I could have met Bakul myself. Oh, how could I know that I would meet you like this and that you would not be knowing about these things! It did not cross my mind then at all.' He remained silent for some time and then started again, 'Your father has said that the boy Partha came to enquire about his illness and stayed at your house for few days, and it was then he had met Bakul for the first time. Now, he is afraid that someone might accuse him of trapping a rich man's son to marry off his daughter in such a way.'

Ron was speechless. Then in the next moment, he realized there was nothing to be surprised at. Given the nature of his father, Ron knew he would think that way only. He became a little angry too;

the way his father had given importance to his principles, his honour and criticism of others, he didn't think with the same importance about his daughter's happiness, her future. A boy like Partha-da, and a family like that! Would he ever get such a match for his daughter? Ron thought about his father.

'And why have the boy's family opposed?' Ron asked sarcastically. Because the bride's family is not rich and do not have social status?'

Prabin did not reply immediately. In the meantime, they had reached the lower part of the hillock of the orange plantation. From there, Ron looked at the sky. Luminous cotton wool-like clouds were moving slowly in the moonlit sky. In the moonlight, the clouds had taken on various hues. Prabin spoke as softly as he could, 'With brothers like us, who would like to marry a girl from our families, Ron?'

Ron suddenly turned and looked at Prabin. In the moonlight, Prabin saw the surprised look on Ron's face. Ron turned his face away from Prabin's gaze; he bit his lower lip and shut his eyes tightly. Yes, this is the reality, he thought, the hard reality. He felt really helpless. What should he do now? What can he do? Only if he could have met Partha-da once, or Bakul. Even if they had met, what would he have done or said anyway?

'When Bakul has accepted his proposal, even if there is opposition from home, Partha said that he would go ahead with the marriage,' Prabin continued. 'He wanted to marry her in court, but Bakul did not want to go ahead with the marriage at that time. She is said to have sought some more time. As to why, I do not know.'

Both of them remained silent for some time. They had walked quite a distance by the road below the orange plantation by then. Ron then turned back and started to return. Keeping his hand on Prabin's back, he said softly, 'Partha-da is really a good man, Dul. Brave. He has a sincere feelings, for us too; it is much deeper than a journalist's curiosity. It would be really nice to have such a man as brother-in-law. I have only one worry, Dul… Partha-da's family is very rich. In a big house, they live in a Sahabi style. Bakul will not be able to adjust to such a family.'

'Nowadays a girl gets married to a boy, not to a household,' Prabin offered his wise thought.

II

A little upstream from the camp site, there was a bend in the little river. At that spot, there were some very large rocks on both sides and flowing through them, the river turned into a fast-flowing foaming rapids for a stretch. And just at the bend a large flat rock—big enough for a man to lie down on—jutted over the river like a hanging platform. Near it was a tall, dome-like rock. Ron and Prabin were talking there; there was not much else to do but talk. It was an existence resembling a suspended state. To that valley of large stone and dwarf trees, tiresome repetitiveness had descended like a thin veil of numbing mist. The beautiful scenery all around, the assurance of danger-free existence, and freedom from the daily terror of being caught in the claws of hunting packs—all these seemed less important as days went by. Ron and Prabin were not unaccustomed to situations like these. They tried to keep the boys busy in long marches, climbing mountains, cultural events, and many more activities…

From the stone platform and the dome rock, one could hear the constant sound of the stream entering the rapids. The water at the base of the stones was quite deep, a deep pool of green water formed there and if one looked closely, *silgharia* fish could be seen swimming in it.

At noon, Prabin came and stretched out face down on the platform rock. Soon, he became enmeshed in deep thought. After some time, Ron also arrived. He carefully climbed the dome rock. Watching Prabin for some time, he said softly, 'What now?' It was a question both to Prabin and himself.

Prabin lifted his head and looked at Ron. Ron had a feeling that an excitement had spread over Prabin. Inside the loose-fitting camouflage fatigues, his whole body had become restless like an uncoiling serpent.

'What are we doing here, Ron? Prabin asked. A sharp, questioning glance focussed on Ron. He did not reply for some time. Then he spoke in a low voice, 'What do you think we are doing, Dul?'

'If I had known the answer, Ron, I would not have asked the question.' Then after a pause he continued, 'I think we are wasting both time and opportunity.'

Ron did not answer. He was little surprised at Prabin's tone.

A pregnant silence descended. Nothing but the sound of flowing water could be heard. Breaking the silence, Prabin started, 'Let us take stock of what we had done in the last three months.'

Ron didn't say anything and Prabin continued, 'In the last three months we have constructed a beautiful camp for staying in this beautiful place incognito. You are correct, Ron, really staying incognito—divorced from the whole world, donning camouflage army fatigues, and carrying weapons in hand, we are an underground army! Whose army? Whom shall we fight and for whom?'

Ron did not reply. He suddenly started to get angry at himself, at Prabin, on the whole situation.

Without answering, he sat brooding on the dome rock, looking at the water flowing at the base of the two large rocks. The water rushed against the rocks producing innumerable bubbles that floated downstream and disappeared.

'In the last three months,' Prabin continued in a grating voice, 'we made the camp, built sentry posts for its protection, drilled regularly, and started a system of regular classes and lectures even though we have nothing new to say to the boys. You went downstream with a detachment, made contact with the villages and built up a system for getting provisions. You had explored the hills and forests of that side.

I have also taken a group upstream in a long expedition. Sometimes by the side of the stream, sometimes through the forests, and sometimes over the uneven tracks on the hills, I have marched and tired my boys out. Every moment, I have kept them under strict discipline—not a single moment have I allowed them to be lazy; and in these 15 days, do you know what I have discovered?

Do you want to hear it? I discovered a small hill surrounded on all sides by the very high hills where sunlight never falls directly. And in that hill of perpetual shadows covered with reeds and bushes—where wild orchids bloom the year-round not on trees, but on the ground, ground orchids—I discovered a waterfall; in a narrow creek of a high hill covered with lush ferns, a stream of water falls from high up. And in the rocks near the waterfall hang innumerable large hives of wild honey bees.

I have discovered these while marching through the hills with the boys, and I discovered lots of questions. What did you discover, Ron?'

'What did I discover?' Ron put the question as if to himself. For some time, he remained silent. Then he started to speak slowly, deliberately, uttering one word at a time, 'Do you know what I discovered, Dul? I discovered that we must resolutely keep moving on the path that we have consciously chosen for ourselves. Only then can we reach our goal.'

'Goal?' Prabin suddenly stood up, like an uncoiling spring. He brought his face near to Ron and asked, 'Goal, Ron? Yes, you are right, when we embarked on this path we had a goal in mind that we believed in—freedom for a small part of a very large country!

Yes, we all believed in that goal. But now, after gathering so much experience, shouldn't we re-examine all the percepts? Shouldn't we try to re-evaluate them? A region with so many nationalities, languages, and religion, can it separate and maintain its independent existence? Can it defend itself from the armies of the international forces, from the greed of the multinationals? Ron, you know all these things, I don't need to tell you all this. Can't we rethink all over again, think about some concept of autonomy? I think it is possible, and possibly desirable too.'

Prabin started panting after speaking for so long.

Ron looked searchingly at Prabin, but did not say anything. Prabin had voiced nothing new, but he had put it courageously with an urgency, and had taken considerable risk in revealing the trajectory of his current thoughts.

Ron looked around at the skyline formed by the hills—the pale cold sky, the darkish deep blue forest, the gurgling stream—and then at Prabin, and said softly, 'I will try to answer your questions, Dul.'

He then looked at the camp under the dwarf trees; the beautifully made bamboo huts could be seen from here. Some boys were gathering at the small opening near the camp. It was time for the sentries to change. Groups of boys were starting to hurry towards the sentry posts to stand guard for the first part of the night. The sergeant was barking some orders.

Some boys were sitting cross-legged on the ground. They would be given training in basic arms; it would be a repetition for the already-trained boys. It was a practice session really—of cleaning, taking apart, and reassembling basic guns and other paraphernalia.

Ron caught hold of Prabin's arm and pulled him towards the camp. His hand felt so lifeless!

Ron started to think to himself. *Is he having some crisis of faith? No, it should not be. He is quite senior, trained, experienced, and a dedicated man. He should not have a crisis of faith. He won't go wayward, he won't turn a traitor. Some genuine questions have appeared in his mind, some doubts have arisen. This is not something altogether abnormal...*

I shall have to discuss it with him.

If it is discussed openly, the doubts in his mind may disappear, but he will have to be watched!

Yes, an eye has to be kept on him.

Ron remembered the trouble Prabin had taken during his illness. How he had constantly stayed with him, encouraged him, reassured him during his moment of crisis. That happened in Kachin, near the Chinese boarder. The long trek through the forests of northern Burma, and through the Death Valley of Hukong, had taken a terrible toll on the boys. Many fell sick; Prabin himself had fallen seriously sick on the way. For two days, Ron had to carry him on his back. But he recovered fast. That plateau-like place near the Chinese border was very cold; it was also winter. Fine dust-like snow had started to fall. Such terrible cold and snowfall was a totally a new experience for the boys. And it was there that Ron had fallen sick.

First, he had a cold with cough. Then the cold settled in his chest. He started having high fevers, and soon, a bad pneumonia developed. Within a week, he got so ill that he could not get up from bed; he could not eat or attend to nature's call unless helped by somebody. He had no idea that illness could make a man so weak and turn him into such a helpless creature. Sometimes, helplessness brought tears into his eyes, and the weakness had sapped his mental strength as well.

Treatment was very backward—practically nonexistent in those border areas. There were no doctors around, but someone had managed to call a health worker of Kachin Liberation Army. The experienced man examined him like a doctor with stethoscope and had diagnosed him with pneumonia.

It was Prabin who stayed with Ron all that time. He had bathed him, helped him attend nature's call, tended to him like a nurse—and like a doctor, even given him the penicillin shots in time. Prabin tried to keep him amused and his spirits up. Ron had discovered a different Prabin then. Instead of the usual unsmiling grumpy man, Prabin had become someone who could laugh at himself and make others laugh too.

He had paid back the debt of me carrying him on my back for two days, Ron thought. No, no, even if I had not done so, he still would have done for me what he did.

Ron had dragged Prabin towards the camp; they took the path below the tall hill and after sometime, started to climb the hill. After climbing up about one third of the hill, they reached a treeless, stony outcropping. There, one could see the mouth of a cave. And if one entered through the narrow neck a little, a widening was reached. It was like a chamber big enough for three-four men to sit and talk. It was cold and dark inside. When the boys had first discovered it, they imagined many romantic notions about the cave. But Ron thought that they were possibly the first men to have entered it. The cave, littered with dead leaves, grass, dust, and with a musty smell, possibly served as lair for bears, tigers, foxes, or snakes.

Ron and Prabin sat on the narrow ledge in front of the cave on this late autumn afternoon. The slanting rays of the sun fell on their faces. From there, the valley below could be seen for a long way. Over the dense forest in front, the tall distant hills appeared hazy blue. The top of the forest appeared like a clumpy carpet. After having passed through the dark bowels of the forest, the sight of its top looking like a clumpy meadow or a carpet evoked inexplicable emotions in Ron's mind. In the slanting slope of one of the hills of the yore was old man Ingti's orange garden; and a little ahead, his village. From the ledge, the camp could also be seen. At the opening in front, some boys were still at the arms training. They appeared so small, like Lilliputians walking here and there.

Ron looked at the sky. The daylight would stay for another one and half hours at best. After that, dusk would envelop the hills in darkness.

Prabin was deeply engrossed in the beauty of the scene. The slanting golden rays of the sun were falling at the top of the tall trees of the forest, and it looked like someone had scattered handfuls of golden dust on a green carpet.

'Dul,' Ron called out softly.

Prabin turned to him. His eyes were now strangely very calm, as if he had made peace with himself and the world. The beauty of nature had calmed him down.

Both of them continued to look at the beautiful scene in front in silence. Now I must start the talk, Ron thought. The doubts and fears in Prabin's mind need to be cleared. Confidence must be brought back to him. How to and from where to start…?'You know, Dul,' Ron started softly, 'in every organization's history there are high and low times, times of crisis. We have crossed such phases. We have seen good times…high times, now we are facing a setback. These are all temporary phases.'

'Who does not know that? It is a natural thing. That is not the problem. The problem is to decide correctly what we ought to do now. Whether we shall follow the old path or, having learned from our experience, search for a new path. The problem is if we have the will and the mental strength to do it. This hiding period is also giving us the time and chance to reflect. Tell me Ron,' Prabin's voice became a little sharp, 'shall we travel the old way and have the same results or do something new?'

'What new?' Ron asked.

'That exactly is what we need to find out together,' Prabin said with great feeling. Then he added, 'Instead of only following the path of armed violent struggle, we also must think of non-violent and democratic struggles also. But this is purely my personal opinion. We must learn about the limitations of underground armed struggle...'

Prabin left his words hanging.

A silence fell between the two.

The sunshine had become quite weak. Only a pale, cold light came out from the setting orange globe. The shadows lengthened and mellowed, and darkness started gathering under the leaves.

'Do you think this new path will lead us to success?' Ron asked.

'There is no guarantee, it can only be known by following it.'

'Exactly,' Ron interrupted, 'there is no guarantee. If we embarked upon a new path now, there is no guarantee of success.'

He stopped and looked at Prabin, whose eyes behind the thick glasses appeared like two deep wells. Then he continued slowly,

'See, Dul, I am not saying that we need not think in a new way, or that our method of work does not require change. But only for sake of change to jump into a new uncharted and uncertain direction—that I oppose, especially at this time.'

'Why at this time?'

'At this time, we are passing through a very difficult and adverse phase. Whatever may be the reasons, we are facing a serious setback. Our enemy is very powerful, and the boys who ate with us from the same plate have now taken up guns against us. To save our strength we have brought the selected boys to this hideout. Who knows how many such camps are located inside the country and outside? In the face of danger, we are protecting ourselves and our strength in this way.

Ron was speaking rapidly; he was a little excited too. 'Remember one thing, Dul, in the face of danger, one must become very resolute. Every job we do, every utterance we make has to be evaluated carefully. In such times, you must be very careful about some members of your own organization too. Do you know what kind of members? Those who are dissatisfied with or without reason, whose acts and utterances are uncertain, those who want to bring some untested ideas into the organization in the guise of solution—you must be careful of such people. Because during a setback, such people spread their own doubts, uncertainties, and weaknesses among others. As a result, the morale of the members of the organization plummets and discipline becomes shaky. Then the organization gets disarrayed.'

After speaking continuously, Ron paused for a while. He drew in the late afternoon air into his chest and said, 'And do you know, Dul, such people also desire the good of the organization in their hearts. That is why they think about new paths; but because they do it at the wrong time and in a wrong way, the result that comes out is the opposite. During a period of setback, we must always guard against all dangerous thoughts and ideas.'

Ron's voice then diminished into a conspiratorial whisper, 'When an idea capable of creating doubts and confusion enters an organization, it can become more dangerous than an undercover spy of the enemy.'

'Does that mean you consider me a dangerous person? I am dissatisfied, beset with doubts, and I carry dangerous ideas. I am like an enemy spy, eh?' Prabin's voice sounded heavy.

'No,' Ron spoke with force. 'Had I thought like that I would not have come here with you and spoken to you like I did. But you must also understand that the things you are speaking about and the ideas you are carrying can really be dangerous; they can really weaken our organization at this time of setback and damage everyone's morale. So, you must be careful that such things don't happen. We are not discussing revolution in a restaurant over a cup of tea. Every day, we are facing death and tackling bullets from our enemy. We must be careful.'

'So now, we must not only censor talk but ideas too,' Prabin commented little sarcastically.

Ron got angry and replied heatedly, 'I don't know why you are thinking like that. I am just telling you the necessity of being cautious, of preserving discipline and loyalty, of becoming resolute.'

Both of them became silent again.

Then Prabin said softly, 'I can understand you, Ron.'

'I knew you would,' Ron said, then added, 'And it is necessary to understand.'

Prabin did not say anything.

It was getting dark. The sun had slid behind the western ranges, and the last of the orange glow was colouring the sky. A few moments later, everything would be dark.

'Let's go, Dul,' Ron said..

'Yes, let us go.'

Both of then hurriedly climbed down the hill towards the camp.

III

Stars appeared in the sky; a bunch of bright stars in a clear sky. Prabin was looking at the sky, deep in thought. Except the sentries on duty, everybody in the camp had gone to bed. Sleep had evaded Prabin for the last few days though; he had not been able to sleep for a pretty long time. When he did drift into it towards morning, he was troubled with weird dreams.

The Great Bear was crystal clear in the sky. It was called the *Kalpurush* in Sanskrit; he did not remember who first showed it to him in the sky. But one thing he did remember was that he used to be very afraid by the very mention of it. If the shadow of the *Kalpurush* falls on someone, the person dies—something of that sort was told to him. And he was very much afraid to venture out of the house at night lest the shadow of the *Kalpurush* fell on him.

There is no reason, no basis of such a childhood fear. But, oh, how powerful was that fear! On starry nights when he had to cross the courtyard at night, he used to cover his head with the round bamboo basket and run as fast as he could.

Looking at the starry sky, Prabin remembered his unfounded childhood fear. Now he is sitting in this valley between the hills, sitting on a rock on the bank of a stream and looking at the sky. The *Kalpurush* has appeared; it is striding over a large part of the night sky! And under its huge spread, so puny and insignificant was his own existence… But he is no longer afraid of the *Kalpurush*. He has long crossed that phase. The reasons for his fears are different now.

Yes, the reasons for his fears are different.

It isn't fear of death—that too had vanished long back. And its place had now been taken over by the fear of failure.

Yes, in his childhood, besides the *Kalpurush*, he was afraid of ghosts and goblins. In school, he was afraid of others laughing at or teasing him; in school, his classmates would really laugh at him.

In middle school, he was really weak and thin; compared to his classmates, he was shorter, too. His parents also worried a lot about his built. Once or twice, they had taken him to visit a doctor. Doctor gave him medicines for worms as well as tonics. His grandmother had brought an amulet for him and fastened it with a black thread around his waist.

Not only that, in high school he had started to suffer from excruciating headaches. Occasionally, he was scolded by his teachers for not being able to read the writing on the black board. He did not talk about this issue at home, even when he had real difficulties with his studies. Therefore, his eye examination was delayed; when his eyes were examined eventually, he was forced to wear thick spectacles.

And for those glasses, he had to face the teasing. Because of his physical built and glasses, Prabin had become withdrawn he started to stay away from his classmates, and from the family too. When his friends went out to play football, he would gather a bunch of fishing rods and go fishing in the swamps. But there was no peace even then. Somebody would shout, 'Oh, shorty, how many fish have you caught?'

A sort of anger, frustration, and hostility started to accumulate inside him; a dislike for his own self developed. And in some hidden recesses of his mind, a sense of inferiority started to grow.

But in high school, he suddenly started to grow. And once he started to grow tall, it did not seem to stop; it was as if his body had started to take revenge for the insults and humiliation heaped on him before. By the time school finals were on, he had become the tallest guy in his class. And while in college, his friends gave him a new nickname: *lenga*, meaning thin and tall.

In college, he realized for the first time that his height was the only positive trait in his physical appearance. But the height failed to give him self-confidence; he remained timorous because of his thin frame.

His sense of inferiority did not disappear.

To overcome his imagined physical—and to some extent mental—disability, he thought of many ways in college. To strengthen the muscles of his body, he did regular yoga and physical exercise. At times, he even did inhuman exertions for body building. After that, he started to learn karate and other martial arts; he soon became quite proficient in these. As a result of all these efforts, changes occurred in his body. Though he never developed the rippling muscles of a body builder, his muscles did become really powerful. His gait also changed; instead of the hesitancy of the past, he started walking with a new-found confidence. People, especially the girls, as well as the boys of his class, started to glance twice when he passed by. But the awareness of people looking at him brought a new hesitancy along with happiness.

Along with his physical efforts, he also tried to impose on him a very strict mental discipline. Sometimes this self-imposed discipline reached the level of self-mortification. Not only did he give up beetle nut and tobacco, he ceased drinking tea too. He tried to drive away all bad thoughts from his mind, especially the sexual awakening so natural for his age. Like his physical growth spurt, his sexual desire and development also occurred fast. All these were a matter of great unease for him; even a natural phenomenon like night fall gave him a guilt feeling for days on end.

But such self-mortification also gave him an inexplicable pleasure. He started to think that he was different and morally superior than his other classmates trapped in the circle of love, girls, and sexuality; he looked down with pity on their commonplace problems of love and heart breaks.

The sense of inadequacy, which so deeply ingrained itself secretly in his mind, drove him to achieve superiority in some aspects of life. That was possibly what had also influenced his decision to join the underground armed organization.

That was the early stage of the organization; only a few selected boys had joined then. They dreamt of a sovereign Assam through armed struggles. That was a very new thing, a very new experience. Joining such an organization reinforced his sense of superiority over and difference from others. He volunteered for all dangerous assignments and plunged headlong into the struggle. And soon, in the way he wanted it to be, he became famous within the organization as an intrepid and a strict disciplinarian leader. His thinness, his thick glasses, everything else faded into insignificance.

But he was not fully satisfied. The insect of inadequacy had not stopped biting still. He wanted to prove his courage and heroism in every action—more so to himself than to others, because the need of proving anything to others had ceased long back.

He never hesitated in showing his toughness in mercilessly destroying his enemies and in maintaining strict organization discipline. He never shied away from doling out the harshest punishment to his colleagues and cadres when the need arose. His friends were quite worried about his harshness.

He became a very different person altogether.

Gradually, he developed a self-confidence which put a stop to his practice of self-mortification; he did not feel the need for strict sexual abstinence anymore and started self-gratification like any other normal boy his age. He also started to read a lot and discuss many things with Ron and other comrades, and it was these readings and discussions which led to the birth of different questions in his mind.

Yes, the questions started from then on.

Sitting on a rock while gazing at the starry sky, Prabin was thinking about all these things. The old memories passed before him like pictures from a disjointed movie. All his colleagues were asleep in the camp, except for the sentries who were awake at the guard posts.

The incident had happened at noon two days ago.

Old man Ingti had suddenly appeared at camp around noon. He went straight to Ron and whispered something in his ears. Ron seemed excited; he came straight to Prabin and said, 'You keep everything ready here, our seniors have come. I am going to bring them here.'

He didn't know why, but the news set off a thumping sensation in his chest.

Ron gave out other necessary instructions, and with four armed soldiers, he set off to receive the leaders.

After the talk he had had with Ron on the ledge before the cave, Prabin had not discussed anything further with him except matters of daily activities. In spite of Ron's natural behaviour, Prabin had the feeling that things were no longer the same. He tried to convince himself that it was a false feeling in his mind but still, he couldn't shake the weird feeling off.

I should have stayed like before. It would have been better if I had continued to act courageously without thinking much, Prabin thought to himself, looking at the fast disappearing figure of Ron. He had inexplicable anxiety till the leaders arrived. He had a premonition that something was going to happen. He felt it in the marrow of his bones, but could not make out exactly what.

He was restless with a sense of uncertainty, and it was only late in the evening he came to know what it was when the leaders revealed it before him and Ron.

'We shall now have to go to foreign shores,' one of the leaders said, adding, 'No, it is not Burma this time. We shall have to go to other places for military training. We have decided that Ron would lead the first 10-member team; Ron, what do you think? Would you be able to?'

Prabin observed that Ron's eyes shone brightly as soon as he heard the proposal.

'Yes, sir, there is no question of not being able to,' Ron spoke in an eager and grateful manner. 'When you have thought it fit to put your confidence in me, I would try my utmost to measure up to your expectations,' he added.

Prabin felt his whole body burning with Ron's words; he got very annoyed at the way he spoke. He was also disappointed at Ron's selection. If somebody had to be sent for military training then considering experience, proficiency, and courage, it was he—not Ron—who should have been selected. In military field, he was far more advanced than Ron on all counts. Had it been some political mission, it would not have mattered. But on a military mission…he felt a bitter taste rising in his mouth.

He carried on hearing the leaders silently; they were speaking about the necessity of advanced military training. Though Prabin was hearing the monologue of the leaders, it did not always register. Different thoughts agitated his mind. He looked at Ron—happiness and excitement brought a glow to his face, an indecent glow! Yes, the shine on Ron's face appeared to be indecent; at least it looked like that to Prabin.

Then they started to discuss who would be in the first group. It would have a leader, a deputy, and eight members. Ron had already been selected as the leader, so they discussed the eight members of the team and he enthusiastically took part in it. He expressed his opinion on each boy clearly and everyone gave great importance to his assessment.

Did Prabin, even for a short while, want to be the deputy leader?

Yes, he wanted it. He thought that he would be offered that position; from the direction the discussions were going, he had that impression. The selection of the deputy was kept to the last.

He would have no problem in working under Ron; he could gather at least that much from the experience of working these last days with him.

Did he want to go to foreign countries for advanced armed training though? It was not that he was very keen to go, but at the same time, it was undeniable that foreign journey for advance training at that time was the most important job before the organization—he surely wanted to be part of it.

When the matter of selection of the deputy leader came, Ron himself proposed his name.

'No. No,' the leaders strongly opposed it. 'We have decided to keep him here,' the leaders said, and started to outline their plans.

Prabin had the feeling that he was seeing the rerun of a frightening movie…the scenes appeared familiar.

We shall need lots of money…' the leader had said, 'lots of it will be required to send the group for advanced training. Money has to be raised here. Since there is no system of regular levy from supporters, money has to be raised by threats, by extortion—just like in the past.'

It meant there was no change, nothing had really changed. The rules of the game were the same, only the field had changed.

Prabin swallowed his anger. He felt a hollow sensation in his chest. Something had vanished, a small something—like the flame of a small lamp—was extinguished.

Nothing had changed.

But what did he expect would change? Was he himself clear about it? Did he know what he was looking for?

Except for some vague and foggy ideas, did he know anything clearly?

Why not, he tried to tell himself, but when he tried to think about it clearly, he stumbled at every step. He knew something was wrong, but what it was eluded him.

No, nothing had changed really. They were moving in the same circle of arms and money.

The 10-member team was chosen; training of the team started soon after.

His work was also outlined. In a few days, he would have to start his work as well. Moving to some safe shelter in the city, he would have to direct the campaign of money collection. The searches and arrests of the past had come down considerably.

But Prabin felt no inner urge. A great tiredness mixed with inexplicable sorrow gradually started to engulf him.

He could no longer find any meaning in his work, and he felt quite lonely and useless.

The morning was very bright.

In the golden warmth of the morning sun, the whole world was aglow.

The leaves had become greener; and the hills, covered in lush vegetation.

The cotton candy clouds were floating playfully in the blue morning sky.

Prabin had met Ron in the morning after he woke up.

'We shall move out tomorrow morning,' Ron said.

Prabin only nodded.

'You seem to be avoiding us, Dul? What is the matter?' Ron suddenly asked.

'Why? Nothing,' Prabin said, taken aback. 'You shall leave, who knows when we will meet again, if at all. It's just that I am feeling sad,' Prabin lied without any effort. Then he wondered if it was really a lie? No, it was not a lie…he really was sad at Ron's imminent departure. Whether they would ever meet again was completely uncertain!

Ron clutched at Prabin's shoulder tightly and looked at him for some time, and his eyes softened with a mist of emotion.

After meeting Ron, Prabin was saddened further; an endless sorrow seemed to envelope him. In that bright morning of warm sunshine, blue skies, and floating white clouds, Prabin felt dejected. He wore his uniform—the patterned camouflage fatigues and the cap with the cover. He put his spare spectacles in the upper pocket of his tunic and his beloved nine mm pistol in the holster. He then started to walk slowly through the rocks and the dwarf trees of the narrow valley for a long distance, and then he returned. His mind was empty; the hustle of the camp made no impression in his mind. The soft hues of nature, the wind, and the busy movements of his companions—nothing touched him anymore. He then slowly started to climb the steep path up the hill and after some time, reached the stony ledge before the cave. He sat down on the grassless place where he had talked with Ron. He sat there and looked at the forest below.

The sun's rays had fallen on the uneven top of the forest through the gaps of the canopy of clouds. That exceedingly beautiful scene also failed to make any impression on his mind.

For a long time, he sat there silently; slowly, his mind filled with a sort of emptiness that transformed into peace. He peeped through the opening of the cave; it was dark inside. He could feel the coldness of the cave from outside as if it was a blinding dark alley.

It was as if he had come to terms with himself and his own life. After some time, he slowly brought out his pistol from the holster.

Pulling the trigger was the only formality left.

The empty cave amplified the sound of the shot many times over, but he did not hear any sound.

His body fell to the side on the cave's mouth.

His left hand clutched a small note addressed to Ron. In it, he had requested Ron to put his body inside the ancient cave and seal its opening permanently.

Now, he would never come out of the blind alley.

IV

The room bore a faint smell of dampness, like that of mouldy old cloth. And the smell wafted up whenever one entered the room. The signs of decay were clear everywhere. Lying on the bed, Ron looked at the walls; for many years, they had not had a coat of limewash. The paint from the woodwork had started peeling off, and the plaster of the walls had fallen off at places as well. And though there were water marks of seepage at the corners, the room was large and quite clean. One entered the room through a door in the verandah; two windows were towards it, and two to the outside. Out of the four windows, only the one near the bed could be opened. After leaving India, Ron had to wait in that hotel room for quite a long time; day after day, a tiring long wait. The arrangements of going abroad for advanced training were not all ready. And so, this faded room had become his address. He had been offered this room as the leader; the rest of the boys stayed in a spacious dormitory.

Ron opened the shutters of the window near the bed. The light of late afternoon sun lit up the room. Ron looked at the gate of the hotel with the thick pillars, the long gravel road coming towards the car parking, the overgrown narrow garden and beyond the wall and the road in front, the rows of houses on the other side. The road was empty; and except for two old men listlessly sitting in the pukka border of the pool in front of one of the houses, nobody was in sight. An old dog with an injured paw limped across the road.

The first day when he had entered the hotel, its rundown condition and unhappy atmosphere depressed him greatly. Even after a few days, his mood had not lightened. Looking at the faded houses on the street, he had a feeling that sometime in the past, this area must have been one of the posh and important areas of the city. The latticed walls along the road, high plinths, wide verandahs and the ornate thick pillars along them pointed to the wealth of their past owners. But for some reason, the neighbourhood must have begun to turn seedy. The houses started to fade due to lack of repair and painting; the gardens turned into overgrown patches, the trees of the compounds became bent, misshapen, lusterless, and the scattered marble statues in the gardens got covered with green algae. It was as if the flow of time took a different course and the street remained like an abandoned blocked stream.

Ron's suspicion was confirmed by the middle-aged servant of the hotel.

'At one point, it became difficult to enter this street because of the parked Buike, Chevrolet, and DeSotos,' the old man said with a grimace. 'Everything became topsy-turvy with the Partition of the country, sahib. Everything broke down. The Hindus migrated out.

Most of the inhabitants of this neighbourhood were Hindus. After the owners moved away, four or five poor Muslim families started living in each of the houses...' he added, making a dismissive gesture.

'This hotel?' Ron asked.

'At one point of time, this house was the garden retreat of a zamindar. The hotel came much later. First, it was an Anglo-Indian sahib who started it, but he could not run it for long. Then, a Hindu trader bought it from him. What a hotel it was at one time! There used to be a jam of horse buggies and cars on the front road. In the evening, large chandeliers were lit in the halls. Oh, how gorgeous it was!'

The old man closed his eyes as if trying to remember the days past.

'And now?' Ron asked.

'Now nobody knows who comes here and who stays.'

'Who runs the hotel?'

'Nobody is sure about that either. Before the Partition, the Hindu trader exchanged this property for the Calcutta home of Amanullah Khan. After his death, his son leased out the hotel; he lives in England. How would he run this hotel here? After that, I don't know who took the lease.'

Have you been here for a long time?'

'Yes, from the days of Khan sahib. Only I am left...other people come and go,' the old man said proudly.

Ron glanced at the room again—foam mattresses on the bed, discoloured carpet on the floor, an old imported colour television set on a peeling plywood cabinet—decay was stamped over everything. One of the speakers on the television must have cracked, because the sound came out rasping.

It seemed as if nobody else except Ron and his team were staying in the hotel. In the small reception counter in the large hall below, two people sat yawning and looking bored the whole day. The bearded old man who talked with him alone seemed to be taking care of the guests: supplying drinking water in the rooms, attending to the guests and, for a small tip, bringing liquor from outside. The cleaners came at a fixed time of the day. The kitchen possibly had few more workers, but Ron had not seen them. During meal times, the old man and one person from the counter would come to serve it. No other guests had come to stay at the hotel after Ron and his boys had come. An oily smell of frying slightly rotten fish always hung around the hotel.

The other boys of his group had gone out for a stroll; the boys of his organization who were originally from this city had taken them out. Ron did not go; he did not feel like it. He stayed back alone in the musty room, looking out of the window to the unhappy road in front and waiting for the boys to return.

Yes, most of the time in his life was spent waiting—waiting for something to happen and the anxiety of the wait. Only the days of his childhood—the days of the primary and middle school—were the real carefree days.

Those days now seemed like a dream.

Whenever he closed his eyes he seemed to see a young boy wearing loose khaki shorts and yellow half-sleeved vest, trying to learn riding the heavy Raleigh cycle of his father in the courtyard of their house, with his brother and sister running behind the cycle. The cycle was quite old. The paint had peeled long back, exposing the rusty frame. The narrow leather saddle had few patches on it. Oh, how joyous were those days! Oh, he had almost forgotten the faces of his brother and sister...

There was waiting even then. Of going from middle to high school, reaching the senior section of the high school where his father taught, then of going to college. At one point, he felt that the mental horizon offered by his rural high school was restrictive. Yes, there was waiting even then, but no anxiety of waiting.

The main task of life now was waiting for something to happen.

They had waited month after month in the Karbi hills for something to happen. They really thought that the situation would change, the military campaign would end, they would no longer have to be on a perpetual run. Something new would start... And Prabin ran out of patience to wait. He could no longer bear the anxiety of waiting. A situation which struck as totally meaningless. All actions appeared absurd, and Dul could not tolerate such a situation. He would not tolerate it and he didn't.

I don't want to try to justify suicide, Ron thought. Then, a barrage of thoughts hit him: But I must try to understand why such a resolute boy suddenly lost his will. What shall I call him? Courageous boy? Traitor? Or something else? Who has given me the right to sit in judgment? Who has made me the judge? Are we not, all of us, passive playthings of an unknown, unfathomable fate? Time is always kicking us like a football from place to place! But don't we have to try to stand up to it? Against this uncaring fate?

Ron had seen a bag of cement kept in Ingti's village house. It was placed on a high wooden stool to save it from the damp. But still, the cement had begun to harden in the moist air. Ron had sent a few boys to bring that bag of cement at any cost. Within a few hours the boys brought the bag, slung on two bamboo poles.

And Ron himself had lain the bloodied body of Dul carefully inside the cave and folded his hands over his chest. And after that, with stones, river-bed sand, and cement, he had sealed off the narrow entrance to the cave. They had interred Prabin permanently in the womb of the mountains.

But his thoughts? His ideas? Had some of it remained embedded in my mind too? Like a flash of light, this thought came to Ron.

The road in front was still deserted. His companions had not returned yet. The whole hotel appeared to be totally silent. His companions tried hard to take him out, but Ron didn't go. He did not have the wish to do so. In the air outside, the smell of raw fish would bother him; he found it intolerable.

Yes, he had left a part of his own existence in the Karbi hills—in that dark cave—and he had carried with him a part of Dul's existence, his thoughts, and his ideas. Leaving a part of himself behind and carrying a load of memories, he was setting out on an unknown and uncertain journey.

Ron suddenly remembered home—his father, mother, brother, and especially his sister, Bakul.

What might Bakul be doing now? Had the matter of her marriage advanced? Had she accepted the marriage proposal? No, she definitely had not done it. He knew she would like to wait for her elder brother to come home once. But was that possible? What might Partha-da be doing? Suddenly, he felt a very strong pull towards home; he wanted to go home and see it once. He would meet everyone and talk his heart out, and he would pull Bakul's tresses lovingly and say, 'Hear me, whatever I order, you shall have to do it.' He would look at Partha-da, clasp his hand tightly and in that gesture, there would be a little gratitude also. He knew that Partha would make Bakul happy. It was not the question of money alone. Ron knew Partha was a stable and a selfish man—having the right amount of selfishness required to build a happy home.

Ron's reverie halted as his companions came back; their chatter floated up from the hall below. Ron returned from the world of his day dreams to the reality of the hotel, and unconsciously, a sigh came out of the chest.

Someone knocked at the door.

'Come, come in,' Ron said.

One of the men from the organization entrusted with foreign work came in with a bright smile.

'Moni, aren't you going back to Assam in a few days?' Ron asked him as he entered.

'Yes, I will leave the day after you leave for training. And you must go in two-three days. I have come to inform you all arrangements have been made.'

'Listen, Moni,' Ron started to speak in an urgent tone, 'You would have to do me a favour. It is entirely my personal work. I will give you a letter that you will have to carry with you and give to my sister in her hostel at Dibrugarh. You don't have to say anything to her except that you have come to deliver a letter. The matter is very urgent, Moni. In some matters, one must not delay...'

V

'Sometimes, I can be very selfish,' Bakul said very softly, 'leading a routine life of classes, timely meals, etc. and here we are—coming out and talking. And my elder brother, nobody knows where he is roaming around. Aren't we very selfish? What a path of no return he has chosen… Death stalking his every step! But do you know what I am most afraid of, Partha? I am afraid that someday, he may be disillusioned due to dashed hopes and be hurt—that is my biggest fear.'

Partha listened silently to Bakul, but did not give any answer. What could he say to comfort her anyway? Whichever way he might try to lighten the situation, he would have to lie. He did not know what the truth was himself; Bakul also knew that. So, he remained silent; he did not feel like giving false consolation.

'Sometimes, I dreamt that my brother had returned. Opening the gate, he was coming home by the path under the *amluckee* tree with tired steps. And in the dead of night, I opened the door for him and broke into uncontrollable sobbing on seeing him. I embraced him tightly. He did not utter a word, but just kept patting my back. I washed his wounds and applied ointment. What a dream it was.

"The sores inside my mind are still festering, Bakul. This time, I have come for a long rest. I shall take rest and think," he said to me in that dream.

And the moment I brought something for him to eat, the police arrived. After that, my brother disappeared; the police also vanished, everything just vanished. Dreams can be so unreasonable; the events you see in them have no rhyme or reason. Where did my brother go, or the police? I could not make out how they disappeared; I only realized that they had vanished,' Bakul went on saying as if she was in trance.

'I see the same dream always, the same dream. Whenever I try to give my brother some food, the police comes; with soft steps, always. I have not seen them even once, never even once.'

Bakul talked, sitting on the ground and embracing her knees. In the afternoon light, the Brahmaputra flowing in front had taken a soft appearance. The waves of the river suddenly shone at places like silver fish. Bakul paid no attention to it; she had even forgotten the presence of Partha sitting near her. She was completely immersed in recalling her dreams.

'Why do I see the same dream in the same sequence?' she suddenly asked. 'Is it that I saw the dream only once? But I feel like I am seeing it every day?'

'The whole thing might be deeply embedded in your mind,' Partha said, gently taking Bakul's hand in his. 'You have such deep-seated worries regarding Ron that you repeatedly keep on thinking the same things. In reality, you have not seen the dream as clearly as you have described it. To the hazy pictures of the dream, you have added your worries and uncertainties, your desire and fears.

Everything you see in dreams doesn't always turn true,' he said softly.

'My brother had to escape,' she said, as if talking to herself. She did not pay much attention to what Partha had said. 'Would escaping be his fate? Escaping from danger! Is there any way to be able to live without not believing in destiny?'

'You have not met Ron for a long time, right?'

'I don't remember how long it has been. He came once, long before I came to the university—for the last time. After that, whatever news I got of him was always through you. When I get to know that you have met him, I always burn with envy.'

'He has not even written?'

'I received a long letter, but that was about six months back. A boy had suddenly appeared at dusk and handed me this letter.'

'But you never not told me about it.'

'Yes, I didn't. When I think about the letter, I feel both happy and sad, but also I get afraid. So, I keep the letter hidden, and read it only surreptitiously.'

'What did Ron write?'

'He wrote many things, Partha. A long, long letter, as if he wanted to compensate for not being able to write frequently with that single letter. He wrote about so many things, his poetry, love, dreams…but never did he mention anything about his own hardship or danger.'

'What we think of as hardship or danger, they do not think it that way. That is their life… What did he write about poetry?

'He has written some new poems. He wrote that he would be sending them soon.'

'And about his love?'

'He wrote that he, too, had fallen in love once, and that love had totally changed his life, his thinking. He wrote that he met this girl in Shillong. And he always keeps thinking whether that interlude of love was real or imaginary. Sometimes it seems to him that it was not true, but an illusion.'

'He met the girl in Shillong?' Partha asked, quite alert.

'He wrote that the girl was very different, extraordinary, in fact. Though she is from these parts of Assam, she is like somebody from a different land. And that he loved the girl so much, so much, that he decided to stay away from her.'

Swaha? It must be. He had written about Swaha only. Ron had written to Bakul about Swaha! Partha felt a storm raging inside. Like a bundle of dried leaves carried by the storm, lots of memories swirled through his mind.

'He loved her so much that he decided to stay away from her,' Partha repeated the words to himself.

'It is for these kind of things I love and respect my elder brother so much,' Bakul said, then continued with emphasis, 'These days when you see so many spineless people all around, it is really something to be able to respect someone. I always think who that girl is! What kind of person she is? The way my brother loved her with all his heart, and that he loved her to an extent where he decided to stay away from her so as to not drag her into danger—it's really something else. Did she love him back with equal fervour? How did she return his love? I want to know that. Oh, only if I could meet this girl once...'

Partha kept silent. He wanted to tell Bakul about Swaha, but rain checked his urge. Why did Ron not tell Bakul about it? His mind suddenly became troubled.

'When I think about my elder brother and the girl he met in Shillong, I feel happy and sad at the same time; at least he came to realize what is the joy and sorrow of love, what is sadness and what sacrifice it calls for…"I cannot support the path they have chosen,' Bakul continued; seemed like she had many things on her mind. 'I cannot support violence, though I know that violence sometimes can become a necessary evil. But evil it is, and violence always begets violence.'

Partha pressed Bakul's hand slightly, and Bakul looked into Partha's eyes. He suddenly felt as if the afternoon river that flowed before them was now flowing in the pupils of her eye.

She smiled slightly and said in a lighter tone, 'It may be that I am really scared...beset with fears of an unknown path and an uncertain future. I don't want to understand everything with reason and arguments, Partha, I want to accept life with my heart and with my emotions. But my elder brother's courage, his indomitable firmness, I respect that.'

Her eyes then brimmed over with tears. She made no move to wipe away her tears. She took Partha's hands, clasped it to her bosom once and then kept it over her folded knees. Then she placed her wet cheek on the back of his hand and pressed over it.

'Had he not been my own brother, I would have fallen in love with him; for such a man, I would have done everything.

Sometimes, I feel like giving up everything—studies, the petty day-to-day events, and go out and do something! Sometimes, I want to involve myself in something worthwhile, do something and give some meaning to existence.'

A light breeze rose from the river, blowing Bakul's long hair. They were sitting on the crook of a stony spar with the timeless Brahmaputra flowing in front. With approaching dusk, the world around was slowly becoming soft and dissolving slowly into the darkness.

Partha drew the silently sobbing Bakul slightly towards him, and they sat in quiet for a longtime holding hands.

Partha suddenly spoke in a voice heavy with emotion, 'Bakul, let us marry soon, very soon.'

His voice had an urgent tone mixed with unspoken fear. He felt that he might lose the girl he had loved so long. He had this feeling for the first time, and he became quite afraid. He couldn't afford to lose her at any cost.

Some silent moments passed. Then Bakul rested her head on his shoulder and then she slowly nodded. Yes! She was consenting with her nod!

A shiver of pure pleasure ran through Partha's whole being.

'Bakul, you have finally consented! It was as if Partha was finding it hard to believe that she had agreed. He lifted her face slowly and gazed into her dark eyes. A faint smell of ripe berries floated up from Bakul and entered his nostrils , and then the smell slowly spread through his body...

They rose from the riverbank and came to the car.

'Bakul, I still can't believe it,' Partha spluttered. Bakul took out a sheaf of papers from her bag and folding it to the last page, offered it to Partha. He started reading in the dim light inside his car. Ron had written that he had reached a crossroads in life, and had chosen one of the ways to travel on; that he was not afraid, but he'd increasingly realized that a human is really like a puppet in the hands of unfathomable and uncontrollable destiny. And that there was no point in rebelling against it, but to not rebel would mean that life had lost all meaning…

Partha read the letter, spellbound:

> My dear Bakul,
>
> Please accept the marriage proposal of Partha-da; I am giving you my blessings, my darling. Don't be unreasonable, and don't delay. Partha-da is a good person and I am confident that both of you would be able to sail together through the turbulences of life and be happy. Just think about how much happiness your marriage would bring to our father, mother, and brother in these sad days—and how happy it would make me!'
>
> I am starting a journey, and I don't know where it will take me. But you should know one thing: your elder brother

> would never lose courage. He won't be afraid of any situation. I have lost the fear of death long ago. Now, I have no fears, because I know I will never vanish away; I would always live, and I shall be reborn as your son…

Partha's eyes moistened. The writing in the letter faded in the dim glow of the dash board. And an explicable emotion suffocated him.

> Where will it end? Where will it end—the history of these stormy times? This tragic drama of confusion and strife, as if a storm has carried on a bundle of fallen leaf, threatening to destabilize their lives. What is he witness to—making of history or the start of a tragic destruction? And maybe, maybe like this, in this uneven way, will advance the days, time, and history. And the chariot wheels of inescapable destiny would run over man's hopes, aspirations, happiness, sorrow, love, and heartbreak, pulverizing them. But who would carry forward the unending struggles of man's dreams against the machinations of blind fate? Who will bring, from amidst death, from the ruins, the good tidings of rebirth of human values, of resurrection of man? Can we respond to that, can we?

Like a movie reel running on fast forward many disjointed and partial images rapidly passed through Partha's mind—Prabhat, Babula, Swaha, Sombori, Bharat Hazarika, Ron, Alok, Bakul, and himself, and many more…

He turned towards Bakul. The faint smell of ripe berries again reached his nose. The fragrance of life…

And closing his eyes, he breathed deeply to take in their fragrance.

ACKNOWLEDGEMENTS

My sincere thanks to the legendary Assamese writer and editor Chandra Prasad Saikia, Dr Indira (Mamoni Roisam) Goswami, and Ms Namita Gokhale, who were always a source of support and solace. Sri Apurva Sarma, Dr Jayanta Rongpi, Sri Manoj Kumar Goswami, Sri Ankur Deka, and Sri Pikumani Dutta hold a special place in my heart for the encouragement they provided. My heartfelt gratitude goes to my readers for their comments and observations while this novel was serialized in original Assamese in the magazine *Goriyoshee*; that stimulated and egged me on to complete it.

Thanks are also due to Atreyee Gohain and Trishna Borah for helping me prepare the first English draft.

Lastly, those without whom this dream of mine would not have been realized: my dear and respected publisher, Sri Nirmalkanti Bhattacharjee, whose vision and support turned this into reality. I am greatly indebted to my dear editor Vibha Chakravarty Kumar, who has so painstakingly edited the manuscript. Her professional approach, commitment, and competence is really exemplary, but overriding all these stands out her genuine love for literature and sterling quality of warm, humane care.